M000086714

Seedless in Seattle

Seedless in Seattle

ROSS O'CARROLL-KELLY
(as told to Paul Howard)

Illustrated by

ALAN CLARKE

PENGUIN
IRELAND

PENGUIN IRELAND

UK | USA | Canada | Ireland | Australia
India | New Zealand |South Africa

Penguin Ireland is part of the Penguin Random House group of companies
whose addresses can be found at global.penguinrandomhouse.com.

First published 2015

001

Copyright © Paul Howard, 2015
Illustrations copyright © Alan Clarke, 2015

The moral right of the author and illustrator has been asserted

Penguin Ireland thanks O'Brien Press for its agreement to Penguin Ireland
using the same design approach and typography, and the same artist,
as O'Brien Press used in the first four Ross O'Carroll-Kelly titles

Set in 12/14.75 pt Dante MT Std
Typeset by Jouve (UK), Milton Keynes
Printed in Great Britain by Clays Ltd, St Ives plc

A CIP catalogue record for this book is available from the British Library

ISBN: 978–1–844–88343–1

www.greenpenguin.co.uk

MIX
Paper from
responsible sources
FSC® C018179

Penguin Random House is committed to a
sustainable future for our business, our readers
and our planet. This book is made from Forest
Stewardship Council® certified paper.

With thanks to Paddy Murray

Contents

Prologue

He's sitting in my seat. That's the first thing I cop when I walk into the dining room. Sorcha's old man is sitting in my seat, at the head of the table, like he's forgotten that this is *my* gaff now and that he's a guest – a non-paying one at that. He even has the balls to chuckle to himself in, like, a *nostalgish* way?

He goes, 'These are the kind of moments you can't pay for, aren't they?'

And I think to myself, well, you certainly can't – you're focking skint.

Sorcha thought it would be a great idea to spend New Year's Eve sitting around the dinner table together – as, like, a family? Except I end up being totally excluded from the conversation.

He's going, 'Oh, we've had some wonderful times in this house, haven't we, girls?'

There's, like, nods and smiles from Sorcha and her sister, who's moving out tomorrow, I'm happy to say – back to the Beacon South Quarter, as it happens. One down, two to go. That's how I feel about Sorcha's family.

'I'm thinking back to all the wonderful New Year's Eves we've had here,' the dick tries to go. 'And the wonderful summers. All those garden parties. It was practically one a week. And, of course, all those wonderful, wonderful Christmases. As a matter of fact, do you remember the year – I think you must have been around eleven, Sorcha – and you decided, in your infinite wisdom, that we should give our Christmas dinner to the homeless? Of course, this was at the very moment your mother was about to serve it up. You made this little speech about the true spirit of Christmas and how, if we really believed in it, we'd go out there on the street and we'd give this wonderful feast of food to people who actually needed it.'

Honor looks up from her iPhone. She goes, 'So you were a sap even then.'

I end up laughing – I know I shouldn't, but I actually do – so I'm the one who ends up getting the filthies from everyone.

He carries on with his story, the knob.

'We wrapped the entire meal in tinfoil,' he goes, 'and we drove into Dublin. Into the *inner* city – do you remember this, Sorcha? – and we handed it all out. Every morsel of it went into the mouths of the homeless, including your mother's sprouts, with the pancetta and the other bits. I can't remember what we had for dinner that night. It was something or other. But I do remember you, Sorcha, looking up from your plate and telling me that the angels in heaven would be smiling down on us tonight.'

'Yeah,' Honor goes, 'thanks for sharing, Granddad.'

I know she's possibly borderline psychotic, but she can also be very funny.

He refuses to take the bait, though.

'As a matter of fact,' he goes, 'I can remember filming the entire thing on the video camera. I must see if I can have it converted onto DVD. There's places that do it, you know.'

I'm throwing the wine into me. There's, like, three hours to go until midnight and the time is already dragging.

Sorcha's old dear walks in, carrying the bird. We're having goose, because the Lalors have always had goose on New Year's Eve.

'I wish you'd let me help you,' Sorcha goes. 'You've been in that kitchen since seven o'clock this morning.'

Her old dear is like, 'I told you, I want you to put your feet up this evening. You've got more than enough on your hands looking after three children.'

Three children.

Honor cops it as well, even though her head is still stuck in her phone. I watch her jaw horden, then her little thumb stop working for, like, three or four seconds.

Then she goes, 'Er, she has *four*?'

She's just like, 'Yes, well . . .' and her voice trails off. I make a grab for the corving knife, except *he* ends up getting there before me, even though it's supposed to be, like, the man of the house who corves the bird.

'Oh my God,' Sorcha goes, 'let's do that thing we used to do where we each name the things we're grateful for from the year just past. For me, it's having three beautiful – oh my God – brand-new, healthy babies and also having my husband delivered safely home from Africa.'

Me and Sorcha smile at each other across the table, which kills *him*, of course. It still snaps his crayons that we've ended up back together.

'Well,' the sister goes, 'I'm not grateful for anything. I'm, like, twenty-eight, no boyfriend, working in Aldi. But at least I'm moving into my own place tomorrow. So I suppose – yeah – that.'

Her old dear goes, 'Well, I'm grateful for my three beautiful grandsons, for my wonderful marriage and for the lesson that money isn't important.'

Especially if you're living off your focking son-in-law, I think. I don't say it, though. What I *actually* say is, 'I'm grateful for my beautiful, beautiful house,' because it's a point worth constantly hammering home to them that it's mine now, not theirs. 'My beautiful – I'm going to say it – wife, who I hope to end up being with forever. I'm grateful for, again, the babies, but can I also throw in a mench for this little one here?' meaning obviously Honor.

The girl rolls her eyes and goes, 'Shut up, you knob.'

Sorcha helps herself to roast potatoes – focking *four*, by the way, even though I manage to bite my lip and not mention it – and she goes, 'What about you, Honor? What are you grateful for?'

Honor goes, 'I'm grateful for the fact that this meal will soon be over and I can go back to my room.'

That ends up being the straw that breaks the camel's blahdy blah. Sorcha's old man goes, 'I don't think anyone wants to spend the last hours of the year listening to your unpleasantness.'

'If you don't like it,' she goes, 'then go and live somewhere else. Except you can't – because, er, you're focking *bankrupt*?'

He ends up totally flipping. 'How dare you use language like that at this table!' he roars at her – as in, like, *really* roars?

We all end up levitating an inch or two off our seats. All except Honor. She doesn't even stir. She has the focking courage of Mafusa.

'It's not your table,' she goes, fixing him with a look. 'It's my *dad's* table?'

I have to say, I don't think I've ever been as proud of my daughter as I am at that precise moment.

'Honor!' Sorcha goes, trying to silence her, even though I'm thinking I actually wouldn't mind hearing more here. 'Leave the table and go to your room!'

Honor's there, 'Er, *happily?*'

She trudges out of the room, dragging her Uggs along the floor, then upstairs she stomps.

And that's when Sorcha's old man turns around to Sorcha and goes, 'When are you seeing that woman?'

Sorcha looks across the table at me, definitely embarrassed – there's, like, something going on here that I don't *know* about?

I'm there, 'Okay, what the fock is this?'

Her old man answers for her. He's like, 'Your daughter needs to see a psychiatrist. I think that much should be obvious.'

I'm there, 'I don't think she does. That's a genuine belief of mine.'

'She infested her school with rats and almost caused Sorcha to lose her babies.'

'*Our* babies.'

He just stares at me – doesn't correct himself.

'Ross,' Sorcha goes, 'Honor is a very, very disturbed young girl. This counsellor – I don't want to use the word psychiatrist, Dad – Siofra Flynn is her name, she might be able to get to the root of why our daughter acts out the way she does.'

I'm like, 'Whoa, whoa, whoa – who the fock is Siofra Flynn? Who is this supposed woman who all of a sudden knows our daughter better than we do?'

'She's an amazing, amazing child psychologist, Ross, and she's written a book called *So Your Kid is a Prick*.'

'*I've* never heard of it.'

'Well, for your information, it's an inspiring book. And I know that because I've taken the time to read it. She's an expert in the area of unspoiling children. She either invented it herself or she was the first one to bring it to Ireland.'

'*Unspoiling* children?'

'Yes, Ross, unspoiling children.'

'So how does it work? When your eight-year-old daughter tells you she wants fourteen hundred snots for a metallic lace dress by Dolce & Gabbana, instead of going, "Yeah, no, I'll stick it on the credit cord," you go, "No, you're not getting it, because you've been a focking nightmare recently"?'

'I know what you're trying to do, Ross.'

'What am I trying to do?'

'You're trying to make it sound like less of a science than it actually is.'

'It just sounds like utter horseshit to me.'

She stands up from the table and from the sideboard she produces the famous book. On the cover, it's a picture of a little boy with a blond, pudding-bowl haircut. The title is – like she said – *So Your Kid is a Prick*, and then underneath it's like, *How to create a better-behaved child*.

'That's actually Siofra's little boy on the cover,' she tries to go. 'His name is Jack. Isn't he – oh my God – so gorgeous?'

I pull a face – unimpressed. I'm there, 'It's a photograph, Sorcha. He could be a little dickhead. All I'm saying is there's no actual proof.'

And he's wearing a turtleneck, I notice. There's no saying how that might affect him in later life.

Sorcha goes, 'The point that Siofra makes in the book, Ross, is that it's never too late to undo the damage you've done by spoiling your child. It's just a matter of introducing new rules, behaviours and parameters. Look at the names of some of the chapters. Stop Apologizing for Disappointments. Don't Debate Your House Rules. Manage Meltdowns. Teach Your Children the Lost Art of Patience. Give Encouragement Instead of Gifts . . .'

I'm there, 'You seem to be suggesting that we've made actual mistakes in the way we've raised our daughter and I genuinely don't think we have.'

Sorcha's old man laughs. He's such a dick.

I'm there, 'Well, if I could turn back the clock, I wouldn't do anything differently. Look, my philosophy has always been, you know, sometimes ugly parents produce good-looking kids and sometimes amazing parents produce kids who are little fockers. No one can explain it. It's genetics. A mystery.'

Sorcha goes, 'We have an appointment, Ross, for the end of January. And bear in mind there's, like, a six-month waiting list to see this woman. The only reason we jumped the queue is because Mum used to play golf with *her* mum in Woodbrook.'

'Her mother plays off a handicap of twelve,' Sorcha's old dear goes – I have no focking idea why.

'There's nothing wrong with her mentally,' I go, standing up from the table. 'She's a bitch. There's a very specific difference.'

'Well, with or without you,' Sorcha's old man goes, loving the sound of his own voice, 'she's going to see this woman and that's all there is to it.'

I call *him* every dick under the sun, then I storm out of the room myself. It's some day for dramatic exits.

Honor, I then discover, is not in her bedroom at all. She's sitting at the top of the stairs, with a face on her as long as Dublin Airport Runway Number One.

I'm there, 'Are you okay?'

She just, like, shrugs.

I go, 'How much of that conversation did you hear?'

She's like, '*All* of it?'

All I can do is just smile at her sadly.

'They all hate me,' she goes, tears in her eyes.

I'm there, 'They don't hate you, Honor. They just think you're, I don't know, damaged.'

'They want to send me to a psychiatrist. They think I'm mental.'

'Well, *I* wouldn't use that word. You heard me defending you in there, I hope. I just think you're either a bitch or a wagon.'

'I'm a bitch.'

'There you are then. That's what I actually said.'

'I could stop any time I wanted to.'

'I believe you.'

'But I don't want to stop. I like being a bitch.'

'That's the whole point, isn't it?'

She suddenly gives me the eyes that no father of a little girl can resist.

'Daddy,' she goes – and she never, ever uses that word to me – 'please don't let them send me to a psychiatrist.'

And in that moment, I'm totally crushed.

'Okay,' I go, on the verge of tears, 'I'm going to make you a promise right now. You won't be going to see this woman, this focking so-called Siofra Flynn they're all banging on about.'

She shakes her head. She's there, 'They're going to make me go.'

I'm like, 'Er, you just heard me use the word "promise", didn't you?'

'Yeah.'

'And when I promise something, I always deliver. I'm on Team Honor. I'm on Team Honor every step of the way. And, hey, I've had an idea.'

'What?'

'Why don't you and me ring in the New Year together – as in, just the two of us? We'll go up to the attic and climb out onto the roof – we can watch the fireworks from up there.'

'You're definitely not going to let them send me to a psychiatrist?'

'Honor, trust me.'

And I can't tell you how much it makes my day to see the corners of her mouth turn upwards into a smile.

I.

The Fock It List

Ealga Gary. Now there's a blast from the literally past. I'm looking at a photograph of her in one of Sorcha's old *VIPs*, at a champagne lunch to raise awareness of – I don't know – something or other, a glass in one hand, the other hand on her hip, sucking her cheeks in so hord it looks like she might swallow her focking ears.

She actually looks like Gal Gadot.

I haven't seen Ealga in maybe twelve or thirteen years. She was in, like, Alex and she used to go to all of our rugby matches. She was mad about me, except we never, like, *did* it? I don't know why. There just wasn't time.

It's, like, a Saturday night and Sorcha and her old pair are at Verdi Requiem in the National Concert Hall, while I'm doing the whole stay-at-home-dad thing. Brian, Johnny and Leo are sleeping soundly upstairs – I can hear them, like, purring away through the baby monitor – and Honor is in her bedroom, trying to provoke a reaction from James Arthur on Twitter by saying hurtful things to him about his face.

I'm having a few cans of the wonder stuff, while flicking through Sorcha's old magazines, looking at photographs of birds, a lot of whom, like Ealga, I recognize – and I end up being genuinely surprised, even depressed, by how few of them I've ridden.

Six birds in, like, twenty *VIPs* is a poor batting average, you'd have to say.

And maybe it's the drink, or maybe it's that me and Sorcha aren't back in the saddle yet after the arrival of the triplets, but I'm suddenly very, very conscious of the fact that I'm thirty-three years old, and I'm thinking about all the opportunities I've missed in my life.

So I grab the laptop, then I open, like, a Word document and I type Ealga Gary's name into it. Then, underneath, I type the name of Morrigan Kennedy, a bird from my *Café en Seine* days, who, like Ealga, had a serious lady boner for me, even though I never got around to her either.

Suddenly, other names stort popping into my head. Cait Bennigan. Aibell Wright. Rachael Aird. Tlachtga Ní Dhuibhir. Fodla Byers. They're coming out of nowhere – names that I associate with regret – and I'm typing them in as fast as my two fingers will allow. Lisa Currie. Thea Donald. Badb O'Crohan. Lisa Strug. Vyvyan Egan. Joyce De Courcy. Hana Peacock. Malorie Miles.

It's at that exact moment that JP rings.

He's like, 'Pint?' and I end up just laughing.

I'm there, 'No can do. Sorcha's at the concert hall with her old pair and I'm doing the whole responsible-adult thing. Here, Dude, do you remember a bird called Ealga Gary?'

'Went to Alex?'

'Big ride.'

'Yeah, what about her?'

'Ah, I don't know. I'm sitting here depressing myself thinking about all the birds I could have ridden in my life but didn't.'

'You rode a lot, Ross.'

'I could have ridden more. I can't help but feel that. I'm actually putting together a list here. Ealga's on it. Then do you remember a bird called Morrigan Kennedy?'

'Was she not . . .'

'Yeah, no, she was never an *actual* lesbian? She was more, you know yourself, half-rice, half-chips.'

'Got you. So who else?'

'Tlachtga Ní Dhuibhir. Badb O'Crohan. Keri Lawless. Joyce De Courcy. Malorie Miles. I don't know if this is some kind of midlife thing I'm going through, but I've suddenly got this irresistible urge to write down the names of all the birds I consider to be basically unfinished business. I don't want to die with regrets. There was another one from Shankill called Something Garrigan with massive chebs whose first name I can't remember – screaming for me.'

He's there, 'So it's, like, a Fock It List?'

Again, I laugh.

I'm like, 'That's a genuinely hilarious line!' and I hit Command and S, and I actually save the file under that name. The Fock It List. JP's very clever when it comes to shit like that. He's the estate agent who described Sean MacDermott Street as 'Dublin's Notting Hill' and called Chorlesland in Greystones 'North Wicklow's very own Hamptons'.

At the top of the page, I put, 'THE FOCK IT LIST!' and then underneath I put, 'Birds I will DEFINITELY ride before I hit forty!' and then me and J-Town spend the next ten or fifteen minutes coming up with more names to add to it.

'Another one is Becky McGrew,' I go. 'How did I never end up riding Becky McGrew?'

Anyway, the thing ends up running to thirty or forty people and it's *as* I'm adding Laura Whitmore to the list – just for the sake of completeness – that I hear the sound of crying. One of the babies has woken up – almost certainly a feed or a nappy change required – and his screams have suddenly woken the other pair.

I'm like, 'Back to reality, Dude – nature calls.'

'Here,' he goes, 'what are you doing next Friday?'

I'm there, 'Er, nothing. And I'm actually owed a night out after this. What are you thinking in terms of?'

'Have you been talking to Fionn?'

'A text on New Year's Eve. Nothing since.'

'He's doing this corporate after-dinner thing in a few weeks. It's in, like, the Double Tree Hilton. We're talking the whole motivational *speaker* vibe? How he survived as a hostage in Uganda and how the coping strategies that got him through those months in captivity can be applied to chartered accountancy.'

'That does *not* sound like a fun night.'

'Dude, he's our friend.'

'And that was going to be my next line. We should definitely support him either way. I presume we'll get in for free?'

'No, let's book a table. Me, you, Oisinn, Christian – the whole crew. Let him know we're there for him.'

'Yeah, no, count me in.'

The old man opens the door, smoking a cigor the size of King Kong's finger.

'House rules,' he goes, in his Caps Lock voice. 'There is to be no talk of Enda Kenny and whether or not we should burn these – inverted commas – bondholder chaps! You know what you and I are like, Ross, when we start debating the great issues of the day. We'd contradict the bloody well Pope!'

I'm there, 'Jesus Christ, let us get in the door before you stort shouting your mouth off, you focking orse clown.'

'And my beautiful granddaughter,' he goes, sweeping her up in his orms. 'Hello, little one! Helen has a little gift for you. I don't know whether to call it a belated Christmas present or an early birthday present.'

'Is it two grand?' Honor goes.

She adores her granddad and you'd have to say that the feeling is mutual.

The old man's like, 'No, it's not two grand.'

'Can I *have* two grand?' she goes.

'I'll tell you what, let's see what's in the safe before you go, shall we?'

He turns around to me then and he goes, 'She reminds me so much of you, Ross!'

I'm like, 'What does that mean – always looking for money?'

'No, I mean in various different ways. It was intended as a compliment, Kicker.'

'Well, it sounded like a dig.'

'It was far from a dig. I was, in point of fact, praising you.'

'Fine. Cool. I'll accept it then.'

He puts Honor down, then we tip down to the kitchen, where Helen is making coffee. 'You couldn't have timed that better,' she goes, giving me a genuinely amazing hug, then doing the same to Honor. 'We've just finished our dinner. You can have dessert with us.'

'Granddad said there was a present,' Honor goes. 'I hope you kept the receipt – in case it's lame.'

Helen goes, 'We'll get you your present in a moment,' because she's actually great with her. 'First, we're going to have the last of the Christmas pudding.'

She brings it to the table.

The smell of brandy always reminds me of playing in the Leinster Schools Senior Cup – mainly because *he* was always focking shit-faced at my matches.

Happy times.

'I was just telling Ross outside,' he goes. 'There is to be no talk about the Irish Bank Resolution Corporation or related issues. You know what we're like when we start discussing the issues of the day. One will say one thing, then the other will come back with something else. Before you know it, you've got a full-scale what's-it on your hands!'

Sometimes, I wish I was actually *genuinely* intelligent, instead of dropped-on-your-head-as-a-baby stupid. Sometimes, when I'm in the cor, I turn on *Newstalk* and I listen to people talking about, I don't know, economics and world affairs and I open and close my mouth and pretend it's me who's saying all that, like, clever shit.

It's nice to sometimes dream.

Helen dishes up the pudding with custard. We horse into it, then Helen takes Honor upstairs to give her this famous present.

I ask the old man if he's heard from the gin-crazed ice-weasel who calls herself my mother.

'We had a lovely card at Christmas,' he goes, 'from that, um, facility she's staying in.'

I'm there, 'Yeah, no, it's called a drying-out clinic?'

'Well, whatever it's called, it's nice to see her retaking control of her life again.'

'If that's what you want to call it.'

'I think, deep down, Ross, your mother is a very lonely woman. I'd love to see her find happiness, perhaps even with a new beau.'

'A new beau?' I go. 'No one would touch her – the unfockable trogdor.'

It ends up sounding a little bit more horsh than I maybe *intended*? He actually seems a bit taken aback by it, but he ends up just changing the subject.

'You and Honor calling in has really given Helen a lift,' he goes. 'She's been rather down in the dumps, don't you know.'

I'm there, 'What's she down about?'

'Erika, of course. We haven't heard so much as a peep from her.'

'What kind of a daughter doesn't bother her hole ringing her old pair on Christmas Day? I'm sorry for saying it – it's just another example of me being prepared to call it.'

'Well, quite. Helen got it into her head that something was the matter. She has wonderful instincts, you see. So two or three days after Christmas, using a thing called Google – oh, it's like being in the FBI, Ross – she managed to track down this Fabrizio chap.'

He's talking about Fabrizio Bettega, the dude that Erika ran away with to Orgentina. He's a tosspot.

'It seems he's running some kind of equestrian school,' he goes, 'in Buenos Aires. Helen spoke to him.'

I'm there, 'And?'

'Well, it seems that he and Erika are no longer – quote-unquote – an item.'

'What?'

'Yes, it seems they broke up some time ago. Which probably explains why she hasn't been in touch.'

'I wouldn't mind, but showjumping isn't even a proper sport – a fact that she seemed happy to overlook. I'd say she's sorry now. So where the fock is she?'

'Fabrizio doesn't know.'

'How can he not know?'

'Oh, don't worry. Helen gave him a bloody earful. Asked him the same thing. How dare you drag our daughter halfway around the world, separate her from her family, then abandon her?'

'Is she still *in* Orgentina?'

'We have no earthly idea. This chap claims he hasn't seen her for the best part of a year.'

'He's a knob-end. I was the first one to go on the record as saying that.'

'We don't know whether she's alive or dead.'

'She wouldn't be dead – would she?'

'Helen's talking about maybe going out there to look for her. It was a sad Christmas for her.'

'Sad for you as well, I'd say.'

He just nods.

I'm there, 'Well, if it's any consolation, we had a pretty horrendous Christmas ourselves.'

He goes, 'I thought I detected a frown line or two! What is it, Kicker?'

'Yeah, no, it's just Sorcha's old man. He's another one – a focking bell-end.'

'Is that so?'

'He's somehow managed to talk Sorcha into bringing Honor to a psychiatrist.'

'A psychiatrist?'

'A behavioural therapist is apparently what she calls herself. She wrote some book.'

'That little girl doesn't need a psychiatrist any more than you do!'

'That's *my* point. She's just a little cow. I don't see why everyone's panicking.'

'Any psychiatrist worth their bloody well salt would tell you, within sixty seconds of meeting Honor, that there's nothing the hell wrong with her.'

'I know I'm quoting myself here, but there's no such thing as bad kids. Some of them are just little fockers. We've got one of those.'

'You're an extraordinary reader of people, if you don't mind my saying so, Ross.'

'That's a lovely thing for me to hear. See, I'm worried.'

'Of course you're worried. I've never heard such stuff and nonsense.'

'I'm just worried this so-called psychiatrist might stort saying shit about the way we've raised her. I'd just hate to end up feeling that I've, I don't know, somehow failed as a father.'

He laughs at even the thought of that.

'Let me tell you something,' he goes, 'as someone who knows a little bit about the subject. There is no such thing as a perfect theory of parenting. It's a myth, Ross – like the lost world of Atlantis and global bloody warming.'

'See, this is the kind of thing I need to hear.'

'A psychiatrist? For a little girl? I've never heard anything so ridiculous in my life!'

'It's horseshit, I agree.'

It's at that exact moment that Honor and Helen return to the kitchen. It turns out the present they bought her was a Lulu Frost statement necklace, which I happen to know cost eight hundred snots, because it was on her original Santa List.

'Oh my God,' Honor goes, 'I *so* heart it!' and the smile on her face as she shows it off convinces me that we were wrong to tell her that it wasn't an appropriate present for a girl of eight going on nine.

So much for Sorcha and her theories.

Honor's like, 'You are – oh my God – *the* best grandfather and step-grandmother ever!'

And my old man smiles, takes Honor's little hand and he's there, 'Let's go and see how much money is in the safe, shall we?'

Dordeen asks me if I want another one of those beers that I drink. She makes three or four attempts to read the name off the can. 'Hymenken' is the closest she gets to it. If they sold it in Lidl – five euros for a tray of focking twelve – she'd know how to say it.

Sorcha tells Honor to stop holding her breath, which is something she does whenever we go to Finglas. As soon as we cross Tara Street Bridge, in fact, she storts breathing in and out at, like, thirty-second intervals.

'I'm conserving my oxygen,' she goes. 'I don't want my brain full of lead.'

She actually means it.

I blame Sorcha for letting her see her entry for the 1994 Young Scientist of the Year Exhibition, which was a comparative study on the air quality between the Northside and Southside of Dublin. See, that's just ammunition for someone like our daughter.

She goes, 'Er, what are we even *doing* here? You do realize, if I develop an accent, it could hurt my future employment prospects?'

Sorcha's there, 'Don't be rude, Honor. We're here to see Ronan and your little niece.'

It suddenly occurs to me, as I'm opening my second can, that having a nephew or niece who's less than seven years younger than you is as working class as backing horses or walking around a supermarket eating food items before you've actually paid for them.

It looks like this is going to be another one of my famous deep-thinking days. Once my brain storts off down that road, I have literally no idea where it's going to end up.

'Thee shoultn't be long,' Dordeen goes. 'Thee've just nipped out for Nicorette.'

We're all cramped into Dordeen's living room, by the way – we're talking me, Sorcha and Honor, Brian, Johnny and Leo in their triple buggy and Dordeen, who continues to watch *Emmerdale* despite the fact that she has visitors.

Sorcha at least makes the effort.

She's like, 'So how was your Christmas, Dordeen?' because she's better at putting on an act than me and Honor. 'Did you have a nice one?'

'Ah,' she goes, 'it was veddy heerd, what wit Kennet being back in priddon. Thee didn't give him the temper doddy release, the doorty bastards. It was lubbly habbin little Rihadda-Burrogan hee-er, but.'

The order in which I'd ride the women out of *Emmerdale* is Katie, then Priya, then Vanessa, then Debbie, then Charity, then Chas. I'd probably ride Laurel as well, if it came up in conversation.

'How's Rihanna-Brogan doing?' Sorcha goes.

Which is, like, a sore *subject*? She lived with us for the guts of twelve months before Dordeen got in Shadden's ear and persuaded her that Finglas is where she should be raised.

'She's depinitely happior,' she goes. 'And that's no offedence to yous. It's just Kulloyinny – is that how you say it?'

'Killiney.'

'Kulloyinny.'

'Killiney.'

'Kulloyinny.'

She's doing it on focking purpose.

She goes, 'It's veddy faahr, idn't it?'

These people judge everything in the world by its proximity to the Broken Arms on the Ballygall Road.

The next thing we hear is the sound of the front door opening and in walks Ronan, followed by Shadden, holding little Rihanna-Brogan – my, I still can't believe it, but *granddaughter*? – in her orms.

It ends up being bear hugs and air-kisses all round.

'You're having another crack at giving up the cigarettes?' I go. 'I'm going to have to say fair focks, Ro.'

He *was* on, like, forty a day, which is a lot for a kid of sixteen.

'Haff to stay offa tum this toyum,' he goes. 'Wanna be arowunt to see me thaughter gurrowing up.'

His accent, I notice, has become about eight times more Dubba-lin since he moved back here.

Shadden hands Rihanna-Brogan to me, then she storts admiring the triplets and Sorcha tells Shadden about her – oh my God – determination to get back to her pre-baby weight, even as she's horsing into the tin of Rover biscuits that Dordeen put out.

I'm not counting, but she's had three Bourbons, two Custard Creams and two pink wafers out of it.

Dordeen goes back to watching her programme and Ro storts catching up with his sister slash half-sister.

'Howiya, Hodor,' he goes. 'Have you a hug for your brutter?'

Honor literally adores Ro, but she hates Shadden for taking him away from us, so she ends up not moving an inch – sort of, like, making *strange*? – until Ro goes, 'Hee-er, doaunt be hoalting your brett like that! You'll turden blue! Come on – breed out!' and he storts tickling her under the orms and suddenly Honor is rolling around the laminate floor, literally helpless with laughter.

It's lovely to see them so close.

'Move back home,' Honor goes, when she's stopped laughing. 'Why do you have to live out here in focking Knacksville?'

Ro's like, 'We've a house out hee-er, Hodor. We're a famdily. Me, Shadden and Rihatta-Burrogan. We're next doe-her – do you want to see it?'

'No, it's probably a hovel.'

He laughs. He's like, 'It's norra hovel. It's nice, so it is.'

'I'd rather not see it,' she goes. 'I think I'd find it too upsetting.'

It's funny, I actually feel exactly the same way.

'How's school?' I end up going.

He's still travelling across town every day to go to Castlerock. He's actually sitting his Junior Cert in June.

He's there, 'School's mustoord, Rosser. The thravellin back and fowert is a birrof a killer, but I do get a chaddence to study on the bus and the Deert.'

The bus and the Dort. Jesus, I've never felt lower in my life.

'I moost show you as well,' he goes. 'Ine arthur been woorking on a perroject bout the East Dodder Roysen. It's an All Arelunt competition and Mister McGahy wants to put me forwurt for it.'

'The Easter Rising?' I go. 'Okay, why does that sound familiar?'

He looks at me, obviously wondering am I for focking real.

He's there, 'Nineteen-hondordun-sixteen. It's the most impowar-tunt event in ear histoddy, Rosser. It's how this cuntoddy gorrits indepentince.'

History was never my strongest subject at school. I was the one who thought the IRB was the IRA's second team.

'Yeah, no, there's definitely another reason it's familiar,' I go. 'The Rising was a whole *big* thing, wasn't it? Are we thinking about the same event?'

'Fifteen-hondord-an-odd eermed Vodunteers seized conthrol of severdoddle buildings in Dublin, inclooting the GPO, and declared Arelunt a Repubalick, inthependent of Beritten.'

I suddenly remember why it's familiar.

I'm there, 'My old man's grandfather – no, wait, his great-grandfather – actually fought in it.'

Ronan's jaw literally drops. He's like, 'Soddy?'

'Yeah, no,' I go, 'he fought in it. The Rising. It's such a random name, isn't it? It's focking ridiculous when you think about it.'

'Hang on, concenthrate a midute, Rosser – are you seerdiously tedding me that a redative of moyen fought in nineteen-hundordun-sixteen?'

'Yeah, the old man's *always* banging on about it. I'm surprised he's never said it to you. Donie Kelly. That was the dude's name.'

'Donie Keddy?'

'Yeah, no, Donie Kelly.'

I can't believe how excited he suddenly is about this news. I find the whole thing incredibly boring. He looks at Shadden. He's like, 'Are you hearton this, Shadden?'

She's there, 'I am, yeah.'

'So what would this fedda be to me, Rosser?'

'Well, like I said, he's your grandfather's great-grandfather. You do the math.'

'So tharrud make him me garreat, garreat, garreat garrantfadder.'

'I'll have to take your word for it.'

'Hee-er, imagine what this'll do for me perroject. A bleaten ancestor of moyen was actually *in* it! Moy Jaysus!'

'You should ring my old man if that's how you feel. He'll fill you in on the whole thing. Bore the focking ears off you.'

'I'll be ringing him, Rosser. Donie Keddy. Ine doyen to foyunt out was he in the GPO – or even Bodan's Middle.'

The health nurse does literally nothing for me – if I had to mork her out of ten, I'd describe her as a five, possibly a six, at the very most. None of which is relevant to the story, but then you know how I like to give you a bit of background colour. The point is that she is very happy with us. She's saying some amazingly complimentary shit about how we're doing as the parents of six-week-old triplets – 'fair focks' being the *general* vibe?

'But you shouldn't have come to the hospital,' she goes. 'We could have arranged a home visit.'

She's a little bit like Hayley from *Coronation Street*, except a Tipperary version?

'The doctor is very happy with how you're healing,' she goes – this is obviously after the Caesarean. 'Like I said, try to take it easy. Let Ross here do all of the housework!'

We all laugh like she said something hilarious. Actually, she did – me doing focking housework. We have two women who do that. Dolores and Lualhati.

'You definitely checked everything?' Sorcha goes, because she's a serious worrier.

The nurse is like, 'Yes, I checked everything.'

'You weighed them – I saw you weigh them.'

'Weighed them. Measured them. Everything is normal.'

'You took the circumferences of their heads, did you? Because I know that's a thing.'

'I did and there's nothing to worry about. I checked their hearing, their vision, their hearts. I checked their arms and their legs, their hands and their feet, for development and motion.'

I'm straight in there. 'Is there any one of them who's more developed than the other two, in terms of, like, co-ordination, reflexes and blah, blah, blah?'

Six weeks old and I'm already trying to work out which one of the three is going to be my number ten. It actually frightens me how much I love my rugby.

'It's too early to make those kind of determinations,' this nurse one goes. It wouldn't be too early if we were in New Zealand – that's all I'm saying. 'But their arms and legs are in perfect working order – like everything else.'

'You definitely checked their vision?' Sorcha goes. 'Because sometimes it's as if Johnny can't see me and I keep getting it into my head that he's, like, possibly *blind*?'

The nurse smiles. She has unbelievable patience. She'd want to – she'll be a long time waiting for a husband.

'Their eyes are fine,' she goes. 'We checked them with a penlight. Their vision is perfectly normal.'

'And their ears – they're not deaf, are they?'

'No, we checked those with an otoscope, like the nose. Nothing abnormal to report.'

'And you checked their mouths and their throats?'

'That's what I was doing with the tongue depressor. No issues there. I checked their thyroid and lymph glands –'

'Their fontanelles? I've been reading a lot about fontanelles.'

'They're fine, too. As is their respiratory function.'

'And their – I don't know the word . . .'

'Genitals?'

'Genitals – I didn't know how to say it. I was going to say dicks.'

'Their genitals are looking very healthy.'

I'm thinking, they *would* be!

'No hernias,' the nurse goes. 'No internal cracks or fissures. Their skin colour is fine. No rashes or lesions. This little one – Leo, isn't it? – he has this birthmark on his face . . .'

Sorcha's like, 'That's not going to be, like, permanent, is it?'

'It'll disappear, probably between six and twelve months. You have three beautiful, perfectly healthy babies.'

'I'm sorry about all the questions. Oh my God, I'm turning into one of those mothers!'

'Don't apologize. That's why I'm here. Now, do you want to ask me anything else?'

And that's when *I* go, 'So, like, when will the weight stort to come off?'

The words are out of my mouth before I realize that I possibly could have phrased it better.

The nurse is like, 'Weight? What weight?'

It's literally the elephant in the room – and that's not me being a wanker. Sorcha piled it on during the final trimester. If I *was* being a wanker, I'd say I'm tempted to ask her to check there isn't still a baby or two in there.

'Are you talking about *my* weight?' Sorcha goes – not a happy rabbit.

I'm like, 'You said it yourself, Sorcha, you were worried would you ever lose it. That magazine you were reading said a lot of birds *don't* after triplets? I'm just saying, this woman wants to hear questions from us and I thought I'd put it out there.'

'I can recommend various diets and exercises,' the nurse goes, except Sorcha's too proud slash embarrassed to listen.

She's like, 'No, I have a lot of books and DVDs.'

Then ten seconds later we've said our thanks and our goodbyes and we're gathering up all of our shit to leave.

We're carrying more baggage than a travelling focking circus. See, one kid is bad enough – you wouldn't believe what comes with three. We're talking bags of nappies. We're talking bags of formula. We're talking bags of toys. I'm like a focking Sherpa carrying them all, because unfortunately Sorcha's still not up to any heavy lifting.

The pram is hilarious. It's, like, the width of the entire hospital corridor and people are having to step out of the way, into stairwells and wards, to let us pass.

Triplets attract a lot of attention from randomers, I've already noticed. There's a lot of women cooing as we push the pram past them, going, 'Ardent thee goer-chuss?' because we're in Holles Street, unfortunately.

We get back to the minivan, which is porked in Merrion Square. I take Johnny, then Leo, then Brian, out of the pram and strap them into their little cor seats, then I fold up the pram and put it into the boot along with all of the other shit. It takes about fifteen minutes and, while I'm doing all of this, Sorcha's going, 'Why did you ask that question about my weight?'

I'm there, 'Babes, you're the one who's been going on about it. You have a two-seat orse – they were *your* words?'

'Ross, it's okay for *me* to say that. But it's not okay for *you* to say it.'

'Okay, I'm hearing you.'

'Unless it bothers you, of course?'

'Bothers me?'

'Me having all this baby weight on me.'

'I don't care what you look like. To me, you're perfect the way you are.'

Your facial expression is all-important when you deliver a line like that.

She goes, 'I *will* lose it, Ross. It's just that it's going to take a bit of

23

time. But I am – Oh! My God! – determined to get my wedding and engagement rings back on before the summer.'

She's got fingers like Elton John at the moment.

I'm there, 'Like I said, Babes, I'll always love you, whatever size you end up.'

'Thanks, Ross.'

'That's me being genuine.'

We hop into the van and off we head. Ten minutes later, we're passing the Tara Towers on the Rock Road and Sorcha goes, 'By the way, don't forget we've got this appointment coming up – to see Siofra.'

I'm like, 'Siofra?'

'Siofra Flynn. *So Your Kid is a Prick?*'

Shit. I'm suddenly thinking about the promise I made to Honor on New Year's Eve.

'Yeah, no,' I go, 'I'm still not convinced we need to go bringing her to see a psychiatrist. Even my old man agrees we're possibly overreacting.'

She's there, 'She put a hundred and twenty rats into the ventilation system of her school, Ross.'

'I know. But I'd still be Scooby Dubious about bringing her to see someone. It's like the song says – why do you have to go and make things so complicated?'

'You're quoting Avril Lavigne?'

'Yes, I am. And I'm also sticking by my original assessment, which is that we've been a brilliant mother and father to the girl. I mean, anything she wants, she instantly gets. We really have been amazing, amazing parents to her.'

We're on the Blackrock Bypass when I suddenly slam on the brakes just as Sorcha at the same time screams.

She's like, 'Hooonnnooorrr!'

We left the girl back at the focking hospital.

I do a quick U-ey. And I don't even wait until we're at the traffic lights. I do a U-ey over the focking median between the two sides of the bypass, causing one oncoming cor to brake and one to swerve to avoid hitting us. I put the foot down and head for town, breaking every red light along the way.

Sorcha's going, 'Oh my God, what are we like? How can we look after three babies when we can't even look after one little girl?'

I'm there, 'Let's not beat ourselves up.'

'I've got – oh my God – *total* baby brain at the moment.'

'We both do. We were up half the night with these three. Anyway, Honor's eight years old now – she needs to stort fending for herself a little bit more. We've enough on our plate.'

'Oh my God, I am *such* a bad mother!'

'I disagree with that analysis.'

'You hear such terrible stories. Oh my God, Ross, I hope she's not . . .'

'Don't think that. Don't even think it.'

It's every parent's worst nightmare that their child will go missing. But if me and Sorcha were being totally honest here, we'd admit that we're twenty-five percent worried about Honor and seventy-five percent worried about whatever poor unfortunate happens to be in her vicinity.

She can say hurtful shit.

'She's going to hold this against me,' Sorcha goes. 'She will, Ross. This will become proof in her mind that we don't give a damn about her.'

I'm like, 'That's why we should possibly lie to her. We'll tell her we knew she was there all along. We saw she was busy texting – actually, she was tweeting, because she showed me a message she sent to Olly Murs telling him he was a shit singer and a sad focking sap – and we just decided, you know, we'd leave her to it and I'd go back and get her once we had the van all loaded up.'

Sorcha goes, 'No, we're not lying to her, Ross. I think we've done more than enough to shatter her faith in adult role models for one day.'

We swing into Merrion Square again. I throw the minivan into a porking space diagonally and I hop out. I don't even bother feeding the meter. I'm like, 'Come on, Sorcha, quick!'

Except she goes, 'Ross, wait – we can't leave three babies on their own in the van.'

'Why, where are they going to go?'

'Ross, we are not leaving three babies unattended in a cor!'

Genuinely, who'd be a parent?

I'm like, 'Okay, you wait here then and *I'll* go?'

Sorcha's like, 'No, because then you'll end up being the hero and Honor will end up blaming me. We'll both go.'

So I end up having to take Leo, Brian and Johnny out of their little cor seats. Holding one in my left orm – picture this, now – and with the other two pressed against my chest with my right orm, I peg it across the road, with Sorcha running after me, going, 'Oh my God, I am *such* a bad person!' over and over and over again.

We reach the waiting room where we left Honor. She looks up from her iPhone and sees us standing there, out of breath from running but with, like, relief written all over our faces.

She gives Sorcha the serious evils – me, less so, I'm happy to say.

'We saw you were busy,' Sorcha automatically goes, 'so we decided to leave you to it and bring everything down to the van, but then we changed our minds and, um . . .'

Honor's not buying it. That much is obvious from her expression. She stands up and walks straight past us, going, 'Yeah, *rull* good parenting, you two!'

Sorcha is on the point of actual tears.

She's like, 'They *still* won't go on,' and she's talking about her wedding and engagement rings. She literally throws them down on the bed. 'Look at the state of my fingers, Ross. I can't even text.'

She has a point.

This was her telling me to buy nappies when I was out yesterday: 'Hrt nsppied.'

I'm there, 'Do you know what you might consider doing?'

She's like, 'What?' already on the big-time defensive.

'Maybe don't have chips with every focking meal.'

No, I don't really say that. What I *actually* say is, 'Exercise – you used to be big into it, remember? There's a place on South William

26

Street that's doing Advanced Hip Hop Yogalates – you give your core a good workout while demanding respect and threatening to pop a cap in the ass of some poot-butt motherfucker.'

'I just don't have the energy,' she goes. 'I got two hours' sleep last night.'

I'm there, 'I know. I got two hours as well, remember?'

She picks up her rings, puts them back in her jewellery drawer and slams it shut in a violent fit.

'Anyway,' she goes, 'get dressed.'

I'm there, 'Er, why am I getting dressed?'

'We have our appointment this afternoon – with Siofra Flynn?'

'Yeah, no, we're not taking Honor to see a psychiatrist slash psychologist. I think I made my position clear the other day.'

'What, when you quoted Avril Lavigne in a discussion about raising our daughter?'

'I'm just saying, I genuinely believe Honor when she says she could stop being a bitch any time she wants. And I still say it's our job as parents to just suck it up.'

'Suck it up? Ross, our daughter doesn't even have a school to go to.'

'I realize that.'

'She doesn't have a school to go to because no school will take her.'

'We'll get her a private tutor.'

'How much money do you think we'd have to pay someone to take on that job?'

She has a point.

'Probably a lot,' I go. 'But we're still not bringing her to a psychiatrist. And the reason we're not bringing her to see her – I might as well tell you – is that I promised her we wouldn't.'

She's like, 'Well, you shouldn't have made that promise.'

'Unfortunately, I did. So that's that then.'

'Well, you're just going to have to *unpromise* her, because we're leaving here in fifteen minutes.'

'Okay, what's Honor going to think of me when I tell her that I'm going to have to go back on what I said?'

'She's going to think you're a liar and an asshole,' I hear this tiny little voice go. 'And she's never going to believe another word that comes out of your focking mouth again.'

She's standing in the doorway of our bedroom, having heard every word of what was just said.

I'm there, 'Honor!' except she just turns on her heel and runs off.

I jump up from the bed and I run after her, except she's faster on her feet than I am – something that's difficult to admit for someone who once beat Denis Hickie in a foot race – and, by the time I get out onto the landing, she's already locked herself in her room and she's telling me through the door that I'm no better than Sorcha's old man and she hopes that I die a horrible death, screaming.

To hear my daughter say that she no longer trusts me sends me suddenly over the edge. This is all *his* doing – as in, Sorcha's old man?

I go downstairs, looking for him – looking for a showdown. I find him in his study, although it's actually *my* focking study when you think about it. It's just that he looks so comfortable in there, sitting behind his old desk, that I end up nearly forgetting that it's not his gaff anymore.

He's on the phone when I burst through the door. I'm like, 'I want a focking word with you.'

He doesn't say anything, just raises his hand in what I think is called a *staying* gesture? 'Excellent,' he goes to whoever is on the other end of the phone. 'My girls are going to be so excited. They're all grown up now, you see. Oh, yes, what you saw on the tape really happened. We gave it all away, then we went home and we had – I think it might have been soup!'

I'm looking around the study. It's exactly as he left it when he sold the house. He must have, like, a couple of thousand books in here, all lined up neatly on these, like, floor-to-ceiling, solid-oak bookshelves.

I've been meaning to get rid of them. I hate the idea of books in the house.

'Yes, I'll pop by tomorrow to collect it,' he tries to go. 'And thank you very much.'

He hangs up and I launch straight into him.

'I made Honor a promise,' I go, jabbing my finger in his general direction. 'I told her that she wouldn't have to go to see this so-called psychiatrist. And because of you getting in Sorcha's ear and persuading her that the girl needs mental help, I've had to break that promise.'

He doesn't say anything – just smiles at me, although it's probably more of a sneer.

I storm out of the room, thinking, I'll get you back for this. And as I do, my phone all of a sudden rings and a bad day gets suddenly worse.

It ends up being Oisinn.

'Dude,' he goes, 'are you sitting down?'

I'm like, 'Sitting down? What are you talking about?'

'Johnny Sexton's leaving Leinster.'

'No, he's not. Stop being ridiculous. He's in contract talks. It'll be sorted.'

'He's just put out a statement, Ross. He's moving to Racing Metro.'

Honor hates me and the reason I know she hates me is that she keeps telling me. She's going, 'I focking hate you,' while we're sitting in the waiting room. 'You said you were on Team Honor.'

I'm there, 'I *am* on Team Honor.'

'No, you're not.'

'Look, I'm *on* Team Honor. I'm on Team Honor all the way. But, unfortunately, I also happen to be on Team Sorcha.'

'You can't *be* on two teams.'

'Actually, you can. I'll give you a quick example. Johnny Sexton. They're saying today that he's moving to France. He's going to be playing his rugby next season for Racing Metro. But if you think he won't also be taking an interest in Leinster's results every week, then . . .'

I hear my voice suddenly crack. I'm still processing the news.

I'm there, ' . . . then you don't know the dude like I know him.'

'Are you focking brain-damaged?' Honor goes.

'No, I'm not brain-damaged.'

'Can you stick to the subject for, like, ten seconds?'

29

'It was a metaphor, that's all.'

While this conversation is taking place, by the way, Sorcha is driving up and down Idrone Terrace, looking for porking.

'Look,' I go, lowering my voice to a whisper, 'just because you have to see this woman doesn't mean you have to tell her anything.'

Honor's like, 'I'm *not* telling her anything.'

'Well, that'd be my advice to you. Tell her fock-all. And if she shows you – I don't know – a piece of paper with a blob on it or a focking squiggle and she asks you what you see when you look at it, say either a rabbit or a butterfly. Because they read shit into shit – that's what they do for a living, bear in mind.'

'I don't *need* your advice?'

'That's good.'

'Because I don't trust anything that comes out of your mouth anyway.'

Sorcha comes running up the stairs, apologizing to the receptionist and making comments about the on-street-porking situation in the centre of Blackrock. The woman smiles and nods like she actually gives a fock, then tells Sorcha that we can go in now.

This *one* – Siofra focking Flynn – is sitting in a leather ormchair when we tip in. She doesn't get up to say hello, just taps the sofa beside her with her hand to tell us to sit down, which is what we end *up* doing?

Sorcha goes, 'I read your book. *So Your Kid is a Prick?* Oh My God, it was, like, *so* an amazing read.'

I love my wife, but she is such a focking crawler.

'Yes,' Siofra just goes, finally looking up from her notes. 'I'm pleased you enjoyed it.'

She wouldn't be the prettiest thing on the buffet, this bird. She's in, like, her late thirties, with red hair which is, like, totally straight and goes down to her waist, a big, pointy hooter and two humungous warts on her face – one on her forehead, the other on her chin – and a body like a melting snowman.

Honor goes, 'Okay, give it to me, Siofra – warts and all,' and I end up bursting out laughing – and it's not me just trying to get back on Honor's good side.

'You are not to speak,' Siofra goes, staring at her, 'other than to answer a direct question. First, I want to talk to your parents,' and then she turns her attention back to me and Sorcha – she's a definite cold fish – and she goes, 'How would you describe your marriage?'

Talk about getting straight to the point.

I'm there, 'Okay, I'll answer that question, Sorcha. I'm going to use the word perfect.'

'No,' Sorcha goes, 'perfect is not the word.'

'Ideal, then.'

'Ross, we've come here for this woman's help. She *can't* help us if we sit here and tell her a pack of lies.'

She was the same at school – a focking swot.

'We've had problems in our marriage,' Sorcha goes and Siofra storts scribbling all this down in her pad. 'We actually broke up for two or three years. Honor and I went to live in the States, where she had – oh my God – a lot of amazing, amazing experiences and got to sample another culture.'

'What was the catalyst for the break-up?'

'Em . . .'

'Was there infidelity in your marriage?'

I'm like, 'No – definitely not.'

'Yes,' Sorcha, at the same time, goes. 'There *was* infidelity.'

Siofra's there, 'Which one of you?'

'It was Ross.'

Sorcha turns and looks at me with her determined face on her. See, I knew this was going to be about pointing the finger of blame at us slash me.

'How many times?' Siofra goes. 'How many times was he unfaithful to you?'

Sorcha's like, 'Should we definitely be talking about this in front of Honor?'

Honor's like, 'Oh my God – hillair!'

'Was it once?' Siofra goes. 'Was it twice? Was it more than twice?'

Sorcha's like, 'It was more than twice, yes.'

'Was it more than five times?'

'I would say it was . . . multiple times.'

31

'Multiple times?'

'I definitely couldn't put a number on it and I doubt if even he could.'

I can't stay quiet for this.

I'm like, 'You're doing a lot of writing there, Siofra – as in, writing a lot of shit down.'

She goes, 'I'm trying to ascertain the level of stability or otherwise in Honor's home environment.'

'Well, I'm just commenting on the fact that you seem to be writing a lot of shit down.'

We're only in the door five minutes and I'm pretty sure I've already been identified as the problem.

She goes, 'And you live with – you told me on the phone – *your* mother and father, Sorcha, is that right?'

Sorcha goes, 'Yes.'

'And you're in *their* home, are you?'

'No, it's actually *ours*? It's the house I grew up in. Oh my God, it has *so* many amazing, amazing memories – but my dad ended up having to sell it because of the whole current economic thing. And Ross's grandmother bought it for us.'

'So *they're* living under *your* roof?'

'I like to think of it as we're all living *together*? We're like one big, happy family.'

Honor laughs. She can't help herself. She goes, 'You don't need to own a Derby winner to know what horseshit smells like.'

It's one of my lines.

I'm there, 'The reason she's saying that, by the way, is because Sorcha's talking through her hole. Her old man hates my basic guts. He thinks she married beneath her.'

'He doesn't think I married beneath me,' Sorcha goes. 'He thinks that I settled.'

'Settled, exactly. And he's no fan of Honor's either – can I just point that out?'

Siofra looks at Sorcha. She's like, 'What is your relationship with your father like?'

'Amazing,' Sorcha goes. 'You've possibly picked up from what Ross said that I'm a definite daddy's girl.'

I'm there, 'Yeah, no, he calls her Princess.'

Honor goes, 'Oh my God, I've just been a little bit sick in my mouth!'

I laugh. No choice.

'I also get on amazingly well with Mum,' Sorcha goes. 'She's actually, like, my best *friend*?'

Siofra turns her eyes to *me* then. She's like, 'And what about you?'

I'm there, 'What about me?'

'What is your relationship with your own parents like?'

'Pretty typical, I would say.'

'Your father?'

'Yeah, no, he can be alright, when he's not trying to be my bezzy mate. And even though he's a total crook.'

'Your father is a crook?'

'Yeah, no, literally. He did time inside for, like, planning corruption and tax evasion. Perverting the course of justice – blah, blah, blah.'

She scribbles every word of this down, by the way.

She's like, 'And what about your mother?'

I'm there, '*She's* just a hound. Her and my old man are divorced, can I just add?'

'Okay. But how would you characterize your relationship with her?'

'Yeah, no, it's fine. On the rare occasions I see her. She's in rehab at the moment, in America. Focking coke-head. And it was a very good friend of mine who got her addicted. He was riding her for a while.'

Even that ends up going into her notes.

I'm there, 'I'm sorry, is all of this actually relevant?'

Sorcha has to stick her Shiva Rose into it then.

'Sorry,' she goes, 'can I just say that I think it *is* relevant, Ross. There's a lot you're not saying here. And one of the things you're not saying is that you are – oh my God – *so* horrible to your parents sometimes. Ross, I hope this room is a space in which we can be honest and open without one of us holding it against the other, but you must have noticed that the way Honor speaks to us is exactly the same way that you speak to your parents?'

Honor's like, 'Great story, Mom!'

And that's when Siofra suddenly closes her pad, puts the top back on her pen and goes, 'Okay, our time is up.'

Sorcha's there, 'Really? Already? I mean, we've only been here, like, ten minutes.'

'I have everything I need.'

I'm there, 'So what happens now – are you going to give us a few pointers?'

'Pointers?' Siofra goes.

'As in, like, dos and don'ts.'

'No, I'm not going to give you *a few pointers*. Unspoiling a child is a lengthy process.'

'Yeah, no, I thought it might be.'

'I'm sensing a lot of hostility and resentment in Honor.'

'Oh my God,' Honor goes, 'you're an absolute genius!'

Siofra goes, 'I don't think it's *unrelated* to her home environment.'

I'm there, 'That sounds very much like you're blaming us.'

'It's not a question of blame. It's a question of identifying modes of behaviour and working to change them.'

'But you're saying we've got to come back again.'

'Of course you've got to come back again. This is just an introductory interview. I want to see Honor twice a week.'

'Twice?' Sorcha goes – she looks at me with genuine concern on her face. I'm thinking, yeah, no, you're the one who opened your big Von focking Trap in the first place.

'Twice a week,' Siofra goes. 'On Mondays, I'll see the three of you as a family. On Fridays, I'll see Honor on her own.'

She stands up, which is our invitation to fock off. We stand up as well.

Sorcha goes, 'It was amazing to meet you. Again, can I just say how much I *loved* your book. I'm actually recommending it to – oh my God – everyone. And can I just say that Jack looks like *such* a lovely little boy.'

Siofra says fock-all.

Honor fixes the woman with a look and goes, 'What's the deal with your hair? Are you one of those weirdos who's, like, never had it cut and gets someone to brush it for you every night because it reminds you of your mother?'

Siofra goes, 'See you next Tuesday.'

Sorcha's like, 'I thought you said Monday?'

And the woman goes, 'Yes, I did.'

'See, this is more like it!' I go.

I'm talking about Christian's plan for the shop unit on Chatham Street that he's ended up stuck with after his sandwich shop was, let's just say, forced to close. From the middle of February, it's going to be, like, a comic book and sci-fi memorabilia store called Boba Fetish.

I'm helping him stack the shelves and I'm going, 'This kind of shop is definitely more you.'

I can feel Lauren just staring at me with, like, a *scowl* on her face? There's a little part of her that will possibly never forgive me for honking in that dude's roll and costing them their submarine roll franchise. I love the girl to bits, but she has trouble sometimes letting shit go.

I'm hanging up the *Star Wars* figures and I end up getting a bit distracted, still thinking about Simon Zebo's flick in Cordiff – a lot of people who saw it thought of me in my prime – then Christian ends up suddenly roaring at me.

'Jesus, how many times do I have to tell you?' he goes. 'Keep the *Vintage Star Wars* series separate from the *Legacy Saga Legends*!'

There's shit I *could* say, but I don't. He's a mate. And he's a mate who happens to be getting a hord time off his dolly right now – because there's a definite atmos between them.

So I just go, '*Vintage* and *Legacy* – yeah, you're totally focking right, Christian,' because that's what mates do.

While *we're* doing all the actual work, Ross Junior, their little son with the famous – I'm going to say it – lisp, is just pulling shit out of random boxes, then leaving it on the floor.

'Can I have thith?' he suddenly goes.

I just happen to look up and it ends up being what I straight away recognize as the Princess Leia slave-girl costume from one of the movies – I can't remember which one.

Lauren's like, 'Yes, Ross, you can have it.'

I try not to react, except my face, as usual, ends up betraying me and Lauren's suddenly looking at me in a challenging way, giving it, 'Have you got a problem, Ross?'

I'm like, 'Yeah, no, there's no problem here.'

She's holding little baby Oliver in her orms. She goes, 'You pulled a face.'

I'm like, 'Well, I didn't realize I pulled a face,' and then I try to change the subject. 'What do you think of the whole Sexton situation, Christian? There must be something we can do.'

He's like, 'From what I hear, the deal is done. The union wouldn't pay him what me and you know he's worth.'

'I find myself just bursting into tears whenever I think about it. It happened the other day in Mothercare in the Stephen's Green Shopping Centre. I was in floods.'

'I'd say there's a lot of people walking around this city feeling the exact same way.'

'I mean, I text him on the morning of every big game: *Eat nerves, shit results*. It's a major port of his preparation.'

'You can still text him, Ross – as long as he's not playing against Leinster.'

'I'd love to deck someone from the union. I don't know who – just someone.'

Little Ross suddenly goes – and bear in mind, this is an actual quote – 'Can I wear thith Printheth Leia cothtume to Debbieth fanthy dreth porthy?'

Lauren is on me like a cat on a bird.

She's like, 'There – you just pulled that face again!'

I'm there, 'Like I said, I didn't pull a face.'

'Yes, you did.'

'Okay, then, I did. Jesus Christ, Lauren, I can't be the only one here who finds it weird. Your son is asking you if he can wear a bikini to a fancy dress porty – albeit a very sexy one. It's focked-up – and it doesn't seem to be something he's growing out of either.'

'What business is it of yours?'

'Oh, pardon me for worrying that he might end up being bullied at school. Jesus, if I was in his class, I'd already be making his life a misery.'

What happens next is un-focking-believable. Christian walks over to little Ross Junior and snatches the Princess Leia slave-girl outfit out of his hands.

'No, you can't have this,' he goes – and bear in mind I've never heard him say no to his son before. 'Choose a costume for a boy. What's wrong with Darth Vader or Qui Gon Jinn?'

Nothing is the obvious answer.

'Or an Ireland jersey,' I go. 'Jesus, I've bought you two or three over the years – *and* a Lions one for Christmas – and I've never seen you wear any of them. That's been very disappointing for me.'

My phone all of a sudden rings, which is good news, because Lauren is about to flip a tit and it's a good excuse for me to step outside for a few minutes and let her hopefully calm down.

The girl has some serious issues – no real surprise, given that her old man is Hennessy Coghlan-O'Hara.

I'm like, 'Hello?' stepping out onto Chatham Street with the phone to my ear.

It ends up being Ronan.

He goes, 'Awreet, Rosser?'

And I'm there, 'Hey, Ro – how the hell are you? Actually, *where* the hell are you?' because I can hear, like, a *buzzing* sound in the background?

He goes, 'Ine getting a tattoo, Rosser.'

Oh, Jesus. The moment that every Southside parent of a Northside child must dread.

I'm there, 'Ronan, getting a tattoo is a massive, massive decision . . .'

He goes, 'I don't need a bleaten lecture, Rosser. Ine fooken sixteen, so I am.'

'Yeah, no, I know. I was just trying to come across as a good father.'

A bird walks by – a ringer for Nicola Peltz – and she gives me a cheeky little smile. I've just got that kind of face.

Ronan goes, 'Hee-er, have you been thalken to me grandda arall?'

I'm there, 'Yeah, no, last night – just about the Sexton situation, which you've probably heard about. Him and Hennessy and one or two others were talking about maybe putting up the money to keep him here, except the deal's apparently already done.'

'I reng him up, Rosser, and I astum about that fedda you were teddin me about – ancestor of moyen what fought in the East Dodder Roysen. And he steerts acton shifty.'

'He's *always* acting shifty. Jesus, Ronan, the first time you ever met your granddad you were talking to him through three inches of prison glass.'

'This was diffordent.'

'He's as iffy as they focking come.'

'Soon as I mentioned Donie Keddy, he steerts saying he couldn't hear me. I was bareaking up. Said he was in a bad aerdia.'

'And you're saying he wasn't?'

'I reng him on the landline, Rosser. He was at howum.'

'Jesus. And Ailesbury Road is definitely *not* a bad area, even if a lot of people living there are in a serious jocker moneywise.'

'So I throyed to ring him back. Ine throying him the last tree dayuz – alls Ine getting is an engayuched towun.'

'Have you tried his mobile?'

'He's not answerdon it. It's like he's avoitun me, Rosser.'

'I'm sure he's not avoiding you.'

'Ine arthur leafon six or sebben messages, but he's not returdon me calls eeder.'

'That doesn't sound like my old man. He loves you – you know that.'

'Sometun's arthur bodderin him, Rosser.'

'Yeah, no, I'll find out what it is. Leave it to me.'

I hang up, then I go back into the shop. And I end up stepping right into the middle of a blazing row between Lauren and Christian.'

He's going, 'Why don't you just say it? You never wanted it to be a comic and sci-fi memorabilia shop in the first place.'

And she's like, 'I'm saying it would have been nice if you'd consulted me.'

This is at, like, the top of their *voices*?

Christian's going, 'I'm trying to make the best of a bad situation.'

And Lauren's there, 'A bad situation caused by your focking friend.'

This is while I'm actually standing there.

And that's when I notice little Ross Junior standing there, sort of, like, silently sobbing to himself, looking at his old dear, then at his old man, then back at his old dear. The poor kid is being torn apart.

I go, 'Hey, Ross, how about me and you head down to Empty Pockets on South Anne Street and let the grown-ups talk? My treat.'

And that's when Lauren turns dog on me. She looks at me and she's like, 'Get the fock out!'

Except before I get a chance to come back with something, Christian goes, 'No, *you* get the fock out!' talking to his own wife.

She goes, 'Excuse me?'

'I mean it, Lauren. I don't want you here. Get out.'

Lauren stares at him for a long time, then she goes, 'Come on – we're going,' and she takes Ross Junior, still sobbing, by the hand and off they storm.

I'm disappointed to see that the kid ends up taking the Princess Leia costume after all.

Sorcha shouts up the stairs – asks me if I'm coming to *watch* this thing? I tell her I'm reading the boys a bedtime story.

She asks Honor the exact same question. From her room, I hear Honor go, 'Yeah, I'd rather eat my own tongue,' which Sorcha takes as an instant no.

They're about to watch this DVD of Sorcha as a kid handing over the family turkey to *Les Misérables*. Her old man has invited a crew around to watch it, including Sorcha's granny, various aunts and uncles, old neighbours, former colleagues from the Law Library and even Father Seamus, the old family friend who married Sorcha's old pair back in whenever the fock it was.

That might be their idea of a fun Saturday night – it's certainly not mine.

And like I said, I'm busy reading to my children.

'It would be an understatement indeed to say that Ross O'Carroll-Kelly was on a different level to every other player on the field in Skerries yesterday,' I go. 'It would be truer to say that he was playing rugby from a different dimension, showing why, at the age of just sixteen, he's already being tipped as a future Ireland number ten . . .'

I know they haven't a bog what I'm actually saying here, but my old man used to read me the Laws of Rugby while I was still in my old dear's whatever. I'm saying it definitely sinks in on *some* level?

'His four tries, not to mention the twenty points he added from the tee, represented only part of the story. Those present who were old enough to have seen one of the truly great Irish fly-halves play likened O'Carroll-Kelly to a young Jack Kyle.'

They're loving it, by the way. Well, Brian's already asleep, but Johnny and Leo are smiling away.

I'm there, 'This is the legendary Gerry Thornley who wrote this, by the way. You'll get to meet him one day. He could tell you some stories about your famous dad!'

Then I feel my eyes suddenly tear up, thinking about how they're never going to get to see Johnny Sexton wearing the blue of Leinster. I've been like this since Oisinn told me the news. I'm even having trouble sleeping in the afternoons.

Sorcha shouts up the stairs. She's like, 'Ross, the DVD player isn't working!'

I'm thinking, who the fock am I – Fix-It Felix?

I'm like, 'Yeah, no, we'll buy another one. I'm halfway through telling a story here, Babes. I'm coming to the good bit.'

She goes, 'Can I hook the laptop up to the TV? It might play on that.'

I'm like, 'Yeah, whatever,' and then I return to the story.

I'm like, 'The only downside to an otherwise exemplary

performance was an unsavoury incident in the second half, when O'Carroll-Kelly – having first intercepted a pass, then run seventy yards to score Castlerock College's fourth try – lifted his jersey to reveal his abdominals to the local support. Admittedly, they had singled him out for some pretty vitriolic personal abuse throughout the match. There is no doubt that if O'Carroll-Kelly can control his temperament, and curb his tendency towards showmanship, we are witnessing the early days in the career of one of the great Irish players of the modern era.'

Oh, holy fock!

This wave of sudden panic hits me. It's like I've been suddenly winded. I can't actually catch my breath. I drop my cuttings book on the floor of the nursery. I stand up, although for a second, I think my legs are actually going to go from under me. I run out onto the landing, then I go down the stairs two at a time, at the same time screaming, 'Don't touch that laptop! Don't touch that focking laptop!'

Except it's already too late.

As I'm pushing the living-room door, the only sound I can hear is Sorcha going, 'Oh my God! Oh my God! Oh my God!' and when I go in, everyone – Sorcha's ninety-something-year-old granny, eighty-something-year-old Father Seamus, plus all of the neighbours and Edmund's Law Library friends – are sitting there in just, like, stunned silence.

I look at the sixty-inch plasma screen on the wall and up there, in letters each as large as your index finger, is the Fock It List.

It actually *says* 'THE FOCK IT LIST!' at the top of the screen. And then underneath, just in case anyone is in any doubt as to what it actually means, it says, 'Birds I will DEFINITELY ride before I hit forty! BOOM!!'

Father Seamus goes, 'Sweet! Merciful! Lord!' and Sorcha's granny – I'm not proud of this – storts sobbing, with her handkerchief held up to her mouth.

And then it goes on to list them – forty-seven names, numbered in order of preference, including, at twenty-two, Sorcha's sister – no name, obviously. It just says, 'Sorcha's sister'.

Other girls are described by appearance. There's 'the lounge bird in the Merrion Inn who looks like Jenna-Louise Coleman except with a knackery accent' and 'that little Slovakian fun-bundle in Costa with the humungous overbloaters who always gives me a Massimo but then only chorges me for a Medio'.

And then – oh, fock, I'm just remembering – some of them have little comments next to their names, such as, 'I'd crawl five miles over borbed wire just to hear her fart through a walkie-talkie' and then, 'I wouldn't throw her out of bed for eating crackers (looks at own dick and goes, "Isn't that right, Crackers?").'

There is a lot of gasping going on. I'm thinking, why are people still reading it if they're, like, shocked by it?

Sorcha's old man goes, 'What in the name of . . .' and then one of his Law Library mates puts his hand on his shoulder to remind him that there's a priest in the room. In the end, all he can say is, 'He needs to be neutered – he needs to be neutered like a bloody dog,' while Father Seamus decides that this is one of those situations that requires an actual prayer.

He stands up and launches into the 'Our Father'. He's all, 'Our Father, who art in heaven, hallowed be Thy name . . .' while Sorcha's granny's breathing becomes suddenly, I don't know, laboured, and one of the neighbours announces that the woman is going into shock. They manoeuvre her into a horizontal position on the old chaise, then Sorcha's old dear and one or two of the neighbours stort loosening her clothing while shouting at her to breathe.

Sorcha turns to me, with tears in her eyes, looking for an explanation.

I go to say something, except I can't find the words. Because there are times in life when there *are* no words? All I can actually say is, 'That list was meant to be, like, hyprothetical.'

'And lead us not into temptation,' the priest goes, 'but deliver us from evil.'

2

The Only Way is Desex

Fionn goes, 'There *were* times when I lost hope,' and everyone in the room is silent. 'There were times when I thought I would never again enjoy the simple pleasures that I'd taken so much for granted. Reading Rimbaud. Enjoying a Sassoferrato masterpiece. Listening to Tchaikovsky's *Variations on a Rococo Theme* . . .'

'For fock's sake,' I go, shaking my head. 'He's losing the room.'

Oisinn shushes me across the table.

I'm like, 'He's dying on his focking feet up there. We need to create a distraction or something.'

We should maybe set off the fire alorm.

But then Fionn goes, 'Sitting on the green at Newtownsmith and watching the sun disappear behind the Joyce Tower. And – I'm going to say it – Hick's sausages.'

Everyone in the room laughs and there's a sudden release of tension. People even clap.

Christian turns to me and goes, 'He's nailing it, Ross. He has them in the palm of his hand.'

I'm there, 'Yeah, no, he's definitely pulled it back.'

Fionn waits for the laughter and the applause to die down, then he goes, 'I did my daily exercises, both physical and mental, even though there were days when I questioned why I should bother. Because, deep down, I knew – as most of you no doubt know, being accountants – that it's when you start losing the will to live due to sheer boredom that you need to stay focused on the goals you've set yourself.'

There's, like, more laughter and more clapping.

And that's when – fair focks – he says it. 'Then, one day, my friends came for me. And this feeds into what I was saying at the top of my speech about the importance of surrounding yourself with competent, goal-minded people you can trust. It was Bobby Kennedy who said of his brother, the late John F. Kennedy: "By God, I'd take his enemies – if I could have his friends." And that's how I feel about my old Castlerock College team-mates, who put their lives on the line to save me. And I'm going to name them, because they're here tonight, sitting at this table over here – Ross O'Carroll-Kelly, Oisinn Wallace, Christian Forde and JP Conroy.'

I let a roar out of me. I can't help it. I'm like, 'Castlerock Über Alles!' at the top of my actual voice, and I end up being shushed by a bird at the next table, an ugly bird with Rachel from *Friends* hair. Actually, you don't see ugly birds with Rachel from *Friends* hair anymore. Back in the nineties, they were everywhere – we used to call them Jennifer Manistons.

'Ssshhh!!!' she has the actual balls to go. 'Ssshhh!!!'

I'm like, 'Fock off – that's *us* he's talking about, you total focking mutt.'

Christian tells me to chillax.

Fionn finishes up. He's like, 'Whether it's surviving six months of captivity in a cellar in Uganda, or surviving in the challenging world of chartered accountancy, it's vital to surround yourself with the right personnel. Thank you for listening.'

There ends up being, like, a *thunderous* round of applause? I'm using that word.

I'm like, 'That's an ovation. That's a definite ovation,' and I stand up and I'm suddenly urging everyone around me to get up as well, going, 'Come on – everyone! On your focking feet, Maniston!'

A lot *do* stand as well.

The night ends up turning into a bit of a broccasion. The last time we were all together like this was Christmas Eve in my gaff. Although after what happened in Africa, we probably did all need a break from each other. Intense is the only way to describe it.

But it's great to see the goys again. We're literally throwing the pints into us and we're all nicely shit-faced.

Fionn tips over to us. He looks well in a tux, in fairness, and I'm not saying that in any kind of gay way. We all tell him we're proud of him.

'You got a bit boring near the end,' I go, 'but you saved yourself with the Hick's sausages line. I was the one who said it should be an ovation. I got them all standing – didn't I, goys?'

They all agree that I did.

'So,' Oisinn goes, 'is this the start of a whole new career for you?'

It's actually a good question.

Fionn goes, 'I don't know. I've had a few requests. And I have to say I get a real buzz out of it. I never got a response like that when I was teaching.'

'I'm not surprised,' I go. 'Banging on about Tchaikovsky and focking Rimbobo. I don't know what was going through your head. But, like I said, the rest of it was actually good – including *our* mench?'

JP is suddenly staring over my left hammer with a surprised look on his face. 'Oh my God,' he goes, 'look who it is!'

I'm there, 'Who?'

'That bird you were talking to me about. She's on the Fock It List.'

'Yeah, don't mention the Fock It List. Sorcha's not a happy rabbit.'

'Is it Ealga Gary?'

'Ealga?'

I turn around and it *is* actually her? Not only that, but she's heading in our direction. Father Fehily used to say that coincidence was the word God used when he wanted to remain anonymous.

I give her one of my famous hero smiles and I go, 'Looking well!' which would be a signature opening line of mine. In this case, it doesn't work, though, because she doesn't even look at me and instead makes a beeline for Fionn.

'Oh! My God!' she goes. 'That was, like, *so* inspirational!'

He's there, 'Oh, well, thank you,' shoving his glasses up on his nose. 'Ealga, isn't it?'

'Yes! I wondered would you remember me!'

'Of course I remember you! We debated against each other!'

'This House would tax goods and services proportionally to the amount of CO_2 they generate.'

'That was it!'

See, this is Fionn's essential problem. He's always had way

too much respect for women. I'd be trying to unhook her bra by now.

Instead, he goes, 'You made an excellent speech yourself that day. I think, in the end, you were the main reason the motion was carried.'

Jesus. I decide to get in there before he frightens the girl off.

'I saw you in *VIP* magazine,' I go. 'I was actually saying to JP that never being with you – as in, like, *with* with? – is one of my definite all-time regrets.'

She totally blanks me. It's weird, roysh, it's as if she doesn't even *remember* me? It's totally focked-up, but she seems to have eyes for only Fionn.

I'll give her sixty seconds before she gets bored and focks off.

She goes, 'I'm here with my sister tonight. She's actually an accountant herself. But I'm involved with the Dublin City Centre Traders Association and we would *love* you to give a talk at our next dinner.'

'Gee whizz!' Fionn goes – I swear to fock, he actually *uses* that word? Then he pushes his glasses up again – Clark focking Kent. 'It's very flattering to be asked.'

'Get used to it,' she goes. 'Right now, as a country, I think we need role models who can help us all to just believe again – as individuals *and* as a nation.'

It'd take a crew of ten men with shovels and biceps like Wreck It Ralph to dig me out of her.

Christian leans over me – he's locked – and he goes, 'What's the Fock It List?'

'Keep your voice down,' I go. 'She's *on* the focking thing.'

'What is it, though?'

'It's just a list I drew up of all the birds I need to ride before I die. Except Sorcha ended up seeing it. As did her entire family. And their friends.'

'Jesus.'

'That's why she had a conniption. She's still not talking to me nearly a week later. I tried telling her that it was only a bit of fun. It's hormless and blah, blah, blah. I probably wouldn't have ridden half of the birds on it.'

I look back to where Fionn and Ealga were chatting a second ago and that's when I discover that they're gone – as in, literally, they're not there anymore. I'm looking around, over both shoulders, going, 'What the fock? Goys, where did they go? I was about to take another run at her.'

And it's JP who nods in the direction of the big double doors at the back of the room and goes, 'Look!'

And I turn around just in time to catch sight of Fionn and Ealga disappearing out of the room, *holding* – I swear to fock – *hands*?

And all I can think is, oh my God, even I, in my prime, never worked as fast as that.

Siofra says she senses tension in the room.

She goes, 'It feels like there's some unresolved issue between the two of you,' and by 'the two of you' she means me and Sorcha.

I'm like, 'I'm sorry to disappoint you, Siofra, but things are going genuinely well at the moment – your Jedi powers obviously aren't as good as you think.'

Sorcha keeps her mouth shut, but I can sense Honor staring at me. I can almost *hear* her smile?

'Well,' Siofra goes, 'I can definitely sense an atmosphere in the room.'

Honor laughs, then goes, 'Oh! My God! If you're not going to tell her, then I will. *He* wrote a list on his laptop of all the women he's going to sleep with!'

The kid has a big mouth.

'Then *she* plugged the laptop into the TV,' she goes, 'and – Hill! Air! – it came up on the actual *screen*? Her granny was crying for, like, two hours solid! The priest had to throw holy water over the TV and the laptop! Oh my God, it was, like, *so* lollers.'

I actually think the priest overreacted. Looking back, he'd possibly agree with that analysis himself.

Sorcha has to toss *her* thoughts into the mix then. You can see where Honor gets it from.

'Yes,' she goes, 'I *am* angry, Siofra. I'm furious with him.'

And I'm there, 'Can I just say in my defence that it was, like, a *fantasy* list? I probably wouldn't have acted on it. And don't tell me birds don't talk about goys in the exact same way because I happen to know they do. Especially when they're all out together on a night out. Girls can be dirty bitches.'

I notice Siofra raise her eyebrows at that line. She promised us a judgement-free environment, just bear in mind.

'My grandmother is ninety years old,' Sorcha goes. 'You could have killed her.'

I'm there, 'Like I said, I heard you and Lauren on the phone a few months ago talking about Bressie. Some of the things that were said. Filthy. I was actually going to say it to you, "Bear in mind, that's another human being you're talking about." But I didn't. My point is, we all have a Fock It List. My only mistake was writing mine down.'

Siofra decides to step in between us then. She's like, 'I'd be interested in finding out the effect that this, shall we say, revelation had on your daughter,' and I'm suddenly sensing that she's coming down more on Sorcha's side than *mine*? 'Honor, how did you feel when you found out your father had this list?'

Honor goes, 'I told you, I thought it was hillair, especially when my stupid bitch of a granny went into shock. They had to give her, like, sugary tea and wrap her in a foil blanket. It was, like, a total lollercaust.'

'Did you feel hurt at all?'

'*Excuse* me?'

'Hurt – that your father would breach your mother's trust in this way?'

'Yeah, right,' she goes, in a really, like, sarcastic way. 'When I said it was lollers, what I was really doing was lying to cover up my pain. Oh my God, you're *so* good at what you do, Siofra! I'm looking around the walls here and I don't see any qualifications. Did you even *go* to college?'

'Why are you focusing on my qualifications, Honor? Why are they an issue for you?'

'Yeah, deflecting a question by asking a question yourself – you're actually *such* a cliché.'

'Is that what I am?'

'You know it is. And, deep down, you hate yourself for it. Or at least you should.'

It's suddenly *my* turn to play the role of peacemaker. 'Yeah, no, that's what Honor does,' I go. 'She lashes out and she ends up saying hurtful things. With me, it's either about my rugby or my ears.'

Siofra goes, 'Let's just move on,' because Honor has obviously touched a nerve. 'Let's talk about unspoiling – what the actual process involves. Do you have a whiteboard at home?'

Sorcha's there, 'We do, Siofra.'

'A board you can write on with a marker, then wipe?'

'I bought it for my finals to keep track of my study schedule.'

'Well, from now on, that's going to be your Honour Board – if you'll excuse the pun. You're going to use it to keep a record of Honor's good behaviour and also those times when her behaviour falls below standards that you consider acceptable.'

'I love the way you don't use the word bad, Siofra. I remember that from your book.'

Honor turns to me and goes, 'I think your wife would be better off using that board to count her daily calorie intake. Hashtag, *obesity* much?'

This we all decide to ignore.

'You're going to reward incidences of good behaviour with two points,' Siofra goes. 'But each and every episode of – again – unacceptable behaviour will incur a two-point deduction. At the end of each week, you'll calculate the points on the board and that will determine the level of pocket money and/or treats that she's given.'

Honor laughs in, like, a really cruel way. She's there, 'Seriously, how much are you paying this woman?'

I was wondering the same thing.

'This is more important than money,' Sorcha goes. 'Siofra, I'm really, really embarrassed.'

Siofra goes, 'Dig out that whiteboard and start unspoiling her today. And you and I, Honor, will start our one-to-one sessions on Friday morning.'

Honor's there, 'Oh my God, some pee just came out in all the excitement.'

'Between now and then, you might do a little homework for me by reflecting on your reasons for infesting your school with rats.'

Honor stands up. 'Please,' she goes, looking at me, 'I can feel my IQ plummeting every second I spend in this woman's company.'

And out the door she goes.

Sorcha is full of apologies. She's like, 'I'm so, so sorry, Siofra.'

And Siofra goes, 'I'm reasonably certain, even at this early stage, that Honor has a condition known as Oppositional Defiant Disorder.'

I'm thinking, no focking shit, Sherlock?

I go, 'You must have seen way worse than her in your time,' looking for her to tell me that she's not as bad as we possibly think, that as parents we're actually nailing it and she'd have to say fair focks.

She doesn't say that, though. She says nothing, except, 'I'll see her on Friday.'

We step outside into the pissing rain and we head back to the cor – Honor walking thirty yords ahead of us.

'Oppositional Defiant Disorder,' Sorcha goes, sounding strangely happy about it. 'Oh my God, she has an actual condition, Ross.'

I'm there, 'I don't know. I'm sticking by my original diagnosis that she's just a nasty piece of work.'

'Well, either way, the unspoiling storts today.'

'I'm still Scooby Dubious. I think I'm on the record as saying that you can't unspoil children any more than you can unspoil milk. Once they're bad, they're bad. We just have to accept that there's nothing we can do, except pray that she emigrates to Australia one day and just, I don't know, pick up the bill for any damage she does in the meantime.'

Honor looks over her shoulder and goes, 'Yeah, I *heard* that?'

The old man goes, 'Isn't that *the* most extraordinary thing?'

We're in his box at the Aviva for Ireland versus England and he's, like, holding little Johnny in his orms.

I've got Brian and Leo on my lap. They're glued to the match.

I'm there, 'What are you crapping on about?'

He's like, 'Well, every time *your* chap, young Sexton, kicks the ball, this little one moves his right foot. There! He just did it again!'

I smile, but then I'm, like, suddenly *sad* again?

I'm there, 'I'm trying not to let it affect me. But I can't believe the boys won't be able to see him week in, week out at the RDS. It just doesn't feel real.'

He goes, 'Your godfather and I are arranging a candlelit vigil out-side the IRFU headquarters once the Six Nations is over. We're going to march from there to the French embassy on Ailesbury Road.'

'What's that going to achieve?'

'Nothing, I expect. It's just a gesture. Let the union know what we think of the whole sorry affair. Isn't that right, Hennessy?'

Hennessy can barely bring himself to even *look* in our direction. He clearly doesn't believe that a corporate box is any place for babies – it's almost as if I've brought a woman in here.

I'm trying to acclimatize the boys to the old Lansdowne Roar – just to make sure they're not fazed by it when they get older.

Hennessy's like, 'Yeah, sure,' then he goes back to watching the match.

I'm there, 'Definitely count me in. For the vigil, I mean. And there's no way Christian, Oisinn, JP and Fionn would miss it either. By the way, why are you avoiding Ronan?'

He's like, 'Who?'

'Er, Ronan? As in your grandson?'

'Oh!' he goes, then he storts – I swear to fock – muttering and stut-tering in a nervous way, going, 'I . . . um . . . I . . . um . . . I . . . um.'

Ro was right. There's something going on and it stinks.

I'm there, 'Dude, you're not returning his calls, which isn't fair. Look, *I* know what you're really like – a complete and utter focking bell-end. But Ronan worships the ground you walk on. And he doesn't understand why you're suddenly blanking him.'

'I've been rather busy,' he goes, 'that's all.'

'That's horseshit and we both know it.'

He becomes suddenly serious then.

'Okay, you might as well hear it,' he goes. 'He's been asking about your great, great grandfather.'

I'm there, 'Yeah, I know. He's doing a school project on the whole, I don't know, big fight thing. Nineteen-fifteen.'

'The Rising.'

'The Rising. I'm still chuckling at that name, by the way.'

'It was you who told him, was it? About old Donie Kelly?'

'I told him his great, great and whatever else grandfather fought in the thing, yeah.'

'Well, I really wish you hadn't, Ross.'

'Why? What's the big deal here?'

'Because now he's asking was the chap in the GPO or was he in Boland's bloody well Mill.'

'And was he?'

'Unfortunately not.'

'Okay – so where actually was he then?'

'He was on the *Helga*.'

'The Helga? What the fock is the Helga?'

'The *Helga* was the ship that blew up Liberty Hall. He was the first gunner on the thing.'

'Okay, so what?'

'What I'm saying is that your great, great grandfather fought in the Easter Rising, Ross – but he fought on the side of the British.'

The penny finally drops.

I'm like, 'You're shitting me.'

He's there, 'I'm not.'

'Ro hates the Brits. It'd kill him if he found that out.'

'Now you know why I haven't been able to talk to him. I don't know how to tell him that old Donie Kelly wasn't anywhere near the GPO. He was firing shells at the bloody thing from further up the Liffey.'

'He sounds like a dick.'

'Perhaps so. But I think that's why the men of our family have always had a certain, shall we say, *sympathy* with the British? The first time you ever heard *The Fields of Athenry* – I'll never forget this; you couldn't have been more than six years old – you told me that you felt sorry for Trevelyan.'

'Trevelyan? Who the fock is Trevelyan?'

'He's the chap who had his bloody well corn stolen! That's why the famous Michael – inverted commas – was transported. "Am I the only one who feels sorry for Trevelyan?" you said. Isn't that right, Hennessy?'

Hennessy mumbles something. Ireland are playing shit, by the way, and I can tell he's putting it down to me bringing three babies in here.

'Straight out, you said it,' the old man goes. 'You felt sorry for Trevelyan. It was in this very stadium, as a matter of fact. Ireland against someone or other. I remember people gasping when you said it. "What an extraordinary little boy," they said. God, I was so proud. Instinctively standing up for the rights of property owners. Yes, our sympathies were always with our guests today – the wonderful English. I mean, if you're going to be colonized by anyone, then why not be colonized by the greatest civilization that has ever amassed an empire? The land of Shakespeare! The land of good manners! The land of cricket!'

I'm there, 'So what am I supposed to tell my son then?'

'Tell him anything you like,' he goes, 'just as long as you don't tell him the truth.'

'The truth would literally kill him.'

'There you are then. Lie, lie, lie – to quote your godfather's advice to me before I took the stand in my corruption trial.'

'I don't know if I *can* lie? Not to Ronan.'

'There are times in life when fictions, fallacies and falsehoods are far more palatable than an inconvenient truth – to quote from your godfather's summing-up during my sentencing hearing.'

'I'm wondering is that true, though? Is lying definitely the best option?'

'You want to protect him, don't you?'

'I'd do anything to protect him. Same as I'd do anything to protect these three.'

'There you are then. I wasn't above telling you the occasional white lie myself if it meant saving you from hurt. I'm going to say two words to you now, Ross. Italia. Ninety.'

'Italia Ninety? What the fock is Italia Ninety?'

'Italia Ninety was a soccer tournament that happened when you were – oh, you must have been ten years old.'

'Well, *I've* never focking heard of it.'

'Precisely. Because I kept you from it. Which was a job and a half, I don't mind telling you, because the whole country went half bloody mad during the thing. Watching *soccer*, Ross! Jackie's Army. All of that. People shaking inflatable shamrocks at you without a by your leave. Shouting, 'Olé, olé, olé!' in the street. Phoning you to tell you – to actually *tell* you – that they were too hungover to come to work. Oh, nothing got done for a month. Hennessy will tell you. Absenteeism was at an all-time high!'

'And this was definitely for *soccer*?'

'Difficult as it is to believe, yes. And I had to protect you from it. I said it to your mother. I said, "If he succumbs to whatever form of collective psychosis has taken over the rest of the country, well, it could spell the end of potentially the greatest number ten of this or any other generation."'

'So you kept it from me?'

'You're damn right I kept you from it! Oh, we kept you home from school for a month. Took the plug off the television. Your mother painted little spots all over your body and we told you that you had the meningitis. Said the same thing to any of your little friends who called to the door.'

I'm there, 'If I'd discovered soccer as a boy, I'd probably be a drug addict by now.'

And he goes, 'There you are then! Whatever you do, Ross, you have to keep Ronan from finding out about the truth.'

Sorcha's old man seems weirdly pleased with himself – why, I've no idea. He's standing at the island in the kitchen, slicing up a stilton-infused Leberwurst from the craft butcher's in Donnybrook Fair, while humming a little tune to himself that I don't instantly recognize.

He's a totally different man from the one who completely lost it over the Fock It List and was practically screaming the

Deliver-Us-Oh-Lords while the priest was saying the Exorcism Prayer over the Sony flatscreen.

I'm like, 'What are you so focking pleased about?' because it's actually annoying me.

'Oh, it's just my way of getting through the day,' he has the actual balls to go, then he goes back to humming, slicing pieces off the Leberwurst and eating them off the sausage knife.

Honor walks in. She grabs a can of Diet Coke from the fridge and goes, 'I've just told Taylor Swift that she's a sad bitch, Niall Horan that he can't sing and Katy Perry that she's an actual mutt without make-up. Seriously, what did we do before Twitter?'

I'm like, 'That's not a bad question,' because it'd definitely make you think.

'I mean, how did we *get* at these people?'

'I'm not sure we even did. A lot of them got away with focking murder.'

Sorcha suddenly arrives into the kitchen then with a collapsible whiteboard, a black Shorpie and a look of resolve on her face that I haven't seen since she led the UCD Philosophical Society's morch on the American embassy to protest against the invasion of either Iran or Iraq – who even remembers now?

She goes, 'Now, you can stop rolling your eyes, Honor, and you can do the same, Ross. You heard what Siofra said. The Honour Board is an essential port of the process.'

Honor turns to me and goes, 'I think your wife is menopausal.'

Sorcha's old man remains surprisingly calm. It's usually lines like that – about his precious daughter – that tip him over the edge.

'So, to begin on a positive note,' Sorcha goes, scribbling on the board, 'you put your breakfast dishes into the dishwasher three mornings this week . . .'

She didn't, by the way. I did it for her.

'So that's six points,' Sorcha goes, her voice all teachery. 'But against that, I'm sorry to say, you tried to shove that girl down the escalators in Dundrum Town Centre.'

'Er, correction,' Honor goes, fighting her corner, 'I tried to trip her. She was wearing a focking *One Direction* T-shirt?'

See, she can be very funny – if *you're* not the one on the other end of it, that is.

'So I'm deducting two points for that,' Sorcha goes, scribbling away on the board. 'Which leaves you with four. And I'm also taking away two points for saying, "Sit down, take the weight off the ground," to me when I walked into your room last night.'

Honor's there, 'I can't help it if you're a porker.'

'It's called baby weight, Honor, and it's very difficult to get rid of.'

'Especially when you're eating a Toblerone a day.'

We're talking lorge ones as well, by the way – Honor *could* make that point as well, but she doesn't.

'Which leaves you with two points,' Sorcha goes. 'And according to the pay scale that I've decided upon, that entitles you to . . . one hundred euros pocket money this week.'

Honor looks at her – I *think* it's a word? – *agog*?

She's like, 'One hundred euros? How the fock am I supposed to live on a hundred euros?'

I always get a little teary when I hear Honor come out with lines that I used as a kid. Seeing your own reflection in your children is one of life's great miracles.

Sorcha goes, 'One hundred euros should be more than sufficient for a girl of eight to live on. We put a roof over your head, we provide you with food and we pay your mobile phone bills. From now on, everything after that is a bonus that has to be earned. And if you swear at me again like that, there's going to be a further two-point deduction.'

Sorcha's old man decides to stick his focking hooter in then. He's there, 'Pardon me for saying it, but one hundred euros is still an obscene amount of money to give to a child of her age. Will I tell you what I'm expected to live on?'

'No,' Honor instantly goes, 'because giving a fock what you think about anything is not actually *in* my job description?'

Sorcha flips. 'Right,' she goes, drawing a huge zero on the whiteboard. 'That's zero points, Honor, because I'm taking two away for speaking to your grandfather like that. And zero points means zero pocket money!'

'Zero,' I go, trying to put a positive spin on things. 'It could be worse. It could be, like, minus-something.'

That's what my old man used to say when my exam results arrived. I think that's why I've ended up with such unshakeable self-belief.

'So it's been a far from ideal first week,' Sorcha goes. 'There's much room for improvement and I'm hoping to see that over the next seven days.'

Honor goes, 'Oh, yeah, like you can bribe me into becoming a good little girl,' and she laughs, which she can well afford to do, because she's still got that two grand my old man gave her a few weeks ago. She goes, 'You're actually a pack of saps,' and then she storms off upstairs, to go back to trolling fock *knows* who?

Sorcha turns to me then. She's there, 'I know you think I'm being hord on her, Ross, but Siofra says in her book that we're doing our children a *disservice* if we let them grow up thinking that rewards are something they're automatically entitled to?'

I don't know what kind of a society we're going to end up with if that idea ever becomes fashionable.

I say nothing, though, except, 'Yeah, no, you seem to know what you're doing, Sorcha,' and I go to leave the room to go and check on the boys, who are having their afternoon nap.

'Hang on, Ross,' Sorcha suddenly goes – this is, like, totally out of the blue. 'I need to talk to you about something, too,' and then I cop her stealing a little look at her old man – like she's expecting him to give her strength to say what she's about to say.

I'm there, 'We're not bringing in the Honour Board for me as well, are we?'

If only it was *just* that.

'That thing on the computer,' she goes.

I'm there, 'Are your talking about the Fock It List?'

'Ross, will you please stop calling it that?'

'I don't know what else to call it. That was its official name.'

'That *thing* I found on the computer – it's made me think.'

'Think? I don't like the sound of this.'

Her old man continues slicing that sausage, I notice, with a massive grin on his face.

Sorcha goes, 'I don't think you have it in you to ever stay loyal to me, Ross.'

I'm there, 'It was a bit of fun – that's all it was. I'm going to stay loyal to you this time. That was a promise I made.'

'Ross, you've said that how many times before?'

'The difference is that this time I actually mean it.'

'You've said that hundreds of times as well. I've given up hoping that you'll ever change.'

'So what are you saying?'

She looks at her old man again. He nods at her, as if to say, 'Be strong now.'

She goes, 'I want you to have a vasectomy.'

I'm like, 'Excuse me?' because I'm in genuine shock.

She goes, 'A vasectomy, Ross,' and she says it like it's nothing.

I'm there, 'And why would I have a vasectomy?'

It's her old man who answers that one.

'Well,' he goes, 'clearly you can't be stopped from philandering, but you *can* be stopped from reproducing. Sorcha doesn't want you to father any more children – either with her *or* with anyone else.'

I laugh. It's all suddenly becoming clear to me now.

'That's why you've been chopping up that sausage,' I go. 'That was a message to me.'

'That's your imagination,' he tries to go.

I'm there, 'Sorcha, can we talk about this in possibly private?'

'Ross,' she goes, 'I'm not going to change my mind. Dad is right. You've got *five* children.'

He's there, 'And those are just the ones we know about.'

I'm like, 'This is him, Babes, he's the one who's put this idea in your head.'

But Sorcha's there, 'Ross, we can't have any more kids. We have our hands full as it is.'

'But a vasectomy is a bit – Jesus, I don't know – a bit drastic, isn't it?'

He continues slicing up the sausage, except I can't even *watch* him now? 'Oh,' he suddenly goes, 'I think I've hit a bit of gristle there,' and then he storts sawing more *vigorously*?

I feel suddenly sick.

I'm like, 'Sorcha, please don't make me do this thing.'

But she just goes, 'No arguments, Ross. You're having a vasectomy and that's all there is to it.'

Christian's jaw is on the literally floor, in all fairness to him. He's there, 'She wants you to have a what?' very much on *my* side?

I'm like, 'Yeah, no, thanks for the support, Dude. Keep that to yourself, by the way.'

This is, like, an hour after he opened the doors of Boba Fetish for the first time.

He's there, 'I'm not going to go broadcasting it.'

I'm like, 'Seriously, Dude, don't even tell the goys. I'm still hoping to somehow worm my way out of it.'

He's like, 'What put this into her head in the first place?'

'What do you think?' I go. 'Focking *him*.'

'I'm presuming you mean her old man?'

'You're presuming right. Jesus, he was slicing up a sausage when Sorcha hit me with the bombshell. And he was humming a tune that I only recognized later was *First Cut is the Deepest*.'

'That's out of order.'

'It's very much out of order.'

'He's obviously trying to emasculate you?'

'Whoa, give me that again. I love new words.'

'Emasculate you. It means, you know, take away your virility. Castrate you.'

'Castrate me? Hang on, they don't cut your actual balls off, do they?'

'I'm talking metaphorically, Ross.'

'Yeah, well, they might as well cut them off as do the other thing.'

I end up working myself up into a bit of a rage about the entire thing. I find a quiet corner of the shop – they're all quiet actually, there's only two people in the focking place – then I ring 11850 and I get the number of a skip-hire company.

A bird answers after four rings.

I'm there, 'I want to rent some skips,' and then I try to work out how many I'll need – as in, like, how many books does this knob-end actually own?

There's, like, ten shelves on three walls of the study, which is roughly thirty shelves. Then there's, like, two hundred or maybe three hundred books on each of those, so I don't know what that works out at. I can't multiply when it's, like, high numbers. It's three hundred times thirty, which is a lot of books – that's all I know.

'I'm going to take a guess and say five skips,' I go. 'Five of the big focking humungous ones as well.'

The bird on the other end tells me she'll have to check whether they have five available and she'll ring me back.

I hang up and wander back over to Christian, who's suddenly talking to some dude across the counter. Try to imagine this goy – he's, like, mid-forties; fat; long hair tied back in a ponytail; little triangle of facial hair under his lip; black floor-length leather coat; wearing leather trousers and motorcycle boots.

And he's going, 'You always said it, my man. You said you'd open your own comic-book store one day!'

Christian's like, 'Ross, this is The Doog. We know each other from hanging out in Forbidden Planet.'

I just shrug. It doesn't affect me one way or the other. I've never been good at pretending to give a fock when I don't.

The so-called Doog goes, 'We actually didn't like each other at the beginning. We had this argument – do you remember what it was about, Christian?'

Christian goes, 'Yes, I do remember what it was about. If you chopped off Bossk's arm, would another one grow in its place? I said it would.'

'And I said what I still say today. Citation needed!'

'Dude, he's a Trandoshan!'

'Citation needed!'

'And all Trandoshans possess the ability to regenerate lost limbs!'

'Citation needed, my friend! Citation needed!'

I have this unbelievable urge to grab his head and smash it through the focking window.

'This is what we're like when we get together,' The Doog goes. 'We'll have to agree not to get into it this weekend, won't we?'

I'm like, 'This weekend?' because we were supposedly all going out on the lash for the Scotland match – we're talking me, we're talking Christian, we're talking Fionn, we're talking JP, we're talking Oisinn.

'There's a comic convention on in Manchester,' Christian goes.

I'm there, 'Excuse me?' because I literally can't believe what I'm hearing.

The Doog has the actual cheek to go, 'Temuera Morrison is going to be there. I'm definitely going to get my Jango Fett helmet signed.'

A grown man still playing with *Star Wars* toys. I end up seeing red. I'm like, 'Yeah, no, shut the fock up, will you? I think we've heard enough from you,' and then I turn to Christian. 'You're missing a day on the lash with your mates – on a Six Nations weekend, I might add – to go to a comic convention with focking Citation Needed here? Is that what you're saying?'

He's there, 'Yeah, that's what I'm saying.'

'Have you told Lauren about this?'

He doesn't get a chance to answer because my phone all of a sudden rings. I've changed my ring tone to Ryle Nugent going, 'Tommmmmy Boooooowwwwe!'

It was one of my better life decisions.

It ends up being the skip company. I step outside this time.

'We don't have five today,' the woman goes. 'But we'd have five for you on Friday.'

And I'm like, 'Yeah, no, Friday is actually perfect. You know what? You've just made my literally week.'

I'm going to have to say fair focks to Fionn and JP. They've arrived out to the gaff with – I shit you not – three pairs of, like, miniature Dubes for Brian, Johnny and Leo.

I actually couldn't think of a better present. I've seriously got the best group of friends in the world.

JP and little Leo are getting on like beer and wasabi peas, by the way. J-Town is talking to him – it's horseshit talk, really – but Leo is laughing his head off and grabbing at his face. I'd love if it happened for JP one day – as in, the whole baby thing. He'd make a genuinely amazing father.

'So have you thought about godparents?' he goes.

And I'm suddenly wondering is that why they're here? Are they angling?

I'm there, 'The talk at the moment is about possibly Leo Cullen to be Leo's godfather, Johnny Sexton to be Johnny's godfather and the Dricmeister General himself to stand for this little dude. I think it'd be a lovely going-away present for Johnno before he heads off to Paris, even though I'm still hoping I wake up and find out the whole thing was a nightmare.'

JP goes, 'You're not bitter then?'

'How could I be? It's Johnny focking Sexton. It'd be nice to let him know, you know, I'm not changing my son's name just because you're going to be playing your rugby for someone else next season. You're still a hero to me and millions like me.'

'Here, do you remember the time you asked Shane Horgan to be Honor's godfather?'

I laugh. That was back in the good old days.

'Then Sorcha said she didn't want some random rugby player,' JP goes, 'and you had to avoid Shaggy for about three years afterwards.'

I'm like, 'I couldn't hurt him. What, the dude who scored *that* try at Croke Park? And the other one at Twickenham? And I still stand by my original analysis – I think Honor would have turned out better if Sorcha had said yes to him.'

'She'd be a totally different kid,' he agrees.

I'm there, 'He wouldn't take shit from her. No focking way.'

'She's funny on Twitter, though – I'm talking about Honor.'

'I'm genuinely afraid to follow her. With a kid like Honor, it's a genuine case of the less you know, the better.'

'The abuse she gives these celebrities. She was the one who called *Little Mix* "Pic n Mix" – this was when they were chubby. She's got, like, eighty thousand followers.'

'Seriously, I don't want to know what she gets up to on social media. That way, if the Feds ever knock on that door, I can genu-inely say I had no idea.'

Fionn's being a bit quiet, by the way. So I go, 'Here, what's the story with that Ealga Gary one?'

This is while I'm putting the Dubes on the boys.

He's there, 'What are you talking about?' pretending not to know.

'Well, she used to be into me,' I go, 'and now she's into you. It's just a bit annoying, that's my point.'

He's there, 'I don't think it's any of your business, Ross, what she . . .'

'Did you ride her?'

'What?'

'And I'm asking that as a yes or no question.'

'It's none of your business.'

'I was thinking of taking a run at her myself that night. That was a focking clever trick you pulled, getting her out of there before I had a chance to hit her with some of my lines. I have to admire you for that.'

'Are we still talking about this?'

'I think she looks like a short-haired version of Gal Gadot and I was on the point of saying that to her.'

'It's a real pity she never got to hear it.'

'The thing you need to bear in mind, Dude, is that it was a pure sympathy ride – and that's if you even got the ride, which is still up for debate. You made a great speech that night. There was a lot of heat around you. I'm saying well done.'

'Yes, thank you, Ross.'

'I would have definitely ridden her that night if you hadn't been in such a hurry to get her out of the room. I'd have hit her with one or two lines – mostly compliments that I already had lined up – and twenty minutes later I'd have been up to my balls in her down in the underground cor pork – like in my Annabel's heyday!'

Oh, fock.

Sorcha is suddenly standing at the door of the nursery. I'm won-dering did she, like, hear any of that?

I decide to just play it cool and hopefully bluff my way out of it.

I'm like, 'Hey, Babes. The goys brought Dubes for the babies –
actual Dubes, look.'

She's like, 'Oh my God, they're so cute!'

'Cute is definitely the word.'

She goes, 'Thank you so much, goys,' head cocked to one side,
smiling from ear to ear.

I think, okay, she mustn't have heard me.

Except then she turns suddenly serious – this is in front of my
friends, bear in mind – and she goes, 'Ross, I'm going to ring the
clinic now and make an appointment for your vasectomy.'

I'm driving through town in Sorcha's famous Nissan focking Leaf,
Pac Manning my way up Kildare Street when, halfway up, I sud-
denly spot Ronan, waiting to cross at the pedestrian lights opposite
Buswells.

I still can't believe the height of him. He must be, like, six-foot tall
now. It seems like no time at all since he was seven years old and
shouting, 'If it's a fooken war you're wanting, then bring it on!' at
the local district court judge in Swords.

I give him a quick blast of the horn to wake him from his little
daydream, then he cops me and I tell him to hop in. I'll drop him
home.

He's like, 'Awreet, Rosser?'

And I'm there, 'Yeah, no, not bad, Ro – not bad at all. Here, why
aren't you at school?' realizing, the second I've said it, how totally
ridiculous that question sounds coming from me.

'Ine arthur been in the Nationiddle Library,' he goes. 'Re-
seerchen.'

He shows me a black, leather-bound notebook, the same kind he
used to use when he was a kid and he'd spend his entire summers
watching the movements of various cash-in-transit vans going
about their business, taking down their licence plates, the number
of personnel they used and the times at which they delivered money
to individual banks.

Like I said, they grow up so fast.

'What exactly are you researching?' I go.

He's like, 'Ine looking for Donie Keddy's nayum in the offishiddle records.'

Oh, fock, I'm suddenly thinking. This shit again.

'And, em, any luck?' I go.

He's there, 'Nuttin. I caddent foyunt any thrace of the fedda. There idn't a Donie Keddy listed addywhere among the combatants.'

'I'm just thinking out loud here, but was this Easter Rising thing definitely as big a deal as everyone seems to be making out? I mean, maybe we should all just get over it.'

'It's the most important date in Arelunt's histoddy, Rosser.'

'Definitely, though?'

'Yeah, definitely. Addyhow, theeve them all listed – all the Vodun-teers what took peert. Like I says to you, he wadn't in the GPO and he wadn't in Boland's Middle. He wadn't in the Fower Cowerts and he wadn't in Jacob's Factoddy.'

'Do you know what I'm just thinking, Ro?'

'What?'

'Maybe my old man made the whole story up.'

'Why would he do that, Rosser?'

'This is a dude who's done actual *jail* time, remember? The judge who sent him down said, "If Charles O'Carroll-Kelly ever caught himself telling the truth, he'd tell three lies to cover up for it." I'm actually just thinking, there probably never even *was* a Donie Kelly. It sounds like a totally made-up name anyway.'

'No, that was he's nayum, Rosser. I got he's beert ceert and evything.'

He shows it to me. I don't know where this kid got his brains, but it definitely wasn't from me.

'See?' he goes. 'Donie Keddy. He was borden in eighteen-hondord-and-noyunty, look.'

I'm there, 'Yeah, it's very interesting if you're into that kind of thing. I'm not sure I agree with *keeping* old stuff like this?'

'What are you thalken about? This is peert of who we eer.'

'Yeah, but what good does any of it do? People going, "Oh, this happened", and then it's, "Oh, that happened". It's all a bit boring is the point I'm trying to make.'

'Do you know what this mee-uns, Rosser?'

'Er, no.'

'It mee-uns that Donie Keddy's conthribution to the fight for Are-lunt's freedom hasn't been recognized.'

'Maybe it's best left that way. Like I said, Ro, my attitude towards history at school was that it was focking ridiculous and there was too much shit to remember. I hope I've succeeded in putting your mind at ease.'

'You habn't, Ross. I need to foyunt out the troot – so I can get he's nayum put on the offishiddle list of Vodunteers what fought for eer independthints.'

That's when he suddenly pulls his jumper off over his head, then rolls up the sleeve of his T-shirt to show me the top of his orm. It's his tattoo. It's not what I *expected*? It's just a list of names.

I'm there, 'Who the fock are these people? Padraig Pearse. Thomas McDonagh. Thomas Clarke. Are they soccer?'

He's like, 'Soccer? They're the Vodunteers that was executed, Rosser, in the sayum battle in which my garreat, garreat, garreat garrantfadder fought.'

'Joseph Plunkett. William Pearse. Edward Daly. I'm sorry to dis-appoint you, but I've never heard of any of these randomers.'

That's when he pulls up his other sleeve and shows me his other orm. It's pretty much the same thing. Seven more names. Eamonn Ceannt and whoever else.

I'm there, 'Dude, when you said you were getting a tattoo, I genuinely thought it was going to be the Manchester soccer logo. Or – yeah, no – Shadden and Rihanna-Brogan's names with, like, a *love*hort? These names don't mean anything to me and I dare say I speak for ninety-nine point nine percent of the population.'

He's like, 'I've to go back, Rosser. Ine getting beerbed woyer and explosions added to them.'

'What about your famous Dubs? Why don't you get a big crest of the Dubs put over the names of these random dudes? Imagine the looks you'll get on Hill 15!'

'No way, Rosser. And I'll tell you what else Ine gonna do. Soon as I foyunt out the stordee, Ine gonna have Donie Keddy's nayum put on me fore-eerm there – wit the Arelunt flag, then, underneat, the woords, "Republican heerdo" '.

Jesus.

My phone all of a sudden goes, 'Tommmmmy Boooooowwwe!'

I answer. It ends up being Sorcha.

She's like, 'Where are you?'

I'm there, 'I'm on the way to Finglas. I ran into Ro in town and I'm dropping him home.'

'The clinic rang back.'

'Okay? And?'

'September.'

'September as in?'

'September is the earliest appointment – for you to have this thing.'

I pull up at a red light on Baggot Street and I punch the air.

I'm like, 'September?' trying to sound like I'm crushed.

She goes, 'I've been ringing different clinics all day yesterday and all day today.'

'God, that's disappointing, isn't it? Genuinely disappointing.'

'Don't give me that. I know what you're thinking, Ross.'

'Okay, what am I thinking?'

'You're thinking September is, like, seven months away. You'll have plenty of time to sweet-talk me around.'

She knows what I'm thinking alright.

I'm there, 'That couldn't be further from my thoughts, Babes. Look, you and your old man seem to think I should have this oper-ation, so I'm prepared to have it. At least this gives you enough time to decide whether or not it's a massive, massive mistake.'

She hangs up. I punch the air again and go, 'Yes!'

Ronan's like, 'What's the stordee?'

'Sorcha wants me to have the snip.'

He laughs. It's funny, I suppose.

He goes, 'They're finally taking Ross O'Cattle-Keddy's balls, what?'

I laugh along.

I'm there, 'Maybe not, Ro. The earliest appointment she can get me is September.'

69

'So you've, what, a seven-munt stay of execushidden,' he goes.

'No, because I know exactly what's going to happen. By the time September rolls around, Brian, Johnny and Leo are going to be nearly a year old. Sorcha is going to miss them being tiny little babies . . .'

'She's not gonna want anutter, Rosser.'

'I think she'll want to keep open the option of possibly one day having more. Cluckiness is nature's way of keeping the species going – that's an example of me being deep.'

All the way to Finglas, I'm just shaking my head, thinking how Father Fehily is obviously looking down on me again.

The receptionist is giving me serious daggers. She says there's a rule about mobile phones in the waiting room. Actually, she doesn't say it – she points at, like, a *sign* that says it?

I mouth the words, 'Yeah, fock off,' to her and I go back to talking to Oisinn.

I'm sure she's thinking, it's no wonder his daughter needs counselling.

Oisinn's telling me about this one-night-stand he had last weekend with some random bird he met on Tinder.

It's a new one on me.

He's there, 'It's, like, a matchmaking app that uses geolocation technology to allow you to set a specific radius and then hook up with people within that radius.'

I'm like, 'Okay, simplify, Dude.'

He laughs. He knows how famously thick I am.

He's there, 'It basically connects you with people nearby who are looking for a date slash casual sex with no questions asked and no promise of a second meeting required.'

'I've had something like that for years,' I go. 'It's called my personality.'

I'm on fire this morning. If Oisinn was here in person, there'd be a high-five for me for that line. There just would.

'See, it's alright for pretty boys like you,' he goes. 'But for dudes like me who get knocked back about thirty times for every one time we click, well, this saves a lot of wasted chatting-up time and embarrassment.'

I'm there, 'So it's kind of like Hailo, except you get a ride instead of a taxi?'

The receptionist sort of, like, tuts to herself. So do one or two others in the waiting room.

Honor suddenly steps out of the, I don't know, consultation room, all smiles.

I'm like, 'Dude, I've got to split. Honor's just come out of her psychiatrist's office. I'll see you in Kielys on Sunday.'

Five minutes later, me and my daughter are in the cor, heading home. *She* has her nose in her phone as per usual, trolling some poor focker or other. I know that Caroline Flack has been making her very angry recently.

I hate to, like, *pry*? I know there's certain shit that gets said in the one-to-one sessions that's supposed to stay in the room, but as we're driving up Stradbrook Road, I can't resist the temptation to go, 'So what's the verdict so far? Has this Siofra one come up with any answers as to what's wrong with you?'

Honor goes, '*You* said there was nothing wrong with me,' straight away on the defensive.

'And I still stand by that. I think what I'm trying to ask is whose side does she seem to be coming down on in terms of which of us, me or Sorcha, is the better parent?'

'It's not about that.'

'Yeah, no, I was only asking. She must be coming down on one side or the other, though. Have there even been hints?'

'No. She just asks me questions, that's all.'

'What kind of questions?'

'Questions about stuff.'

'Again, what kind of stuff?'

'Just stuff.'

'Like why you put all those rats in your school?'

'Yeah.'

'And did you mention to her that I was against the idea of sending you to a non-fee-paying school in the first place?'

'No, I just said it was a shit school. They gave out free milk and they said prayers. '

'I'd just be interested to know whether she thinks I'm nailing it as a parent or not – and whether there are any areas I could improve on.'

'Everything doesn't have to be about you.'

'That's one way of looking at it, I suppose. Anyway, Honor, I have a little treat for you.'

'Is it money?'

Her little hopeful face – they break your hort at that age.

'No,' I go, 'it's not money. Even though I know you're probably a bit short of moo since this unspoiling bullshit came in.'

She goes, 'If it's not money, you've already lost my interest. Hashtag, snore.'

And I'm there, 'Well, you might change your mind when you find out.'

We pull into the driveway and I notice that they've arrived. I'm talking about the *skips* I ordered?

'We're going to burn all of your grandfather's books,' I go.

I can't even begin to describe the happiness that comes over her face.

She's like, 'What?'

I'm there, 'Oh, you heard right, kid.'

She goes, 'Oh! My! God!' and I suddenly feel like the best father in the world.

We go into the gaff – Sorcha and her old pair have gone to the Handweavers for lunch, taking the boys with them – and we head for the study. I grab an ormful of books from a shelf and Honor does the same and we carry them out and drop them into one of the skips. Then we go back inside for more.

Honor's like, 'Oh my God, this is *so* lollers.'

I'm there, 'I told you it was going to be good, didn't I?'

'This is one of the best things we've ever done together.'

'That's a lovely thing for me to hear, Honor. Never worry about saying stuff like that to me.'

'I can't wait to see *his* face – he's such an orsehole.'

'I hate books. I genuinely do.'

'Why does he need so many anyway?'

'Er, *my* point? It's not right for *anyone* to be this much into books. I don't focking trust it.'

'It's going to be so funny when he finds out.'

'I'm thinking of turning the room into, like, a gym. Just in case I go back to playing rugby, which is a definite possibility, by the way. Actually, it'd be good for your old dear as well – she could do with putting in a few hours. Although obviously don't mention to her that I said that.'

'Oh my God, she's *so* fat.'

'She knows her way around the Domino's menu is probably a nicer way to say it.'

It takes us an hour and a half to carry all of the books outside and they end up filling all five skips. The really nice thing is that we're chatting away the entire time, properly getting on with each other.

It's lovely – that's what I'm trying to say.

We go down to the shed and I grab the can of petrol that we keep for the lawnmower. I know you shouldn't technically *give* kids petrol, but Honor insists – 'I said *I'm* focking doing it!' – on dousing the books herself.

She makes sure they all get a good soaking, then I tell her to take a step backwards, doing the whole responsible parent bit.

I strike a match and I drop it into the first skip. There's a sudden *whoof*. I can't believe how quickly the entire thing goes up and I end up having to jump backwards a couple of feet.

'Oh! My God!' Honor goes.

I turn around and I'm like, 'Do you mean that in a good way?'

She's there, 'Er, *yes*?' and then she looks at my face and just, like, bursts out laughing. She's there, 'Oh my God, your eyebrows are gone!'

I'm there, 'What?'

She goes, 'You've singed off your eyebrows, you sap!'

She takes a photograph of me with her iPhone, then she shows it to me. She's right. My eyebrows are gone, my face is black and my quiff is singed to the point that it looks like actual *pubic* hair?

The two of us end up laughing – I'm not exaggerating here – for five minutes solid.

Honor goes, 'Oh my God, let's do a selfie!' and she holds her iPhone at orm's length and takes a photograph of us standing in front of the blazing skip, the two of us unable to keep a straight face as we think about Sorcha's old man and what his reaction is going to be.

'Okay, gimme the juice box again,' Honor goes.

She has all the lingo.

I hand her the can and she douses the books in the four other skips. I keep getting fits of giggles, which then sets Honor off as well.

We're both actually *sore* from laughing?

I light the other four skips, one by one, making sure to stand well back this time. We take a few more selfies and she posts them on Twitter, along with a message saying, 'Me and my dad just burned 4,000 books. LOL!' and it's the 'me and my dad' bit that really touches me.

I'd like to think that in years to come, Honor will look back and say, 'You know what? I'm glad I had that moment with the old man.'

'Shit!' I go after about fifteen minutes, because the smoke is getting unbelievably thick and I realize that I can't see Killiney Bay anymore. I can't even see the end of the gorden. I'm actually storting to choke a bit and I'm wondering should I have asked them to put the skips a bit further away from the gaff.

One of the neighbours is suddenly shouting through the hedge, going, 'What the hell is going on? What are you burning in there?'

That number of books creates a massive amount of smoke – trust me.

I turn around to Honor and I go, 'This is possibly not good for our lungs,' because I'm seriously coughing and spluttering at this stage and so is she. 'Maybe we should go inside and watch it from your bedroom.'

She goes, 'Wait there for a minute!' and she runs inside. Sixty seconds later, she reappears with a book that we totally forgot about.

So Your Kid is a Prick by Siofra Flynn.

Honor tosses it onto the fire, then we stand there, covering our noses and mouths, staring at the photograph of Siofra's goody-goody son with the blond, pudding-bowl hair and the turtleneck, as the flames wrap themselves around him and the book turns black.

Sorcha waits until the fire brigade have left before she turns her attention to me.

She goes, 'Oh! My! God!'

I'm there, 'That's possibly a bit of an overreaction, Babes.'

'An overreaction? Three units of the Dublin Fire Brigade?'

'One would have been enough. The neighbours must have totally exaggerated it.'

'The smoke was visible from Howth. We couldn't see six feet in front of us from the bottom of Killiney Hill Road.'

She's, like, full-on Elin Nordegren angry.

I'm there, 'Let's be honest with each other, Sorcha. I think this is about more than just a bit of smoke.'

She goes, 'Of course it's about more than just the smoke! You burned my dad's library!'

'Well, technically, it wasn't your old man's library. It came as part of the house. Which made it mine slash *ours*?'

'You *burned* four thousand books!'

'It was actually me and Honor who did it. And that's not me grassing her up.'

'Why would you do something like that?'

'I just don't like having books lying around the house.'

'Some of them were James Joyce and George Bernard Shaw second and third editions.'

'Yeah, I don't know who either of those people are – that was a real tumbleweed moment, Sorcha.'

'Some of them were worth – oh my God – *so* much money.'

'Like I said, you're either into books or you're not.'

'You know my dad is upstairs in literally tears?'

'It gives me no pleasure whatsoever to know that.'

Honor shouts down the stairs, '*I think it's focking lollers, can I just say?*'

I'm there, 'I'm only laughing because she's *making* me laugh?'

Sorcha ends up just shaking her head. I think she's still a little bit in shock.

She's there, 'I can't believe you would encourage our daughter to burn literature.'

'She didn't need a lot of encouragement,' I go. 'And there's no point continuing on this conversation, because they're gone now – and it's like a definite weight has been lifted from my shoulders. Did I mention that I'm going to turn the room into a gym for my possible comeback? I was thinking of getting some of Father Fehily's famous motivational quotes framed and stuck on the walls. *Rugby doesn't build character – it reveals it. The reason most people don't recognize opportunity when it arrives is because it usually comes dressed up as hard work.*'

She just stares at me and goes, 'Get out of my sight, Ross. We'll talk about this with Siofra next week.'

Scotland. Focking Scotland. They never beat anyone, except we've just been handed our orses by them. I'm giving my analysis in Kielys and it's as hord-hitting as you'd expect from someone who's never behind the door when it comes to calling it.

I'm like, 'Kidney has to go. I know I said nice shit about him when we won the Grand Slam and whatever else. But I was never one hundred percent convinced. How many Ireland schools teams did he leave me off back in the day?'

Fionn's there, 'All of them.'

I'm like, 'I rest my case.'

JP goes, 'He certainly seemed to have a blind-spot where you were concerned,' which is a nice thing for me to hear, even though the dude *could* be ripping the piss, because he's hammered – as we *all* are? 'He didn't bring you to the U-19 World Cup either.'

I'm there, 'There you are then. I've been questioning his judgement of players since – when *was* that? – 1998?'

'And even though he would possibly argue that his decision not to bring you to France was vindicated by the fact that they actually won the tournament, I always look back on that as the moment when Ireland lost potentially the greatest player in the history of the game – someone who would have made a massive difference today.'

I stare at him for a few seconds. He seems to be serious.

'Yeah, no, I'll accept that,' I go. 'He brought Brian O'Driscoll and he didn't bring me. Unfortunately for me, I liked a drink. That's the difference between success and failure at this level, I suppose. It's millimetres. I think even Drico would accept that he was the lucky one.'

Oisinn arrives over with the pints.

'By the way,' I go, 'I'm celebrating tonight – remember that whole vasectomy thing?'

Oisinn's like, 'Vasectomy thing?' because he's the only one who hasn't heard. 'What's this about?'

I'm there, 'Yeah, no, I never told you. Sorcha's old man is trying to have me neutered, as he calls it, because I'm such a dirty dog. But it turns out the waiting list for the op is something ridiculous. The earliest I can get it done is September.'

JP goes, 'September? That gives you a lot of time to sweet-talk Sorcha around.'

'You're smelling what I'm stepping in, Dude! You're smelling what I'm stepping in!'

JP lifts his glass. He's like, 'Here's to the Irish health service!' and I laugh and return the toast.

Fionn, I notice, is all of a sudden looking over my shoulder – there's obviously someone more interesting behind me.

I turn around and it ends up being this bird called Lucy Markham, a bird we all knew from Knackery Doo back in the day – thick as a fock-ing embassy hedge, but an absolute cracker in terms of, like, *looks*?

She's coming over to us – except it's not me, JP or even Oisinn she's interested in.

She goes, 'Fionn?' and I'm just standing there thinking, okay, this is becoming ridiculous now. 'I don't know if you remember, we did drama together when we were in, like, primary school?'

Under normal circumstances, a bird like Lucy wouldn't look twice at someone like Fionn. She's a ringer, bear in mind, for Sammy Winward, except probably more horsey-looking.

I quite like horsey-looking birds.

'I remember you,' Fionn goes. 'I think you were also in girl guides with my sister.'

She's there, 'I *was* in girl guides with your sister!'

'Eleanor.'

'Eleanor – that's right!'

Focking spare me. I decide to get in there to show Fionn how a real player operates.

'I was a big admirer of yours back in the day,' I go, fixing her with a look – you know the look I mean. 'I don't know if you remember the time you were waiting at the bus stop opposite Foxrock Church. You were all dressed up to go out somewhere with your mates and I flew through a puddle in the old Z4 and drenched the focking lot of you!'

Except this line seems to just go over her head. She flashes her upper veneers at me in what passes for a smile in this port of the world, then goes back to talking to Fionn, clearly smitten.

'When you were kidnapped,' she goes, 'I said to my mom, "Oh! My God! I hope he's okay! We were really, really good friends in drama!"'

He's like, 'That's very sweet – thank you.'

'You are, like, so brave to come through something like that.'

All of a sudden, six or seven other birds stort shuffling over – they're all Lucy's friends. Suddenly, they're all telling him the same shit – they knew him through this club or that person or this society in UCD – crowding around him like seagulls waiting for chum to be tossed.

Me, JP and Oisinn end up being literally pushed to one side, left there on our Tobler.

'Yeah, no, we were in Africa as well,' I try to go. 'As a matter of fact, I was the one who did the majority of the rescuing. Fionn was crying like a focking girl because he thought we were going to be shot.'

But my lines are totally wasted on these people. No one even looks at me.

Oisinn makes a pretty gallant attempt to pick one of the weaker ones off the edge of the pack. I'm pretty sure she's called Sarah Jane something or other and she's a focking disgrace – a horrendous underbite and a chest as flat as a dead man's ECG – but even *she* has no interest in the rest of us. Oisinn tells her that *Neroli Portofino* is actually his favourite perfume at the moment – which isn't actually *bad* in terms of an opening line? – but she just says thanks and turns her attention, like the rest of them, back to Fionn.

Oisinn takes this surprisingly well, considering this was supposed to be a goys' night out.

'We're wasting our time,' he eventually goes, taking a sudden interest in his iPhone. 'We can't compete with that. I'm going to grab a takeaway.'

I'm there, 'Eating's cheating, Dude.'

'I'm not talking about food.'

It turns out he's talking about Tinder again.

I'm like, 'Dude, no one who considers himself a serious player needs to use a dating app.'

He shows me his screen. He goes, 'What do you think of her?'

It's a bird with short, red hair.

I shrug. I'm like, 'Average.'

He goes, 'Average is good enough for me. Goodnight, gents.'

I'm there, 'Dude, you can't just abandon ship. We're on a supposed night out.'

'She just messaged me. She's in Bellamy's. I'm out of here.'

Out the door he goes. I grab what's left of his pint figuring, waste not, want not.

I turn to JP and I'm like, 'So it's just us,' except this *look* suddenly crosses his face?

I'm there, 'Okay, what?'

He goes, 'I said I might meet up with Chloe.'

'Chloe? As in, "Chloe and Sophie" Chloe?'

'Yeah, no, she's at a porty in Greystones.'

'Focking Chloe? Are you seeing her or something?'

'I'm not seeing her. I've just, you know, seen her once or twice.'

Jesus, I think. He can do better than Chloe. She's been cocked more times than Elmer Fudd's shotgun.

I'm there, 'So you're bailing on me as well?'

81

He goes, 'Why don't you come with me?'

'What, just to stop you feeling guilty? Fock that. No, I'm going to stay here to try to stop Fionn making a fool of himself, like the true friend that I am.'

So then *he* focks off as well, leaving me *completely* on my Tobler, standing on the edge of Fionn's suddenly harem of women, like a literally spare knob.

I'm listening to Fionn and he's full of it. 'I knew from day one,' he goes, pushing his glasses up on his nose, 'that if I was going to survive this experience, I would have to stay physically fit and intellectually alert.'

'Here, Specsavers,' I suddenly go, 'tell them about me riding that female guard – the one who looked like Forest Whitaker – to try to win our freedom.'

And Lucy looks over her shoulder at me and goes, 'I'm not trying to be rude, but we're actually trying to have a *conversation* here?'

And I suddenly realize, mad as it sounds, that these birds have literally no interest in me whatsoever. Fionn has totally humiliated me and usually it's the other way around.

So I turn around and I walk out of there, out onto the Donnybrook Road, to try to grab an Andy McNab.

And no one – and I mean no one – even notices that I've gone.

3.

Who Killed Liberty Hall?

I can't believe Sorcha's old man is still busting Honor's hump about his ridiculous focking books. She's well able for him, in fairness to her.

I'm in the gym – which is what I'm now calling the study – just doing a few sit-ups, and I can hear the two of them going at it in the kitchen.

He's going, 'Do you have any idea of the value of those books you destroyed?'

And she's giving it, 'D. F. K., D. F. C.,' which I know, from personal experience, stands for Don't Focking Know, Don't Focking Care.

He's like, 'There were books in that library that were worth up to ten thousand euros each. And I resisted the temptation to sell them, even when I was facing bankruptcy.'

She's like, 'That's life in the big city, Grandpappy. Deal with it.'

Honor doesn't take Sweet Honey Iced Tea from anyone. I respect her for that.

I hear Sorcha go, 'Honor, if you speak to your grandfather again like that, I will be deducting two points from the Honour Board – and believe me, Honor, you don't have many to lose this week.'

I end up having a little chuckle to myself, then I finish my sit-ups – 300 in total – and I tip down to the kitchen to see if the kid needs a bit of back-up.

The kitchen is a scene of mayhem. Seriously, try having triplets – it's like a focking comet hits your house every day. There's, like, toys and all sorts strewn everywhere. Sorcha's old man is making an effort to tidy them up. Honor is staring into the fridge, tutting because there's fock-all in there she wants to eat. Sorcha is sitting at the table, feeding Johnny. Brian is lying on his play-mat – I like to think he's working himself up to do his first sit-up – while Leo is lying on his front next to him, going, 'Ah-goo, ah-goo, ah-goo,' being vocal, like any good captain.

It's amazing, roysh, because all three of their heads turn to me the second they hear my voice.

I'm there, 'I've just given myself an unbelievable talking-to.'

Sorcha's old man is bending down to pick up a rattle – he looks up at me. He's still seriously pissed about those books.

'While I was doing my sit-ups in your old office,' I go, 'I gave myself a little pep talk. It was, like, tears streaming down your face stuff as well.'

I make a big show of running my hands up and down my abs, like a Romanian busker fingering the keys of his accordion, then I stort talking about the kind of equipment I'm going to buy for the new gym.

I'm giving it, 'Treadmill. Weights bench. Definitely going to get a rowing machine,' and at the same time – I'm going to admit it – I'm staring at Sorcha, looking for a flicker of interest from her. If her orse was a carry-on bag, it'd have to go in the hold.

Sorcha's old man says nothing. He bends down to pick up a miniature rugby ball – you can tell from the way he does it that he's never handled one, miniature or otherwise, before. We're talking zero technique.

I stort showboating then, ripping the serious pistachio out of him, not knowing that the dude has an actual cord to play.

I'm going, 'I'm also thinking about dusting off your old exercise bike, Sorcha, and maybe getting a set of kettle bells. There's teams like Seapoint who would love to have someone like me in their firsts. Burning those books might end up being the best decision I ever made in terms of my rugby career.'

That's when he suddenly stands up to his full height again and looks at me, a smile on his lips.

'I have some good news for you,' he tries to go.

I'm there, 'What, you're finally moving out, are you? No real loss there.'

Honor picks up Brian and storts chatting to him. She's going, 'Hello there, little brother! Hello there, little brother!'

She's good with him, although I can see Sorcha keeping one nervous eye on her.

'I'm not going anywhere,' Sorcha's old man goes. 'I'm sorry to disappoint you. No, what I was going to say was that I've been racking my brains trying to come up with a way around this dilemma of yours – this ridiculous waiting list to have you sterilized.'

Sorcha goes, 'Dad, don't call it that. That's only going to escalate things.'

I'm there, 'September – yeah, no, bummer,' still not having a clue what direction this conversation is about to take. 'It'll probably have all been forgotten about by then.'

'Well, as it happens,' he goes, 'I had a drink with an old friend of mine last night. Arthur Minihan. I handled his divorce. Saved him a fortune, as it happens.'

'This is riveting stuff. I'd say the evening must have just flown by, did it?'

'He owes me a favour, you see. I had no intention of ever calling it in. But, well, he never fails to remind me when we see each other. You'll never guess what he does for a living!'

'I can't wait to hear. This is real edge of your focking seat stuff, this.'

'He's a surgeon!'

I can feel the hairs on my Jeff Beck suddenly standing to attention.

'What?' I go.

He's like, 'And do you know what area of surgery he specializes in?'

'You're going to say he does vasectomies.'

'He does vasectomies!'

'This is actually bullshit.'

'I mean, what are the chances that I should find myself enjoying a drink with him in the same week that you're struggling to find a surgeon to perform just such an operation at short notice?'

'You met him for a drink on purpose, knowing.'

'Hill! Air!' Honor goes – I actually thought she was on *my* side?

'Well, either way,' Sorcha goes, 'the upshot is that *he's* going to do the operation, Ross. He's booked you in for the 28th of May.'

All that work I did talking to myself, boosting my confidence – it's all gone to waste now.

All I can think to say is, 'The 28th of May is, like, three days after the RaboDirect Pro12 final – in other words, Johnny Sexton's last-ever game for Leinster?'

Sorcha's old man goes, 'So?'

I decide not to even bother engaging with him. He knows liter-ally fock-all about the game. I turn to Sorcha. I'm like, 'Babes, that's going to be a difficult enough week for me. Emotionally, I'm going to be all over the focking place. I think maybe we should stick with the original plan of September. It's actually a quieter time rugby-wise.'

'No,' she goes, 'it's happening in May.'

'May seems a bit sudden. I think I'll take a rain-check and go with September.'

'Ross, you're having the operation in May. I mean it. Otherwise it's *you* who's going to be moving out.'

'There will be no violence here today,' the old man goes. He's wear-ing his famous Cole Haan camel-hair coat, and his hat and his face are sort of, like, flickering in the candlelight. 'This will be a peaceful protest.'

There must be, like, three or four hundred of us gathered outside the French embassy on Ailesbury Road.

'Angry as we are,' he goes, 'we must not descend to hooliganism.'

'The focking French,' someone shouts, totally ignoring the fact that the vast majority of people here own holiday homes in either Brittany or Provence. 'We shouldn't buy any more of their cheese. We should picket, I don't know, Sheridan's – in fact, anywhere that insists on selling it.'

The old man just shakes his head.

He's there, 'While the temptation, I know, is to lash out, let us not forget that our argument isn't with the French. They are our friends. A lot of us spend three or four months of the year there.'

You can see people nodding and generally calming down.

He goes, 'And, as I'm often wont to say to the inestimable Hennessy Coghlan-O'Hara, what would John Shanahan's famous Angus beef be without a bottle of Château Lafite Rothschild for company?'

That gets a cheer and an actual round of applause. You can see why he topped the poll when he ran for Dún Laoghaire-Rathdown County Council.

'They love him,' Hennessy goes, as if reading my mind. He's standing over my right hammer. 'I said it in 1990. He could have followed Haughey, if that's what he'd wanted.'

I'm there, 'Yeah, no, it's pretty inspiring stuff alright.'

'Our argument,' the old man goes, 'is not with the French. And it's certainly not with the notion of a free market European economy in which workers are permitted to – inverted commas – *ply their trade* wherever they so wish. Our argument is with the Irish Rugby Football Union, who have allowed one of the greatest number tens this country has ever produced to slip through their fingers – and, let's be honest, they have a history of doing that.'

He looks straight at me when he says it. I feel a lot of hands suddenly patting me on the back – we're talking Oisinn, we're talking JP, we're talking One F from *The Stor*.

Everyone's going, 'He's talking about you, Ross!'

Someone shouts, 'Your son was the greatest waste of natural talent that Irish rugby has ever seen. Even Declan Kidney said it.'

It's definitely one of the proudest moments of my life. You can say what you want about my old man – he always had *the* most incredible belief in me. None of it was justified, of course. But he was always there on the sidelines, telling everyone within a one-kilometre radius at the top of his voice that they were watching the next Tony Ward, even on those very rare days when I couldn't hit sand if I fell off a camel.

I spot Christian, standing about fifteen, maybe twenty feet away. He looks upset. We're all upset. But I get the impression it's not about this.

I push the stroller over to him. I'm like, 'You look like shit. What's the Jack?'

He's there, 'Nothing,' keeping his voice down, so Hennessy doesn't hear him. 'I slept in the shop last night, that's all.'

'In the shop? We're talking Boba Fetish?'

'The night before as well. I had another row with Lauren.'

I'm seriously worried about them. The girl could do with copping the fock on.

I'm there, 'Was it about you going to Manchester with Citation focking Needed?'

He goes, 'Yeah. And other things.'

He's hammered, by the way – six o'clock in the evening, even though I'm in no position to judge.

Totally out of the blue, he goes, 'She went out last Friday night.'

'Out?' I go. 'Out where?'

'*Out* out. Got all dressed up and said that she was entitled to a life, too.'

'But she's, like, married,' I go, because I'm very old-fashioned in a lot of ways. 'She should be at home looking after the kids.'

'She arrived home at, like, two o'clock in the morning,' he goes. 'I asked her where she was and she said it was none of my business.'

'You don't think she's having an affair, do you?'

'I don't know. I'm saying it's possible.'

The old man suddenly goes, 'Will you follow me, ladies and gentlemen?' even though there are no actual women there – he's just covering all the bases. 'Will you follow me to the headquarters of the Irish Rugby Football Union, where we will give the bean-counting apparatchiks who run Irish rugby a demonstration of the depth of feeling that exists on this issue?'

'Will there be hymns?' someone shouts – presumably a Protestant.

The old man goes, 'Oh, there'll be hymns alright! And there'll be a few stories told, no doubt, about our favourite Johnny Sexton moments.'

'Obviously the Heineken Cup final against the Northampton Saints in 2011 stands out in the memory!' someone shouts. 'He did most of the talking at half-time! He's the one who got them to believe the match was still winnable!'

Someone else shouts, 'His cross-field pass for Isa Nacewa's try against the Scorlets last year was simply sublime! There's no other word for it! So was his forty-five-metre drop goal in the same match!'

It's pretty heady stuff.

All around me, people are lighting their candles. Someone storts singing *A Change is Gonna Come*, except changing the opening line to, 'I was born by the river, near the RDS – and just like that river, I've been Leinster ever since.'

Everyone joins in. There's some incredible voices in the crowd. Like I said – Protestants.

I check the boys are okay, then I put my orm around Christian's shoulder. He grabs one handle of the stroller and I grab the other and we stort pushing it, walking behind a humungous banner that Oisinn and JP made for the occasion. It just says, 'Let's Bring Sexy Back!'

And we morch to Lansdowne Road. We morch as a tribe. Because that's what we are. We are Leinster. This is us.

Although a lot of people do end up either driving or getting taxis – because it's got to be, what, three kilometres away?

Siofra is clearly a fan of books – that's judging by her reaction.

She's there, 'You *burned* four thousand books?'

She's looking at me like I'm a focking rabbit playing hopscotch.

I'm like, 'Yeah, no, and I'm sick of having to defend myself for it.'

Sorcha's there, 'I'm only mentioning it, Siofra, just in case you picked up on an atmosphere between us, like you did before. I remember what you said in your book about always ensuring that the lines of communication are clear.'

'You did the right thing mentioning it,' Siofra goes.

Honor actually laughs. She's like, 'Yeah, don't *even*! She's been storing it up for days – couldn't wait for today to arrive so she could come in here and tell you all about it.'

You don't get to be Head Girl in Mount Anville without having a streak of something in you.

Siofra keeps her eyes fixed on me. She goes, 'Can we talk about these books?'

I'm there, 'These books, as you call them, seem to be an issue with a lot of people – why, I don't know. They're something I've never been into. I'd nearly ban them.'

'I should mention as well,' Sorcha goes, 'that Ross involved Honor in the act – as in, the *actual* act? He let her douse them with petrol.'

Honor's there, 'Oh my God, you are such a knob,' taking her old man's side – it's a lovely thing for me to hear. 'Could your focking head *be* any further up this woman's orse?'

'I can't believe he gave our daughter actual petrol,' Sorcha goes. 'I should also mention that a lot of the books were very valuable. There were a lot of second and third editions. And a lot of them had – oh my God – *so* much sentimental meaning for me. They were, like, a huge part of my childhood. My dad had everything by Charles Dickens. Practically everything the Brontë sisters ever wrote.'

'See, this is what it's been like for me,' I go. 'Her just randomly throwing out the names of people I've never heard of, expecting to get a reaction.'

Sorcha's there, 'I can't believe you're actually proud of what you did – destroying literature. It's like something from – oh my God – Cambodia in the 1970s.'

'I've read three books in my life – Bernard Jackman's autobiography and Leo Cullen's autobiography twice. That's a fact. That's out there.'

'This was revenge. You only did it because my dad suggested you have a vasectomy.'

Siofra storts scribbling in her notepad like a focking lunatic – see, her crew think everything comes back to a man's obsession with his own dick.

I'm there, 'Maybe I just don't want to have a vasectomy, Sorcha – have you considered that?'

'It's the responsible thing to do,' she tries to go. 'We have three newborn babies – *and* a daughter.'

'My *mom* is very concerned about the population problem,' Honor goes, 'even as she adds to it.'

Siofra stops writing. She's there, 'Ross, I want to ask you a question?'

I'm there, 'Yeah, no, shoot for the stors, Siofra – because I think we've already decided that I'm the villain in this whole thing.'

'Do you see any similarity between Honor's behaviour and yours?'

'Okay, where's this going?'

'Honor infesting her school with rats and you burning your father-in-law's books.'

'I honestly don't see the connection.'

'Both, I would suggest, were acts of wanton destruction. Both – at least, according to Sorcha – were motivated by vengeance.'

'You're reaching, Siofra.'

'You don't think there's any common thread connecting the way you act and the way Honor acts?'

'You're embarrassing yourself, Siofra. Seriously. Stop it.'

There's, like, thirty seconds of silence then, in which fock-all gets said. I wouldn't be a huge fan of silence, but Siofra is big into it, because it gives us an opportunity to – get this – reflect, something else I have literally no interest in.

'Perhaps think about it between now and our next session,' Siofra goes.

I'm there, 'I don't need to think about it. Because I know that whatever way she's turned out has nothing to do with me. That's no offence, Honor.'

'Just think about it.'

'Well, I'm probably not going to think about it – and I'm telling you that now, Siofra, just to spare you any disappointment later on.'

They want you to stort doubting yourself, these people. That's how they get into your head.

She's like, 'Maybe just ask yourself the question then.'

I'm there, 'I've never asked myself a question in my life and I'm not about to stort now.'

She touches the wart on her chin – something I've noticed her do whenever she's challenged.

'Let's move on,' she goes, 'and discuss how you're progressing with the unspoiling.'

Sorcha's there, 'Oh my God, *so* well, Siofra.'

'Tell me about the last seven days. You're still using the Honour Board?'

'Yes, we are.'

'And did Honor have any credit at the end of the week?'

'Unfortunately not, Siofra. Her behaviour this week fell far below what I would consider the acceptable standard. She told me I had an orse like a –'

'You don't have to tell me exactly what she said. All I need to know is that you made good on the deal that she only receives rewards if her instances of good behaviour outweigh her instances of unacceptable behaviour.'

'Absolutely, Siofra! In fact, yesterday is a perfect example of that. Honor told me she wanted new Uggs – even though I bought her new Uggs for Christmas.'

'There's focking stains on them,' Honor goes. 'Because you made me go to Finglas in the focking rain.'

'There's a tiny water stain on one of them, Siofra, where she stepped in a puddle. You wouldn't even notice it. So I said, "No, I'm not buying you new Uggs, Honor, because buying you new Uggs would be an unnecessary indulgence – and you haven't earned any unnecessary indulgences this week." I was quoting directly from your book.'

Siofra's like, 'How did Honor react?'

'I'll answer that,' Honor goes. 'I called her a fat focking heifer. She was eating a pizza at three o'clock in the afternoon and she wonders why she can only fit into sweatpants. Hashtag – er, can someone *padlock* that focking freezer?'

I'm taking a sudden interest in my fingernails, not wanting to come down on either side.

She had that pizza one hour before her dinner, I could point out.

'She wasn't at all pleased,' Sorcha goes. 'She shouted some things and stomped about the house.'

'And how did you deal with that?'

'I did exactly what you suggested in *So Your Kid is a Prick*. I said, "While I recognize that you're disappointed – and I can actually *empathize* with those feelings? – the rules of the Honour Board are not open to debate."'

'Try to stick with that formula of words.'

'Then she started shouting, "I hate you! I hate you! I hope Dad dies, so that you'll be a lonely single mother." Sorry, I know you don't want me to go into specifics about what was actually said.'

'But you held firm.'

'I did, Siofra. I managed her meltdown – like you said *you* do with gorgeous little Jack – by refusing to engage with it.'

'Did it work?'

'I'm happy to say it did.'

'No, it didn't,' Honor goes – because she loves having the last word. 'I went upstairs and poured red nail vornish all over *your* Uggs. To see how happy *you'd* be walking around with stains on them.'

'Yes, she did do that,' Sorcha goes, 'and I've already deducted two points from next week's total.'

Siofra smiles at Sorcha – I shit you not – and goes, 'Just keep going the way you're going. It sounds to me like you're doing great!'

I'm back in the gym – well, it will *be* a gym when I've got more than Sorcha's old exercise bike in it – and I'm doing yet more sit-ups, dedicating these babies to *The Saturdays*. I do a hundred for Frankie Sandford, then a hundred for Mollie King, then a hundred for Rochelle Humes, then a hundred for Vanessa White, then a hundred for Una Healy.

I refuse to call her Una Foden, by the way – I wouldn't give your man the acknowledgement.

I finish up and I towel myself down. I'm thinking I might even do the *Sugababes* in the afternoon, all four line-ups if I'm up to it.

Suddenly, I hear, 'Tommmmmy Boooooowwwe!'

It's a number I don't instantly recognize, but I make the mistake of stupidly answering it and it ends up being Tom McGahy, Ronan's school principal and a dick of the highest order.

He goes, 'Hello?'

I can't believe he's suddenly in my head just as I was thinking about rooting Heidi Range.

I'm there, 'What the fock do *you* want?' because he's always hated my guts, going way back to my school days, when he told me to stort putting my school work ahead of my rugby and Father Fehily made him apologize to me in front of the entire school.

He goes, 'I want to talk to you about Ronan.'

I'm there, 'Is this about his tattoos?'

'What tattoos?'

Oh, shit.

'Nothing,' I go. 'Forget I said anything. What about him?'

'Well,' he goes, 'where is he?'

'I don't know where the fock he is. I presume he's at school.'

'Then you presume wrong. Because he's not here. In fact, he's been marked absent for the past two weeks.'

'I know he's been spending a lot of time in the library in town. I wouldn't sweat it.'

'He's supposed to be sitting his Junior Certificate in June. But, like you, he's allowed himself to become distracted by extracurricular things.'

'Dude, you need to get over that bollocking that Fehily gave you. It was a long time ago.'

'I've spoken to some of his teachers. As far I can see, he hasn't opened a book since Christmas – not a school book anyway.'

'Ronan's sixteen. He's a grown man. Why are you telling me all of this?'

'Because you've been filling his head with lies.'

'Lies?'

'He's become obsessed with finding this ancestor whom you told him was a combatant in the 1916 Easter Rising.'

Whom. That'll tell you what kind of man you're dealing with.

I'm there, 'It's not a lie. He actually fought in the thing.'

'Not according to the records,' he tries to go. 'I've been through them myself. You could save your son a lot of anguish – not to mention a lot of time that would be better spent on his studies – by telling him the truth now.'

'Listen to me, you focking whom-freak, I don't need you – a toss-pot and a tosser – to tell me how to raise my son. I play it as I see it. You'd know that about me if you knew where the rugby field even *was* back in the day.'

Five hundred sit-ups and I'm already thinking crazy thoughts about maybe coming back!

McGahy says something very odd then. 'Bear in mind,' he goes, 'that all of this is being noted.'

I'm there, 'Noted? What do you mean by noted?'

'I'm saying there may come a day, very, very soon, when you have to rely on my good nature.'

'Yeah, I seriously focking doubt that. Like I said, keep your hooter out of my family's business. You prick with ears.'

I hang up on him, then I wander down to the kitchen. Sorcha is sitting at the table, feeding Brian his formula, while Leo is goo-goo-gagging away and Johnny is screaming his lungs out in his little chair.

He's off his food at the moment. I know it's a weird thing to say, but I think the whole Sexton thing is affecting him as much as it's affecting me.

'Ross,' Sorcha goes, sounding pissed off, 'can you please help me here?'

I'm there, 'Yeah, no worries,' and I pick the little dude up and stort bouncing him up and down in my orms, at the same time going, 'What's up with my little Kicker? What's up with my little Kicker, eh?' and he eventually stops crying. I've got a genuine gift. There's no doubt that he's going to grow up to worship me – just like his namesake, I could say!

While she's feeding Leo, I *should* mention, Sorcha is also eating slices of Kilmeaden cheddar straight out of the packet.

'That old exercise bike of yours cleaned up very well,' I go, trying to be subtle. 'Most of the rust came off it.'

Sorcha just stares at me, having already decided that it's a dig. 'This is my lunch,' she tries to go.

'I'm just saying that Lualhati did a good job cleaning it.' It's going to be one of those fair focks conversations.

'I didn't have time to make a sandwich, because I'm busy trying to raise three babies while you're off doing . . . *push-ups*.'

'Sit-ups.'

'Yeah, like there's a *difference*?'

Someone needs a nappy change. That's not another dig at Sorcha. I'm actually talking about Brian. There's a hell of a hum coming from his general postcode.

I'm there, 'I'll get it,' just to show her I'm prepared to pull my weight.

I put Johnny back in his chair, then I pick up Brian, lie him down on the changing mat and get down to business.

'By the way,' I go, 'who's Lauren hanging out with these days?'

Sorcha's like, 'Lauren? What do you mean?'

'It's just Christian said she went out last week – as in, like, *out* out? You're her best friend. I just thought if she was, you know, having an affair, you'd probably be the first person she'd tell.'

I open the nappy. Jesus, the focking smell.

'Lauren wouldn't have an affair,' Sorcha goes, genuinely laughing at the idea.

I'm there, 'How do you know?'

'She's not the type.'

'Well,' I go, wiping down the little dude's bottom, 'all I know is that Christian is sleeping on the floor of his shop.'

'They're having a lot of problems – I know that much.'

I grab a new nappy.

I'm there, 'See, that can happen when the magic goes out of a relationship,' and I let it hang there in the air for a few seconds. I stick the new nappy on. I'm good at it. 'Here, speaking of which . . .'

'Okay,' Sorcha goes, 'all of this has been a segue into what?'

'I was just going to say that we should maybe go back to having regular, you know, fun and games.'

I just think if she remembered how good I am between the sheets, she might drop the whole vasectomy thing. If it ain't broke, blahdy, blahdy, blah.

'Ross,' she tries to go, 'I've just had triplets.'

I'm like, 'Yeah, no, that was three and a half months ago. I mean, how long do they recommend before you get back in the saddle?'

It's the wrong choice of words.

She reaches across the table and she picks up something, which turns out to be a DVD. She practically throws it at me. I manage to catch it, even though I'm changing Brian.

Hand–eye co-ordination is something you never lose.

'I want you to watch that,' she goes.

I'm there, 'What is it?' reasonably enough.

'It's a film that the clinic sent, guiding you through the procedure, the effects and the risks.'

'Sorcha, I'm still not a hundred percent convinced about this whole vasectomy thing.'

'It's happening, Ross. There is no debate about this.'

I tell Sorcha I'm going out. It's, like, Paddy's weekend. Ireland are playing Italy in Rome tomorrow and Oisinn and JP are keen to hear my analysis as to where Ireland go from here over a few scoops.

She looks at me like I've just said *the* most ridiculous thing in the world.

'But I've ordered an Indian,' she goes.

I don't comment on that either way.

I'm just there, 'This is kind of important, Babes. It's a question of, would I be prepared to see Joe Schmidt replace Declan Kidney and lose whatever he brings to Leinster?'

She goes, 'Ross, you have three newborn babies.'

'Er, they're *asleep*?'

'What I mean is, you can't keep up this bachelor lifestyle forever.'

'Sorcha, it's the last weekend of the Six Nations. It's very much a crossroads for Irish rugby.'

She stares hord at me. She's like, 'Did you watch that DVD?'

I'm there, 'Not yet. I definitely will, though.'

'I mean it, Ross, this has got to stop. It's all very well for Oisinn and JP – they're single and they don't have children.'

'Against that, I would say that they very much rely on my analysis. It's Ireland's worst Six Nations for I don't know how long.'

She stares hord at me again for a good ten seconds. Then she's like, 'Go then. I'll save you some chicken dhansk.'

She won't, of course. She'll horse the focking lot – that's as sure as we're going to be handed our orses in Rome tomorrow.

I grab an old Jo and I head for town – a man with a definite plan. I'm not meeting the goys at all. You possibly guessed that.

I whip out my phone.

Oisinn texted me a photograph last night of his latest Tinder date and she wasn't actually bad. She was a little bit like Amy Willerton, although profile pictures can be sometimes misleading and she might *actually* be mud-hog ugly.

But that's when I had the idea – which, at the time, seemed like the best idea that I'd ever had in my life.

It ended up being pretty easy to join Tinder. All you really need is a Facebook account. So I set up obviously a fake one under the name of Richie McCaw – hilarious!

For my actual profile pic, I took off my shirt, flexed my abs – actually, I didn't *need* to flex them, because they're as tight as wet jeans at the moment – and I took a few selfies of just my abdominal area. I downloaded the Tinder app, then literally sixty seconds later, I was part of the GPS non-committal sex revolution.

The taxi drops me off in town. And suddenly I'm standing on Grafton Street and I'm thinking, okay, Oisinn, let's see how good this supposed app is.

I hit the button and literally nothing happens for the first, like, sixty seconds. Then my phone all of a sudden storts throwing me pictures of birds in the immediate vicinity who like what they see and want a piece.

Unfortunately, most of them end up being pigs. You'd have to admire their optimism, though.

I quickly flick through them. It's, like, no, no, no, no, no, no, no, whoa!

She's nice. Ursula McKeever.

I check through her other photos. She might be a focking munter who just happened to be having a good hair day. That can happen. What's that line from that film that we used to watch in college? Even a stopped clock tells the right time twice a day.

No, she's nice. It would only be a slight exaggeration to say she looks like Roxanne Pallett.

I click and she obviously does, too, because my phone tells me I've made a match. It asks me if I want to, like, *message* her? I'm thinking, yeah, no, why not? So I do.

It turns out she's drinking in Bruxelles, which happens to be one of my favourite spots. So I tell her I'm very much nearby and yeah, no, maybe I'll pop in and *see* her?

I wander around there, thinking to myself, this is it – this is the reason we put satellites in space. Everything comes back to sex really.

I'm at a serious advantage, of course. Ursula not knowing what I actually look like means I can check out the merchandise without committing to buying it.

So it's very much a case of hashtag winning, as my daughter would say.

I head for Bruxelles and in I go. The place is rammers – like I said, it's Paddy's weekend – but I spot Ursula straight away. She's in a little huddle with, like, two or three friends and they're all looking at her phone and sort of, like, giggling – obviously wondering am I an Abercrombie & Fitch model or something – then looking around them, obviously wondering who, in this sweating mosh pit of humanity, it might be.

I check out the goods from, like, ten feet away and I'm happy with what I see. If anything, her photograph doesn't do her *justice*?

I walk up to her and I go, 'Hey,' laying on the chorm thick.

She's instantly embarrassed. This is obviously *her* first time on Tinder as well.

But her embarrassment is nothing compared to my surprise when she opens that beautiful little mouth of hers and *the* thickest bogger accent I've ever heard comes out.

She there's, 'By my oath, I don't believe it! Are *you* Richie McCaw?'

I actually take a couple of steps backwards and stare at her, just blinking. It's like on *X Factor* when some focking homeless mong ends up having a voice like Katherine Jenkins and all the judges end up having to go, 'Jesus, I wasn't expecting that – not from a focking bet-down, light-switch licker like you.'

This is that situation in reverse – a complete and utter ride who opens her mouth and the voice of Peig focking Sayers comes spilling out.

I'm like, 'Yeah, no, I'm Richie McCaw,' still holding back a little.

'I'm *saw* embirissed,' she goes. 'We were pleein with the epp on my phawn and Nuala here saw the picture of you with your six-peck . . .'

I'm there, 'It's actually an *eight*-pack?'

'And she hit the button. I tried to cencel it – by my baptism, I did – but I didn't knaw hoe. I'm *saw* sorry to have wasted your time, Sir.'

Now, I should mention that my impression of country birds was once probably much the same as yours. You go beyond Naas and it's all women in shawls and men's shoes dreaming of moving to Dublin to work in the V.H.I. But this Ursula bird is proof that things are definitely changing. A lot of it is down to improved diet.

'Well, since I'm here,' I go, 'why don't I buy you a drink?'

I can't describe the delight on her face. It's like she's just stepped out of Busárus and she's seeing two-storey buildings for the first time.

'I'll have a pint of Bulmers,' she goes.

I can do better than that – and I do! I buy them *each* a pint of Bulmers – her and her three mucker mates. That's what an operator I am. And it's not long before Ursula's – I don't know if you want to call them – *inhibitions* stort to melt away?

She's telling me about Malachy, her ex, who told her he loved her, but it turned out that he didn't, not *really*, and she sheds one or two beer tears, and I'm pulling my most understanding expression and telling her that the most difficult thing she faces is learning to trust again – but trust she must, because otherwise what future is there for, I don't know, the Earth? Then she's telling me about leaving her home in Galway to move to Dublin to work in the claims deportment of the V.H.I. – see, I knew it! – and I rub the top of her orm in a sympathetic way when she tells me she has a big family and she sometimes misses them. I even laugh along when she mocks me about Dublin's prospects in this year's All Ireland – 'Donegal are the men will knock smoke out of you' – like I *give* a fock one way or the other?

The friends are all impressed by me – I'm putting on a bit of a show, in fairness to me – and after a couple of hours, when Copper Face Jacks gets inevitably mentioned, the birds enter into a little huddle. Ursula knows that to bring someone with my looks into Coppers is to risk losing me in the first ten minutes.

But at the same time, she's having doubts, because I hear one of her friends tell her to hold her whisht, wouldn't she be a fool to think that Malachy isn't out doing the selfsame thing this very night – 'it's not keening for you, he'll be, the dirty slattern – and let him chew on this for fear he'd be hungry' – and isn't she entitled to a bit of fun with a fella who seems to be very genuine and the vein of poetry coming out of his very mouth?

Okay, there's a chance I'm possibly exaggerating the accent. But, seriously, you'd wonder how these four ever found their way across the Shannon.

After a few minutes of consultation, Ursula turns around to me and goes, 'I'm ectually tired. I might hid beck. Do you want to come with me? For a coffee?'

Malachy has been totally forgotten. When you ride someone just to get over an ex, it's called a Sexorcism. That's just for your own education.

I'm like, 'Yeah, no, just a quick coffee and then I'll be on my way,' letting her know that my time is valuable. 'I have to be up early in the morning.'

She lives in Rathmines. A lot of them do. When we get into her gaff – it's, like, a flat more than an aportment – she insists on going through the unnecessary foreplay of actually *making* coffee, while I stort giving her little compliments about her hair and her body, again to keep her mind focused on the direction this evening is headed.

I've got seriously blue balls here. The last time I had Ant and Decs was with Joyce slash Forest Whitaker, bear in mind, as a focking prisoner in Unganga Nanga.

She's suddenly having doubts, though. While we're kissing in the kitchen, she keeps going, 'This is rendom. It's, like, *saw* rendom.'

And I'm going, 'For me, Ursula, there are times for questioning yourself and there are times when you should just, I don't know, go with the moment – feelings and blah, blah, blah. We're going to have to be quick, though, because I've got rugby training in the morning.'

It doesn't put her mind at ease, though. She suddenly puts her hand on my chest and pushes me away, going, 'Naw, it's too soon.'

I'm there, 'Too soon?'

'After Malachy.'

Focking Malachy. I'd deck him if he was here.

I'm like, 'Another way of looking at it is that a handy way of getting over someone is to ride someone else.'

'By my oath, I would like nothing more,' she goes. 'And you make very fine words. But I don't knaw you whill enough yit.'

'I can't think of a better way to get to know someone than to ride them.'

I've got the gift of the gab – there's no doubt about that.

'Naw,' she goes. 'I'd put a lie on my soul if I said I wasn't sorry I wasted your time this night.'

I roll my eyes.

I'm there, 'Yeah, no, you did,' grabbing my jacket. 'You took me off the focking field of play tonight – and for fock-all!'

'I'm sorry you're upsit. There's naw need for you to gaw. We could watch a fillum!'

'A focking *fillum*? You must think you're in a dream or something. You've already wasted enough of my precious time. I might as well have stayed home with my wife and kids.'

'The *vas deferens*,' the dude goes, 'is the part of the male penis that transports sperm from the epididymis to the ejaculatory ducts in anticipation of ejaculation.'

Jesus.

There's, like, an illustration on the screen of a man's – again, I know this isn't the actual *medical* term for it? – but mickey. It'd nearly give you a complex as well. The dude is hung like a focking Hoover hose.

'During a vasectomy, the *vas deferens* from each testicle is severed and then clamped to prevent sperm from entering into the seminal stream, thereby preventing fertilization from occurring.'

I feel myself suddenly cross my legs at the mention of severing and clamping anything in that region.

'It can take several months after a vasectomy for all of the remaining sperm to be ejaculated or reabsorbed into the body. It is recommended that you use an alternative method of birth control until you have a semen sample test that reveals a zero sperm count.'

Sorcha's old man steps into the living room at the exact moment the dude mentions a zero sperm count. I make a grab for the DVD remote, except he manages to whip it off the table before I can reach it.

'No,' he goes, loving my sudden embarrassment, 'please don't turn it off on my account.'

Of course I don't want him to see that he's winning, so I pretend that it doesn't bother me. I just shrug as he sits down on the sofa beside me and goes, 'I'm actually rather curious as to whether there'll be pain.'

There's, like, a doctor in full scrubs on the screen, checking the shorpness of a scalpel, which I don't think it was strictly necessary to show.

The dude doing the voiceover goes, 'The procedure is relatively simple. The testicles and scrotum are cleaned with an antiseptic, then shaved.'

I don't need to tell you how focked-up it is to be watching something like this with your father-in-law, but I crack on that it doesn't bother me. I can't show him any sign of weakness.

'Each *vas deferens* is located by touch and a local anaesthetic is injected into the area.'

'Local,' Sorcha's old man goes, determined to see the bright side. 'So you'll probably be conscious.'

I feel my stomach suddenly lurch.

'Using the scalpel,' the dude on the TV goes, 'the surgeon makes one or two small openings in the scrotum. Through these openings, the two *vas deferens* tubes are cut.'

Oh, Jesus, I think I *am* going to vom.

'The two ends of the *vas deferens* are then tied, stitched or sealed, using heat to cauterize them closed. The *vas deferens* is then replaced inside the scrotum and the scrotum is then stitched up.'

I'm *definitely* going to vom. I suddenly jump up from the sofa.

Sorcha's old man goes, 'Are you okay? Are you going to be sick?'

I don't say a word. I can't trust myself to even open my mouth. I run out of the room and down the hall to the little jacks under the stairs. In I go. I drop to my knees, whip up the lid and stort spewing like the Bellagio fountains.

After five minutes of, like, uninterrupted hurling, I wipe my mouth with the back of my hand, then I sit with my back against the wall, trying to get my breath back.

'Are you ready?' Sorcha goes.

She's spent the last fifteen minutes putting Brian, Johnny, Leo and the rest of the travelling roadshow into the cor and now she's looking at me – I'm going to take a chance that this is an actual word – but *expectedly*?

I'm like, 'Ready? What are you talking about? Ready for what?'

'Don't tell me you've forgotten,' she goes. 'We have an appointment at the school.'

This is literally the first I'm hearing about it.

'Ross,' she tries to go, 'I've reminded you about this at least three times.'

The really annoying thing from my POV is that I hear her constantly laughing with Lauren and her other friends about how she has, like, baby brain at the moment – yet when I pull her up on stuff, she can never just admit, 'Yeah, no, I've got shite between my ears right now. Sorry, Ross.'

I'm there, 'What school are we even talking about?'

And that's when she says it.

She goes, 'Castlerock College.'

I get this sudden feeling of, I don't know, *dread*?

I'm there, 'Er, what the fock even *is* this interview, Babes?'

'We need to get the boys registered,' she goes, 'for secondary school.'

'*Secondary* school? Jesus Christ – they're four months old.'

'Four months is actually late. Do you have any idea how tough the competition for places is?'

'It just seems a bit focking ridiculous to me.'

'Well, ridiculous or not, we want our children to get an amazing, amazing education – and you've always said you wanted them to go to Castlerock.'

I ask the question already knowing the answer. I'm there, 'So, um, who are we actually meeting?'

She goes, 'Tom McGahy.'

He knew. He focking *knew* when I was abusing him on the phone – calling him a dick and all the rest of it – that this appointment was in his diary. And yet he never told me – that's focking sneaky, you'd have to admit.

'Ross,' she goes, 'go upstairs and put a shirt on,' which is what I end up *having* to do? 'Honor, come on, we're all going – into the minivan.'

I can hear Honor downstairs go, 'Are you deaf as well as fat? I said I'm staying here.'

'And I said you're *not* staying here,' Sorcha goes. 'And if you insist on speaking to me in that way, I'll be putting a minus-two on the Honour Board before the day is out.'

Honor walks out to the minivan, rolling her eyes and shaking her head and dragging her feet and texting, while I follow, doing pretty much the same thing.

Ten seconds later, we're on the road.

We haven't driven very far when Honor – out of the blue – goes, 'So how many points do I need to get new Uggs?'

Sorcha's like, 'If you could finish a week with *any* points on the board, Honor, I think I'd be happy.'

I'm thinking about McGahy, wondering will he have forgotten that I called him a whom-freak and a prick with ears and all sorts of other shit. He won't have, of course. He's famous for bearing grudges and it's only been a few days.

Honor goes, 'I can't believe you'd let me go out in Uggs that are wrecked,' staring at the back of her mother's head. 'You're such a scabby bitch.'

Sorcha's like, 'Keep talking that way, Honor, and there will be a deduction.'

'You know you have a bald patch? It's all that peroxide you put in your hair. When you're forty, you're going to have a comb-over.'

See, it's times like this when actually *giving* Honor stuff is a good idea – it distracts her from the business of being evil.

'Well, luckily,' Sorcha goes, 'I don't have to listen to you being unpleasant to me,' and she sticks her iPhone ear buds into her ears. 'I'm going to have another listen to this song.'

The *song* – so-called – is being sung by Garret, by the way, as in Garret who's married to Claire from Bray of all places? It's called *The Power of Three* and it's actually about Brian, Johnny and Leo. They wrote it – as in Garret and Claire – then went to an actual studio in Canada to record it, *him* singing and playing the guitar and *her* doing backing vocals, the pair of focking saps.

It's actually a brilliant song, although I'd never admit that.

I continue driving. I can feel Honor staring at the back of *my* head now and it's obvious that she's trying to come up with something horrible to say to me.

She's like, 'Buy me the boots.'

I'm there, 'I'd love to – genuinely, Honor – but I can't. Although it's nice to know that you see me as the good cop in the whole good cop, bad cop situation.'

'Where's your rugby tactics book, by the way?'

'It's back home in the gym. I left it on the weights bench.'

I bought a weights bench, by the way.

She goes, 'Will it be there when you come back, do you think?'

I'm suddenly there, 'Honor, please don't do anything to that book. All of my thoughts about rugby are in it. I'm begging you.'

'Buy me the boots. That fat sap beside you doesn't need to know.'

While this conversation is taking place, Sorcha is, at the top of her voice, going, 'THIS IS – OH MY GOD – *SO* AN AMAZING SONG!' shouting the way you do when you've got earphones in. 'THEY SHOULD ACTUALLY RELEASE THIS!'

I pull a face that says they'd only be wasting everyone's time.

'Buy me the boots,' Honor goes.

I'm there, 'I'm sorry, Honor. Your old dear is very much of the view that things have to be earned to be appreciated, so it looks like we're sticking with that for now.'

I pull up at a red light on Rochestown Avenue and I go to check my voicemail messages, mainly just to kill the conversation with Honor dead.

I hit 171 and I hold the phone to my ear.

'*ME AND YOU ARE STRONGER WHEN IT'S MORE THAN YOU AND ME*,' Sorcha goes. '*THE WORLD DOESN'T* STAND A CHANCE AGAINST THE POWER OF THREE. GARRET'S LYRICS ARE – OH MY GOD – *ACTUALLY* DEEP!'

The next thing I hear is, 'You have one new voice message,' except the voice isn't in my left ear. It's coming through the cor speakers, because Sorcha obviously took it upon herself to synch my phone with the hands-free kit in the focking minivan.

And that's when I hear a voice that sends my blood instantly cold.

It's like, 'Howiya, this is Ursula – Ursula from the other night?'

Behind me, Honor goes, 'Oh! My! God!' the delight already obvious in her voice.

I'm suddenly hitting random buttons on my phone, trying to switch it off, except I *can't*?

'Er, I'm just ringing to say,' Ursula goes, 'that I'm sorry I upsit you the other night. It was a fine thing to meet you and I enjoyed kissing you and I wouldn't be putting a lie on my soul if I said I was as light in my head as a puck goat after it. It's a pity you couldn't stee for the fillum. I hope your rugby metch the next day wint whill.'

'Rugby match!' Honor goes. 'Hill! Air!'

I look sideways at Sorcha. She's going, '*TOGETHER THROUGH LIFE, THROUGH GOOD TIMES AND STRIFE! I ACTUALLY THINK IT'S LIKE A SIMON AND GORFUNKEL SONG!*'

I'm looking at the phone, thinking, okay, how do I take the battery out? Honor, at the same time, is laughing in a really cruel way and Ursula's voice is still echoing around the minivan, going, 'I also just wanted to say thenk you for being so nice. I've been thinking about what you sid – about all leds not being the same and how I just need to become bitter at spotting the good ones. By my baptism, thet was what I needed to hear – indeed and indeed. I'd love to see you again if thet's possible. Maybe give me a call.'

At the exact moment that the call ends, Sorcha presses pause on her iPhone and goes, 'Oh my God, that is *so* the nicest present anyone has ever given me. Imagine sitting down and writing a song and then recording it.'

I'm there, 'I know. They must have fock-all else to do.'

'Well, I'm going to listen to it again . . .'

She presses play on her iPhone and she's suddenly singing along again. Honor leans forward and, in my ear, she goes, 'I want those focking boots.'

And what else am I going to say except, 'Yeah, no, cool – I've a feeling you're going to get them.'

We take Brian, Johnny and Leo out of the van and we put them into their stroller, the size of a scrummaging machine, an operation that takes about fifteen minutes.

When it's done, Sorcha goes, 'Come on, Honor,' except Honor doesn't move.

She's like, 'I'm going to stay here, thank you,' staring at her iPhone screen.

'We are *not* leaving you on your own in the minivan.'

Honor doesn't even look at me. She just goes, 'Speak to your wife, will you?'

And what choice do I have, except to go, 'I think she has a point, Sorcha. She looks pretty busy there. What are you doing, Honor?'

She goes, 'I'm online shopping.'

'There are you are, Babes. I think it'd be better all round if she *didn't* come in with us? It's going to be hord enough persuading McGahy to take three little Ross O'Carroll-Kellys without her loosing her mouth off at him.'

Sorcha considers this for a few seconds, then goes, 'Okay, you can stay here.'

Then she turns and storts pushing our eight-feet-wide stroller in the direction of the main school building.

'I don't know where she's getting the money to online shop,' Sorcha goes. 'She hasn't completed a week with a single point on the Honour Board since we storted seeing Siofra.'

I'm there, 'I think she's got my self-belief, though – that's nice to see.'

'Well, she can compile all the wish lists she wants. She won't be getting anything until her behaviour dramatically improves.'

I'm like, 'Yeah, no, good point, Sorcha,' and into the school we go.

McGahy is delighted to see us coming.

He's there, 'Good morning,' obviously loving the power he suddenly has over me. 'Come into my office.'

It turns out we can't, because the stroller is too wide to fit through the door. It's too wide to fit through most doors. I don't know why this comes as a constant surprise to Sorcha.

'Can we talk out here?' Sorcha goes, meaning outside in the corridor.

He's like, 'Yes, of course!' and then, after an awkward silence, he goes, 'So – why did you ask to see me?'

He knows why we asked to see him. He's just going to make us say it, so he can have the pleasure of telling us to go fock ourselves.

Sorcha, in her best Mount Anville voice, goes, 'Well, like I said to you on the phone, we have three beautiful little boys – as you can see – and they're going to be storting on solids soon, so obviously we're storting to think in terms of, like, secondary schools for them. Now, I realize we've possibly left it late . . .'

'It's not too late . . .'

I look at McGahy and I'm like, 'Are you serious?'

I don't know why I end up getting suckered by him.

He goes, 'Let me finish, please. It's not too late for me to tell you that we are unfortunately closed for admissions.'

See, that's what a complete and utter dick he is.

Sorcha's there, 'This would be, like, 2026 we're talking about?'

He goes, 'Yes, 2026. All full. What a pity.'

'Well, what about 2027? I'm thinking, Ross, they could do an extra year in Montessori. I've read that can be actually *beneficial* for a child's development?'

'Unfortunately,' he goes 'we're full for 2027 as well.'

Sorcha looks suddenly puzzled. She's obviously doing the maths in her head. 'Full for 2027? But presumably those children . . . haven't even been born yet.'

He goes, 'Some of them haven't even been conceived. But that's how seriously *their* parents take their children's education.'

A look crosses Sorcha's face that I straight away recognize as shame. She goes, 'I knew we should have done this a year ago, Ross, when I missed a period.'

I hate seeing Sorcha upset – especially because this is personal, between me and this knob-head – so I end up basically losing it. I'm like, 'Where the fock are our kids *supposed* to go to school then?'

McGahy – and I'm quoting him word for word here – goes, 'There's always Blackrock. Or Clongowes.'

'There was a time, when this school had actual priests calling the shots, when I could have taken off one of my Dubes and beaten you to death for saying that. Father Fehily wouldn't have even called the Feds. Him and the other priests would have dragged you outside and buried you in a focking hole behind the boiler-house.'

Sorcha looks at me sadly and goes, 'There's no alternative, Ross – it's our fault for leaving it so late.'

She turns the stroller around and she walks away. Two passing students hold open the double doors for her and she pushes the boys out through it and she storts heading back to the cor, hating herself.

I'm left standing there, weighing up whether or not I should deck this focker just as a way of having the last word. I'm actually making a fist when he turns around to me and goes, 'Of course, I could be persuaded to *find* some room on the list if you were to do something for me.'

It's certainly my day for being bribed.

I'm there, 'You're a total and utter dick. I hope you know that.'

He goes, 'Ronan is one of the brightest pupils in this school. He's going to fail his exams this summer unless he ends this wild goose chase he's on to find this war hero ancestor who never even existed.'

'He did exist.'

'Well, why isn't his name in the records?'

'Look, he existed and he was a hero. It's just, well, he was a hero for the other side.'

'What?'

That's shocked him.

I'm there, 'Yeah, no, he was in the British Ormy. He was the one who blew up Something Hall, presumably trying to end this whole thing. I mean, they were making shit of O'Connell Street – might be half of what's wrong with it today.'

He goes, 'You're telling me he was on the *Helga*?'

'He was the first gunner, apparently. We've always been leadership material, you see.'

'You need to tell Ronan that.'

'I'm not telling him.'

'His exams start in nine weeks' time. He needs to know the truth.'

'The truth will break his hort . . . but then, against that, I'd rather see my children raised by wolves than send them to Clongowes.'

'So you *will* tell him?'

'Leave it with me. You dick.'

I walk into Honor's room holding the big cordboard box with Ugg Australia on the side and her little face lights up.

Actually, it doesn't – that'd be wishful thinking on my port. She barely even looks up from her phone.

She goes, 'Put them on the chair over there,' talking to me like I'm the staff. Dolores and Lualhati, in other words. 'I'll look at them when I'm ready.'

I actually put them on the bed and I go, 'Just to let you know, Honor, you're only getting these boots on one condition.'

She looks up at me and her eyes narrow to, like, *slits*?

'You're not in a position to talk about conditions,' she goes. 'Do you want me to tell Mum what I heard in the cor?'

'I don't think you'd do that. I'm going to call your bluff on that one.'

She stares hord at me, then at the top of her voice goes, 'Mom!'

I'm like, 'Okay, okay – you win.'

Sorcha shouts up the stairs. 'What is it, Honor? I'm feeding the boys.'

Honor goes, 'I just wanted to talk to you about something. Something that's been troubling me.'

'Just give me a second.'

I'm there, 'Honor, I said okay. Please, look, that message you heard, I think it might have actually been a wrong number. I didn't recognize the voice.'

She goes, 'Why did you buy me Uggs then?'

'Alright, I do know the girl. She's actually an old friend of mine – plutonic – and I happened to be helping her through a break-up.'

'By kissing her?'

'They weren't those kind of kisses.'

'Yeah, don't *even*.'

'Please, I'm begging you. It was totally innocent.'

She goes, 'Why don't you play the message for *her* then?' meaning Sorcha. 'She'll be up here in a second.'

I'm there, 'I'd be scared she'd get the wrong impression – just like you have.'

'I want them in black as well.'

'What?'

'My black Uggs are storting to look scuzzy. I want them in black as well.'

'Jesus, we're supposed to be *unspoiling* you.'

'Er, spare me. That was never going to work. The damage is already done.'

'Yeah, no, that's always been my line.'

'I want black ones. Go and buy me them now.'

'Honor, it's seven o'clock in the evening.'

'Mom!' she shouts. 'I have to tell you this thing! It's about Dad!'

Sorcha goes, 'Honor, just give me a second and I'll be up!'

I'm there, 'Okay, I'll get you the black ones.'

She's like, 'Go now. Dundrum is still open.'

I sit down on the side of her bed and I go, 'Look, just hang on a second – can I just ask you to do something for me? Let's not call it a condition, because you didn't react well to that word when I said it the first time. Let's just call it a favour.'

'I have a rule. I never do anything for anyone.'

'I know – and I respect you for that. But this could actually benefit you as well.'

'Okay, I'm going to listen to you *while* I'm texting? Just so it's not a complete waste of my time.'

'Yeah, you do that. All I was going to ask is that maybe you might, you know, make an effort not to be such a bitch all of the time.'

'Excuse me?'

'And I'm saying that as someone who knows there's nothing actually wrong with you – you just enjoy being cruel and horrible to people.'

'Yeah, eyes glazing over.'

'I'm saying I don't think this Honour Board thing is going to work either. But it could be months before Sorcha realizes that. You know what your old dear's like with her ridiculous notions. Remember that time she had us praying to Holy God every night to say thank you for all the things we had in life? How long did that last?'

'Too long.'

'But it was eventually forgotten about, wasn't it? This will be the same. But, unfortunately, we're all going to have to go through the motions – seeing this Siofra focking what's-her-name twice a week, for week *after* week – until this thing either works or doesn't work.'

'It's not *going* to work.'

115

'Look, *I* know that and *you* know that. But why don't you just pretend that it's working?'

'And why would I do that?'

'So we don't have to keep going to see this supposed psychiatrist.'

'Hmmm.'

'Think about it, Honor. I don't mind still spoiling you – as long as you hide whatever I buy you in the eaves there, because Sorcha would have kittens if she found out. I don't mind even throwing you the odd grand. But you could help by maybe, like I said, being less of a weapon generally.'

'I'm not making my bed every morning.'

'I'll make your bed for you.'

'Domestic servitude isn't my thing.'

'Look, I'll make your bed for you. And I'll continue putting your dishes in the dishwasher for you. All I'm asking, Honor, is that you maybe don't swear at your granddad – even though he deserves it – and you don't call your mother names for being overweight.'

'She's obese.'

'She's fat – I think we'd best leave it at that.'

She lifts the lid off the Uggs box, pulls out one of the boots and storts inspecting it closely. When she can't find anything wrong with it, she puts it back into the box.

'Let me get this straight,' she goes. 'You're asking me to pretend to be a good little girl?'

'I know that's a massive, massive challenge.'

'No, it isn't. It's easy.'

She does this kind of, like, fake smile then and she flutters her little eyelashes at me. Looking at her, it would be possible to mistake her for a normal little girl.

She's like, 'See?'

I'm there, 'So you're saying you could definitely do it?'

'If you buy me everything I want, yes.'

'This is muesli to my ears, Honor. If we can convince Sorcha that you're cured, we'll never have to see this Siofra one again.'

'I want white cordigan Uggs as well, by the way.'

'Hey, let's not get greedy, now. There *are* limits.'

She shouts, 'Mooom, hurry! I need to tell you this thing!'

And I suddenly hear Sorcha's footsteps coming up the stairs. She's going, 'I'm coming, I'm coming.'

I'm there, 'Okay, you win – I'll get you the black ones and the white cordigan ones.'

And it's only then that I remember the Uggs box on the bed. I slam the lid back on it and I shove it into the eaves, just as Sorcha arrives into the room, out of breath from the walk up fourteen stairs.

'What is it?' Sorcha goes. 'What's this thing that's so important?'

My hort is beating so hord it feels like it's going to come out of my chest.

But Honor flashes her the same fake smile she gave me and goes, 'I just wanted to say that I have the best dad in the world.'

It gives me a lovely, warm feeling, even though I know it's total horseshit.

Sorcha looks at me with genuine delight on her face.

Then Honor goes, 'And I have the best mom, too!'

Ronan answers the phone in, like, a low *whisper*?

I'm like, 'Hey, Ro – where the fock are you?' because I can barely hear the dude.

He goes, 'Ine in Glasnebbon, Rosser.'

I'm like, 'Glasnevin? What the fock is in Glasnevin?'

'Glasnebbon Cemetoddy,' he goes. 'Ine here since seben o'clock tus morden. Still on the thrail of this fedda.'

'Will you be there for a while?'

'Ine gonna be hee-er till thee shut the gates tonight – same as last night and the night befower.'

Jesus.

I type Glasnevin into the satnav.

Forty-five minutes later, I'm actually there, throwing Sorcha's Nissan focking Leaf into a porking space, before tipping inside. After fifteen minutes of walking around, I somehow manage to find Ro, sitting on a bench amidst all these millions of headstones, with a big stack of folders next to him that's as thick as a DBS repeat student.

He's wearing his little wife-beater vest, even though it's still Morch, and he's freezing his tits off. But the important thing from his point of view is that the names of his supposed Volunteers are visible for everyone to see. I notice he's also had the borbed wire and the explosions added, though not – I'm relieved to see – the name of the famous Donie Kelly.

I'm like, 'Hey, Ro!' and he looks up from a map he's sort of, like, examining.

He's there, 'Ah, howiya, Rosser. Ine still looking for eer friend.'

'Yeah, no, you seem to be obsessed. I can't believe I'm about to say these words, but I'm storting to worry about your school work, Ro.'

'Doatunt be. Ine on top of me skewill woork.'

'This whole thing has gone too far, Ro. Why can't you just accept that you're never going to find him?'

'He's beddied hee-er, Rosser?'

'Is he?'

'They're *all* beddied hee-er. Michael Cottons. Eamon Debba Leerda. Constidence Meerka Vidic. Hee-er, do you know who's ober theer? Baredda Been. Lorta Meercy on him.'

'I've never heard of any of those people.'

'Rosser, you need to leern about your histoddy.'

'I disagree. I think there'd be a lot less trouble in the world if everyone just put the focking olden days behind them. That's just an example of me calling it.'

'You caddent know where you're going, Rosser, if you doatunt know where you're from.'

'I know where I'm from. Torquay Road.'

'Not originally, you werdent. Eer past is impowertant, Rosser. One day, me own thaughter is gonna come to steert aston me about her famidy three. What am I supposed to say to her?'

'Say to her the same thing that I'm about to say to you – how about I buy you a cor?'

'A keer?'

'A cor, yeah. It's focking ridiculous that you don't have a set of wheels.'

'Ine only sixteen, Rosser.'

'Even so.'

'Ine too young to hab a thriving licence.'

'Don't get pulled over then. That'd be my advice. Yeah, no, a cor is exactly what you need. I hate thinking about you on public transport. Come on, let's go and see Frank Keane – see will he sort you out with a little Beamer.'

'I caddent give up now, Rosser – not when Ine this close.'

'I'm offering to buy you a Beamer – right now.'

'This is the most exciting thing what's ebber happened to me, but.'

I take a deep breath, then I ask him if I can sit down.

'Fooken cowerse,' he goes – because we get on like Pormesan and pears.

He moves his big stack of paperwork and I reverse-pork the old glutes onto the bench beside him. Who'd be a father? I sometimes ask myself that. Then I remember that it's one of the few things – other than obviously rugby – that I'm excellent at.

'Ro,' I go, 'I've got something to tell you and there's a possibility that you're not going to like it.'

He's like, 'What is it, Rosser?'

'Okay, you can blame my old man for this, because he's the one who opened his big focking mouth in the first place. Look, this Donie Kelly dude – he *did* actually fight in this whole, you know, thing.'

'The East Dodder Roysen.'

'Yeah, I'm never going to get used to calling it that, so they might as well stort calling it something else. But, yes, he fought in it. It's just that, well, he was coming at it from a different angle to a lot of other people.'

'I was thinking he must have been. Was he peert of the crew what throyed to take over Thrinity Coddidge, but he got shot by a doorty Ordinge fook and he had to go on the run, injured?'

'I'd love to say yes to you, Ro. I really would.'

'Was he mebbe woorking as a sniper on the roof of the Jacobs factoddy, and he escaped, then went under cubber, which is why he wadn't counthed among the combatants?'

'Again, it's a no.'

This is even more difficult than the chat we had about the birds and the bees. What an eye-opener that was for me, by the way.

I'm like, 'Ro, look, the truth of the matter is that, well, the reason he's not on any of the official lists is that he was on a boat.'

He goes, 'A boat?'

'Yeah, no, a boat called the *Helga*?'

The only reason I remember the name is because Sorcha once hired a nanny called Helga – she had tits like a roofer's nail bag and a face like a yak eating chips.

Ro goes, 'He couldna been on the *Helga*, Rosser. Shuren the *Helga* was a Brit boat.'

I'm there, 'Yeah, no, so I believe.'

'So was he a spoy on it, was he, Rosser?'

He's in for one hell of a land here. But I've no choice other than to just tell him.

'He was actually a gunner on the *Helga*,' I go. 'First gunner, though, if that's any consolation to you.'

His face is suddenly as long as a double bass.

'Are you teddon me,' he goes, 'that moy garreat, garreat, garreat garrantfadder . . . foyered on the Vodunteers?'

'Well, they *were* making shit of the place,' I go. 'This is from the information I've been given.'

'You're teddon me he was a fooken thraithor?'

'He probably wouldn't have considered himself a traitor, Ro. He just happened to be on the other side.'

'He was borden in Arelunt and he fought on the soyid of the Brits – that makes him a fooken thraithor in moy books.'

'Maybe he wasn't on anyone's side – that's another way of thinking about it. Maybe he was just trying to keep the peace. Maybe he was firing those guns, going, "Whoa! Everyone just chill!" '

Ronan doesn't answer me and I can't even bring myself to look at him. A few seconds later, I hear him quietly sobbing to himself.

I'm there, 'My point is, Ro, that all of this happened a long, long time ago. No one really knows for sure what happened. History is mostly just guesswork.'

He stands up and he picks up his folders and he carries them – we're talking, like, months and months of research – over to a big, black dumpster and drops them all inside.

He wipes his tears away with an open palm and goes, 'Ine the descendant of a fooken thraithor? How am I gonna tell me thaughter?'

I'm there, 'I would say *don't*. Keep it to yourself would be my advice.'

'How could I keep sometin like that from me owen flesh and blood? The fact that she comes from doorty fooken thraithor stock – a man who turdened he's back on he's own cuntoddy.'

'Let me put it to you another way, Ro. In ten years' time, do you honestly think anyone's going to be still talking about this thing that supposedly happened? By the time she's a teenager, it'll be long forgotten. Trust me.'

He storts walking away from me then. I'm like, 'Ro, this is not as big a deal as you think.'

But he goes, 'I've doorty fooken turden-coat blood in me,' and then he storts running in the direction of the exit gate.

I shout after him. I'm like, 'Ro, I'll buy you a cor – it'll make up for all of this,' my voice sounding suddenly very southside here among the headstones.

Ro doesn't stop, except only once, to look over his shoulder and go, 'I wish I was nebber borden into this famidy.'

Sorcha is sitting in the kitchen, feeding Leo. At the same time, she's staring at what's left of a box of Mister Kipling Cherry Bakewells, presumably wondering is it worth putting them back into the cupboard or should she just horse the last two.

'By the way,' she goes, '*what* is going on with Honor?'

I'm like, 'What do you mean?'

'She said thank you to me when I poured out her granola this morning. At first I thought I might have misheard her, but then when I poured her juice, she said it again. She said *thank you*, Ross.'

'I don't think I've ever heard her say those words.'

'And then when my dad walked into the kitchen and said, "Good

123

morning", she didn't say something horrible under her breath. She just totally blanked him.'

'That's a definite breakthrough.'

'Breakthrough is right. Do you know what this means?'

'We don't have to go to see Siofra anymore?'

'I'm saying the opposite, Ross. I'm saying it's working. The actual *unspoiling*?'

I'm thinking, tell my focking Mastercord bill that. I've just shelled out nine hundred snots on a Moncler 'Nantes' fur coat, ninety snots on a pair of Polo Ralph Lauren leggings and three hundred snots for a pair of Wildfox mirrored sunnies for the girl.

She goes, 'I told you Siofra was a genius, Ross.'

I'm there, 'Yeah, no, she's certainly that. By the way, I'm, er, heading out.'

I've decided to give Tinder another crack.

Sorcha's like, 'Out where? Ross, it's nine o'clock at night.'

And I'm there, 'I, em, said I'd meet Christian for a chat. It sounds like things are getting worse there.'

She straight away buys it. That's how much goodness is in the girl. I don't deserve her. But, against that, my balls are focking blue.

Ten seconds later, I'm out of the door and Hailoing a taxi on the Vico Road. Half an hour after that, I'm sitting in The Bailey, making short work of a pint of Ken while staring at my phone.

Richie McCaw needs company.

Tinder storts throwing faces at me – the usual rogues gallery of crobats, heifers and 3am beauty queens. I end up having to flick through thirty or forty of these before I come across one that I like the definite look of.

Ariane Natin. It sounds like a made-up name, although who actually cares? The girl is hotter than two squirrels humping in a wool sock.

It's, like, a black-and-white photo of the girl, side on, looking all moody, with lips like Angelina and cheekbones shorp enough to shear off an afternoon's growth of stubble.

I say I'll take it. Thirty seconds later – definitely keen – she does the same and then I message her to tell her I'm in The Bailey. She says she'll be there in, like, five minutes.

I'm thinking, okay, I may feel bad after doing this, but at the same time I'm trying to remember the traditional love cheat's mantra – conscience only lasts until Tuesday.

I knock back a mouthful of the golden wonder and I stare at the door until it eventually swings open. And in that moment I end up literally spitting Heineken all over myself.

It's actually still dribbling down my face and onto my chin as I stare at my date and she stares back at me, as shocked to see me as I am to see her.

I was right. Ariane Natin *is* a made-up name? Ariane Natin is Lauren.

4.

Gone Goy

Lauren looks at me like I've just vomited on a baby or something. In fairness, I probably look at her in much the same *way*?

She puts her hand over her mouth and goes, 'No! No! No! No! No! No! No!' over and over and over again.

I tell her to at least *try* to hold it together? This is in front of a pub full of people, bear in mind.

She goes, 'You? Of all the focking . . .' and her voice trails off.

It's weird. She's just been caught doing the dirt on Christian – or at least that was, like, her *intention*? – but what she's most upset about is that her blind date turned out to be me.

It's a good job I'm not sensitive.

I'm there, 'Like I said, Lauren, let's try to keep our shit together here. I'm every bit as shocked as you.'

She goes, '*You*, though?' tears streaming down her face. She probably hates herself for not being able to resist my photograph. I've got abs like focking speed bumps these days, in fairness to me.

I'm there, 'Lauren, come on. Sit down,' and that's what she ends up doing, not beside me, though – opposite me, so if anyone walks in, she can pass this off as just, like, a random encounter.

I'm there, 'Can I get you a drink? And that's not a line I'm feeding you. No strings attached.'

She's there, 'What do you mean, no strings attached?'

'As in, I wouldn't expect anything in return.'

'You wouldn't be getting anything in return.'

'We're on the same page then.'

'You're married.'

'I hate to point out the obvious, Lauren, but so are you.'

In other words, stalemate. There's, like, silence between us then for ten, maybe twenty seconds.

'I'll have a glass of white wine,' she goes. 'A Sancerre, if they have one.'

I tell a passing lounge girl. A looker.

Lauren shakes her head and laughs in, like, a *bitter* way? She goes, 'Okay, this is – officially – *the* worst moment of my life.'

I'm there, 'It's a very good photograph of me and I'm saying that in your defence. Would you believe me if I told you I wasn't even flexing in that picture?'

'You are such an arsehole.'

'Like I said, Lauren, there's a pair of us in it. Where did you get that photograph, by the way? The one of you?'

She goes, 'It was taken in Paris,' and she says it in a really, like, *shifty* way?

I'm like, 'When, ten years ago? You're seriously taking the piss using that as your profile picture.'

'It's me.'

'I'm just saying the picture does you a lot of justice.'

Her wine arrives. She throws a mouthful into her. I wouldn't say it even touches her throat on the way down.

I'm there, 'Hey, I'm just making the point.'

We sit there, again saying nothing. I can tell that she's thinking about Christian.

'I don't do this,' she tries to go. 'As in, I don't make a *habit* of it? I was just, I don't know, curious more than anything.'

I laugh. 'Lauren,' I go, 'I'm not judging you. We're both in the same boat here.'

She roars at me then. She's like, 'Don't you dare! Don't you focking dare try to establish some . . .'

'Some what?'

'Some, I don't know, moral equivalence between me and you. I'm nothing like you.'

'Hey, we've both been caught offside, in case it's escaped your attention.'

127

'I said I was curious, that's all. Whereas you're a serial focking cheater.'

'You don't get to look down your nose at me, Lauren. Not anymore. You got torted up tonight – left your husband and kids at home – with the intention of hooking up with some total randomer. The girl who never tires of reminding Christian what a complete and utter dick *I* am.'

She necks the rest of her wine and almost in the same movement nods at the lounge bird to ask for another.

Lauren actually looks well. Like I said, she's made a real effort. Her hair is up in a bun and that black shirt she's wearing really shows off her jobes. Not that I'm planning to try something. She's married to my best friend – although I did ride *his* old dear back in the day.

Her second glass of wine arrives.

'Me and Christian have been having . . . problems,' she goes.

I'm there, 'I know he slept in the shop once or twice.'

'He took himself off to some ridiculous comic convention.'

'With Citation focking Needed. I don't know if you've had the pleasure. He's a knob. Then again, I don't fully blame Christian wanting to get away from you. You seem to be busting his balls on a pretty much permanent basis these days.'

'You don't know anything about our marriage.'

'I know he's trying to make a go of things with the new shop.'

'He didn't even ask me.'

'Maybe he thought you'd say no. Have you thought about that?'

'I was entitled to say no. It was supposed to be *our* shop.'

'Look, the whole *Star Wars* thing, I'm going to be honest with you, Lauren, I don't get it either. *Star Wars*, *Star Trek* – focked-up or not, that's what the dude is into. You just have to accept him for who he is.'

She turns up her nose like she smells something, I don't know, decomposing.

She's there, 'Do you think I need marital advice from someone like you?'

'It wasn't marital advice,' I go. 'It was an observation.'

'From a man who's been cheating on his wife for their entire marriage. Longer.'

'Twenty-four hours ago, I would have taken that from you. Not anymore, Lauren. You're in no position to cast whatever they're called – is it dispersions? – on my record.'

Again, there's more silence, then eventually she goes, 'So what happens now?'

I'm like, 'What do you mean?' wondering am I suddenly misreading the situation.

She's there, 'What I mean is, what do you want to do?'

'Look,' I go, 'I'm not saying I'm not flattered, Lauren. You're a definite looker, but you're married to my best friend.'

The punch comes from nowhere. And it *is* a punch – not a slap – straight in the mouth. I can honestly say I haven't been hit that hord since the night I asked for a mojito in Flannery's in Limerick. My head snaps backwards and I fall off the chair onto the floor, blood pouring from my lip.

And suddenly Lauren is, like, bearing down on me. 'I meant are we going to tell Christian and Sorcha?' she goes.

My focking mouth.

I'm like, 'No – my policy has always been deny, deny, deny.'

My lip is focked here.

'*I'm very flattered,*' she goes, imitating me – making me sound like I'm slow or something. 'You will never, ever get that lucky.'

Then she throws what's left of her wine in my face, turns on her heel and disappears off into the night.

I'm in the kitchen, mixing formula for the babies. Sorcha does a double-take when she sees me. 'Oh my God,' she goes, 'what happened to your mouth?'

She misses nothing. It'd be hord to miss. It's swollen up like a baboon's orse.

'I was, em, in a bit of a scrap,' I go, having to think on my feet. 'Yeah, no, with Fergus McFadden.'

She's like, 'Fergus McFadden? *The* Fergus McFadden?'

'He's just Fergus McFadden to me. I wouldn't give him the focking pleasure.'

'Are you saying he hit you?'

'I said one or two things about Clongowes that he didn't like the sound of and he reacted – just as I would have done if the shoe was on the other foot.'

She's making bacon and butterscotch breakfast muffins, although most of the bacon she's fried is going straight into her focking mouth, I notice, rather than into the actual cake mix.

There's things I could say, but I don't. I'm showing incredible restraint, you'd have to agree.

She's there, 'Are you ever going to grow out of the whole school rivalry thing?'

'Probably not,' I go. 'Because it's too important. It's the reason I can't walk past either of the Kearneys without giving them a serious shoulder nudge, yet fifteen minutes later I'm buying them pints and telling them that they're two of my favourite Leinster players. It's, like, hatred, except *mixed* with respect?'

Sorcha's old man looks up from his *Irish Times* and tuts – as in, like, *properly* tuts. 'Thirty-three years of age,' he goes, 'and brawling in the street like a yob.'

I'm there, 'What would you know? You never went to a rugby school.'

He actually did. He went to Michael's, but I love getting that dig in.

Sorcha goes, 'It's actually making me question whether or not we should be sending the boys to Castlerock after all.'

McGahy rang yesterday to say that he'd found three vacancies he didn't know he had for the year 2026. Ronan's totally devastated, but at least he's back at school. Breaking one son's hort was the price of guaranteeing the others a decent second-level education.

'Still,' Sorcha's old man goes, 'maybe this operation will quieten you down.'

I'm like, 'What's that supposed to mean?'

Sorcha's old dear is pacing the kitchen, trying to get Brian to stop crying. It's possibly hunger, the poor kid. She goes, 'Now don't you two start. I don't think I could bear to listen to you going at it again.'

I'm there, 'No, I'd like to know what your husband meant by that line.'

He goes, 'Well, I've heard that cutting off the supply of sperm leads to a dramatic drop in one's testosterone levels – and all-round virility, as a matter of fact.'

'That better be horseshit you're spouting.'

'Happens with bulls after they've been neutered. Without the means necessary to reproduce, they've been known to just, well, keel over and die – from lethargy.'

Sorcha's old dear goes, 'Edmund, that really is enough!'

And that's when Honor walks into the kitchen.

'Something smells delicious!' she goes.

I swear to fock – those are her exact words. It's surprising enough for Sorcha to actually look up. 'Yes,' she goes, 'I'm making my bacon and butterscotch breakfast muffins.'

Honor's like, 'Must be the bacon I can smell! I'm really looking forward to them! You're *so* an amazing cook, Mom!'

Sorcha turns to me with a big ridiculous grin on her face – she's like someone from Roscommon having the Internet explained to them for the first time.

'Now don't you dare wash those baking dishes!' Honor goes. 'I'll do that as soon as the muffins are in the oven! First, I'm going to go and tidy my bedroom!'

And off she goes. I notice Sorcha's old man looking at her over the top of his glasses.

'Oh my God,' Sorcha goes as soon as she leaves the room. 'She called me Mom! And she wasn't saying it in a mean way either!'

'Well, I don't buy it,' her old man goes. 'She's up to something.'

Sorcha throws the muffins into the pre-heated oven. She's like, 'I actually think you're wrong. I think the unspoiling is definitely having an effect.'

I'm there, 'Yeah, no, she definitely seems less of a bitch. Let's hope she's turned a corner and that'll be the end of that.'

Now her old man is staring at *me*. I decide to get out of there. I tip up the stairs.

I'm thinking about what he said – about me possibly losing my *virility*? – and I get this sudden urge to, I don't know, flee. To where, I have no idea. But I head for our bedroom and I open the top drawer in my bedside locker and I see my passport lying there. I whip it out and I automatically slip it into the pocket of my chinos – no real idea why. I just want to have it with me in case I decide that I can't go through with this thing and I have to bolt.

Then I tip back down the hallway and I stand in the frame of Honor's bedroom door. She's lying on her bed, texting someone. 'Oh my God,' she goes when she sees me, 'the last thing that woman needs is more focking bacon! Hashtag, lardons. Hashtag, lardass.'

I'm there, 'Honor, I think you should maybe row it back a little bit.'

'Excuse me?'

'You're possibly over-egging it. You can't be the girl from *The Exorcist* one day, then Hannah Montana the next. *He's* already suspicious. He thinks you're up to something. So wash the dishes by all means, but still say the odd horrible thing. Call him a knob or a focktard or something. Just let the occasional one slip out and then be all sorry, like it's a setback or something.'

She's like, 'Fine,' and then, in the same breath, she goes, 'I've seen a pair of dungarees I want.'

I'm like, 'Dungarees?'

'Except they're, like, shorts. They cost four hundred euros and they have them in BTs.'

'Four hundred euros?'

'I'll tell Mom about that woman.'

'Okay, I'll get them for you.'

'Would it not be simpler if you just gave me your credit cord number and I could order the things I want myself?'

'That's not going to happen, Honor.'

'It was worth a try.'

'Just make sure this stuff goes into the eaves. Then you can sort of, like, slip things into your wardrobe gradually, over time, so your old dear doesn't cop.'

'I'm not an idiot.'

The next thing I hear is, 'Tommmmmy Boooooowwwe!' and I get, like, an instant fright. I'm totally paranoid today. Every time my phone goes off, I'm terrified that it's going to be Christian, thinking maybe Lauren went home and confessed everything. But when I check the screen, it ends up being Shadden. I answer, relieved, although my relief doesn't last long.

She's in, like, tears on the other end of the phone.

She goes, 'Your arthur barreaking he's heert, so you are.'

I'm like, 'Whoa, Shadden – he had to know the truth.'

'He's not bleaten sleeping, Rosser. He's pacing the flowur at night, saying, "I've doorty, turden-coat blood in me vayuns." He didn't hab a drop of thrink on Good Friday. And now he's back on the smokes.'

Okay, I'm not taking the rap for that. I've seen the photographs from the day he storted primary school. If you look at his jumper closely, you can make out the outline of ten Johnny Blue in his shirt pocket.

She goes, 'He's eeben talking about getting he's tattoos lazered offum.'

I'm there, 'In fairness, Shadden, I wasn't a hundred percent in favour of him being tattooed in the first place.'

'He lubbed them tattoos. Now he says he dudn't deserb them. He says he's blood is yeddow.'

'His blood isn't yellow.'

'That's what he thinks. You have to talk to him, Rosser.'

'I've already tried. You've seen where it got me.'

'Will you throy again, but? Your the oatenly one who can get troo to him. He woorships you, so he does.'

'Does he?'

'You know he does.'

'What kind of stuff has he said?'

'He just looks up to you. You're his heerdo.'

'Okay, that's an unbelievable boost you've just given me. When's he getting these tattoos removed?'

'The day arthur tomoddow.'

'Okay, I'm going to fix this.'

'He's apposed to be sitting he's June Yidder Ceert in a few weeks, Rosser.'

'Like I said, Shadden, I'll fix it.'

Because I've had an actual idea.

I stick my head around the door of the shop. Christian is down the back with a price gun, stickering a box of Avengers action figures. He looks up. He seems pleased to see me, which is a good sign.

I'm there, 'How's it going, Dude?'

And he's like, 'Yeah, no, quiet this morning.'

Quiet is the understatement of the century. The shop is empty – no sign of even The Doog.

Lauren obviously said fock-all to him about what happened, so I slip around the door and into the shop.

I go, 'Dude, do you know anything about geology?'

He looks at me, confused.

He's there, 'It's, like, rocks and shit, isn't it?'

I'm there, 'Okay, not geology, then. Which is the one that's all about, like, your ancestors and shit?'

'That's genealogy.'

'Say that word again.'

'Genealogy.'

'Okay, that's not all *that* different from what I originally said?'

'Well, that's what it's called.'

'Genealogy?'

'Genealogy.'

'Okay, next question – where would I find out about it?'

'Are you drunk, Ross?'

'Dude, it's eleven o'clock in the morning.'

'My question still stands.'

'No, I'm not drunk.'

'It's just that you're acting really weird.'

'Okay, I'll tell you what it is. Ronan was doing this – I don't know what you'd call it – a *project*, during the course of which he found out that his great, great, great grandfather betrayed his country.'

'How did he betray his country?'

'Okay, random – have you ever heard of a thing called the Rising?'

134

'Are you talking about the *Easter* Rising?'

'Jesus, am I the only one who this is news to? Okay, so it turns out that while it was going on, this relative of ours – going way, way back – blew up a big building with loads of these supposed rebels in it.'

'Fock.'

'Fock is right. So Ronan is obviously devastated.'

'I'm not surprised. He's very proud of his Irishness.'

'Yeah, no, unfortunately so.'

'So why are you asking me about genealogy?'

'I've had one of my world famous ideas. I just thought if I could find someone else in our family tree, going back however many years, who was an *actual* hero, then I could show my son that he doesn't have traitor's blood in his veins.'

'Have you talked to Fionn?'

'I don't want to have to ask him for a favour. He's already a bit full of himself at the moment.'

Christian suddenly stops stickering.

He's there, 'You should go to the National Library. It's on – what's that street? Is it Kildare Street?'

'Yeah, it is! I saw Ronan coming out of there a few weeks back.'

'That's where all the Americans go to trace their Irish ancestry. They'll be able to help you in there.'

I'm like, 'Christian, I owe you one,' and I turn to go.

And that's when he says it – totally out of left field. He goes, 'She's definitely having an affair.'

I turn around. Believe me, it takes every ounce of insincerity in my character to look him in the eye and go, 'We've been through this. Lauren wouldn't have an affair. What are you basing this on?'

He's there, 'The fact that she went out the other night dressed like she was going on a date.'

She *did* look well. I think I mentioned that.

He goes, 'She said she was meeting her friend from college, Pamela.'

I'm like, 'There you are then – you can put your mind at rest.'

'But Pamela rang the gaff about an hour after she went out. It turns out she wasn't meeting her at all.'

'Maybe they got their dates mixed up.'

'When Lauren came home, I said to her, "How was Pamela?" and she said, "Great form."'

'There could be two Pamelas. Is anyone considering that fact?'

'Why are you defending her, Ross?'

'I wouldn't say I'm defending her. I'm just offering her the benefit of the doubt – as you should. A marriage should be based on trust.'

Jesus. I wouldn't be able to look at myself in the mirror if I didn't look so good.

'Then,' he goes, 'there's the other thing.'

I'm like, 'What other thing?'

'She downloaded the Tinder app on her phone.'

I wonder is it too much to ask for just one stress-free day?

'Tinder?' I try to go. 'No, you've lost me there. Let's move on.'

He's like, 'Tinder, Ross. It's that app that Oisinn uses to hook up with randomers.'

'You think that's what Lauren is doing? Hooking up with randomers?'

'Why else would she have the app on her phone?'

'Maybe she accidentally downloaded it.'

'I don't think so.'

'Well, maybe it's just something you should forget about. Leave well enough alone.'

'Trust me,' he goes, waving the price gun at me. 'If it's the last thing I do, I'm going to find out the truth.'

The dude in the library might as well be talking French for all I understand of what he says.

'Records for the nineteenth century come in two forms,' he goes. 'For births, deaths and marriages that took place after 1864, you should be able to find civil certificates at the General Records Office. Prior to 1864, you'll be relying on parish registers in order to find baptismal and marriage records. And in that case, it's helpful to know the county and preferably the parish in which they originated.'

You can imagine me, I'm sure, nodding away like the dog off the focking Churchill Insurance ad.

'So,' the dude goes, 'what's the name of the relative you're trying to trace?'

I'm there, 'Yeah, no, I don't *have* a name?'

'Well, do you have an address – the name of a village or a townland?'

'This is all very specific, if you don't mind me saying. The whole point is, I don't know *who* I'm looking for? All I'm trying to do is find one apple on my family tree that isn't rotten to the focking core.'

Now *he's* not following *me*. He's stroking his beard, going, 'Errr . . .'

I'm like, 'Okay, if it narrows the search down for you, I'm looking for someone – I don't care how many centuries back I have to go – who did something that was, like, heroic – namely, killing British people.'

'But you don't have a name?'

'I don't even know if they exist.'

'Do you know roughly what time period we're dealing with?'

'Dude, I thought this information would have all been computerized.'

'Well, computerized or not, you have to know what you're looking for. Can I ask you, what's *your* surname?'

'Does that mean my second name?'

'Your second name, yes.'

'As it happens, I've got two. O'Carroll and Kelly. O'Carroll is my old dear's maiden name – she's a focking drunk – and Kelly is my old man's name.'

'Okay, wait here.'

He disappears into the back.

There's a bird standing beside me with glasses and a fantastic set of butatoes, going through a box of index cords. Birds can be smort *and* pretty. There's cases.

'I thought everything would have been focking computerized,' I go, although I don't say it in a chatting-up kind of way – I'm just making pleasant conversation. 'It's the year two thousand and whatever it is – information's supposed to be at the tip of our fingers. I'll use Wikipedia as an example.'

She doesn't say anything, just flashes me one of those Trinity College undergraduate smiles – all teeth, no sincerity – and goes back to her cords.

It's, like, fifteen minutes before the library dude returns and when he does I can't actually believe my eyes. He's pushing one of those, like, two-wheel hand trolleys that you see, I don't know, removals men using and it's stacked high with all these large, green, leather-bound ledgers. There must be, like, twenty of them.

That's actually what I say.

I'm there, 'There must be, like, twenty of them.'

And the dude goes, 'This is just to start you off. There's another, what, seventy or eighty back there as well. That's what I'm trying to tell you – it's needle in a haystack stuff.'

My hort literally sinks.

I'm there, 'Er, okay,' sort of, like, hesitating. 'I'm, er, just going to go for a quick wizz first,' and I slip out of the reading room and down the stairs, no intention of actually *going* for a piss? I just need an excuse to get out of the room so I can fock off home.

Memories of my Leaving Cert come flooding back.

I'm about to go out the door, out onto Kildare Street, when I hear Ryle Nugent screaming the name of Ireland's number fourteen. I answer my phone. It ends up being my old man. He's half shit-faced. I can tell by his volume.

'I'm sitting in the Horse Shoe Bar with your godfather,' he goes – this is his opening line, bear in mind – 'enjoying a couple of Death in the Afternoons, as Hennessy likes to call them. We were discussing the rights and wrongs of austerity economics and who should pop into my mind, only you. I said to Hennessy, "Ross will have a take on this and it'll be something obtuse yet suitably caustic – you see if it's not!"'

I'm there, 'I'm halfway down Kildare Street. You could hang up the phone and I could probably still hear you.'

'Kildare Street?' he goes. 'What the hell are you doing on Kildare Street?'

'I'm in the National Library.'

'Did you just say you were *in* the National Library?'

'*In* it, yeah.'

'Not *outside* it?'

'Sorry, why is it so hord to picture me in a library? What the fock is wrong with everyone?'

'Nothing at all. That's the wonderful thing about you, Kicker – you're never done improving your mind. What, might I ask, is your current field of study?'

'If you must know, I was trying to trace our family's geological roots.'

'Were you indeed?'

'I had to tell Ronan the truth about his great, great, great grand-father. The poor kid is crushed. He thinks he has traitor's blood in him. He's talking about having his tattoos removed?'

'Tattoos?'

'Yeah, no, don't ask. I just thought if I could find someone in the family – a grandfather, a great grandfather, a great, great grandfather – who wasn't a dick, some dude who was a hero for, I don't know, killing some other dude, then Ronan could be proud of his, I think it's a word, *heritage*?'

I hear the old man sigh.

Then he goes, 'You could write the book on how to be a good father, Ross. And I don't know where you learned it from, because, God knows, I wasn't any kind of role model.'

I'm there, 'You shouldn't have any more to drink.'

I hear him turn to, presumably, Hennessy and go, 'He's looking up the family tree to try to find someone who performed an act of heroism for his country.'

I hear Hennessy go, 'Do they keep records from the Middle Ages?' and the old man laughs.

'Oh, Hennessy,' he goes, 'you'd humour a dying man!' and then he gets back on the phone to me. 'So, how goes the investigation thus far, Kicker?'

I'm like, 'Shit, since you're asking,' and I'm on the point of telling him that I've already given up and I'm about to fock off home, when he goes, 'You see, that's another one of your great qualities, Ross – you were the same on the rugby field – you simply refuse to quit.'

I'm a sucker for a compliment, especially one I don't deserve.

I'm like, 'Yeah, no, I am a bit like that alright.'

He goes, 'Well, you're dogged, you see. Like what's it called? Yes, a badger. When it sinks its teeth into something.'

I feel this sudden wave of, I don't know, guilt at throwing in the towel so easily. And that's when he goes, 'Do you know something – stay where you are. I'm on my way.'

I'm like, 'What?'

'Yes, indeed, Ross! We've seen what one O'Carroll-Kelly is capable of doing! Imagine what two can do working together! Bloody hell!'

I try to go, 'Er, no, I don't want to put you to any trouble – stay in the Shelbourne, you focking pisshead,' except he's already hung up on me. And then I have no choice but to peg it back upstairs to the reading room.

I grab one of the leather-bound ledgers off the trolley and I bring it over to a desk and I'm pretending to be reading it when he suddenly walks into the reading room, squinting his eyes to try to find me, smelling like a focking distillery with his face all red.

There's this face I sometimes pull to make it look like I'm thinking. It's sort of, like, a *pained* expression? I do that while I'm running my finger over random lines on the page – not a clue what any of them means, by the way.

He's suddenly standing over me.

'Look at that!' he goes, at the top of his voice. 'You're so engrossed in your labours that you didn't even see me come in!'

I look up.

I'm there, 'Oh, it's you.'

He grabs a chair from another table and drags it over, the legs scratching off the wooden floor. One or two people look up and he raises his hand and sort of, like, mouths a silent apology.

'So,' he goes, in what he presumes, in his shit-faced state, is a whisper, 'what approach are you taking?'

I'm like, 'Approach?'

'Yes, what's this book you're reading?'

'To be honest, I haven't a clue. There's, like, a hundred of them.

I'm just going to go through them all, line by line, to see does something pop out.'

'You've got a mind like a computer, Ross.'

'I'll take that as a compliment.'

'A computer!'

I go back to work – or at least I pretend to – while he continues to stare at me for a good sixty seconds, sighing and shaking his head in admiration.

'I suppose I'd better give you a dig-out,' he goes.

I'm like, 'There's a massive stack of these books up there and he's got, I don't know, I think he said eighty more of them somewhere else.'

'Well, I might, um, come at it from a different angle to you, Ross. I've got a fairly good idea what I'm looking for.'

He stands up and walks up to the counter, leaving a vapour of cognac fumes in his wake. He storts shooting the breeze with the librarian dude and thirty seconds later I hear the dude laugh out loud.

People genuinely love my old man for some reason.

The dude disappears off somewhere, my old man looks over his shoulder at me and I go back to dragging my finger over the meaningless words in the ledger.

Five minutes later, he's back with a ledger of his own, except this one is smaller and it's covered in, like, *red* leather?

'You see, there *was* someone in the family who did something,' he goes. 'Or so it was always rumoured.'

We end up sharing the desk. He opens the book and licks his fingers to turn the pages.

I'm there, 'We've only really got today to find something. He's having his tattoos removed tomorrow.'

He goes, 'Don't you worry. I checked with our friend up there at the desk. They're open late tonight. With two O'Carroll-Kelly brains working on it, we're bound to turn up something before the day is over.'

We both go to work – well, one of us pretending to – and every so often the old man makes a noise like 'Hmmm' or 'Aha!' and one or two times he goes, 'Interesting. Very interesting.'

'I'm having a vasectomy,' I go.

I don't know why I tell him at that moment. I don't know why I tell him at all. I just blurt it out.

The old man looks up from his book. 'A *vasectomy*?' he goes, like I've just told him I'm having a sex change.

Then again, I might as well be.

I'm there, 'Yeah, no, I've got five kids now. Sorcha thinks we shouldn't have any more, even though it was actually her old man's idea.'

The old man doesn't say anything for a few seconds.

'Look,' he eventually goes, 'I don't want to interfere in your marriage, Ross, but in my experience – old-fashioned as it sounds – a lion must be the master of his own savannah.'

I'm there, 'Okay, what are you talking about?'

'I'm talking about Edmund, of course. I mean, all this nonsense about sending Honor to a psychiatrist. What, that precious little girl? And now it seems he's telling his daughter that her husband should have the – inverted commas – snip.'

'Are you saying I should tell him to go fock himself?'

'I'm saying that you know a thing or two about leadership, Ross. Need I remind you that you captained Castlerock College to victory in a certain Leinster Schools Senior Cup year?'

'It was 1999.'

'And how do you think you'd have fared if Christian or Oisinn or Barry Conroy's young chap had started giving out instructions during one of your world famous team talks?'

'I'd have decked them.'

'Precisely.'

'They'd have been decked.'

'*Uno duce, una voce*, as P. J. used to say.'

He can be great, my old man – although I'd never make the mistake of letting him know.

I'm there, 'Anyway, stop focking blabbing on, will you? We've got work to do.'

'Don't worry,' he goes, flashing me a shit-faced smile, 'I've already found what I was looking for.'

*

The place is called Laseroff and it's somewhere on the North Circular Road – that's according to Shadden – although I've driven up and down it six times at this stage and I still haven't found it and now I'm storting to panic, roysh, because Ronan's appointment is for ten o'clock and it's already, like, one minute *to*?

The address is supposedly nine hundred and something, although I'm expecting it to be, I don't know, some kind of hospital building, not the dingy basement that it actually ends up being. But I suddenly spot the sign out of the corner of my eye and I throw Sorcha's Nissan focking Leaf into a non-existent porking space with two wheels on the kerb.

It's like, 'Laseroff – Proven and Effective Tattoo Removal', and then underneath, 'Erase that ex's name from your life – and your body!'

They're like a different species on this side of the city.

I grab the manila envelope off the passenger seat and in I go.

I try the door, except it's locked, so I end up hammering on it with my hand, going, 'Leave those tattoos alone! Don't you focking remove my son's tattoos!'

I'm suddenly buzzed in.

Through the reception area I run. A woman wearing a headset tries to stop me, but on I go – not a focking clue where I'm headed – but my feet take me down a flight of stairs to, like I said, a *basement*? There's a door in front of me with the word 'Surgery' on it and I go through it like I'm tackling Leigh Halfpenny.

God, I hate Leigh Halfpenny.

Ronan is lying on a white leather bed, wearing a black, wife-beater vest, showing off his scrawny upper orms, while a dude in a long white coat stands over him, painting over the names of the supposed Volunteers with a disinfectant swab.

Ronan's pretty surprised to see me. He's like, 'Rosser? What the fook are you doing here?'

I'm there, 'I'm here to stop you making the worst mistake of your life,' which is probably overstating it slightly. You've got to bear in mind that I'm high on adrenaline.

'This is Pavel,' he goes, introducing me to the doctor dude – *if* that's what he even is?

I'm there, 'Alright, Pavel? Ro, you don't have to do this.'

'Ine a descendant of a doorty, threacherous fooker,' he goes. 'I habn't the right to weer the nayums of them brave heerdos on me eerm.'

I'm there, 'What if I told you that you do?' and I hold up the manila envelope.

He goes, 'What's that, Rosser?'

I'm like, 'Pavel, give us a minute here, will you?' and Pavel goes, 'Of course,' and then focks off out of the room.

I'm there, 'I spent the entire day yesterday in that famous National Library of yours.'

He's like, 'What?'

'Now don't stort worrying your head about me.'

'Ine bound to woody, Rosser – what were *you* doing in there?'

'Believe it or not, I was doing some research on our family history.'

I don't mention that my old man helped me, which is possibly wrong of me, but the way I look at it is, fock him.

Ronan turns his head away.

'Famidy of turden-coat scoombag fooks,' he goes.

I'm there, 'Well, not all of them, it turns out.'

I reach into the envelope and I pull out the little pile of documents.

I'm like, 'For instance, Ro, were you aware that there was another big Irish battle – in seventeen something-something?'

He goes, 'The Unirit Oyrishmen Rebeddion – seventeen hundord and noyunty-eight, Rosser.'

I'm there, 'Er, yeah, that's the one,' because it sounds *kind* of right?

From the pile of documents, I pull out a pencil drawing of a man with a big nose and a mullet swinging by his neck from the branch of a tree. I hand it to Ro.

He goes, 'Who's this sham?'

I laugh.

I'm there, 'His name was Edward John Kelly. He was your great, great, great, great – and whatever else – grandfather. He beat two

British soldiers to death with a rock at the Battle of Arklow and he supposedly stabbed another in the throat with a pike although the second one was never proven.'

'You're fooken habben me on.'

'I'm not. Arklow was a place very near Brittas Bay. It's actually still there. I got my hands on a map. I'm a little bit in awe of myself, if I have to be honest.'

'So what happened to the fedda, Rosser?'

'They hanged him. Well, they called it *half* hanging? They tightened a rope around your neck, then loosened it when you went unconscious. Then they woke you up and did it again. It was to try to get information out of you.'

'Did he rat addyone out, Rosser?'

'I'm proud to tell you, Ro, that the answer is no. Which is why they then ended up *actually* hanging him?'

His face lights up.

He goes, 'He was a marthur, Rosser. A marthur to the cause.'

I'm there, 'I knew you'd be pleased.'

I hand him all the documents.

'There's, like, birth certificates, maps, newspaper cuttings, all sorts of shit in there,' I go. 'He's buried in Wexford, of all places. I was thinking, you know, if you changed your mind about getting those tattoos removed, me and you could maybe drive down there now and check out his grave?'

Ronan doesn't say anything. His head is turned away again. After a second or two, I realize that he's crying.

I'm there, 'Are you okay, Ro?'

He turns his head back to me. There's, like, tears running down his face. He goes, 'You did all that woork, Rosser – for me?'

I'm there, 'I'd do anything for you, Ro . . . Jesus.'

He wipes away his tears with an open palm. He goes, 'You doorty looken . . . Ah, you caught me unaweers, is all.'

I laugh. See, he hates anyone seeing any sign of weakness in him.

I'm there, 'So will we tell Pavel that you've changed your mind and maybe hit the N11?'

He looks at me in a way that I can't even put into words.

'Mon,' he goes, jumping up off the bed and throwing on his Dublin GAA tracksuit top, 'let's get on the roawut.'

Sorcha is all smiles as she sets up the whiteboard in the kitchen. Honor is smiling, too, although the strain of all the pleases and thank yous and excuse mes and sorrys she's had to say in the past week is storting to tell in her starey eyes and the tense lines around her mouth.

This is hord for her. No one's disputing that.

'Now,' Sorcha goes, 'I've been looking forward to today, Honor, because you have had – I think we can safely say – your best week yet!'

Honor goes, 'Yay!' somehow managing to make it sound like she *means* it?

'You washed those baking dishes for me,' Sorcha goes, scribbling it down on the board, 'which means you get two points. You tidied your room, which is another two – that makes four. And you helped me carry the shopping in from the car and I'm going to give you another two for that, which makes six altogether. Now, in the debit column, when your granddad asked you to lower the volume on the TV in case you woke your brothers, you called him . . . Okay, I'm not going to use the word.'

'Fockpig,' Honor goes. 'I called him a fockpig.'

'Well, I wasn't going to say it. The point is that you recognized immediately that it was wrong.'

'It slipped out.'

'Well, according to Siofra's book, there are always going to be slip-ups and reversions to the old behaviours. But I'm still going to have to take away two points for that one. Which gives us a grand total of . . .'

Drum roll.

She goes, ' . . . four points!'

I'm like, 'Four! I'm going to have to say fair focks, Honor!'

And *she* goes, 'Thanks, Dad! I'm kicking myself over the two I lost! I'll just have to make an even bigger effort next week!'

Sorcha's there, 'You're doing amazing, Honor! Oh my God, you so are! So four points equals two hundred euros in pocket money.'

Honor smiles and shrugs. It's not a fortune, but it's better than a kick in the orse with a golf shoe.

'So well done!' Sorcha goes, then she folds away the whiteboard and brings it back upstairs.

As soon as she's out of the room, Honor turns to me and goes, 'Two hundred euros? How the fock am I supposed to live on that?'

I'm there, 'It's not a lot, I'll grant you. But I'll get you anything you want – that was our agreement.'

'Well, I want a pair of Stella sunglasses.'

'I'll get you them.'

'You've no choice.'

'I realize that. But don't forget, Honor, that you have to keep your side of the bargain.'

'Er, I'm *being* good?'

'It's not only about being good, Honor. It's also about being convincing. Pulling the wool over Sorcha's eyes is easy. God, I've been doing it all my life. But you've got to persuade Siofra that this isn't just an act.'

'Siofra's a knob.'

'I agree with that analysis. She's a dope, but she's not a fool. Just don't overdo it when you're having your one-to-ones with each other. Just tell her you're sorry about all the bad shit you did and from now on you just want to do good shit.'

'I don't need you to tell me what to say.'

'I'm just giving you one or two pointers. Bear in mind, Honor, that if we can convince her that you've been unspoiled, our next session could be our last.'

She's there, 'Leave it to me,' and off she goes upstairs.

I open the fridge and I stare into it for a good thirty seconds, trying to decide what to eat.

That's when Sorcha's old man walks in. 'Four points,' he goes.

I'm there, 'Yeah, no, we're proud parents today.'

'I'm still not sure I buy it.'

'It's not whether you buy it, Edmund. It's whether Sorcha and Siofra buy it.'

That puts him back in his box – for about ten seconds anyway.

147

I suddenly notice that he's got some kind of, like, *document* in his hands?

'I've just been reading this,' he goes, showing it to me.

He's gagging for me to ask what it is. I decide not to give him the pleasure. But then I change my mind and I go, 'Okay, what is it?'

He smiles. He's there, 'It's your life insurance policy.'

I'm like, 'Why are you reading that?'

'Well, it's just that you're having this operation next week . . .'

'It's more of a procedure than an operation.'

'And anaesthetic is notoriously unreliable.'

'No, it's not.'

'People *have* died under anaesthesia – that's all I'm saying.'

'Yeah, no, I'm presuming rare cases.'

'Well, it's at least some comfort to know that if you don't wake up after the operation, Sorcha will be in for a windfall of three point four million euros.'

'You're just trying to put the shits up me.'

'I'm sure that kind of money would soften the blow of losing you.'

'You're trying to put the shits up me because I burned your ridiculous books. You big focking . . . book head.'

I walk out of the kitchen, leaving him obviously spitting nails that I've managed to get the last word in. I whip my phone out and I notice that I've three missed calls from the old man. I ring him back.

'Three missed calls?' I go. 'If you were a bird, I'd call you a focking stalker.'

He's there, 'How did you get on – with young Ronan?'

'Yeah, no, he was delighted. We drove down to Wexford to see where this dude was buried. Then we went to Arklow and found, roughly, where they hung the focker from a tree.'

'That's wonderful.'

'Yeah, no, it was actually quite interesting. There's also this place called – this is going to make you laugh – *Vinegar* Hill. They've got, like, a *museumy* thing there? I actually learned loads of facts. I mean, I'd forgotten them all by the time we got back to the cor. But Ro took it all in. You know what his brain is like.'

'Well, Ross, I just wanted to say thank you!'

He sounds, I don't know, excited about something. Or he could be half trashed again.

I'm there, 'Why are you thanking me?'

'Because, Ross, you are my inspiration. The wind beneath my proverbial what-have-yous. This thing you did for Ronan. The lengths you were prepared to go to just to make him happy. Well, it got me thinking about your sister . . .'

'Erika?'

'I got home. Had a couple of drinks . . .'

'Jesus, you were already mashed when I met you.'

'Told Helen the story. You in the National Library. Looking up all sorts. We started talking about what a wonderful father you are . . .'

'I would say it's definitely a thing I've cracked.'

'And then we started talking about Erika, as we often do, and, well, we both became rather teary – and I thought to myself, in the same situation, What Would Ross Do? I posed that question. And Helen said, "He'd get on a plane and he'd go to Argentina and he'd find her and he'd bring her home."'

'Well, I went to Umbongo and found Fionn, so that's actually a good assessment by Helen.'

'So that's what we are going to do. We've booked our tickets, Ross. Monday evening, we fly out. I should have asked you did you want to come with us?'

'Monday? I can't. I've got this supposed vasectomy thing the next day.'

'What, that's still happening, is it? Oh well, it was just a thought. Anyway, must go. Packing to do.'

'Winning the Rabo Pro12,' I go, 'is a bit like riding a really good-looking bird from the inner city. It's actually pretty fantastic while it's happening, but as soon as it's over, no one wants to discuss it.'

Christian goes, 'We're staying for the presentation, aren't we?'

He's hammered – as per usual these days.

And I'm there, 'Of course we're staying for the presentation. I've said all along we're going to give Johnny Sexton a proper send-off. Jesus, we owe him that.'

This is us in the RDS, by the way – the famous Dublin Fortress. We're talking me. We're talking Christian. We're talking JP. We're talking Oisinn. We're talking Fionn.

We've beaten Ulster out the focking gate, but it's a day – I'm going to use the word – *tinged* with sadness? Because we're saying goodbye to a couple of old friends today. Not only Johnno, but Isa as well.

We've been with them through the good times and even some of the bad.

Oisinn's wiping away tears, the big old softie. JP puts his orm around his shoulder. He's like, 'Come on, Big O – it's okay.'

Oisinn's there, 'It'll never be the same again.'

'I know,' JP tries to go, 'but maybe it'll be better. We're losing Sexy. But did you see Ian Madigan out there today?'

I'm actually proud of Mads. He's the closest thing I have to a protégé – until my boys grow up, of course. And, like Johnno, he'd have a massive amount of respect for everything I could have achieved in the game but didn't.

JP goes, 'Ross, what was that thing Father Fehily used to say? Sometimes good things come to an end so better things can come to a beginning.'

Oisinn nods. He knows it makes sense. I stort thinking about my operation in two days' time, wondering will I still believe those words on Tuesday night?

The final whistle blows. We watch them collect the Cup and do a lap of honour. Johnno sees me in the stand and he gives me a little nod and a wink as if to say, your support has been unbelievable and that's one of the main reasons it's so hord to leave. But leave he must.

And leave *we* must.

Ten minutes later, we're walking up Anglesea Road towards Kielys and I notice that Christian is especially quiet. I know the dude well enough to know that it has fock-all to do with the great man moving to Paris. There's something else on his mind. The trick with

Christian is to let him know you're there for him and he generally tells you what's eating him in his own good time.

'So what the fock's wrong with you?' I go, giving him a little gentle encouragement.

He's like, 'What do you mean?'

'What do I mean? You were drinking two pints for every one I drank in there. And I was drinking pretty fast. Come on – spill.'

He goes, 'I did something terrible last night.'

I'm like, 'Tell me what it was. I'll be the judge of that.'

'I checked Lauren's phone.'

Oh shit, I think. Oh focking shit.

I'm like, 'Yeah, no, that's bang out of order, Dude.'

He goes, 'It's been driving me mad, Ross. The thought of her meeting another man.'

'You don't know for a fact that she did.'

'Remember I told you she downloaded the Tinder app?'

'Er, vaguely. Very, very vaguely.'

'Well, I checked the history on it. She met this dude in The Bailey. Richie McCaw.'

'Richie McCaw? Richie McCaw lives in New Zealand, Christian.'

'Yeah, I know that.'

'So how is Lauren meeting him in The Bailey? You're losing the plot, Dude.'

'It's obviously not *the* Richie McCaw! It's just somebody's user-name.'

'Well, either way, I think you're being ridiculous.'

'His profile picture is a shot of his abs. I mean, what a focking dickhead.'

'You don't know if he's a dickhead. He could be a really good goy and maybe nothing happened between them.'

'No, I need to find out who he is.'

'My advice to you would be forgive and forget. I mean, *you* went off to that comic convention with that fockwit who hangs around your shop.'

'How is that the same thing?'

'I'm not saying it's the same thing. I'm saying you've both done things in your marriage you possibly regret. A bit like me and Sorcha – until we decided to draw a line under the past. Any birds I cheated on her with before a certain date, she can't say anything about them. It was, like, a sexual amnesty. You should do the same. Patch it up. Even just for Oliver and little Ross's sake.'

He doesn't say anything. We reach Kielys and it's, like, pints all round. It ends up being a pretty good night, even if I do end up having to watch girls, again, throwing themselves constantly at Fionn.

Seriously, they come at him in waves, telling him how – oh my God – brave he is and how they saw him give a talk at the Irish Dental Association's annual conference in the NCH, or the Google town hall in the Convention Centre, or the Carrickmines Croquet and Lawn Tennis Club's annual dinner dance in Bewley's Hotel, and what a total – *oh my God* – inspiration he is, especially in these times when it's nothing but bad news about the economy.

He's lapping it up, of course. And at no point during the evening does he turn around and go, 'Oh, by the way, you see this handsome bastard here? He deserves most of the credit, because he saved my life.'

I try not to let it bother me.

Anyway, at some point towards the end of the night, he's standing there with a pint in either hand – the old closing-time handcuffs, as we call them – and he says *the* most un-Fionn-like thing to me.

He goes, 'I could have any woman I wanted in this pub tonight.'

I'm like, 'No, you couldn't.'

He could. He really is that hot right now. He reminds me of myself back in the day. There's no need for him to be a dick about it, though.

He goes, 'I think we both know it's true.'

I'm like, 'Maybe it is true. It won't last forever, though – bear that in mind. I think what I'm saying is, enjoy it while it lasts.'

'Oh, I intend to. When I look back on all those years when it was you and JP and Christian getting all the girls . . .'

'You were a nerd. That was the hand you were dealt.'

'I've just decided, you know, I'm actually going to enjoy this.'

I offer him a bit of advice then, just as a friend. I'm like, 'Just don't let it go to your head.'

He doesn't answer me. He's smiling across the bor at a bird who looks like Kendall Jenner, except with bigger Lulus.

That's the point of the evening when I get the tap on the shoulder from JP.

I'm like, 'Alright, Dude?'

'Ross,' he goes, 'we all know you're going into hospital on Tuesday to have this, you know, vasectomy.'

I'm like, 'Yeah, no, keep your focking voice down, will you? I don't want half the world to know.'

'So we clubbed together and got you a present.'

Oisinn suddenly throws his orms around me, pinning *my* orms to my side? The focker is as strong as Richardt Strauss and I literally can't move. JP puts something over my head, which I straight away recognize as one of those, like, lampshades they put on dogs to stop them licking themselves when they take their balls.

Everyone in Kielys is laughing. I'm, like, kicking and screaming, trying to wriggle free, but Oisinn's grip is too strong. He can still bench-press something ridiculous.

JP fastens the thing around my neck and I can just about see over the top of it. I'm looking at a pub full of people with their iPhones out, taking photographs and actually filming the Rossmeister General – wearing a focking booster collar.

Oisinn releases me and gives me a shove forward.

He goes, 'It's been a bad week for Leinster rugby – there's no doubt about that. Johnny Sexton's going to Paris and, in forty-eight hours' time, they're taking Ross O'Carroll-Kelly's balls.'

I'm having to stretch my neck to see over the top of the collar. There's, like, laughter and camera phone flashes and one word suddenly enters my head.

That word is, Fock.

'The first thing I want to say to you,' Sorcha goes, 'is thank you, Siofra. From the bottom of my hort – *our* horts – thank you, thank you, thank you.'

153

Siofra seems a bit surprised by this outburst, although she takes the focking compliment all the same, I notice.

'Sit down,' she goes, all smiles. 'Why are you thanking me?'

'Because,' Sorcha goes, 'you're a miracle worker! You're an *actual* miracle worker?'

Siofra's there, 'So we're still seeing progress, are we?' delighted with herself, the patronizing fock-wench.

'Er, progress would be an understatement,' Sorcha goes. 'Isn't that right, Ross?'

I'm like, 'Er, yeah, no, she's definitely less of a bitch.'

'Oh my God, she's a completely changed person, Ross! She's no longer hostile. She's no longer cheeky. She's helpful around the house. She hordly ever swears, apart from the occasional F-word that slips out and the C-word two Fridays ago.'

'Like I said to you at our very first meeting,' Siofra goes, 'if you stick to the unspoiling programme laid out in *So Your Kid is a Prick*, then results *will* follow.'

What a focking spoofer. I nearly feel like blurting out the truth, just to wipe the smug look off her face.

Sorcha goes, 'Do you know what the really lovely thing is, Siofra? For the first time since she was born, Honor and I have been able to enjoy the same kind of relationship that I had with *my* mom growing up? We're actually becoming, like, best *friends*?'

While all of this is going on, I should mention, Honor is sitting there with her hands on her lap and the biggest butter-wouldn't-melt smile you've ever seen on her face.

I'm thinking to myself, it's too much – it's definitely too much.

'And what about you, Honor?' Siofra goes. 'Are you happy?'

Honor nods, slowly and, I don't know, *deliberately*?

She goes, 'I'm *very* happy, Siofra. Oh my God, it's like I've come out from under a spell or something. I look back now and I think about the person I used to be and I'm *actually* ashamed? Because I can see now how destructive my behaviour was.'

I can't even look at Siofra. I'm thinking, she's going to know this has been totally rehearsed. She's a supposedly clever woman.

'I realize now that a lot of my problems were down to getting things too easily,' Honor goes. 'I didn't have to work for them, so I didn't, like, *appreciate* them? I'm not saying that I'm, like, an angel all of a sudden. This is work for me. I'm going to have bad days – like anyone else. But I'm going to try to become a better person every day. And the reward – like Mum said – is that I suddenly have a new best friend.'

She smiles at Sorcha.

I'm thinking, she's blown it. She's focking blown it. Siofra's no fool – certainly judging from the prices she chorges. Sorcha might have bought this crock, but there's no way Siofra will.

But then it turns out she actually *has*?

I'm waiting for her to say, 'Hey, kid, don't shit a shitter,' except, instead, she goes, 'That's lovely to hear.'

That's what a complete and utter focking chancer the woman is.

She goes, 'That's lovely to hear. I have to say, Honor, I've seen a lot of progress, too, in our weekly one-to-ones that made me hopeful that you'd turned a corner.'

So I suddenly stand up, seeing my chance.

I'm like, 'Well, thanks for fixing her, Siofra. I'm going to say fair focks. We'd definitely consider recommending you to other people whose kids are bitches. Or bastards – they could be boys. Come on, Sorcha, let's go.'

Except Siofra's on it like an Easter bonnet.

'It's way too early to think of Honor as being *fixed*,' she goes. 'Her behaviour has improved and that's obviously very encouraging. And she certainly seems to be sincere in her stated desire to become a better-behaved young person.'

I'm like, 'There's a "but" coming – come on, let's hear the but.'

'I think any change in Honor's behaviour can only be accurately assessed over a longer period of time.'

'Of course you do – because it means more ching for you, you focking bluffer.'

Sorcha goes, 'Ross!' because she can be such a fool for people.

I'm there, 'Hey, I'm calling it as I see it. You've heard Honor mention that she's all better now. She was a focking nightmare for a long time and now she's not. That's good enough for me.'

'I would suggest,' Siofra goes, 'that you continue to use the Honour Board and keep our weekly appointments – both the family sessions *and* the one-to-ones – until August.'

I'm like, 'August? It's focking May.'

'I know what month it is.'

'You're saying we're going to be coming here for the entire focking summer?'

I look at Honor. She manages to hide her true feelings behind a hey-ho smile, but I know that in her mind she's pulling my fingernails out with her teeth.

'Don't listen to my husband,' Sorcha goes. 'We are committed to the programme, Siofra, and we're going to see it through.'

When we leave the office, Sorcha goes off for a hit and miss and that's when Honor opens up on me. She goes, 'You focking said if I pretended to be good, I wouldn't have to come anymore.'

I'm there, 'That's what I thought.'

'Do you have any idea how hord it is for me to be nice?'

'It's a massive, massive ask – I realize that.'

'And it turns out I've just been wasting my focking time.'

'Stick with it, Honor – for a few more months.'

'I want things.'

'I'll buy you things.'

'I'm going to make a list. Eight things. No, twelve.'

'I'll get you them.'

'I know you will. Because if you don't, I'll tell *her* that you've been buying me things all along – and I'll tell her about that phone call you got.'

Off she stomps, out to the cor.

I'm standing there thinking, okay, I don't need this. I seriously don't need it. I'm supposed to be having, like, major surgery tomorrow. And that's when Sorcha comes out of the jacks and goes, 'Oh my God, I totally forgot – my dad wants to meet you later!'

I'm like, 'Meet me? We live in the same gaff – worse focking luck.'

'No, he wants to meet you for, like, a drink.'

'A drink?'

'In Sandycove. It's a nice thing, isn't it?'

'I don't get why he wants to meet me for a drink, though.'

'Does it matter why? Why don't you just go with it, Ross? Maybe he wants to show you – yeah, before you go under the knife tomorrow – that there's, like, no hord *feelings*?'

I'm there, 'I doubt it. I seriously focking doubt it.'

He's standing at the bor in Fitzgerald's watching the end of the *Six One News* with – focking ridiculous – a gin and tonic in his hand.

My opening line is a cracker.

'Yeah, no,' I go, 'I'll have a drink if you're buying – but make it a man's drink.'

He's raging and he has no answer to it. He's just there, 'Hello, Ross.'

'Beer me,' I go to the borman. 'Heineken,' and then I turn back to *him* and I'm like, 'Okay, what's the deal here? What's this about?'

He smiles at me, except it's, like, *fake*?

He goes, 'I'd like to talk to you about, well, declaring a truce.'

I'm there, 'A truce? You're the one who's been on my case since day one – I mean, constantly telling Sorcha that she was too good for me.'

'Look, you and I are never going to be friends. But that's often the way with father-in-laws and son-in-laws. And, yes, I'm not going to deny it, I still think my daughter married beneath her when she married you . . .'

'This is you making peace, is it?'

'But we both *love* Sorcha – you in your way, hard as it is for me to fathom sometimes, and me in mine.'

Gin and tonic. The focking Dowager Countess of Grantham drinks gin and tonic.

I'm there, 'Agreed.'

And Sally Webster.

He goes, 'This war of attrition that you and I have been waging can't continue. All this tit-for-tat doesn't make for a happy home environment. You and Sorcha have three lovely children to think about.'

I'm there, 'We actually have *four* lovely children?'

But he just sips his drink – doesn't respond.

He goes, 'You and I will never be friends, Ross. But I'm going to pay you a compliment now.'

I'm like, 'Go on, this should be good.'

'If anything *were* to happen to you while you were on the operating table . . .'

'Sorcha would get three point four mills – you already mentioned.'

' . . . I was going to say, Sorcha's life would never be the same again.'

I just nod. 'Okay,' I go, 'I'm going to accept that.'

He sticks out his hand – he has a woman's hands – and he goes, 'A truce?'

And I'm like, 'Okay – a truce it is then.'

We finish shaking and I'm suddenly thinking, okay, now I need to get out of here before this becomes awkward. I put my pint to my lips with the intention of, like, knocking it back in one and that's when I hear a voice from across the pub go, 'Ross! O'Carroll! Kelly! As I live . . . and breathe!'

I turn my head to see this old dude – he's got to be, I don't know, seventy years old – coming out of the jacks. I sort of, like, turn away and look at Sorcha's old man as if to say, okay, who's this focking random weirdo? Probably another one of my old man's mates.

The dude goes, 'I saw you play . . . for Castlerock College . . . oh, many, many . . . many, many moons ago . . . and I turned to the chap . . . who happened to be standing beside me . . . and I said to him . . . I said, "Remember this moment – because we are watching the next . . . the next Mike Gibson!"'

The dude is hammered, in case you haven't worked that out yet. Seven o'clock in the evening and off his tits. But like I said, I love a pat on the back.

I'm there going, 'Yeah, no, like you said – it was a long time ago,' and at the same time I'm looking at Sorcha's old man as if to say, 'See – there *are* people out there who remember the things I did on the rugby field.'

'Newbridge College,' this dude goes. 'That's who . . . who you were playing . . . I said to the chap standing next to me, "Remember this moment . . . we are looking at the next Mike Gibson!" '

I turn to Sorcha's old man.

'Sorry about this,' I go. 'Happens from time to time. A lot of people have made the Mike Gibson comparison, by the way. Jack Kyle is the other one that always gets mentioned.'

He nods, even though he knows fock-all about rugby. At the same time, he whips out his phone and goes, 'I have an important call to make. I'll leave you to chat with your fan!'

I roll my eyes as if to say, you know, this is a bit of a pain, but it's a port of the game – goes with the territory, you could say.

He goes outside, out onto the Sandycove Road, his phone clamped to his ear.

The old dude is obviously one of those annoying drunks who attach themselves to randomers in a pub and sponge drinks off them all night. But, even taking that into account, he's saying a lot of nice shit about my rugby, so I end up offering to get a round in.

He asks for a pint *and* a chaser?

And at the same time, he's going, 'Newbridge College . . . it was the final, wasn't it?'

I'm there, 'Yeah, no, I'm just trying to cast my mind back here.'

I'm doing the whole false modesty thing.

He goes, 'You won it on your own . . . the final . . . By! A! Mile! I said to the chap next to me . . . I said, "Remember this moment . . . because . . . because we are looking at the next Mike Gibson."'

I'm there, 'You certainly seem to know your rugby.'

'I do . . . I love rugby.'

After ten or fifteen minutes of this, I'm looking over my shoulder for Sorcha's old man, except there's still no *sign* of him?

I decide to – fock it – get another round in. A pint for me and a pint and a short for the old dude, who at some point goes, 'What happened to you?'

I'm there, 'Excuse me?'

'I watched . . . I watched for your name . . . every time the Ireland squad was announced. Ross O'Carroll . . . O'Carroll-Kelly . . . I watched for your name.'

'I would answer your question by saying a combination of bad luck, injuries and telling Warren Gatland a few home truths one night in the Berkeley Court in 2001. And I'll be proved right about him in the long run – mork my words.'

'Mike Gibson . . . that's who you were like . . .'

'Yeah, no, so you keep saying. Can you be more specific about the qualities that made me a great player in your opinion?'

'Pace . . .'

'Yeah, no, I definitely had pace.'

'Hands . . .'

'Hands – okay, obviously hands.'

'And you knew . . . you knew how to manage a game . . . how to manage a game . . . Mike Gibson.'

My nose storts twitching. I'm suddenly getting a horrendous whiff of piss. I look down and I notice, to my total disgust, that the dude has, like, soiled his actual trousers.

'Get him out of here!' the borman suddenly shouts – *not* a happy bunny?

I'm there, 'Yeah, no, I'm not actually *with* him? He's just an admirer.'

'Out!' he roars.

And because there's no one else in the pub, it automatically falls to me to help. So what else can I do except put his orm around my shoulder and sort of, like, usher him out of the pub?

'Mike Gibson,' he keeps going. 'I said it . . . Mike Gibson . . .'

Outside, the air hits him pretty hord. I can see him swaying backwards and forwards and it's like he might topple over at any second.

I'm there, 'You never mentioned my kicking, by the way. I had a ninety-two percent success rate in Leinster Schools Senior Cup matches. There's not many have that – Rog, Johnno and Mads included.'

The dude puts one hand against the wall to steady himself, then suddenly – without, like, *any* pre-warning? – he storts spewing his guts up, all over the path. I end up having to jump backwards to stop my Dubes being pebble-dashed.

I'm like, 'For fock's sake!' and at the same time, roysh, I'm looking over both shoulders, wondering would it be bad form for me to just, like, abandon him here? I don't actually know the dude. I mean, yes, he's a major fan – he's made that much clear – but I owe him fock-all.

I'm like, 'Where do you live?' but he's too out of it to even hear me.

I'm on the point of just, like, bailing on him when Sorcha's old man suddenly reappears.

He sort of, like, chuckles to himself and goes, 'Dear, oh, dear!'

And I'm there, 'It happened very suddenly. One minute he was talking about what a disgrace it was that I never actually made it in the game of rugby – when others with less talent did – and the next minute he was chucking his lunch.'

And that's when Sorcha's old man says it. 'Come on,' he goes – this is to the drunk dude, 'let's get you home – you've got work tomorrow.'

And the dude looks at Sorcha's old man – vom all over his boat race, bear in mind – and he goes, 'Thanks, Edmund . . .'

As you can imagine, roysh, I'm a bit *thrown* by this?

I'm like, 'Hang on, do you two actually know each other?'

And Sorcha's old man goes, 'Well, of course we do! This is my friend, Arthur! He's operating on you in the morning!'

It would not be an exaggeration to say that my blood runs literally cold at that moment. I'm like, 'But he can't . . . he can't operate on me – look at the focking state of him!'

Sorcha's old man goes, 'Oh, you'd be shocked at Arthur's powers of recovery. This is just an average night for him.'

Shit is suddenly becoming clear to me here. I'm there, 'You . . . you brought him on the lash . . . you brought him on the lash knowing he was going to be operating on me.'

'Like I said,' he goes, 'Arthur's been doing this for years. Although I have noticed in the last year or two that he's started to develop the shakes the day after a session like this.'

'You even had *me* plying with him drink.'

'I played nine holes with him in Delgany before Christmas.

Couldn't hit the ball. There was one shot – he had to take four swings at it. *And* it was a putt!'

'You offered me a truce. You said if anything happened to me on the operating table, Sorcha's life would never be the same again.'

'What I meant was it would be better! She could finally be all the things she could have been if she'd never met you.'

'You've stitched me up.'

He laughs. 'No,' he goes, 'that's actually Arthur's job. Provided his hand is steady enough!'

I get this sudden tightness in my chest and my breathing is suddenly all, I don't know, *uneven*? I realize straight away that I'm having a basic panic attack.

'Come on,' Sorcha's old man goes, lightly slapping the old dude's face, 'let's see can we get a taxi to take you home.'

I stort walking backwards, off the kerb and onto the road. A cor has to swerve to avoid creaming me. The driver gives me an angry blast of his horn, but I barely hear him, because I'm going, 'No way! No focking way!' over and over again.

And then I hear a voice shouting Tommy Bowe's name in my pocket. I answer without even checking the caller ID. It ends up being my old man. His opening words are, 'We are engaged to the La Reina del Plata!'

I'm like, 'What the fock are you shitting on about?' because I'm actually still in *shock* here?

He goes, 'Helen and I are starting out for *La Paris de Sudamérica*!'

I'm there, 'Okay, I'm hanging up on you now, you fock-tool.'

'I'm saying we're leaving for Buenos Aires, Ross! To try to find your sister! I was just saying to Helen again what a pity it is that young Kicker isn't coming with us! What a team that'd make, eh, Ross?'

My hand automatically reaches for my trouser pocket and suddenly, for the first time, I can see a way out of this thing. Through my chinos, I can feel the outline of my passport and I take it as an instant sign.

I'm like, 'Give your focking orse a rest for two seconds, will you? What time is your flight?'

'It's a nine p.m. flight to Heathrow,' he goes. 'Then it's overnight to Ministro Pistarini and the devil take the hindmost! Hurrah!'

'I'll see you at the airport,' I hear myself go. 'I'm coming with you.'

5.

Don't Cry for Me, Orgentina

I'm like, 'Step aside, coffee – this is a job for alcohol!'

The air hostess smiles as she hands me the two whiskeys, although the line wasn't *for* her benefit? It was intended for the little honey across the aisle who's a ringer for Florence Brudenell-Bruce.

When the trolley is pushed away, I go, 'So where are *you* off to, pretty lady?'

There's no doubt I have a way about me.

She goes, 'I beg your pardon?'

She's English – not one of the slutty ones either.

I'm there, 'I was just asking where you were going – break the ice, blah, blah, blah.'

She's like, 'I'm going to Boonoth Airketh – like everyone else on board.'

'Yeah, no, like I said, I was only really making conversation. It's mad that, isn't it?'

'What's mad?'

'Just the way you pronounced Buenos Aires.'

'How did I pronounce it?'

'You said Boonoth Airketh.'

'Well, that's how the locals pronounce it.'

'Yeah, I'm agreeing with you. I'm just saying, you know, it's okay to say Boonoth Airketh and Barthelona the way the locals say it. But if you pronounced the name of, I don't know, some town in Africa the way the people there say it, you'd be called a racist. Every so often, I get like this. I call them my deep-thinking days.'

'Hmmm.'

'So you've obviously been to this place before if you're pronouncing it like that?'

'Yes, I'm studying in Boonoth Airketh.'

'I'm going to say fair focks. Can you recommend any good nightclubs – for example, where do you tend to socialize yourself?'

She goes, 'I don't really go out much. I mostly stay home with my boyfriend,' and then she pulls her iPod out of the seat pocket in front of her and puts her buds in her ears to signal that the conversation is over.

It's called being cock-blocked by Steve Jobs.

I turn to the old man, who's had his nose in his *Irish Times* since we left London. 'In a lot of cultures,' I go, 'what she just did would be considered rude.'

He doesn't even hear me.

He just goes, 'There's talk of water metering now – on top of the bloody property tax! Frankfurt's way or Labour's way indeed!'

I'm there, 'Okay, I need to get this whiskey into me – otherwise, I'm going to end up focking you through that emergency door over there.'

I drink the first one straight from the little bottle and that's when I notice that Helen – in the window seat, on the other side of the old man – is just, like, staring at me.

'Ross,' she goes, 'are you sure Sorcha agreed to you going on this trip?'

Jesus. She kept asking me the same shit on the flight to Heathrow, except then it was, 'Does Sorcha know where you are?'

I was still a bit shit-faced from Fitzgerald's, in fairness to me. I possibly still am.

The old man looks up from his newspaper. 'Of course she knows where he is!' he goes. 'You don't think he'd just get on a plane to Argentina without mentioning it to his good lady wife, do you? Good Lord, Helen, give the chap *some* credit!'

I don't say anything. I switch on the little TV and I flick through the movies. *Argo. Django Unchained. Zero Dork Thirty.* There's none I haven't seen. I might watch *ParaNorman* again.

I think for a couple of minutes, then I go, 'Can you make phone calls from flights?'

Helen's like, 'You *didn't* tell Sorcha, did you?'

I'm there, 'Yeah, no, I'm pretty *sure* I did? It's just, I don't know, maybe she was a bit distracted when I mentioned it. She's got a brain like pâté at the moment. I probably should double-check with her whether she heard me or not.'

The old man pops the handset out of his orm rest. He goes, 'Actually, you can make calls on these things, don't you know! The wonders of modern technology! Very expensive, though!'

I snatch it out of his hand.

I'm like, 'You're good for it, I'm sure,' then I stick in his credit cord number and I dial the gaff.

Sorcha's old man answers on about the twentieth ring. I have no idea what time it is back home, but it sounds like he's just woken up.

He goes, 'Where the hell are you?'

I turn the TV onto the map channel, which shows you the plane's position. We're over, like, some sea – possibly an ocean. 'Hord to say,' I go. 'Put me on to my wife.'

He's there, 'You'd better be at that bloody hospital in the morning.'

I'm like, 'Go and get her – this is costing my old man a fortune.'

It's a good four or five minutes before Sorcha gets on the phone – and even then she sounds half asleep.

'Ross,' she goes, 'it's four o'clock in the morning.'

'Yeah, no, I thought I'd just, um, give you a ring.'

'Where are you?'

'Did I not mention?'

Helen is staring at me.

'Ross, are you drunk?' Sorcha goes. 'Oh my God, you're supposed to be having surgery in a few hours.'

I'm there, 'Yeah, no, I know you're going to laugh at this, Sorcha.'

'Laugh?'

'I'm on an airplane.'

'An airplane? An airplane where?'

'Well, we're over water at the moment, but we're heading for Orgentina.'

'You're joking, aren't you?'

'I'm not joking, Babes.'

166

'Ross, please tell me you're joking.'

'It was a real spur of the moment decision, if that's any consolation to you. The old man and Helen were going anyway to try to find Erika. And they thought I might be able to give them a dig-out. I found Fionn, bear in mind.'

She's literally lost for words. I can picture her lips working like she's trying to blow bubbles with no gum in her mouth.

I'm there, 'I couldn't go through with it, Sorcha – as in, the vasectomy?'

A few people turn around in their seats. I'm having to shout to be heard over the sound of the engine.

I'm like, 'I met your old man for that drink last night. He brought along the surgeon who was supposed to do the op. Got him shit-faced. There was no way I was letting him near my dick with a scalpel. I panicked. I knew I had to get out of the country.'

I'm suddenly the centre of attention on the flight. Honestly, have people not got anything going on in their *own* lives? Even my old man is suddenly glued to what's being said.

Sorcha goes, 'Ross, the second you get off that plane, I want you to get another one and get back here immediately.'

I'm like, 'I can't do that, Babes. I'm very much a man on a mission here – and that mission is to find my sister.'

She's there, 'Ross, you have a wife and four children!'

And I go, 'Sorry, you're breaking up, Sorcha – it's a terrible line,' and I end up just hanging up on her, because it's very difficult to get through to the girl when she's being hysterical.

I hand the phone slash handset back to my old man and I go, 'Job done,' and then I look up at all the people turned around in their seats and I go, 'Yeah, the show's over, people.'

I love a buffet breakfast. I like to give the metabolism a good workout, giving it all sorts of random shit to deal with – prosciutto and cheese, followed by a bowl of melon balls with yoghurt, followed by sausage, egg and beans, followed by three croissants and possibly a Danish.

'So,' the old man goes, 'where are we going to start this search?'

Helen doesn't say anything. She's in a serious fouler and I'm saying that as one of her biggest fans. When we landed, she wanted to put me on the next flight back to London, except we ended up having, like, a blazing row in the baggage hall.

I was like, 'I'm not going back, Helen, to have some old focker take a knife to my nuts, so you can get that idea out of your head. Anyway, I have a job to do here and that job is to find my sister slash half-sister.'

She wasn't happy. She's still not happy. She's not even eating.

'I was up in the night,' the old man goes. 'Jetlag, don't you know! I went to the business centre. Chap in there helped me get on the famous Internet and we printed out the addresses of local saddlers, veterinary practices, equine centres – that type of thing.'

Helen's like, 'What was the point of that?'

'Well, horses, of course! I know she's not with this Fabrizio chap anymore. But you and I both know how much Erika loves our four-legged friends. *Equus ferus caballus*, if you'll permit me! Thought we could show her photograph around. Explain the state of play. Our daughter. Lost contact and so forth. We'll ask them has she been in – and, if so, we'll ask them if they might tell us where she lives.'

Helen goes, 'Do you have any idea how many people live in this city?'

'I expect it's rather a lot.'

'Three million.'

'Yes, I thought it might have been in that – inverted commas – ballpark. Well, the sooner we get started, the better, eh?'

I rub my two hands together and I go, 'Okay, let's do this thing!'

Helen stands up from the table, at the same time giving my old man a look, then she walks straight out of the restaurant.

The old man storts acting all, I don't know, *shifty* then?

He's there, 'Perhaps, um, you might stay here, Ross. Spend the day getting yourself acclimatized. I noticed they have Heineken on draught in the bar.'

I'm like, 'Heineken? Is that all you think I am?'

'Please don't take offence.'

'A piss-head who can't pass a set of focking beer pumps? Dude, I'm here for the same reason as you and Helen. To try to find Erika.'

'It's just that Helen is rather concerned that you've abandoned Sorcha and the children just to get out of having this, well, procedure.'

'I'm tempted to say Sofa King what?'

'Look, I'll talk to Helen.'

'Heineken on focking draft. It's a good job I'm not sensitive.'

'I'll talk to Helen and I'll explain that whatever upset we're feeling at Erika's disappearance, well, you're bound to be feeling it, too.'

'That's why I'm here.'

'Don't worry, Kicker, I shall talk her round.'

Off he goes.

I fock off back to my room. I lie on the bed and I sort of, like, *nap* for an hour? Then I switch on the TV and I flick through the channels, except they're all in, like, Orgentinian and obviously I don't have a word. There's, like, some kind of, I don't know, daytime soap opera on and I watch it for a good ten minutes – people just going, 'Tha-tha-tha-tha-tha-tha-tha!' to each other – and I laugh out loud, thinking, 'How do they even understand each other – or are they just pretending to?'

Then I'm suddenly thinking about Heineken and quietly cursing my old man for putting the idea in my head.

I check the time on my phone. It's, like, twelve o'clock in the day. In Ireland, it's even later. Whatever way you look at it, it's a respectable hour for the first of the day.

I tip down to the bor.

The dude behind the bor is called Sergio – or at least that's according to his badge.

'Heineken,' I go. 'Pint.'

He pulls it for me, at the same time taking a massive interest in the crest on the jersey I happen to be wearing.

He's like, 'What eez?'

I laugh. I'm there, 'It's Leinster. I thought this was supposed to be a rugby country.'

'Len?'

'Leinster.'

'Lenstra.'

'Lein-*ster*. Lein-*ster*. Felipe Contepomi?'

'Felipe?'

'Contepomi? He was one of your crew. Played for us. Doesn't matter.'

This country seems to do its own thing language-wise.

He goes, 'Theez, I don't know.'

I'm like, 'That's why I said forget it. Doesn't matter.'

'You like sock air?'

'Excuse me?'

'Sock air – do you like?'

'The opposite. Are you trying to say soccer?'

'Sock air, yes.'

'I'd focking ban it. That's how much I hate it.'

'Baneet?'

'Ban it.'

'Lionel Messi.'

'I don't know what you're saying.'

'Lionel. Messi.'

'Yeah, no, still nothing – let's agree to differ.'

And there the conversation ends.

Ten minutes later, I order another Heineken – no words, this time – which I end up sinking in, like, three mouthfuls, then I'm suddenly trying to decide between going back to the room for another nap, or going out and possibly exploring Buenos Aires.

And being, at hort, an adventurer, I decide to do the latter – in other words, the second of those two things.

The city ends up being humungous. The Avenue Something de Somethingo is the main drag – I suppose the locals would look on it as *their* O'Connell Street? – and it's, like, fourteen traffic lanes wide.

I walk up and down it, just taking in the sights.

One of the things I instantly love about Buenos Aires is that no one knows me here. I know certain people – I'm talking about mainly my critics – would hear me say that and go, 'Er, no one knows you in Dublin either,' but it's genuinely nice to be able to just walk around without people looking at me, then under their breath going, 'That's the goy who very nearly made it as a rugby player but didn't for various reasons – not all of them his fault.'

The women are tremendous. I literally fall in love six times in the first twenty minutes after I step out of the Intercontinental Hotel. A lot of them are of a type, you might say – tall, long, dork hair, massive jiggers and lips that could suck a papaya up a Pringles tube.

It'd be very easy to get distracted, but I have a job to do, which is obviously to find Erika. While my old man and Helen are checking out, I don't know, horsey places, I stort checking out the kind of places that *I'd* expect to find my sister – in other words, shops.

Whenever I close my eyes and try to imagine her now, I picture her swanning around whatever the equivalent of BTs is here, spending money on threads.

I hit about five serious high-end deportment stores, scouring their shoe, jewellery and fine fur deportments, showing my most recent photograph of her on my phone to various shop staff, none of who seems to know her.

Once, I actually think I spot her and I end up following this girl who went into a changing room with a red Roland Mouret sheath dress – except when I whip back the curtain and go, 'I bet you weren't expecting this!' it ends up not being her at all and she storts screaming at the top of her voice – and who could blame her?

I show another shop bird – a girl in her twenties with great noogies, who looks a little bit like Olivia Munn – the photograph and she seems to straight away recognize her. '*Si!*' she goes. '*Si!*' which is their word for yes – same as in Spanish – and then she goes, 'Theez way! Theez way!' and she leads me across the floor of the shop, through the racks and racks of clothes, and I stort to get actually excited, thinking, 'What are the chances of her being here on the very day I happened to swing by?' but then this Olivia Nunn one stops in front of a big display of coats and goes, 'Theez?' and she takes my phone and she looks at the photograph again and I realize that she thinks I'm looking to buy the coat that Erika is wearing.

I'm like, 'No, no, no – I ham looking to find theez girl!'

I manage to make myself understood.

'Theez girl?' she goes.

I'm like, '*Si*. She heez my seester slash half-seester. She heez somewhere een Boonoth Airketh.'

She stares at the photograph for a long time and I go, 'I'll tell you what – forget it,' getting suddenly frustrated. 'Seriously, it doesn't matter.'

Ten seconds later, I'm on the down escalator, thinking, fock it, I'll go back to the hotel for another pint of Heineken, before grabbing a late afternoon nap. Inventing the siesta is possibly the greatest day's work that mankind has ever done.

That's when this Olivia Nunn one – fock it, I'm just going to *call* her Olivia Nunn – shouts at me from the top of the escalator. She's like, 'Whait! Meester – whait!'

It turns out that she thinks she recognizes her. '*Calle Florida!*' she keeps going. '*Calle Florida!*'

I'm like, 'Florida? Are you trying to say she's gone to Florida?'

'No, no. Come. Come. Theez.'

She leads me out of the deportment store and up the road, then around one or two corners, until we come to a street which it turns out is actually *called* what she was trying to say – in other words, *Calle Florida*.

'I theenk,' she goes, pointing to a little boutique, which is called *Ninos*.

I'm there, 'What? You think she's in there?'

'I theenk. I don't know.'

Then off she trots.

I tip over to the shop and I look in the window. There's a bird in there who's a ringer for Erika alright. But then I have to be sure. I don't want to be wrong again and this time end up being arrested. I watch her picking up items of clothing, looking at them, then folding them and putting them back. She's wearing, like, a grey wool dress, cut short, tights and a pair of prostiboots.

Suddenly, I'm sure.

I push open the door and in I go. She doesn't, like, *see* me at first? She's, like, too engrossed in the clothes.

I go, 'Hello, Erika!'

I swear to fock, she turns around and it's like she's just seen a ghost. Which is exactly what I am, I suppose. A ghost from her past.

She goes, 'What the what?' and what she actually means is, 'What the fock?'

I'm there, 'I'm sorry, I didn't mean to scare you. You're looking well,' and I'm saying that as a blood relative.

'What are you . . . what the fock are you doing here?'

She's busted and disgusted.

I'm there, 'We came here to look for you – and it looks like I'm the one who found you.'

She also *smells* lovely, by the way.

She goes, 'Maybe I didn't want to be found . . . who's *we*?'

She's actually, like, *shouting* now?

I'm there, 'We, in this case, is me, your old dear and my old man – well, he's your old man as well.'

She goes, 'Where are they?'

'They're around.'

'Do they know I'm here?'

'Calm down, Erika!'

'I asked you do they know I'm here?'

'No! I only just spotted you ten focking seconds ago!'

'You are not to tell them you found me! I mean it, Ross!'

It's at that exact moment that the manageress, having heard our raised voices, suddenly arrives over and says something to Erika in a language that I straight away recognize as *not* English. She seems to be, like, giving out yords to her – I'm presuming for causing a disturbance. But instead of telling her to go and sit on her thumb, which is what the old her would have done, Erika says something to her in the local lingo, which seems to be some kind of apology.

The manageress woman literally scowls at her, then turns and walks away – and that's when the penny finally drops.

'Oh my God,' I go, 'are you actually *working* here?'

She's there, 'It's not a big deal, Ross. Can you please leave?'

'I can't believe you've been reduced to this – working for a living.'

'If you don't go now, I'm going to get the sack.'

'I never thought you'd stoop so low. I know about Fabrizio, by the way. I know he dumped you.'

'How?'

'Your old dear rang him at Christmas. He told her you weren't together anymore.'

'You don't have to sound so pleased about it.'

'Don't worry, I'm not going to say I told you so, even though I did predict it, if you remember. So what actually happened?'

'It doesn't matter what happened. We wanted different things.'

'Namely?'

'I wanted to get married and have children. He wanted to fock a woman called Camilla Lacobellis behind my back.'

'See, I knew it. One player recognizes another – like I said, I spotted it a mile off.'

'You have to go, Ross.'

She storts shoving me towards the door of the shop.

I'm like, 'Whoa, I'm not going anywhere.'

She's there, 'Ross, I have to work.'

'Well, when will I see you again?'

'You don't need to see me again. You found me. Tell Mum and Dad I'm alive, then you can all go home.'

'They'll want to know where I saw you.'

'You are *not* to tell them!'

'The plan is to bring you back to Ireland.'

'I'm not going back to Ireland.'

'Because you're too proud? Because you don't want people to know you got dumped and ended up working in a clothes shop?'

'Goodbye, Ross.'

'You're not getting rid of me that easily. I want to have a proper talk with you.'

'There's nothing to say.'

'I'm talking about lunch – that's all.'

She doesn't say anything.

I'm there, 'The alternative is that I go back to the hotel now and I tell your old pair exactly where to find you.'

'You're such a wanker.'

'Lunch.'

She stares at me for a good, like, ten seconds. 'Pick me up here tomorrow at two. I have an hour – that's all.'

I'm there, 'Okay.'

'And don't you focking dare tell my mum and dad that you found me.'

I go to hug her. In fact, I *do* hug her – except she doesn't respond. Her body goes stiff. It's like trying to be affectionate to someone with *rigor mortis.*

I pull away.

I'm there, 'And by the way, if it's any consolation, I think Fabrizio is the real loser in all of this. He obviously didn't realize what he had in his hands. A girl who's amazing looks-wise – also intelligent, great little body . . .'

'Oh my God, you are so weird.'

'Yeah, no, I know. I'll see you tomorrow at two.'

The girl restocking the cold meats on the breakfast buffet table gives me a lovely little smile.

I go, 'Hey!' just to let her know she has my attention in that French maid clobber.

I'm one of those dudes who doesn't consider scoring birds in other countries to be actual cheating. It's just road ass.

It is what it is.

She finishes laying out the meats, then off she focks.

I grab some smoked salmon, a custard Danish and a hord-boiled egg, then I tip over to the table where the old man and Helen are sitting, having already finished breakfast.

I'm like, 'Morning.'

The old man goes, 'Here he comes! They don't make number tens like this chap anymore and, if there was any justice in the world, he'd be sitting at home this morning waiting for the announcement of the Lions squad!'

It's a lovely thing to hear.

I'm like, 'Shut your big focking air raid siren mouth, will you? Jesus, I could hear you in the focking lift!'

He's all, 'Absolutely, Ross! Quite right!'

Helen goes, 'Good morning, Ross,' and she's being definitely nicer to me now than she was last night.

I'm like, 'Hey, Helen.'

I'm on the record as saying I think she's a cool person – a hundred times nicer than that gin-addicted, rubber-faced scrat who calls herself my mother.

'Ross,' she goes, just to prove it, 'I wanted to apologize to you . . .'

I'm like, 'Yeah, no, Helen, you don't have to – you've been like a second mother to me. Blah, blah, blah.'

'I was tired after the flight. And, well, I'm in quite a heightened emotional state anyway.'

'Apology accepted.'

'It's just not knowing where my daughter is and whether she's safe – well, it's killing me.'

Shit. Suddenly, I feel like the biggest dick in the world.

'Erika's fine,' I go. 'Don't you worry about that.'

She's there, 'We don't know that, Ross. We don't know that for sure.'

'I do. I definitely do. I have this, I don't know, weird ability to, like, *sense* shit? Some people call it ESB.'

The old man goes, 'We walked the bloody legs off ourselves yesterday, Ross.'

I'm there, 'You're saying you had no luck?'

'We met a chap in a saddlers who said he knew her. Or rather she came in once or twice with Fabrizio. He hasn't seen her for about a year. What about you, Ross – what did you do?'

'Believe it or not, I had a good mooch around myself. I actually came at it from a different angle to you two. I was thinking, okay, what else is Erika into aport from horses – and the answer my brain came up with was shopping.'

'Shopping?'

'Yeah, no, she's big into shopping. Helen knows what I'm talking about. So I went around the various different deportment stores, trying to see was she in there, like, *buying* shit?'

'And was she? I'm sorry. Silly question. If you found her, you'd have told us, of course.'

I take a bite out of my custard Danish. I go, 'Hmmm,' and I stare out the window.

Helen goes, 'Thank you for trying, Ross.'

I decide to quickly change the subject. I'm there, 'So where did you two go last night? I didn't see you in the bor.'

The old man goes, 'We took a stroll up to the famous Plaza de Mayo.'

'The what?'

'The Plaza de Mayo is the main square in the centre of the city. It's always been a sort of focal-point of political life here. I suppose you could describe it as *their* Molesworth Street.'

Helen goes, 'I wanted to see the handkerchiefs painted on the ground.'

I'm like, 'Er, okay.'

'It was the Mothers of the Disappeared, Ross. During the years of the military junta, tens of thousands of people went missing in this country. Their mothers organized themselves and they marched regularly, demanding to know what happened to their children. It seemed kind of appropriate to us.'

I just nod. It's actually a bit boring.

I'm there, 'Yeah, no, I might check that out alright. Thanks for the tip.'

The old man goes, 'Of course, it's where you'll also find the famous Casa Rosada, where Evita stood and famously addressed the poor people of Argentina.'

I'm there, 'Did you say Evita?'

'That's right – María Eva Duarte de Perón!'

'Was that *actual*?'

'What do you mean?'

'I mean was she, like, a real person? I thought that movie was made up – like that play about Munster beating the All Blacks.'

'Oh, no – it was based on real events, Ross.'

'That's so random.'

'She was married to the famous Juan Perón, who wasn't all bad – for a dictator with Nazi sympathies. He was one of South America's better leaders, I would have thought.'

'Is that where we are – *South* America?'

'That's right! América del Sur!'

All of a sudden, I hear, 'Tommmmmy Boooooowwwe!'

I look at my phone. Sorcha's face is suddenly filling the screen. She doesn't look happy. I know it's a photograph, but it's a reminder of how pissed off she is with me right now. I consider not answering it. I actually go, 'Yeah, no, I'm not sure if I need that headache right now.'

Except then I catch Helen staring at me across the table, so I think, yeah, no, I possibly *should* answer it?

So I do.

I stand up from the table and I go, 'Hey, Sorcha – greetings from *South* America.'

I head back to the buffet table. I pick up a hord-boiled egg.

Sorcha goes, 'I've booked you a flight. It's the one o'clock from Buenos Aires to Heathrow. You probably should think about heading for the airport now.'

I'm like, 'Sorcha, I'm not coming home – not yet.'

I can hear babies crying in the background. I'm not a total iceberg. I don't envy her that shit.

She goes, 'Look, Ross, I talked to my dad. He admitted everything. He knows he was out of order getting that surgeon drunk. He was still upset about his books. But it doesn't change the fact that you need to come home and you need to have this operation.'

I end up just blurting it out. Well, first I check that the old man and Helen are definitely out of earshot. *Then* I blurt it out.

I'm like, 'I found her.'

She goes, 'What?'

'I found her – as in, Erika?'

'Oh! My God!'

'She's here. I met her yesterday.'

'Ross, that's like, oh my God!'

'Yeah, no, you've *made* that point?'

'And how does she look? Is she really thin?'

'She looks well – and I'm not going to say any more than that because we're related.'

'I actually don't believe it.'

She seems genuinely pleased – their differences suddenly forgotten.

'I was the one who actually tracked her down,' I go. 'The hero of the hour and blah, blah, blah.'

She goes, 'Helen and Chorles must be – oh my God – *so* relieved!'

I'm there, 'Errr . . .'

'What?'

'Yeah, no, I haven't *told* them yet?'

'You can't keep something like that from them.'

'See, the thing is, she doesn't want to see them.'

'Ross, *you* don't get to make that decision. Helen is entitled to know that her daughter is safe.'

'Well, I just figured, you know, if I tell them where she is, then Erika might do another runner. There's also something else . . .'

'What?'

'You might not want to hear this.'

'Ross, she's my best friend.'

'All I'll say is I don't think Helen and the old man would want to see her the way she is now.'

'Oh my God, is she . . .'

'She's *working*, Sorcha. She's working in a shop.'

'Erika? Working?'

'Exactly. This is the level that this so-called Fabrizio has reduced her to.'

'Ross, I need time to process this.'

'We all do. That's why I'm saying that I should possibly stay here for now. I need to build up her trust, then convince her that if she comes home, she won't be judged – even though I was the one who said the thing with Fabrizio wouldn't last pissing time.'

There's, like, silence on the end of the line for a good ten seconds. Then she goes, 'Okay, stay there. But you're still having a vasectomy when you come home.'

I'm there, 'We'll certainly discuss it again.'

'We miss you. Honor really misses you.'

'Does she?'

'Oh my God, I can't believe the change that has come over her. I put her hair in a plait last night!'

'Jesus.'

'She actually let me, Ross. Oh my God, it reminded me so much of when *I* was a little girl and my mum used to put *my* hair in a plait. And the way she's been speaking to me, Ross!'

'Good? Bad?'

'Good! It's "Mommy this" and "Mommy that" and "please" and "thank you". I know you were dubious, Ross, but you'd have to agree that Siofra is amazing.'

'She's something alright.'

'I actually used the word genius when I saw her today. Hang on. Honor wants to talk to you. Ross, give Erika my love. Tell her – oh my God – to get in touch when she's ready, either by text or e-mail or Facebook or Twitter.'

I hear the phone being handed over, then ten seconds later I hear Honor's voice. 'What the fock?' is her opening line.

I'm there, 'I'm sorry, Honor, I had to get out of Dodge. I'm in a place called Orgentina, looking for your Auntie Erika!'

'Yeah, I'm really struggling to give a shit what you're doing right now. I'll be sure to let you know if that changes.'

'I can hear you're upset.'

'She plaited my hair last night.'

'No one's saying that's right, Honor. It's just one of the things you're going to have to put up with.'

'There's some things I want.'

'Are there many of them?'

'What the fock kind of question is that?'

'I'm sorry.'

'There's seven things. I want them and you're not here to get them for me.'

'I'll get you them when I come home – does that work for you?'

'No, it doesn't work for me. Because I want them now.'

'I don't really see what I can do from over here. I'm in the South of America.'

And that's when she says it.

She goes, 'Give me your credit cord number.'

I'm there, 'I'm not giving you my credit cord number.'

'Do you want me to tell Mum that you kissed that other woman?'

'Jesus, Honor.'

'Give me your credit cord number.'

I whip out my wallet and I read off the number, the expiry date and three-digit security code off my Mastercord.

Then she hangs up without saying even a word of thanks.

Erika looks amazing. I'm going to have to stop thinking like that. She actually orders in the local language – tenderloin for me, a goat's cheese something or other for her and a bottle of Malbec. It's sexy. I'll leave it at that.

'They're beautiful,' she goes.

For a second, I actually think she's talking about my guns. I'm wearing a tight black shirt that does a great job showcasing them.

I'm like, 'They're a lot work – I'm not denying that.'

She goes, 'Of course they're work, Ross. It's three little babies.'

The penny suddenly drops.

I'm there, 'Yeah, no, they're definitely worth it. The payback will hopefully come when they get older. Rugby – blah, blah, blah. How did you know about them?'

She shrugs.

'Facebook,' she goes.

I'm there, 'I thought you'd given it up. The last thing you posted was, like, a year ago.'

'I still look at Sorcha's profile. I'm still interested.'

'I always say that Facebook is good for stalking – but *not* stalking? Does that make sense?'

'Not really, no. I mean, I don't have the energy or the interest to follow the things that pass for thoughts in your mind.'

'I can understand that. Even I find it tiring. So if you're still following her on Facebook, you'll have seen that she's, em, changed a bit.'

'She's put on a lot of weight, hasn't she?'

'I'm glad you said it. If I say shit like that, I'm automatically a dick.'

We're, like, sitting outside – it's some restaurant that Erika likes – even though it's pretty cold.

June is apparently winter here. I don't know what focking lunatic decided that.

A basket of bread arrives. I grab a roll, cut it in half and butter it.

'So what's with the names?' she goes.

I'm there, 'The names?'

'Brian, Johnny and Leo.'

'Yeah, no, *I* chose the names?'

'Yeah, I guessed that much. It's just I thought Sorcha would have named them after – I don't know, whatever – prisoners of conscience or environmental activists. Didn't she have a teddy bear called Steve Biko?'

'She still has it. Steve focking Biko.'

The two of us laugh. We both love the girl, but she does leave herself open to having the piss ripped.

'Yeah, no,' I go, 'I just put my foot down. I said Cullen, Sexton and O'Driscoll are genuine heroes of mine and I want that recognized or acknowledged or whatever you want to call it. No debate.'

'I presumed she was so grateful to have you back from Africa that she let you have your own way for, what, about a week?'

'There might have been a little bit of that as well. You know about Fionn being kidnapped then?'

'Like I said, I'm still interested. Do you mind if I smoke?'

I think about it for a few seconds and she just, like, glowers at me.

I'm like, 'Yeah, no, fire ahead.'

I'm still terrified of the girl. She takes a packet of Marlboro Lights out of her bag. She takes one out and lights it.

'Yeah, no,' I go, 'I wondered did you know about Fionn. I was thinking, does she feel maybe feel guilty about jilting him at the altar, given that *that* was the reason he ended up going to Africa in the first place. I think what I'm trying to say – and this isn't to be a wanker – is that he would never have been kidnapped if you hadn't dicked him around so badly and I hoped you weren't blaming yourself.'

'I treated him badly. He didn't deserve that. He was always the nicest out of all of you.'

'That's a view. You're entitled to it.'

'The cleverest, the sweetest, the most real.'

'Well, you wouldn't recognize him now. He's riding all around him. Do you remember a bird called Ealga Gary?'

'No. Vaguely.'

'It's pissing me off. That's the point I'm trying to make there. He's suddenly this celebrity survivor. I sometimes wish you had married him.'

'It wouldn't have lasted.'

'Yeah, no, I predicted that. I also predicted the other thing. Focking Fabrizio. Does he still class showjumping as a sport in the same way that rugby is a sport?'

'I have no idea.'

'Because that's what he said to me once and there were witnesses. So you haven't seen him – as in, you're not in touch?'

'No, we're not in touch.'

'Do you remember the time I kept calling him Febreze-io in the Merrion Inn and he wanted to deck me? In his focking dreams, of course.'

'Yes, Ross, I think about that day all the time.'

She doesn't. She's being a bitch. Our lunches arrive. Mine is swimming in blood. They don't actually cook steak in this country – they just call time of death and slap it on the plate. It's how I love it.

'Random one,' I go. 'You remember that movie *Evita* – Madonna was in it?'

She's like, 'What about it?'

'Did you know that was actual?'

'What do you mean by actual?'

'As in, it actually happened. They probably didn't sing every second focking word to each other. But Evita was a real person. Isn't that the most random thing you've ever heard in your life?'

She doesn't say anything, just twists what's left of her cigarette in the ashtray.

'So what happened with Fabrizio?' I go. 'Are you going to tell me?'

She's there, 'I told you yesterday.'

'I wouldn't mind hearing it in a bit more detail.'

'Why do you need the details, Ross?'

'Just background. You mentioned another woman. Isabel something.'

'Camilla Lacobellis.'

'That was it. Who is she?'

'She's no one. She's from this family – they're a famous show-jumping family. He's in business with them. They run an equestrian centre together. The one where he trains.'

'*Trains* is a hilarious word, but I'm going to let it go. I think what I'm trying to ask is, is she hot?'

'She's rich and she's connected. I think that's probably more the attraction for Fabrizio.'

'Can I quote you a line from *Romeo and Juliet*?'

Erika looks surprised. She even laughs. She's like, 'Er, okay – if you want.'

I'm there, 'If you can fall for chains of silver – you can fall for chains of gold.'

'That's, er, very deep, Ross.'

'It's a song I've always loved. So how did you find they were doing, you know, the nasty-nasty?'

'He started being not very nice to me – presumably just after he discovered he liked having sex with her more than he liked having sex with me. Typical man – didn't have the moral courage to just tell me. Decided that the easiest way to handle it was to be a complete asshole to me for six months so that *I'd* finish it with *him*.'

'Girls do that as well. I'm sorry to interrupt your story. But girls do it as well.'

'Anyway, I suspected something was going on, so I followed him one day. I saw them going into a hotel.'

'Did you actually catch them going at it?'

'Why does everything have to be a movie scene for you, Ross?'

'I don't know. I really don't.'

I finish my steak, then I push my plate to one side. 'Okay, next question,' I go. 'When are you coming home?'

I'm possibly a bit pissed at this stage.

She lights another Marlboro Light. She hasn't touched her lunch, by the way.

She's like, 'I'm not.'

I'm there, 'Not? As in, not ever?'

'My life is here now. I'm happy.'

'You couldn't be happy. Jesus, Erika, you're working.'

'I *like* working.'

'I wish you could hear yourself say that. The reason you don't want to go home is that you're scared of the humiliation. Did you hear about Erika Joseph? Ran away on her wedding day with a showjumper who fancied himself as a bit of a player, then ended up getting dumped herself – what, two years later?'

'That's not it.'

'That *is* it. And that's the reason you don't want to see Helen and that's the reason you don't want to see the old man. Because they told you you were making a mistake when you left Fionn, even though I personally thought he was punching well above his weight. Yet another thing I'm on the record as saying.'

I feel suddenly bad then.

'I'm sorry,' I go. 'It's just that I can see what this is doing to your old dear. Him as well. It's killing them, Erika.'

She goes, 'I'm not completely hortless, Ross. I do think about that.'

'But you won't let me tell them I found you?'

'They won't understand my reasons for wanting to stay here.'

'That'd make three of us.'

'My work is here.'

'Jesus, you could do that job in Dundrum. Horvey Nichs – any of those shops would love to have you working there. *If* that's what you're suddenly into.'

'My life is here. Amelie is here.'

'Who the fock is Amelie?'

'She's a little baby I nanny for.'

'You're nannying as well?'

'Yes, I'm nannying as well.'

'Jesus, Erika – I genuinely didn't think you'd have fallen this low.'

'I happen to be very happy, Ross.'

'Er, *two* jobs? That's how poor people carry on. When they finally make good, you hear them going, "Back when my life was shit, I used to have to work two jobs." Are you hoping that *he'll* take you back?'

'*I* finished with *him*, Ross.'

'You know what I'm trying to say. Are you hoping he eventually dumps this Camilla Whatever the Fock so you can step back in there?'

'Believe me, I hope I never lay eyes on him again.'

'They're not going to stop looking for you, Erika – as in, Helen and the old man?'

'You need to persuade them.'

'They're not going to just go home. Did you know they're engaged, by the way?'

'Yes, I knew that.'

'Heard about it on Facebook – don't tell me. Well, your old dear won't get married unless you're actually there. If you could just, I don't know, swallow your pride for once in your life.'

She goes, 'I've got to get back to work.'

She reaches across the table, picks up my iPhone and puts her new number into my contacts book.

'I'm trusting you with this,' she goes. 'Don't you focking dare give it to Mum and Dad.'

I'm like, 'Yeah, no, I won't.'

'Ring me, okay?'

'I will.'

'Because it was nice to see you. Once I got over the initial shock.'

'It was nice to see you, too.'

She stands up and I stand up. She gives me a hug. Jesus, I'm as hord as a chimney-sweep's brush here.

I go, 'What perfume is that, am I allowed to innocently ask? Is it the Jean Patou one that I've always liked?'

She doesn't answer me. I watch her leave – her orse like two perfect melon balls – as she disappears into the busy lunchtime crowd.

I ask if it has a sunroof. I love a sunroof. Where I come from, a sunroof is almost a human right. He says yes, it has a sunroof.

I'm at the cor rental desk in the hotel, by the way. I'm actually banjoed from all the walking I've been doing and I've decided what I really need is a set of wheels – specifically a humungous, silver Chevrolet Tahoe – to get around.

Bear in mind that for the past six months I haven't driven anything except Sorcha's Nissan Leaf and that focking ridiculous minivan we bought. I think, in cor terms, I've also got blue balls.

I hand the dude my credit cord and it's at that exact moment that I hear the old man's voice behind me.

He's like, 'There he is! You saw the Lions squad, I take it!'

'Yeah, no,' I go. 'I checked it on my phone when I woke up.'

It's mad, I realize, but there's always that tiny port of my brain that thinks, "You never know."'

'I was saying to Helen,' he goes, 'that even if you had a professional contract and were playing the best rugby of your bloody well life, Gatland wouldn't have taken you to Australia. You two have history, remember.'

'That's a nice thing to hear,' I go.

'I meant every word of it. What are you doing, Ross – renting a car?'

'Yeah, no, it certainly focking looks like it, doesn't it?'

'Decided to widen the perimeter of the search area, have you?'

'Something like that. I was also thinking of taking a drive out to where Felipe Contepomi grew up. Be sort of, like, a *pilgrimage* for me?'

'What a wonderful idea!'

The dude behind the counter hands me the keys and the rental agreement and he tells me the number of the porking bay in the basement where I'll find it.

'Well,' the old man goes, 'Helen and I have been in the business centre since six o'clock this morning, printing these things out.'

He hands me an A4 sheet of paper with Erika's face on it, then some words in the local lingo that I presume mean, 'Missing!' and then some more writing and then the old man's phone number.

'Thought we might start posting them around the city – train stations and lampposts and so forth. Do you fancy joining us?'

I'm like, 'Er, no, I won't actually. I think I'll just continue going at it from my own angle.'

'Okay,' he goes, disappointed, but trying to stay cheery. 'Good luck with your search!'

And I'm like, 'Yeah, no, whatever,' and off he focks.

It's as I'm waiting for the lift, roysh, that I just so happen to look to my left and, against the wall, there's, like, a display of leaflets, intended for tourists – day trips to water porks, parrot sanctuaries and blahdy blah-blah. But there's one leaflet in particular that catches my eye. It's got, like, a horse on the front of it.

It ends up being a flier for the Orgentine Equestrian Championships at the Something de Something Something this weekend. The main attraction – hilariously – seems to be Olympic gold medalist Fabrizio Bettega on his horse, *Ushuaia*, and I'm thinking, yeah, no, whatever lifts your luggage, people. Jumping over things on an animal has about as much to do with sport as jumping over things on a motorbike. There's, like, a photograph of him as well, looking all pleased with himself, the totally delusional focktard.

I stop, roysh, because my eyes are suddenly fixed on the photograph next to his one. It's of a woman. At a guess, I'd say she's in her late forties, possibly even early fifties. Chunky is a word you'd use to describe her if you were being kind – black hair with a straight fringe, literally no neck and a face that would frighten a police horse. I actually laugh out loud, not so much at the photograph – more at the caption underneath.

It's Camilla Lacobellis.

She has the beginnings of a must-dash as well, unless it's just a bad photograph – and that's me trying to give the woman the benefit of the doubt.

I'm thinking, he dumped Erika . . . for that!

I'm trying to imagine the humiliation the girl must have felt – as a proud girl and also a bitch – to lose the supposed love of her life to a woman who looks like someone shaved Adam Jones and rouged his focking cheeks.

And as I'm standing there staring at her photograph, you can probably imagine what comes into my head. I'm suddenly thinking the obvious. If I rode her, it'd be something to hold over him. It'd also be revenge for Erika, of course.

I look at the bottom of the flier. There's, like, an address on it for Fabrizio and Camilla's equestrian school. They seem to be one of the, I don't know, *sponsors* of the event? It's like, Boulevard General Alberto Guglielmone, Las Cañitas, Buenos Aires.

I go back up to my room. I pick up my black shirt – I'd class it as a scoring shirt – and I give it a quick sniff test. It's definitely good for another wear. I throw it on, then I have a splash of Paco Rabanne *Invictus* and I brush my teeth.

I look at myself in the mirror and I like what I see.

I give myself the guns in a way that says, 'Okay, player, let's do this thing.'

The satnav brings me right to the gates of the equestrian school, which happen to be open. I drive through them, then up the gravel driveway, still not knowing how I'm going to play this thing, but at the same time one hundred percent confident in my ability to do the right things under pressure, like I always did on the field of battle.

I pull up in front of this, like, massive sprawling gaff and I'm thinking, okay, hopefully *he's* not here – but if he is, I'll just deck him and be on my way.

Suddenly, I hear this tapping and I turn to find Camilla's face filling the entire window on the driver's side. I get such a fright that I end up pretty much levitating off the seat. She's like something out of a focking horror movie and the photograph on the flier actually did her a hell of a lot of favours.

She says something to me in the local lingo.

I wind down the window, going, 'Er, no speako.'

She's like, 'Hengleesh?'

And I'm there, 'Slash Irish, yeah.'

She goes, 'Why hyou har here?'

I blurt out the first thing that comes into my mind. I'm there, 'I wanted to buy some hay.'

Hay? Okay, where the fock did that come from?

Luckily, she doesn't hear me – or maybe she *mishears* me, because then she goes, 'Hyou har journaleest?'

I'm there, 'Yeah, no, I *am* a journalist – that's what I meant. I wanted to write an article about your whole, I suppose, set-up.'

'Set-up,' she goes, like she's discovered a new word and wants to memorize it. 'Set-up. Set-up.'

I'm there, 'It means your whole thing. I'd love to take a look around and ask you a few questions. Is it the horses that do all of the actual work? That kind of thing.'

'What heez hyour nim?'

'It's Ross.'

'Ross.'

'Ross O'Carroll-Kelly.'

'And what heez pepper?'

'You mightn't have heard of it. It's the, em, *Foxrock Bugle*?'

Okay, that's not bad.

She goes, '*Focks ruck . . .*'

'*Foxrock Bugle*,' I go. 'It's a massive paper in Ireland.'

'Iarlant.'

'Ireland, yeah.'

'Hyou come from Iarlant to write theez?'

'No, I came over here to write an orticle about a dude called Felipe Contepomi?'

'I don't know.'

'Well, he's what you'd call a *real* sporting hero? My, I don't know, editor said that while I was here I should do an orticle on show-jumping. The odd time, we put it on the sports pages – for a laugh.'

I notice her checking out my biceps. I think I mentioned that they look fantastic in this shirt.

She's like, 'Okay, heez good – welcome,' which is my cue to get out of the cor.

We shake hands – she has a focking grip like Dean Mumm – and then she storts giving me the guided tour of the place, telling me how long it's been there, how many horses she has, how many supposed Olympic champions she's trained – just boring stuff.

'Hyou like horses?' she goes.

She has a bit of a husky voice, like she could do with clearing her chest.

I'm there, 'Not really. I find them a bit boring and there's something about them I also don't trust.'

It's while she's showing me around that I stort to pick up what would have to be described as a vibe from Camilla. It's very subtle at first, but once or twice, when I stick my head into a stable or even a horsebox, pretending to take an actual interest in what goes on here, I catch Camilla checking out my orse, which looks well in these trousers, in fairness to the woman.

I know a lot of people are probably thinking, yeah, no, typical Ross, thinks the entire female population wants to pop those famous chino buttons of his. But trust me.

Father Fehily used to say that men with the worst motives are usually the best judges of character. And, like I said, I get the instant impression from Camilla – in the slightly longing way that her eyes keep drifting south to my pecs – that she's a bit of a man-eater. And her preference, as we already know, is for young blood.

I'm there, 'I suppose the other reason the – what did I say? – *Foxrock Bugle* want me to write about this place is because of the whole Irish angle. The famous Febreze-io Bettega operates out of here, doesn't he?'

'Yes, he heez may – how to say? – partner?'

'Yeah, no, like I said, there's the whole Irish angle. He went out with an Irish bird for a little while. I'm saying he had an Irish *girlfriend*?'

'But now,' she goes, a definite twinkle in her eye, 'he does not have Ireesh girlfriend.'

She laughs in a cruel way.

I may be a feminist, but I have never wanted to spite-ride a woman like I want to spite-ride this one.

'Is, em, Febreze-io here today?' I go, making sure to keep saying his name like that.

She's like, 'No,' and then, with a suggestive half-smile, she goes, 'We haff the place alone.'

See, I told you. I instantly know when a woman is filthy. Actually, a huge percentage of showjumping types are like that – think of what goes on around the Dublin Horse Show.

Of course, the big question, as usual, is when to pull the trigger. Even when a bird is definitely into you, it's sometimes hord to gauge the right time to make your move, especially if you're both sober. I have, from time to time, lunged twenty or thirty seconds too early and ended up with a girl's palm paying a flying visit to my face.

So I play it cool.

'Maybe we should at least try to keep it professional,' I go, turning my back on her – we're in the middle of some kind of yord. 'I think I owe it to my readers.'

The next thing that happens is unbelievable. Now, I've known some forward birds in my time – a bird who knows what she wants can sometimes be a good thing – but this is a definite first, even for a man with my vast experience with the deadlier of the species.

She hooks her index finger into one of the belt loops at the back of my chinos and she yanks me backwards towards her. She's surprisingly strong for a short bird – she could drag Fosi Pala'amo into touch. She grabs me by the waist, then turns me around until I'm facing her.

'Why hyou look here?' she goes.

She taps her chest. She has massive bazoos – that's her one upside.

She's there, 'I talk to hyou and hyou not look heen may face – hyou look heen may chest.'

I'm terrible. I do that – especially if the boat isn't great.

I go, 'It's probably shyness.'

She's there, 'Shine nuss?'

'No, shyness. I get like that if I'm incredibly, incredibly attracted to a woman.'

192

'Hyou harr hattracted?'

'Is that not obvious?'

'Pear haps a lidl.'

God, this woman is barely a mammal. I've often regretting having sex with certain birds, but this is one of those times when you *pregret* it?

'At the same time,' I go, 'I'm trying to be professional here. I came here to supposedly interview you. I can't very well just . . . And then the other thing is, well, I know you're attached. I wouldn't want to cut another man's lunch, no matter who that man was.'

She grips my biceps with her two hands and gives them a decent squeeze.

She goes, 'Theez, I like.'

I'm there, 'Yeah, they're one of the things that always get complimented.'

She's staring at me – and at the same time salivating like a dog loose in Nandos.

She grabs me very violently by the back of the head and our mouths are suddenly locked together. We kiss for about thirty seconds and then, when she thinks a decent interval has passed, she makes a grab for the old holiday money.

I'm like, 'Whoa, not here!' because, like I said, we're outdoors.

She goes, 'We can do heet here!' and she points to a nearby stable. The woman is an animal.

I'm there, 'No – your bedroom. Let's go to your bedroom.'

She thinks about it for, like, five seconds, then she practically runs me into the gaff and up the stairs in a headlock.

Now, if there's one thing that I've been consistent about over the years, it's my point-blank refusal to discuss what goes on within the four sacred walls of the bedroom – or wherever I happen to ride someone. A lot of this is out of respect to the girls involved and it's always been an orticle of faith for me.

But what I *will* say, just for the purposes of the story, is that as soon as we get into that bedroom, Camilla is all over me like a wet shower curtain. She pushes me backwards onto the bed, her lips all over mine, as we race through preliminaries.

She's one ugly sow – I can't say that enough times.

She takes off her wellies and her bodywarmer, then storts kissing me again, while fumbling blindly with my chino buttons like a woman trying to pick a two-euro coin out of a pocket full of change. All the time, she's telling me that she loves young men and that she wanted me the second she saw me.

It's not all one-way traffic, by the way. Two minutes in and I have the hand in the old baccy pouch, telling her that she's the spits of Candice Swanepoel, which is a lie, but with bigger clankers, which is true.

She's having the time of her life, can I just mention?

Being the age she obviously is, she ends up being a bit, you know – the nicest way I can think to put it is that having sex with her is like waving a hot dog at a festival.

To cut a long story short, we end up going at it like zoo monkeys, her toes curled like a jester's shoes as she screams her *Ave Marias* at the beamed ceiling above our heads. Once or twice, Fabrizio's name slips out of my mouth, but in the heat of the moment – and with her half praying, half swearing at the top of her lungs – she doesn't hear me and I end up getting away with it.

We seal the deal and there isn't a peep of complaint out of her as she suddenly collapses into a deep sleep, snoring like a focking elephant seal. I turn over, so I don't have to look at her face, and at the same, I'm thinking, yeah, no, hurry home, Fabrizio.

I end up having a bit of a snooze myself. Then about two hours later, I'm having a root through Camilla's knicker drawer for a screwvenir of the occasion, when all of a sudden I hear the front door slam.

Camilla hears it, too, because she's suddenly sitting bolt upright in the bed.

I'm there, 'It sounds to me like your man is home.'

Her hand goes over her mouth. She storts uttering – presumably – curses in the local lingo. *Jésus* gets a mench. So does his mother.

She goes, 'Now hyou must leaf!'

I'm there, 'Too late. It sounds to me like he's already coming up the stairs.'

She jumps out of the bed and tears open the curtains.

Now, I know more about windows than everyone who has ever worked for Bill Gates combined. I've climbed through more than you've probably cleaned. But for once I have no intention of taking the coward's way out.

'Plees!' Camilla is going, trying to cover those big baby dinners of hers with her dressing-gown. 'Hyou must go.'

I'm standing there, stork naked, by the way.

I'm there, 'I'm not going anywhere. I want to see this focker's face when he finds out I took you to the shake shop.'

'Plees – he wheel keel hyou!'

I laugh.

I'm like, 'Yeah, no, give me a break – what's he going to do, run over me on his focking horse?'

I can hear him coming along the, I don't know, passageway outside.

'He heez athlete,' she tries to go. 'Sportsman.'

And I'm there, 'Focking sportsman – you're all kidding your-selves!'

I stand facing the door, just making sure that the dude gets the full frontal view when he walks through it. I watch the handle of the door go down, then I put my two hands on my hips, ready for him, and I flex my stomach muscles.

No, I don't flex my stomach muscles. I don't need to flex my stomach muscles.

Camilla is already shouting apologies at him through the door and through her sobs. The door flies open and he's suddenly stand-ing in front of me, his mouth slung open in shock.

Although it's nothing compared to *my* shock?

Because it's not Fabrizio. It's just some random bald dude.

I'm like, 'What the fock?' suddenly bending down to, like, gather up my clothes. 'What the *actual* fock?'

The dude is suddenly shouting something at me in the native

tongue, his face *literally* puce red? He's working himself up into a bit of a rage. He looks mad enough to either kill me with his bare hands or have a hort attack on the spot and I'd guess that the odds are pretty even on which one it's going to be.

All of a sudden, Camilla makes a run for him. She throws her orms around him, pinning *his* orms to his side? Then she storts shouting something at me and it takes a few seconds for me to realize that what she's actually doing here is taking him out of the game to create space for me to run – the same thing that Kevin Maggs used to do for Brian O'Driscoll back in the day, although obviously *on* the field?

God, I would have loved to have played on the same team as Kevin Maggs.

I don't wait any longer. I see the opening and I'm gone, bending down to scoop up my clothes, then pulling them on me, as I go down the stairs three at a time and get the fock out of there as fast as my feet and my Chevrolet Tahoe can carry me.

Erika answers the phone sounding *already* pissed off?

She's like, 'Ross, what the fock do you want?'

It's just like old times.

I'm there, 'I was just wondering where you were. I called in to the shop and they said you weren't in today.'

'I'm minding Amelie,' she goes. 'What do you want?'

'Er, I was wondering did you fancy meeting up?'

I'm actually still a bit shaky after what happened this morning.

She goes, 'Like I told you, Ross, I'm working.'

I'm there, 'Come on, Erika, minding a baby isn't working.'

I wouldn't want Sorcha to ever know I said that.

I'm like, 'Where are you?'

She's there, 'Ross.'

'Erika, this is kind of important. I need to ask you something.'

She sighs. But at the same time, she knows I'm not going to give up.

'I'm in the Bosques de Palermo,' she goes.

I'm like, 'Er, okay.'

'It's a pork, Ross.'

'Can you text that to me, so then I can stick it directly into the satnav.'

She sighs again, then hangs up, but ten seconds later, my phone beeps with the name of the pork and the address. I'm there in fifteen minutes.

I spot her from, like, fifty yords away. She's sitting on a bench, feeding this famous baby its bottle. I morch straight up to her. She goes, 'Seriously, Ross, I really don't think we need to see each other every day.'

I pull the flier out of my inside pocket, open it out and hand it to her without saying a word. I sit down beside her as she gives it the quick once-over. Then she's like, 'Okay, what?'

I'm there, 'Is that the Camilla Lacobellis that Fabrizio dumped you for?'

She goes, 'No.'

'Are you saying definitely no? Look at the photograph again.'

'Jesus, Ross, I don't need to look at it again. That's her mother.'

'You're shitting me.'

'Actually, she's uglier in real life. That photograph does her a lot of favours.'

'So why the fock is she called Camilla as well?'

'You've never heard of a mother and daughter with the same name?'

'For fock's sake. This is some bullshit.'

'What are you talking about?'

'Yeah, no, nothing. It's just focking ridiculous – both called the same thing.'

'The mother is Fabrizio's partner – he bought into the equestrian school about eighteen months ago. I don't think she's, you know, all there.'

'She's definitely not all there. Going around with the same name as her daughter. She'd want to cop herself on.'

Erika looks suddenly confused. She's like, 'What did you do?'

I'm there, 'Nothing.'

'Ross,' she goes, 'what did you do?'

'I'm like, 'Okay, I rode her.'

She goes, 'What?' at the same time laughing.

'I thought I was doing you a favour.'

'How was that doing me a favour?'

'Because I thought the shmugly hogger was his focking girlfriend.'

'You thought Fabrizio dumped me for *her*?'

'That's why I was upset for you. The focking head on her. But I thought, well, if I at least ride her, that evens things out a bit from a family point of view.'

'Ross, this woman has a screw loose.'

'Yeah, I realize that now, Erika.'

'You're unbelievable.'

'Yeah, no, I'm definitely a filth bag – you have to say that about me.'

'I don't want to talk about this anymore. It's one of the most upsetting things I've ever heard.'

We end up both sitting there in silence for a good, like, thirty seconds.

'It's mad seeing you with a baby,' I go. 'And I'm only saying that because I remember how much you despised children.'

She's there, 'Do you want to hold her?'

'Yeah, go on. I'm actually amazing with kids. They just seem to love me.'

She hands her to me. She's a seriously cute little thing. It suddenly hits me how much I miss the boys.

I'm like, 'What did you say her name was?'

She goes, 'Amelie.'

I'm guessing she's about the same age as Brian, Johnny and Leo.

I make some random noises and Amelie smiles and reaches for my face.

'See?' I go. 'They just instantly connect with me. It's like a gift that I've been given, along with all my other qualities.'

Erika's there, 'I better get her back. Serena and Arturo will be home.'

'Serena and Arturo? What do *they* do?'

'They're barristers.'

'Brainiacs, in other words. And where's home?'

'It's about a ten-minute walk from here.'

'I could drop you. You'd want to see what I'm driving – I know you were always a big fan of cors back in the day.'

'I like walking.'

'Okay, cool. Can I maybe walk with you?'

'If you want.'

She takes Amelie from me and puts her into her little stroller, then we set off, through the streets of Buenos Aires, for the gaff where Amelie's old pair live.

She goes, 'You definitely haven't said anything to Mum and Dad, have you? About me being here?'

I'm there, 'I said I wouldn't and I haven't . . . I, em, might have mentioned it to Sorcha, though.'

'What?'

'She's my wife, Erika. I don't have any secrets from her. Well, that's not strictly true. What I mean is she was putting me under pressure to come home and I had to quickly come up with a reason to stay. She was genuinely delighted – when I told her I found you.'

'That's nice.'

'Which is mad, because she hated you when you went away. But then she instantly wanted to know everything. Were you still thin? Like I said – everything!'

'I do miss her.'

'Well, she misses you. I can tell you that for a fact. You were her best friend. I'm having to pick up a lot of the slack.'

'You mentioning *Evita* the other day reminded me of something. It's just a funny story. We were in, like, fifth year and this rumour went around that I was, you know, having sex with boys.'

'Jesus. And were you?'

'Of course I was. Anyway, you know what girls are like. Wasn't long before Sister Luke heard about it – Erika Joseph is sexually active, shock, horror. So she sat me down and asked me was it true and I just thought, fock it, I'll shock this bitch. I said yes. So she decides then that I should go for a test – to see did I have an

STD – and that Sorcha, as the fifth-year head prefect, should bring me into town for it.'

'I never heard this story before.'

'Of course, Sister Luke has no idea how much an STD test costs. I just chanced my arm and said two hundred pounds and she gave it to me. Two hundred pounds – this was in, like, 1996.'

'And did you go for the test?'

'No, I'd never had *unprotected* sex. I'm not an idiot. So I just spent the money on shoes. Then we went to see *Evita* in the afternoon. I think it was the first time Sorcha had ever done anything bold in her life. All the way through the film, she kept saying, "Please, Erika, we've had our fun – now let's go back to school!"'

'She's a real goody-goody alright. So what did you tell Sister Whatever?'

'I just said I paid for the test, but the queue was too long. So the following week she sent us back again.'

'Hilarious.'

'Another two hundred pounds.'

'And what movie was it the second time?'

'I think it was *The Mirror Has Two Faces* . . . Okay, this is the house.'

We've stopped outside this humungous gaff that looks like the kind of gaff you see on Northumberland Road – we're talking big gorden, we're talking massive bay windows, we're talking three storeys plus a basement.

I wait outside on the road while Erika brings Amelie in. A woman in her – I'm guessing – late thirties opens the door. She's not exactly a looker, but she's definitely worth the detour, as it says in all the guidebooks. They talk for a few seconds, then the woman gives Erika a huge hug and the woman takes Amelie inside.

We walk back to the city centre, neither of us saying much.

After a while, Erika goes, 'Okay, I've changed my mind. I want to know – what happened in the house?'

I laugh.

I'm like, 'Not a lot. *He* walked in on us.'

'Who?' she goes. 'Fabrizio?'

'No, the husband.'

'Oh my God.'

'Yeah, that was pretty much *my* thought at the time as well.'

'He's as unhinged as she is.'

'She said he was some kind of athlete.'

'I think he won an Olympic medal for fencing. Maybe a bronze.'

'Fencing? Jesus, the things that pass for sport in this country. It's pissing me off.'

'Poor Camilla. I wonder how she explained that one away.'

'Hey, it's not the first time I've left a gaff with my clothes in my orms and my bare orse showing. I dare say it won't be the last.'

She's in, like, knots laughing. It's nice.

We're suddenly back in the city centre. She's like, 'I have to go.'

I'm there, 'Do you want to maybe grab a bit of dinner?'

'No, I've got some things to do.'

'Okay, we'll maybe do it another night.'

We kiss each other goodbye and not in a weird way. It's the way any half-brother and half-sister would kiss each other. Then I make my way back to the cor. I sit into it and I pull out my keys and that's when this suddenly *weird* feeling comes over me?

It's hord to describe it. It's just a sudden sense I get that something isn't right – like the wave of panic that comes over you when you remember that you've left, I don't know, a window open or the cor unlocked.

It's Amelie. Jesus Christ, it's Amelie.

I can't believe I didn't see it at the time, but I can certainly see it now. Her face. Her little face. She has *her* features. *Her* features and *his* colouring.

I'm sitting there with my mouth wide open, literally unable to move.

I have no idea who the fock that woman was who took Amelie into her gaff. But that baby girl is Erika and Fabrizio's daughter.

6.

A Dummy Pass

My phone rings while I'm sitting at the bor. It's, like, an Irish number – one I don't recognize? – but I answer it anyway. I'm there, 'Hello?'

A woman in a singsong voice goes, 'Hi, this is Julie from the Mastercard Fraud Team.'

I'm there, 'Hello, Julie from the Mastercord Fraud Team,' flirting my orse off with her.

I'll never change. I don't think anyone would want me to.

She goes, 'I'm ringing because we've noticed some unusual activity on your account recently. Do you mind if I run through some recent transactions with you?'

She's got a lovely tone to her voice. I'm there, 'Yeah, no, fire away, Julie.'

'Okay,' she goes, 'there's one from this morning from Harrods dot com for £849 sterling.'

'What?'

'There's another one from last night – again it's Harrods dot com – for £975 sterling. There's one from the day before yesterday for Ticketmaster dot com – that's for €180 euro. There was also a purchase made that same day – Tiffany & Co . . .'

'Tiffany? Shut the front door!'

'That was for €760 euro. Then there's Brown Thomas – an online purchase – for €1,400 euro. Then the same day there's another purchase from a website called *Petit Tresor* dot com and that's for €770 euro.'

'I don't focking believe it.'

'So you're confirming that there has been fraud on this account?'

'No, that's not fraud. I mean, I don't know of any thief who could go through my money that fast. That kind of damage could only be the work of a wife or a daughter.'

'Right.'

'And in this case it's a daughter.'

I can't describe to you how suddenly pissed off I am.

'Okay,' she goes, 'would you like to put a block on that card?'

I'm there, 'I would genuinely love to say yes to you – unfortunately, the kid *has* shit on me?'

She seems a bit taken aback by that statement.

I'm like, 'Just tell me how much is on the cord.'

She's there, 'Well, the current balance on the account is . . . €11,074 euro.'

'And what's my limit?'

'It's €11,300 euro.'

'So she's not going to be able to fit anything else on that cord?'

'You're €226 euro from your ceiling.'

'It's basically maxed out, in other words?'

'Unless you make a payment.'

'Yeah, no, I won't be doing that. Five grand in three focking days. Paris Hilton wouldn't spend that. Thanks for your help, Julie.'

I hang up, then I ask Sergio for another pint of Ken. While he's pulling it, I knock back what's left of my last one.

I've been sitting here all evening, thinking about Erika and obviously Amelie. I've been trying to ring the girl every, like, five minutes, except she's not answering her phone, and from the number of missed calls she's had from me, she's probably twigged that *I've* twigged?

I've a mind like an electric cor. I'm focking slow, but I get there eventually.

I try her one more time. Again, it goes straight to her voicemail. That's thirty-eight times now. She could probably take out some kind of injunction against me if I wasn't a blood relative.

'I thought I'd find you in here!'

The old man's voice suddenly fills the bor.

'Sergio,' he goes, 'I'll have one of my famous brandies when you're ready.'

Sergio pours it for him and the old man hands him an American fifty-dollar bill, then waves his finger at him to let him know that he doesn't want change. From the look on Sergio's face, you can tell that his day has just been well and truly made.

'So what did you do today?' the old man goes.

And I'm thinking, Ah, you know, the usual. I rode a fifty-year-old woman you wouldn't kick in a ruck, ran testicles-swinging from the gaff when her husband walked in on us and found out that my daughter has been spending my money like it's 2005 all over again. Oh, and by the way, I found out that *your* daughter has a secret love child that she for some reason handed over to a random stranger this afternoon.

I don't actually say any of that, though. I just go, 'Yeah, no, I just drove around, seeing could I see her. No luck.'

I know I should tell him about Erika – about knowing where she is, at least. He's, like, *entitled* to know? I mean, he's *her* old man as much as he is mine. But then I promised her I wouldn't say shit.

And on top of that, I need some answers before I make a decision as to what I'm going to do.

Firstly, is it *her* actual baby? Secondly, who was that woman who took her on the doorstep? And thirdly, just generally what the fock?

I'm like, 'Where's Helen?'

He goes, 'She's got one of her famous migraines, I'm afraid. I think it's just the stress of it all.'

I'm there, 'It's a shit state of affairs – there's no denying that.'

'She is absolutely convinced that there's something seriously wrong. She said it was a mother's intuition – this was the phrase she used – and I wouldn't know the first thing about it. She said a mother knows instinctively when her child needs her and she knows that this is the case now.'

This is the moment. It's here. The time when I should tell him. I should pick my phone up off the bor and go, 'This is her new number,' or I should tell him the name of the shop where she's working, or give him the address where Erika handed over his granddaughter to a total stranger three or four hours ago.

But I don't.

All I go is, 'Mine's a Heineken, since you're asking,' like the use-less excuse for a son that I am.

'Forty-nine missed calls?' Erika goes. 'Is there something wrong with you?'

There possibly is. I've been waiting outside her work since, like, half-eight this morning and she obviously only storts at ten.

I'm there, 'I wouldn't have had to ring you forty-nine times if you'd answered your phone just once.'

She's like, 'I told you I was busy last night.'

'Well, I needed to talk to you,' I go. 'I actually *still* need to talk to you?'

She tries to walk straight past me, into the shop.

So I go, 'Erika, I know about Amelie.'

That gets her definite attention.

'Amelie?' she has the balls to go. 'What about her?'

I'm like, 'You're not her nanny. You're her mother.'

'Her mother? Yeah, I think all those tackles you took on the rugby field have damaged your brain.'

'I think there's possibly something in that. But, at the same time, I'm not wrong, Erika. I can see you in her – *and* him, unfortunately.'

The woman who owns the shop suddenly steps outside – her face screwed up like her tongue's made of wasabi. She says something in foreign, which I don't understand.

Erika looks at me and goes, 'She wants to know should she ring the police?'

Because our voices *were* raised.

I'm there, 'Yeah, no, try that. And when I'm hauled in, my one phone call will be to my old man, to tell him that I found you and that you're working here. Oh, and also that he's a grandfather for the sixth time.'

Erika thinks about it for a few seconds, then says something back to the woman in gibberish, which I take to mean, 'No, actually don't bother your hole ringing them – but I might need a moment here.'

The woman goes back into the shop.

'She's your daughter,' I go. 'It took a while for the penny to drop, as it usually does with me. But you can't deny it.'

She's there, 'So she's my daughter – so what?'

'Why did you try to hide that fact from me?'

'Why would I tell you?'

'Er, I'm your *brother*?'

'You're not my brother. We just happen to have the same father.'

'See, this is what you do when you're challenged – you lash out, not caring who you hurt.'

'We've never been close.'

'I disagree. I think there's always been a connection.'

'An accident of biology – that's all we have in common.'

'Does Fabrizio know?'

'Know what?'

'Er, about your *own* accident of biology? I'm asking does he know he has a daughter?'

'No. I never told him. And I never will tell him.'

'Well, if I see him, he's still getting decked. One thing will follow the other. Count on it.'

She's there, 'Just go home, Ross. Go back to Ireland,' and as she goes to step past me, I hear a slight, I don't know, *catch* in her voice?

I'm like, 'Who was that woman?'

She doesn't answer me.

I'm there, 'I could always, you know, knock on her door and ask *her* what the fock is going on.'

When she turns around and looks at me again, she has tears in her eyes.

She goes, 'Why did you have to come here? Why did you have to come here and ruin everything?' and that's when she suddenly becomes hysterical. She storts slapping me across the face with her two hands and I end up having to grab her in, like, a bear hug, pinning her two orms to her side. I sort of, like, waltz her over to this concrete bench a few feet away, all the time going, 'It's okay, Erika. It's going to be okay.'

Then I sort of, like, manoeuvre her into a sitting position and, by the time I let go of her, she's as docile as a Scottish prop. And *like* a

Scottish prop, all she wants to do is put her orms around my shoulders and cry.

I'm rubbing her back, going, 'It's okay, Erika. You're too proud. That's always been your basic problem.'

She eventually pulls away from me. Her make-up is all over the shop. She dabs at it with the back of her hand.

She goes, 'It was all arranged. It was all arranged and then you had to focking walk in with your size twelve feet.'

'They're size ten. What was all arranged?'

'I was going away.'

'Where?'

'It doesn't matter.'

'Hey, I'm asking.'

'I was going to Seattle . . . It's in America.'

'I'm not an idiot, Erika. I've seen everything that Meg Ryan has ever been in.'

'It was going to be a new start. And you had to focking ruin it.'

I'm there, 'Erika, who was that woman? You need to answer me.'

'She's Amelie's foster mum.'

'*Foster* mum?'

'She's had her for the past three or four months. I take her two or three afternoons a week – just to help us all adjust to the idea.'

'Whoa, what do you mean by foster mum? Are you saying you were planning to give your baby away?'

'I *am* planning to give my baby away.'

'Erika, you can't.'

'I don't *have* those instincts. Maternal instincts. You saw me with her.'

'I saw you with her and I thought, holy shit, she's really good with her – and this is a woman who always said children disgusted her. Sickened you, was I think the expression you used.'

'I don't want her, Ross.'

'You don't mean that.'

'Every time I look at her, I see . . . him.'

'*He's* going to be decked. *He's* going to be the subject of a decking. That's guaranteed. So what's all this about Seattle?'

'Nothing. I have friends there. I'm going. Start again.'

'Erika, that's just how you're feeling now. Trust me. Jesus, you've been on your own all this time, coping with this shit. You know?'

Fock, *I'm* even crying now.

I'm there, 'But the good news is that you're not alone anymore. Come back to Ireland and bring her with you. You can live with us. There's nothing *but* empty rooms in that house. What about that, Erika? Amelie could grow up in the same house as her cousins. Oh, they're three little bruisers, Erika – I can't wait for you to meet them. She can watch them make their debut for Ireland one day. And you'd have your best friend back.'

'Sorcha wouldn't want me living with you.'

'Are you mad? She focking idolizes you – always did. Although you're bound to make *my* life hell. What, the two of you together, in my ear the whole time? I wouldn't *give* a shit, though. And Honor as well. I mean, she's a focking nightmare of a kid, but she has her moments. And she can be very funny, even while she's being, you know, a cow.'

Erika sniffs, then storts nodding her head.

I'm like, 'Yeah? You'll come back to Ireland? The two of you?'

She nods and this feeling of sudden joy comes over me.

I'm there, 'I'll ring my old man and tell him the news,' loving the feeling – if I'm being honest – of being the man of the moment yet again.

'No, wait,' she goes. 'You've got to give me some time.'

I'm like, 'Why do you need time?'

'Because it's all too much! I can't see Mum and Dad now. I have to build myself up to it.'

'Yeah, no, cool.'

'Just give me twenty-four hours, okay?'

'Okay.'

'Pick me up here, tomorrow at lunchtime. I'll have my bags packed and Amelie will be with me.'

Sorcha goes, 'Ross, I have *the* most amazing news!'

I'm like, 'Yeah, no, Sorcha, *I* was actually ringing to tell *you* something?' but there's no shutting her up once she gets on a roll. Don't marry an All Ireland debating champion is not a bad bit of advice.

She's there, 'I told you how Honor's been behaving this week. She's got, like, fourteen points on the Honour Board and last night we watched *Mary Poppins* together for the first time! Do you remember I told you it was me and *my* Mom's favourite movie when I was a little girl?'

I'm like, 'Sorcha . . .'

'So I was telling Siofra all of this today. I mean, she actually agrees that Honor is now almost totally unspoiled. And she said – wait for it, Ross – that she would write a letter to Mount Anville, on *actual* headed notepaper – she's a doctor, Ross, or she *has* a doctorate – asking them to accept her back into the school. I think they'll say yes, Ross, because they're really, really decent, but if they don't I was thinking we could take them to court.'

'Sorcha,' I go, 'will you shut the fock up babbling for, like, ten seconds?'

'Excuse me?'

'Erika has a kid.'

'What?'

'Exactly. She had a baby. A little girl.'

'Oh! My God!'

'Her name's Amelie. It's *his* – except he doesn't know?'

'When? I mean, how old is she?'

'Same age as the boys.'

'Oh my God!'

'I know.'

'Is she already back at her pre-baby weight? And don't tell her I asked you that.'

'I don't know – I didn't ask her to step on a focking scales. Look, the thing is, Sorcha, she's not coping well. She was about to give her away.'

'Give her away? As in, like, her baby?'

'Yeah, no, to this couple. They're, like, fostering her. They're barristers or something. They've a nice gaff, in their defence.'

'She can't just give her baby away.'

'Well, she's not going to now because I stepped in. She was thinking of going to the States to make a fresh stort. Would have been the biggest mistake of her life. Luckily, I stopped her.'

'Ross, you're amazing.'

'I know. I'm going to learn to take a compliment for once, because I've definitely done well here.'

'What did Helen and Chorles say?'

'Yeah, no, they don't know yet.'

'Ross, you have to tell them!'

'Erika just needs to get her shit together before she can face them. She's got to build herself up to it.'

'What weight would you say she is, Ross? Just between ourselves.'

'I've no idea, Sorcha. Look, what I'm ringing to say is that she's coming home with us tomorrow. Her and Amelie. And obviously they're going to need somewhere to live – that's presuming she doesn't want to live with Helen and the old man, which I'm pretty sure is the case, because she thinks they'll never forgive her for famously dumping Fionn at the altar.'

'She could live here, Ross.'

'That's what I told her. I was actually hoping you'd say that.'

'We've all these empty bedrooms.'

'Exactly.'

'And Amelie could grow up here with all her cousins. Oh my God, I'd have my best friend back!'

'She was telling me all about the time the nun sent the two of you into town for the STD test and you went to see *Evita*.'

'Oh my God, I remember!'

'It's going to be like that again – like old times.'

'Ross, you're incredible.'

'Like I said, I'm actually patting myself on the back here.'

She goes, 'Oh, wait, Honor wants to have a word.'

I'm like, 'Er, no, Sorcha, I'll see her in a day or two,' and I quickly hang up.

*

Helen looks so miserable when her risotto arrives that I want to tell her the news, that I found Erika and that she has a beautiful little baby girl and they're coming home with us tomorrow. But then I made Erika a promise, so I keep my mouth shut while Helen plays with her dinner and says she knows – just *knows* – that Erika is in some kind of distress.

All I go is, 'I think you're wrong, Helen. I actually think everything is going to be fine.'

The old man goes, 'There you are then!' like it's automatically proof of something. 'Ross here has wonderful instincts, Helen. He was like that on the rugby field, too – had this ability to foresee events that Gerry Thornley once described as preternatural.'

It doesn't seem to put Helen's mind at ease.

'I know my daughter,' she goes, 'and I know she needs me.'

We sit there in the hotel restaurant eating our dinner in silence.

The old man tries to kick-stort the conversation again by going, 'Did you see Michael D. has criticized the politics of austerity in the *Financial Times*, Ross?'

I'm like, 'Er, no.'

'Wants reform of the European Central Bank. I must drop the interview up to your room. I'd be interested in hearing your thoughts on whether or not the chap overstepped his remit as President.'

It's at that exact point that I hear what would have to be described as a kerfuffle on the far side of the restaurant. I can hear, like, the *maître d'* shouting, then two or three more raised voices – a woman's, a man's, then a waiter's – and I'm about to crack a joke about how someone else isn't happy with the risotto, when suddenly the shouts turn to screams and a man comes chorging into the restaurant brandishing what looks very much to me like a sword.

The old man goes, 'Hello – what's all this how-do-you-do?'

And suddenly my hort is beating so fast that I think it might explode. Because I realize that the man who's heading in the general direction of our table with his sword raised and murder in his eyes is the same man who walked into the bedroom and caught me pretty much tupping his wife.

The old man goes, 'What the . . . is he coming over here, Ross?'

I look around for something I could possibly belt him over the head with – Camilla's husband, not the old man – except I'm not *quick* enough? The dude is suddenly right in front of me, his sword stretched across the table, its shorp tip pressed against my Adam's apple, just daring me to move.

Yeah, no, I remember Erika mentioning that he was a fencer.

'Hyou!' the dude goes. '*Bastardo! Bastardo!*'

I'm sitting there, literally frozen in my seat. I'm thinking, how did he find me? Fock, I must have told Camilla where I was staying – I actually did, because I mentioned that I was in one of the suites.

There are, like, gasps from all the other, I don't know, diners. The old man picks his napkin off his lap and throws it down on the table. He goes, 'What the hell is all of this about?'

Helen is just sitting there with a shocked look on her face and a forkful of risotto suspended in the air about six inches from her mouth.

'He make fuck with my hwife!' the dude goes.

Oh, Jesus – *she* suddenly arrives in then, going, '*No! No! No! Pleece! No! Pleece no!*' and then she stands next to him, her right hand clutched to her hort, wailing something in the local gobbledygook, which I presume is some kind of plea for my life.

The old man goes, 'He make what?' because he's looking at Camilla and he's obviously thinking, deep down, there's no focking way Ross rode that.

'Fuck!' the dude goes. 'He make fuck and now he die!'

He pushes the tip of the sword and I feel the skin in my neck strain like it's about to break.

'Well, it's clearly a case of mistaken identity!' the old man goes, always prepared to see the good in me. 'I mean, we've only been in this country, what, three days?'

What can I tell you? I'm a tough dog to keep on the porch.

'I hknow heem!' the dude goes. 'Thees woman heez – how to say? – mental in head, but she heez steel my hwife. You make fuck and I keel hyou.'

I'm still sitting there, too terrified to even move.

The next thing I hear is a girl's voice going, 'Papa, no! Papa, no!'

They're big on focking drama, these people. Madonna got them spot-on.

Across the restaurant floor comes this girl – or it's probably more accurate to say the most beautiful girl I have ever laid eyes on. The only way to do her justice would be to describe her as Irina Shayk, except with an even better body. She's so thin, her tits are in single file. And I instantly know that this is the Camilla Lacobellis that Fabrizio dumped Erika for.

How this pair of focking eyesores produced a daughter who looks like that is a debate we'll have to leave for another day.

Like I said, the girl – absolute ride – is giving it, 'Papa, no! Papa, no!' and I use the distraction to suddenly flick the blade of the sword away with the back of my hand and, almost in the same motion, grab a silver tray from the next table to act as, like, a shield.

I jump to my feet and stort backing away. The dude sort of, like, stalks after me, knees bent, back straight and his sword orm stretched out in front of him, like you see in the Olympics.

He sort of, like, lunges at me with the sword and I manage to, like, block it with the tray. The sound of steel on steel puts the genuine shits up me.

'You make fuck!' he goes. 'I keel!'

The old man's going, 'Security!' at the top of his voice. 'Can we get some bloody well security in here? We're paying guests!'

The dude goes for me again, except not with a lunge this time – it's more of a *slashing* motion? I sort of, like, bend backwards, *Matrix*-style, to avoid the blade and it cuts clean through a net curtain.

Missing me seems to make him even madder. He roars something at me in the local lingo and then makes a run at me, swinging the sword like a focking lunatic – slashes and lunges and whatever else is going. I'm, like, backing away the whole time, blocking the blows with the tray, or ducking them so that he ends up doing serious damage to the furniture.

Everyone in the restaurant is screaming and running for cover at this stage.

215

'There will be a complaint,' the old man is shouting, 'to the Irish consul about this!'

The dude is throwing aside tables and chairs to get at me. There's, like, the sound of glass breaking and plates smashing and furniture splintering as he keeps coming, his blade whistling past my face and crashing into the metal tray so hord that I can feel the vibrations up my orms.

The restaurant is suddenly a mess. There's, like, broken glass and spilled flowers and furniture stuffing and feathers and food everywhere.

I'm doing an incredible job defending myself, to be fair to me. That is until the moment when I manage to step on a broken wine carafe and I suddenly find myself stumbling backwards, my legs all bandy, unable to break my fall. I hit the deck with a thud and the mad focker is suddenly standing over me, laughing now – victory, his – the point of his sword just an inch from my nose.

I'm cross-eyed looking at it, genuinely thinking that this is it. This is the moment when the Rossmeister's years of being a bit too free and easy with his own sabre finally catch up with him.

It's literally a case of live by the sword, die by the sword.

I close my eyes, *resolved* to it? And then I hear this bump and I open my eyes and I realize that someone has tackled the lunatic. They're suddenly rolling around on the ground, then the sword is somehow pulled from the dude's hand and it goes flying across the restaurant floor.

Three security gords then appear and they sort of, like, wrestle the focking headbanger out of there, his ugly wife following them, begging them not to hurt him.

I turn around to say thank you to whoever it was that just saved my literally life. And that's when I get the biggest surprise of the evening – although it's nothing compared to the shock that *he* ends up getting?

He's like, 'Russ?'

It's focking Fabrizio.

I'm there, 'Jesus Christ, why did it have to be you?'

The old man is going, 'It's *him*! What the bloody hell is going on?' while Helen is going, 'Where is she? Where is my daughter?'

But Fabrizio doesn't hear her. He's still struggling with the shock of seeing me there. He goes, 'You? It was you?' and then his confused look turns into a smile. 'You haff sex with Camilla's mothare?'

He laughs, then he says something in the local nonsense to the other Camilla, obviously explaining who I am, because I hear Erika's name get mentioned.

That's when Helen suddenly steps forward, giving it, 'I asked you a question! Where is my daughter?'

It's the first time he's actually noticed her. He's there, 'Meesiss Josuff. Why are you . . .'

'Where is she?' she goes. 'Where's my daughter?'

'I halready tell you when you reeng. I know nussink. We harr not togezzare now.'

'You took my daughter away from her family, from her friends, from her fiancé and you brought her here! And the last thing you said to me was that you'd look after her – where is she?'

'I don't know. I haff not seen her for halmost one year.'

Helen bursts into tears and goes running from the restaurant. My old man runs after her.

I'm there, 'I said you were a tool right from the beginning.'

He goes, 'You haff sex weeth Camilla's mothare – you harr seek in head.'

Even the woman's own daughter is disgusted at the thought of anyone wanting to give her old dear a rattle.

'Hanimal!' she calls me.

'Now, I go home,' *he* goes. 'I haff competition this weekend.'

I try to get the last word in by going, 'Yeah, it's not a focking sport, Fabrizio. I'm sticking by that assessment.'

'Well, I haff Holympic medal for proof.'

'Olympic medal or not, I'm going to get you back for what you did to my sister. That's a focking promise.'

I set off early to collect Erika. That's how *excited* I am? I actually walk to the shop and I look in the window, but I don't see her in there, then I realize that I'm, like, more than an hour early. She said, like, lunchtime and it's only, like, half-eleven.

So I grab a crappycino in the little coffee shop a few doors down. To pass the time, I borrow a pen from one of the waitresses, then on the back of a napkin I write down the names of the players – one to fifteen – that I'd pick to stort for the Lions against Australia.

Hilariously, there end up being nine Irish players in the team and no English players!

Then I stort to think about how I'd break the news to the likes of Owen Farrell and Billy focking Twelvetrees that they're not even on the bench! I'd actually look them straight in the eye and let them have it: 'You've been pissing me off for years, Farrell. Everything about you. The hair. Everything. As a matter of fact, the only reason I stuck you in the original squad was so I could have the pleasure of dropping you later on. Now get out of my sight, you focking dickhead. And send Billy focking Twelvetrees in. Twelve trees, no mates.'

I end up getting a bit giddy. I actually stort laughing out loud, just thinking about the poor dude's face when he finds out that I've dragged him all the way to Australia just to tell him to fock off as well. The waitress asks me if I'm okay and I tell her yeah, no, I'm fine.

I'm like, 'Yeah, no, I'm just in scintillating form.'

I knock back the rest of my coffee, then I stick my team selections in my pocket, thinking there'll be time enough to pick my XV for the Second and Third Tests on the flight home. I settle the bill, leaving a ridiculously generous tip, then I head back to Erika's shop.

Again, I don't see her through the window, but I think nothing of it. In I go. The owner is there. I think I already mentioned that she's just okay looks-wise. She'd be a six. But then again I'm heteroflexible – I'd ride anything!

'Is, em, Erika ready?' I go.

She's like, 'What?'

I'm changing that six to a five and a half.

'Erika,' I go. 'I'm supposably *meeting* her here?'

She's like, 'No, gone. She heez gone.'

'She couldn't be gone. Like I said, I'm supposably *meeting* her?'

'Yesterday, she hask for weeches and she gone.'

Oh, shit.

I'm like, 'No, no, no, no, no, no, no, no, no, no . . .'

'Yes,' the woman goes. 'Yes.'

I suddenly feel like Munster must have felt after they signed Clinton Huppert. Focking suckered.

I'm there, 'She knew. She knew what she was going to do, that's why she asked me to wait twenty-four hours.'

The woman goes, 'She leaf letter for man who come.'

She roots around under the counter, then she pulls out an envelope, which she hands to me. I tear it open and I pull out the note inside.

It's like, 'You ruined it, Ross. I will never, ever forgive you for that. You fucking ruined everything.'

There's not even any kisses at the bottom.

I scrunch the note up and I drop it on the floor. I step out of the shop onto Florida Street, totally dazed.

I suddenly remember that I have Erika's number. I try it, but of course she's not going to make the mistake of answering. It rings seven or eight times, then it goes to her voicemail.

Then I'm trying to think of that barrister couple's address, except I can't remember it. All I know is that it looked like Northumberland Road, although that's obviously not a lot of good to me.

But then I remember that we walked there from the pork, the address of which is in the satnav. If I can find my way back to the bench where I met Erika that day, then I can definitely find the gaff from there.

I run back to the hotel.

I spot the old man and Helen in the lobby and they spot me. The old man tries to talk to me. He's like, 'Ross, we really need to . . .'

And I'm there, 'I can't explain. I will, but not now.'

I peg it down to the cor pork and I hop into the old Chevrolet Tahoe. I go through my previous destinations. *Bosques de Palermo.* That was it.

The drive takes fifteen minutes. I'm there in ten. I pork, then I retrace my steps back to the bench, then from there to the gaff where I watched Erika hand over Amelie to a total randomer.

I walk up to the front door and I knock. But when no one imme-diately answers, I end up totally losing it. I stort kicking the door, going, 'Give her to me! Give her to me!'

The next thing I hear is the sound of feet running through the hallway and the door flies open. There's a dude standing there. He looks a little bit like David Duchovny. He obviously thinks I'm just some random headbanger trying to kick his front door down, so he goes to grab me by the scruff of my Lions jersey, except I just brush his hand aside, then I shove him up against the wall and I go into the gaff.

I chorge down the hallway to the kitchen. I push the door.

She's standing there – the woman that Erika handed Amelie to the other day. She obviously saw me, too, because I notice a flicker of, I don't know, recognition in her face.

The next thing I feel is this, like, almighty crack across the back of my head. I stagger forward, then I turn around and I realize that the dude has hit me over the head with, like, a sweeping brush.

The woman shouts something at him in the local lingo. I'm pre-suming she's telling him who exactly I am, because he suddenly puts the brush down and storts talking to me in, like, English.

He goes, 'What hyou want?'

He has the actual balls to say that. Barristers here are obviously as full of themselves as barristers back home.

I'm there, 'What I want is my niece.'

He goes, 'Niece?'

'Yeah, no, my *sister's* baby? Amelie. Is she upstairs, sleeping?'

They stort chatting away – again, in the local lingo. Sometimes I hate the fact that I grew up in a country where there's no need to learn other languages.

Eventually, he goes, 'Your seester hasks hus to fostare Hamelie, *si*?'

I'm there, 'No, it's not *si*. It's not *si* by any means. The girl is not in the right state of mind to make that decision. She's scared and on her own and possibly depressed.'

And that's when I notice that the dude's wife is crying.

She goes, 'She has left Hargentina. She come hlast night and she say deal is hover. She take Amelie and go to hairport.'

I'm like, 'The hairport?'

The dude then goes, 'Theez heez ferry bad for hus. She say we can hadopt Amelie. She heez ferry heppy with theez decision. We are ferry heppy, too. She lives with us for four days of effery week. We luff her like she heez our child. Then Erika comes last night and says she chenge her mind. Takes bebby. Today, we haff broken heart. Now, I hask hyou to leaf.'

I suddenly feel like the biggest dick in the world.

I'm there, 'Did she mention where she was taking her?'

He goes, 'I said leaf. Now.'

The old man knocks on the door. I'm like, 'Yeah, no, it's open.'

In he comes, Helen behind him.

He's there, 'I got your message. You said you had something to tell us.'

And I'm there, 'Dad?' which I never usually call him. 'Helen? Okay, I don't know where to stort. Okay, maybe with the good news. You have a granddaughter. Amelie is her name.'

The old man is like, 'Granddaughter? What the hell is going on?'

I tell them to sit down, except they can't – they're too in *shock*?

I decide to tell them the story from the beginning.

I'm there, 'Look, I've been seeing Erika behind your backs. And obviously I don't mean seeing her in *that* way, although I don't think either of us would deny there was an attraction before we found out we were related. Yeah, no, I actually found her on day one. She was working in a clothes shop not a million miles from here. That's how low she'd sunk.'

Helen is not a happy hamster. 'We've just spent three days combing every inch of this city,' she goes, 'from early in the morning until late in the evening, putting her photograph up on lampposts, showing it to strangers. You watched us come back here every night, exhausted and upset, not knowing if she was alive or dead. And all the time, you knew where she was?'

I'm there, 'I realize the point you're trying to make, Helen. But Erika asked me not to say anything to you.'

'How dare you! How bloody dare you!'

The old man steps in then. He's like, 'Okay, let's just hear the chap out, Helen.'

I'm there, 'Erika swore me to secrecy. She was afraid that if you found her, you'd try to talk her into going back home.'

'Of course we would,' the old man goes. 'It's where she belongs.'

'Like I said, she was working in a clothes shop. I think there was a part of her that didn't want you to see her like that. Serving people. You know how much she hates people.'

Helen goes, 'Where is she now? Where's Erika?'

'Yeah, no, I'm getting to that, if you'll give me a chance. Erika mentioned that she was doing a bit of nannying on the side. You can imagine what a shock this was to me. Of all the types of people that Erika despised, babies were always top of the list. Then I met her out and about – it was in a pork – and she had this little girl with her. Anyway, it was only later that the penny dropped – the likeness. I suddenly copped it – shit, that's *her* actual baby.'

Helen literally roars at me. 'That's when you should have told us!' she goes. 'You should have told us then!'

'She was going to give her away. There was this couple. Barristers. They were, like, looking after her three or four days a week. Fostering was the word that was used. Erika was going to actually give her to them, except I talked her around. I thought I did. She said she was going to come home with us. She just needed twenty-four hours to get her head straight before she could face either of you. Little did I know that she was planning to peg it.'

Helen's like, 'So where has she gone?'

I'm there, 'There's no point in shouting at me, Helen.'

'I want to know where she is!'

'She went to . . . hang on . . . it's a Meg Ryan movie. *When Harry Met* focking *Sally* keeps popping into my head for some reason. Seattle! That's it! Seattle was the talk!'

She really loses it with me then. She's like, 'If you'd told us, we could have stopped her! We could have stopped her and she'd be here now!'

The old man goes, 'Now, calm yourself, Helen, and let's think about what the chap said. When we arrived here three days ago, we didn't know where Erika was and we didn't know that she had a baby and that she was about to hand her over to some strange – barristers, did you say, Ross? Now, we've a fair idea that she might be in Seattle and that her baby is at least still with her. Ross is the hero here, Helen.'

Except Helen's not ready to forgive and forget. Not yet. She'll come around, though. She's always been a major supporter of mine.

I'm there, 'So what happens now? I was thinking we should possibly head for Seattle. Continue the search.'

'No,' the old man goes. 'We'll go home. Regroup.'

I'm there, 'Helen, I'm sorry I never mentioned that I knew where Erika was.'

Except she doesn't say a word. She just turns her back on me and walks out of the room.

'Brace yourself!' Sorcha goes.

I'm like, 'Yeah, no, I'm definitely listening.'

It's, like, ten o'clock on a Saturday morning and I'm wandering up some random street in Buenos Aires, looking for somewhere that does a decent eggs Benedict.

She goes, 'They've said they'll take her back!'

I'm there, 'Who? What are you talking about?'

'Mount Anville, Ross. They said they'd take Honor back. It was Siofra's letter. That's what decided it.'

'Yeah, no, that's great news.'

I woke up this morning to three more abusive messages from the kid. The last one was just, 'Oh my God, you are so focking dead.'

Sorcha goes, 'They rang yesterday and said they'd be happy to welcome her back to the school in September. I told them that she's – Oh! My God! – a totally changed girl.'

'Like I said, it's amazing.'

'Yearbook Committee. Duologue Drama Workshops. Mother–Daughter Pancake Breakfasts. It's all ahead of her, Ross. Are you at the airport?'

'Er, not exactly – quite a bit has happened in the last twenty-four, Babes.'

She suddenly sounds worried.

She's like, 'Oh my God, what?'

I'm there, 'Yeah, no, Erika's not coming home with us. She's gone.'

'Gone?'

'Pegged it. Tricked me into thinking she was going to come home with us, then the second my back was turned she snatched Amelie, then she headed for the airport. I'm presuming it's, like, Seattle she's gone to – unless that was another red heron.'

'Wait a minute – you're saying she *snatched* Amelie?'

'Yeah, no, she took her back from that couple who were hoping to adopt her. Told them she'd changed her mind. And they're obviously devo.'

'Oh my God!'

'And guess who's ended up being the bad goy in all of this?'

'Who?'

'Me, of course. Helen had a total focking conniption when she found out that I knew where Erika was and didn't say anything.'

'Ross, you should have told her – oh my God, I said that to you.'

'Hey, this is all down to him. Focking Fabrizio. I saw him, by the way.'

'What?'

'He showed up at the hotel.'

'Oh my God. How did he know where you were staying?'

'It, em, doesn't matter. The only thing I'm sad about is that I never got the chance to deck him.'

'Ross, you know how I feel about violence. We're actually reading Vera Brittain's *Testament of Youth* in my book club at the moment.'

'I'm sticking by what I said. He's riding in the Orgentine Equestrian Championships – so-called – today. I was actually reading about it online. He's going for, like, his seventh national title in a row. I'd love to somehow fock it up for him.'

'Just get yourself home, Ross.'

'Yeah, no, we'll probably be leaving tonight.'

And that's when I suddenly find myself staring in the window of

224

a shop called Beagle Marine. It's, like, a sailing *supplies* shop? It reminds me of that place in Dún Laoghaire, next to the Meadows & Byrne. They do like, wetsuits and life jackets and sailing boots and flares.

And they do something else that suddenly catches my eye.

I'm like, 'Sorcha, I have to go. Give Honor and the boys my love. And tell them I'll see them tomorrow.'

The women in Orgentina are some of the most beautiful in the world. And I'm a bit angry with myself that the only one I rode while I was here was a complete focking truffle-pig. But then showjumping – despite having nothing to do with sport – has always attracted beautiful women. I'm thinking about the birds you see hanging around Ballsbridge during the second weekend in August – solid jawlines, proper Protestant names and that filthy look in their eyes that tells you that anything might happen here if you keep the French Mortinis coming.

Well, they're exactly the same in this country.

I'm sitting next to this bird who's wearing a pair of jodhpurs so tight, you could count the change in her pocket.

'God, I love showjumping,' I go, making conversation, but also playing the role of a fan. 'Those people who say that it's just sitting on an animal and letting him do all the focking work – where are they today, that's what I want to know?'

She smiles at me.

She's like, 'Heenglish?'

I'm there, 'Irish.'

'Ireesh?'

'Yeah, no, it's kind of the same thing. They like to pretend it's not, but there's no real difference between us.'

I'm just glad Ronan isn't here to hear me say that.

Seventy snots I paid for this seat, but it was worth every cent. I'm right at the very front, literally within spitting distance of the Horse Obstacle Course, where I've so far seen six animals go around with not a focking clue that there's even a human on their backs.

The rule is that whichever horse knocks over the least number of fences, then the rich kid who bought the horse for a six-figure sum – and is literally piggybacking on its talent – is declared the winner.

I turn to the bird beside me and I'm like, 'So what do they call you? *What hees hyour hname?*'

'Laurina,' she goes. 'And you harr?'

I'm there, 'I'm Ross,' and I lean in to do the whole air-kissing thing. I tell her that in Ireland it's traditional to do eight – four on each cheek – and she actually believes me.

She's wearing Versace *Bright Crystal* and I'm suddenly horder than a dinner lady's orm.

I'm there, 'It's lovely to meet you. So who are you here to see today?'

She's like, 'May seester heez Mercedes Larroquette. She heez jumping next.'

'Your sister?'

'Seester, yes.'

See, that just goes to prove my point. How can it be a sport if men and women compete against each other at exactly the same level? If this is a sport, then so is writing poetry and, I don't know, playing Buckaroo.

A whistle blows. Then out she comes. Mercedes Larroquette. A big focking ride, like her skin and blister beside me. She's on, like, a white horse.

Suddenly, without any pre-warning, Laurina puts her hand on my knee, gripping it hord. Then she suddenly remembers herself. She's like, 'I ham surrey,' quickly pulling her hand away. 'I get – how to say – vary nerfoos when my seester compete.'

I grab her hand and put it back on my knee.

I'm like, 'Hey, if it helps, then my advice would be to just go with it.'

I'm very understanding.

The horse that Mercedes is sitting on is called *Rio Tercero*. He ends up doing well. His back hooves clip a couple of fences – and Laurina digs her fingers deep into my leg both times – but only one bor actually falls, which puts the horse into the overall lead. Laurina throws her orms around my neck and gives me a huge hug.

'I ham so heppy!' she goes. 'Hyou harr my goot luck, yes!'

God, I wish I was staying another day. I'd focking ride her like Tony McCoy.

Suddenly, my phone vibrates in my pocket. I answer it and it ends up being the old man. It sounds like he's in a bit of a panic.

He's like, 'Where the hell are you, Kicker? We're about to leave for the airport.'

I'm there, 'Calm down. I'm going to make my own way there. I've got something to do here, then I'm going to drop the rental cor back at the airport.'

'Where are you, Ross? You sound like you're at a rugby match.'

I laugh. I'm like, 'Dude, this is as far from a rugby match as it's possible to be. I'll see you at the airport.'

I hang up and I go, 'So who's up next?' already *knowing* the answer? I bought a programme.

'Heez Fabrizio Bettega,' she goes.

I'm like, 'Febreze?' because I can't actually help myself.

She's there 'No, no – eez Fabrizio.'

I'm like, 'Febreze-io.'

'Fabrizio Bettega.'

'Like I said, I've never heard of him.'

'He heez Olympic weener. He also ween theez competition seex times.'

I look across to the other side of the Horse Obstacle Course and I can see Camilla, the absolute lasher, with her old dear – face like a focking cage-fighter – waiting for him to ride out.

'I'm going to be honest,' I go, 'he sounds like a bit of a dick. As in, not a nice goy? I still hope your sister stops him winning his seventh.'

'No,' she goes, 'I theenk he wheel ween. He heez – how to say – favoureet?'

And I'm like, 'Well, I've just got a sneaking suspicion that today's not going to be his day.'

The whistle blows, then out he comes. There's, like, a huge cheer for him and he sort of, like, waves to the crowd, full of himself – I know I'm one to talk. I'd probably have my shirt off by now, kissing my guns.

There ends up being, like, a standing ovation then – the dude is obviously a hero to these poor, deluded focks – and he rides around the edge of the Horse Obstacle Course, waving his riding cap at them. Even Laurina buys into his bullshit. She's, like, clapping as hord as the rest of them as he rides past. I put my head down so he doesn't cop me.

Then the crowd is suddenly silent and he's getting ready to do his round, psyching himself up. The horse sort of, like, shuffles its feet, sending up little clouds of dirt, then he sort of, like, snorts. There's, like, unbelievable tension in the air. The whistle blows, Fabrizio digs his heels into the animal's sides – unnecessarily, I would have thought – and they're suddenly off, heading for the first fence.

They're over it without any problems. He's obviously a good horse. Then the second, third and fourth present no difficulties either and you can nearly hear the crowd willing him over them.

The horse's rear hooves clip the top of the fifth. The top bor wobbles and the entire audience holds its breath, expecting it to fall, except it doesn't.

It's probably held on by focking magnets, I think.

He actually storts showboating then, looking back over his shoulder at the fence and pulling a 'Phew!' face for the crowd. They all laugh and applaud – they obviously love a showman, these people – and then they're suddenly deathly silent as the horse gears up to jump the sixth.

I feel my jacket, just to make sure the thing is still in there.

He's got, like, three more fences to jump, the first of which is literally eight feet in front of me. I can actually see a little smug smile on Fabrizio's face as he turns the horse around and gets ready to run at it.

He sticks his heels into the animal's sides again and the horse storts building up speed. And that's when I whip it out.

The little foghorn I picked up in Beagle Marine.

I stand up, knowing timing is all-important here. A few people behind me stort shouting at me, presumably to sit down because I'm blocking their view. I wait until the horse is, like, eight feet in front of the fence, then I let him have it.

BBBBBBRRRRRRRRRRRRNNNNNN!

The horse gets such a fright that actual shit comes out of its orse. And he runs – I swear to fock – straight through the fence, sending the bors and wooden boxes flying everywhere. Fabrizio has become, I don't know, *unseated*? He's hanging off the horse, his orms wrapped around its neck as the animal – seriously spooked now – storts running around the outside of the Horse Obstacle Course.

He drags Fabrizio for, like, an entire circuit, before Fabrizio manages to get his foot out of the stirrup and is then dumped, with the sickening sound of bone breaking, onto the ground directly in front of us.

It's his orm. He's, like, clutching it and howling in agony.

I know I have to get out of here, because the atmosphere is turning suddenly ugly. People are shouting at me – wanting to know, I presume, what the fock? Even Laurina is going, 'Why hyou do theez?'

That's not important right now. All that matters is that Fabrizio knows that it was me. I call his name, just as the medics are arriving on the scene to tend to him. He looks at me and I meet his eye and I show him the foghorn and I mouth the word, 'Decked!'

Then someone suddenly shoves me from behind and I turn around and it's a little dude who looks mad enough to kill me with his two hands. I look over his shoulder and three security gords are making their way along the row towards me.

So I turn around and I get the fock out of there as fast as I can run. Which is very fast – ask Denis Hickie.

But before I do, I turn to Laurina and I go, 'I'd love to stay. But I've got a plane to catch.'

She's got, like, a look of shock on her face. I kiss her on the lips and then I'm out of there.

So we arrive home, having basically failed.

No Erika, no Amelie and Helen so pissed off with me that she refused to even sit near me on the flight from Buenos Aires to London and again from London to Dublin. Her and the old man flew first class and I sat – if you can believe this – in economy.

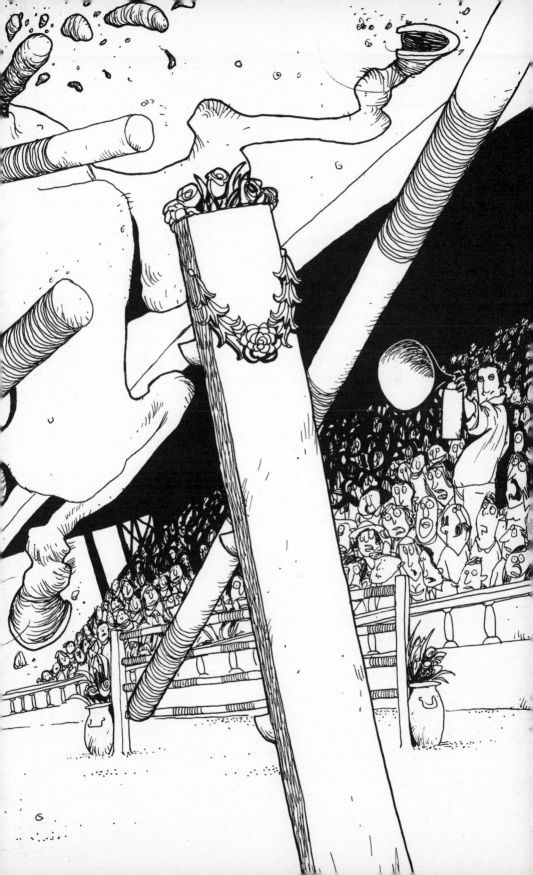

Sorcha is there to greet us at the airport. She's made the effort as well. She's wearing her good Stella McCortney blazer, although I can't help but notice that she's bursting out of it. I don't want to be a dick, but the girl looks like she's put on half a stone in weight in the less-than-a-week since I've been away. She's got jowls like the dog from *Turner and Hooch* and an orse like Wyatt Crockett.

But, like I said, I don't want to be a dick.

She goes, 'Oh my God, I *so* missed you!' the whole me-doing-a-runner-when-I-was-supposed-to-be-having-the-snip totally forgotten.

The old man and Helen suddenly walk through the arrivals gate behind me. Sorcha rushes to them.

She's all, 'Hi, Chorles! Hi, Helen. I'm so sorry about Erika!'

I tip over to Honor, who's standing a few yords away with the three boys in the big, wide stroller, smiling so sweetly that it looks like her face is sore. She's going to give herself an embolism.

'God, I missed you,' I go, kissing her on top of the head. 'It's great news about your old school having you back as well, isn't it?'

Then I crouch down on, like, my hunkers and say hello to Brian, Johnny and Leo.

'Did you get my voice messages?' Honor goes through gritted teeth.

I'm like, 'Yes, I did. I have to say, you know a lot of colourful swear words. You'll fit back in at Mount Anville in no time.'

'You credit cord was declined.'

'Yeah, no, I'm aware of that.'

'It's maxed out.'

'That's what tends to happen, Honor, when you spend five Ks in, like, three days?'

'Well, you need to pay it off. There's things I want to buy.'

'I'm not going to pay it off. I gave you that number in a moment of weakness. You bought, like, five Ks' worth of shit in three days, Honor. There's limits. That's the point I'm trying to make.'

She just, like, glares at me.

When all the welcome homes are done and dusted, we stort making our way towards the cor pork, Helen still not talking to me and Honor kicking the back of my heels every twenty or thirty steps to try to trip me up. But the old man is telling me that I played an absolute blinder as usual, even though we didn't get the result we wanted.

They head for their cor. Helen doesn't even say goodbye to me. I'm banjoed. I need my bed.

We get back to the minivan and Sorcha suddenly remembers that she hasn't paid for our porking. She heads off in search of a machine while I take the boys out of their stroller and stort strapping them into their cor seats.

While I'm doing this, Honor is just, like, staring at me. 'You're *actually* serious?' she goes. 'You're not going to pay that credit cord bill?'

I'm there, 'Not only that, Honor, I'm actually going to cancel the cord. Money doesn't just fall from the skies, Honor. It has to be actually earned.'

I don't know where this shit comes from. Maybe I'm taking it out on Honor because Helen is giving me such a hord time. Or maybe it's just jetlag. Either way, I'm certainly not in my right mind.

She's there, '*Excuse* me?'

'Look,' I go, 'I think you did pretty well out of the deal. You pretended to be good, you fooled Siofra into thinking that you're not a bitch anymore and you got back into Mount Anville. And in return you got, what, nearly eleven grand's worth of clobber? That's not a bad result for you, Honor.'

'I want my own credit cord.'

'You didn't think I was going to go on just, like, buying you shit indefinitely, did you? Like I said, there's, like, limits. I also don't want you growing up thinking that someone is always going to be there to pick up the tab for you. I mean, I'm going to have to ask my old man for the shekels to pay off that bill.'

'I'll tell Mum that you've been buying me things behind her back.'

'I'll just deny it. I'll say you used my credit cord without my permission.'

'I'll tell her you kissed that woman.'

'You do that and I'll accidentally on purpose find your stash of

233

clothes in the eaves of the house. I'll go, "Oh my God, look at all this stuff, Sorcha! She stole my Mastercord details – she was putting all this shit on it while I was away!" And then she'll send it all back to where it came from. And you wouldn't want that, I suspect.'

I suddenly spot Sorcha walking back across the cor pork with the ticket in her hand.

Honor smiles again – for *her* benefit rather than *mine*?

I'm there, 'Like I said, you did well out of the deal, Honor. Accept that.'

But literally a shiver runs up my spine when she turns around to me and goes, 'Oh my God, you've just made an enemy out of me. That's going to be the biggest mistake of your miserable life.'

7.

The Fraud of the Rings

I ask Ronan how he's fixed and what I mean is fixed for the Junior Cert, which storts tomorrow morning.

'Ine a bit nerbous,' he goes, 'but there's nuttin I habn't cubbered.'

I'm there, 'Do you know what's good for nerves? A few beers. Will I get you a can?'

He goes, 'No! Moy Jaysus, Rosser, I doatunt want be going into me foorst exam with a bleaten hangover.'

Er, *I* did.

I'm there, 'You're definitely sure, because I was thinking of having one myself.'

He's like, 'No, tomoddow's too impowertant, Rosser.'

'Hey, you know best. Just to say that I drank the night before all of my exams. But, then again, you know how that went!'

They arrived about an hour ago. Ronan and Shadden with Rihanna-Brogan, then Shadden's old dear, Dordeen, with her daughter Kadden's two kids, Lamar, who's seven, and Tequila, who's six.

They're upstairs in, like, Honor's room, doing God knows what. It's, like, four weeks since I got back from Orgentina and Honor hasn't delivered on her threat of revenge for cutting off her line of credit. But every so often I catch her smiling at me insanely, like she's got some horrible torture in store for me.

Sorcha is telling Shadden and Dordeen that she's storted making her own baby food, by waterless-cooking root vegetables – obviously all organic and locally grown. This seems to piss Dordeen off for no good reason. She stares at Johnny, Leo and Brian, all playing happily on the floor, already capable of sitting upright and supporting themselves, by the way, about four weeks ahead of schedule.

She goes, 'I stiddle tink tree is too meddy,' like having triplets was a choice we actually made.

I'm there, 'What the fock are we supposed to do – put one or two of them in the *Buy and Sell*?'

She smiles – delighted with herself for getting a reaction out of me. That'll teach us for feeding our children something other than chips and TK red lemonade.

'I call as I see,' she goes. 'People eeder like that, or thee dowaunt like it.'

I'm there, 'Actually, there's a third category, Dordeen – people who think you're a focking brainless councilite skank.'

Yeah, no, I don't really say that. But I'm just about to when Honor suddenly pops her head around the kitchen door.

She's like, 'Hiii!' in her put-on *cute* voice?

Sorcha goes, 'Hello, Honor – are you all playing nicely together?'

Honor's like, 'Yes, Mommy. We're getting on really, really well. Em, can I bring one of the boys upstairs?'

I'm about to say no – it's out of the focking question, except Sorcha gets in there before me and she goes, 'Oh my God, of course you can!'

Honor heads straight for Johnny, who's holding his little rugby ball in his two hands, staring at it as if mesmerized by it. Honor bends down and picks him up off his play mat.

She's like, 'Which one is this?' staring straight at me. She knows full focking well which one it is.

'That's Johnny,' Sorcha goes.

Honor's like, 'Come on, Johnny – your big sister is going to bring you upstairs to play! Thanks, Mom!'

Honor gives me a sly smile as she disappears out of the kitchen, then back upstairs.

'She's like a different child,' Sorcha goes. 'Isn't she, Ross?'

I'm like, 'Er, she certainly *seems* to be? It's early days, though – she *could* easily turn bad again.'

I'm suddenly picturing her, dropping my little number ten on his head – accidentally on purpose – or even doing something to damage his kicking leg.

Sorcha goes, 'You remember what she was like before, Dordeen?'

Dordeen's there, 'She was a little fooken wagon. Ine soddy for having to say it.'

'There were certainly aspects of her behaviour that fell below what Ross and I considered socially acceptable.'

'Idn't she the one what put the rats in her skewill? That was in the *Heddild* and evvyting.'

'Well, we don't talk about it anymore. We took her to see this amazing, amazing behavioural therapist and one of the most important things she taught us was that we shouldn't keep a score cord of past transgressions. Every new day is a blank page.'

'Yeah, whatebber you say.'

Honor wouldn't have to *break* Johnny's leg to ruin his future career. She could do something to, I don't know, manipulate his hip – something subtle to knock it out of alignment, something we possibly wouldn't notice until his Junior Cup year.

Or maybe I'm just being paranoid.

'Hee-er, Rosser,' Ronan goes – he's holding Rihanna-Brogan in his orms, by the way – 'hab a listen to this. She's saying lowauts of new words, reet, but cos she's arthur spending half her life in Kulloyney and half in Fingerless, her accent is a birra boat.'

Shadden goes, 'This is veddy fuddy, so it is.'

'Hee-er, Rihatta-Burrogan,' Ronan goes, 'what did you hab for yisser breakfast this morden?'

Rihanna-Brogan goes, 'Poddidge.'

Me and Sorcha laugh – you'd have to.

'Reet,' Ronan goes, 'so that's normal, reet? Now, hab a listen to this. Rihatta-Burrogan, what's yisser favourite foowut in the wurdled?'

And Rihanna-Brogan, in the most unbelievable Vico Road accent, goes, 'Frittaaawta!'

Ronan and Shadden both laugh. Me and Sorcha laugh as well. It's like those Nigerian taxi drivers you sometimes get who've managed to pick up a Dublin knacker accent – it's genuinely funny.

Not to Dordeen, though.

'A little geerl of her ayuch,' she goes, 'shoultn't eeben know what a bleaten frittata is!'

Sorcha's like, 'There's nothing elitist about frittata, Dordeen – it's just a crustless quiche,' but it's a waste of time talking to the woman. You might as well read your cor manual into a focking cave.

'I doatunt want her being buddied when she steerts skewill,' she tries to go. 'She needs to forget evvyting she leerned when she was libbin out hee-er.'

Or a toe. All Honor would need to do is damage the big toe on Johnny's standing foot – I'm talking about, like, a sprain? – so that when he storts walking, he's going to be wary of putting pressure on it and that will totally mess up his head when it comes to his kicking later on.

I suddenly don't give a fock if I'm being paranoid.

'I'm, er, just going to check on the kids,' I go, sounding weirdly grown up.

Sorcha goes, 'I'm sure they're fine, Ross!'

It's like she doesn't even remember what our lives were like before she heard the words Siofra Flynn.

I'm there, 'Yeah, no, I'll look in on them anyway.'

Up the stairs I go, as quietly as I possibly can. I tiptoe along the landing slash passageway to Honor's room and I sort of, like, push the door open a crack, so that I can see in.

I stand there for, like, ten or twenty seconds, watching and listening. They're playing away like any normal kids. And it's a huge relief to see that Lamar, rather than Honor, is holding Johnny.

I end up having a bit of a chuckle watching them, just the happy innocence of kids having fun together. They're playing a game called Here Comes the Bride – the same game that probably we all played as kids. Honor is pretending to be the priest and Lamar and Tequila – despite being brother and sister – are playing the happy couple on their wedding day.

They needed the baby because it's apparently a Northside wedding and Honor has also persuaded Tequila to put a cushion up the front of her dress for added, I don't know, *authenticity*?

'By the power vested in me,' Honor goes, 'I now pronounce you man and wife. You may kiss your sister.'

I suddenly relax – the shoulders literally drop – and I decide to just leave them to it. Down the stairs I go, actually smiling to myself.

Sorcha's like, 'Are they okay?'

I'm there, 'Yeah, no, they're playing Love and Marriage.'

And everyone – even Dordeen – goes, 'Awww!'

I don't bother mentioning that the bride and groom are very closely related and that *she's* pregnant with their second kid, because I'm sure Dordeen would find a way to take offence.

Sorcha goes, 'It's like she's turned into this – oh my God – model child. Who's for banoffee pie?'

Dordeen goes, 'The which?' because we've already had Sorcha's Double-Double Chocolate Cake with crème focking fraiche – *and* her Brazil nut brownies.

Sorcha goes, 'It's banana, cream and toffee, Dordeen – on pastry!' and then she suddenly turns to me. 'Why are you staring at my stomach, Ross?'

I'm there, 'I wasn't.'

'You were – and you *still* are!'

'Yeah, no, it must be, like, an unconscience thing?'

It's Ronan who breaks the sudden tension.

'I habn't room,' he goes, 'for anutter thing. Fact, we'd bethor be headin back.'

Shadden goes, 'Tanks, Sudeka. It was good to gerrum away from the bukes – eeben for a few hours.'

We all end up saying our goodbyes in the hallway. Dordeen says she wouldn't make a habit of coming out here and I tell her that's good because we won't be making a habit of inviting her.

Sorcha calls up the stairs to Honor that her brother is going home. There's, like, the sound of feet and Honor comes chorging down the stairs, followed by Tequila and Lamar, who's still holding Johnny.

He hands him to me. I give a quick inspection. Nothing seems to be broken.

Honor throws her orms around Ronan, gives him a massive, massive hug and at the same time goes, 'Good luck in your exams!'

He's like, 'Ah, tanks, Hodor.'

And I'm there, 'Yeah, no, I second that. I hope it goes well, Ro. And even if it doesn't, bear in mind that I don't have a single qualification to my name.'

It ends up being a genuine tumbleweed moment.

Out the door and down to the Dort station they go. Tequila and Lamar seem happy enough. For a minute or so, I allow myself to think, yeah, no, maybe Honor *has* somehow changed?

But then I catch her looking at me, over her shoulder, as she's walking back up the stairs. And from that look, I instantly know that she's done something – something truly focking terrible – and I just don't know what it is yet.

It has to be said, the Queensland Reds are making the Lions work here. It's way too focking close and I don't know why Warren Gatland doesn't just throw Paul O'Connell on – *and* Johnny Sexton while he's at it.

Because he knows fock-all about the sport of rugby, I remind myself.

My phone suddenly goes. I've changed the ring tone to Ryle Nugent going, 'It's Kearney time!'

It ends up being Christian.

He's like, 'Are you watching this?'

He's obviously ringing for my analysis.

I'm there, 'Yeah, no, they're definitely making us sweat. Lot of heavy hits out there. Tommy Bowe is going to be a massive, massive loss and I'd be pretty worried about the lack of attacking fluency out there, just with an eye on the three Tests.'

He's like, 'Hmmm,' and it's straight away obvious that he's ringing for something other than my rugby expertise.

I'm there, 'Is everything okay, Dude?' and I'm thinking, please don't let this be about Lauren and the whole Tinder thing. I genuinely don't think I could take any more stress in my life right now.

'I was thinking about what you said a few weeks ago,' he goes, 'about Lauren and the whole Tinder thing.'

I'm there, 'Er, what did I say again? Just refresh my mind.'

'You said I should just forget about it. You said I shouldn't bother trying to find out who this mystery man of hers was.'

'I still think it's good advice.'

'So I've spent the last few weeks thinking, why would Ross say that? I mean, why is he so keen that I should ignore the fact that Lauren went on a date with another man and possibly cheated on me? And then the answer suddenly hit me.'

'You're breaking up there, Dude.'

'Ross has been through a separation – a separation that almost ended in divorce. But he fixed his marriage. In other words, he knows what he's talking about.'

'Jesus Christ, Dude, I can't tell you what a relief it is for me to hear you say that.'

'He knows that if you're going to make something work, you have to put a lid on the past and forget about it.'

'See, I'm constantly reminding Sorcha to do that.'

'I mean, *I've* made mistakes.'

'Going to that comic convention with Citation focking Needed. I hate to bring that up.'

'Anyway, the good news is that we're doing something about it, Ross. Me and Lauren.'

'What?'

'We've been seeing this marriage guidance counsellor. It's going well.'

I can't tell you the sense of relief that suddenly comes over me.

I'm like, 'Dude, I'm going to have to say fair focks.'

'By the way,' he goes, 'have you seen Fionn since you came back from Argentina?'

'Er, no. Actually, Oisinn asked me the same thing yesterday – what's the craic?'

'I won't spoil the surprise. Just tell me if you notice anything different about him.'

And that's how he leaves it.

Of course, it's not long before the curiosity gets the better of me. I text Fionn, asking him what he's up to, and he texts me back straight away to say that he's watching the match in The Queens in Dalkey. I tell him I'm on my way.

I'm there in, like, ten minutes. I throw the cor into the church cor pork, then I tip across the road.

I end up hearing him before I actually see him.

'Dude,' he shouts, which is unusual in itself, because I don't think Fionn has ever called me that in all the years I've known him. 'Pint of the obvious?'

I'm like, 'Er, yeah,' and that's when I suddenly see him, although it's a miracle that I even recognize him, because he looks fock-all like the Fionn I've known since we were pretty much kids.

The first thing I notice is that he's not wearing his glasses. *And* he's got a new haircut – we're talking blade four at the sides and a quiff at the front that'd nearly rival mine. He's wearing – I shit you not – chinos, a light blue Ralph with the collar up and Dubes, which I've never seen him wear before.

He hands me a pint. 'Here,' he goes, 'get a smile on,' which is one of *my* famous phrases?

I'm like, 'Where the fock are your glasses?'

He goes, 'I don't wear them anymore. I'm getting my eyes lasered.'

I've heard birds say they think he's actually quite handsome without them, although I think he actually looks a bit, you know, slow.

I'm there, 'You're *getting* them lasered? Can you even see right now?'

'Hey, I can see well enough,' he goes. 'Although I'm in a serious jocker today.'

A serious jocker? I swear to God, it's like some evil spirit has possessed him. And that's when it suddenly hits me. Fionn is turning into Ross O'Carroll-Kelly.

He goes, 'I did another corporate last night. Mastercard – up in Leopardstown. Had them eating out of my focking hand. Here, do you remember a bird called Joyce De Courcy?'

I'm like, 'Joyce De Courcy? Yeah, no, she's on the Fock It List.'

'What's the Fock It List?'

'Do you not remember I told you? It's a list I drew up of all the birds I plan to hopefully one day ride.'

He laughs in, like, a really *cruel* way?

'Dude,' he goes, 'I'm sorry to have to tell you this – I got there before you.'

I don't focking believe it. He even gives me the guns when he says it.

He goes, 'She spent three hours last night bouncing up and down on me like I was focking a Pilates ball. Then another two hours this morning. I gave her a serious workout. Although I have to say, she's being a bit of a Klingon. What do you do when they won't fock off the following morning?'

I look to my right and I notice her coming back from the Josh Ritter.

She goes, 'Oh, hi!' fake-smiling me.

I'm there, 'Hey, Joyce. You possibly remember me – Ross O'Carroll-Kelly?'

'Oh my God,' she goes. 'Rugby!'

And I'm like, 'Yeah, no, thanks,' because it's nice that people still remember.

I'm about to ask her if I can get her a drink when Fionn – totally out of the blue – goes, 'It's time you thought about maybe hitting the road, Joyce.'

As he's saying this, he's checking out his quiff in the mirror behind the bor.

Joyce is a bit, I don't know, taken aback by his bluntness. She goes, 'I was actually thinking we might get some lunch. They do amazing food here.'

Fionn goes, 'Are you focking terminally slow or are you just hard of understanding?'

This is Fionn, bear in mind. I think *I'm* more in shock than Joyce.

He goes, 'Dermot O'Leary has his orm around your shoulder and he's going, "Let's look back at your best bits!" Do you get what I'm saying? It's over. You're leaving the stage. You're thanking the judges and you're saying, "This isn't the end of Insert Name of Artist here."'

She looks at him, just shaking her head, tears in her eyes. She goes, 'You're a focking asshole.'

'If I was a focking asshole,' he goes, making sure his shirt collar is up, 'I wouldn't have Hailoed a taxi for you. It's outside now. Have a nice life.'

I'm there, 'Is this not weird?'

We're sitting in, like, Shanahan's on the Green, waiting for Christian and Lauren to arrive.

'In what way is it weird?' Sorcha goes. 'We're meeting two of our – oh my God – best friends for dinner.'

It's weird because I haven't set eyes on Lauren since our famous date night.

'It's just I know they've been having a lot of troubles,' I go, 'and I'm just wondering will it be maybe awkward?'

Sorcha goes, 'No, because Lauren said that things couldn't be better between them at the moment! The whole marriage guidance thing is going – oh my God – *so* well!'

I look up in time to see them walking across the restaurant floor towards us, hand in hand, Christian all smiles, Lauren looking a bit sheepish – very like me, I suppose. We do the whole air-kissing thing. Lauren sort of, like, stiffens when I touch her. Has it occurred to her, I wonder, that *I'm* possibly embarrassed about what happened as well?

We all sit down.

'So,' Sorcha goes, 'who's looking after little Ross and Oliver tonight?'

Christian goes, 'Lauren's old man,' and I sort of, like, smile to myself at the idea of Hennessy minding children. He'll be teaching them how to hide money offshore, no doubt. 'What about *your* little bruisers?'

Sorcha goes, 'Yeah, no, Mum and Dad. Oh my God, I literally don't know how we'd cope without them. Three is, like, *so* much work. But let's not make tonight about that. Let's hope we never turn into those kind of parents who only know how to talk about their children!'

We all laugh and then there's, like, thirty seconds of total silence between us.

'I thought the Lions did very well against the Waratahs this morning,' I go, to try to reboot the conversation. 'Sexton took his try very well. I'd still have him kicking ahead of Leigh Halfpenny and that's not just because I consider him a friend.'

Lauren goes, 'Sorcha, how are the babies?'

Sorcha's like, 'Oh my God, I can't believe how quickly they're growing! Leo is already standing on his own, isn't he, Ross?'

I'm there, 'Yeah, no, he's a definite leader.'

'I'm actually remembering at the moment how the middle of the first year is *the* most sociable time for babies. They're learning to smile, laugh, squeal – any way they can communicate. Brian is definitely going to be the extrovert. I think Johnny is going to be the thinker. He's always – oh my God – lost in his own little world. And then Leo, like Ross said, he's the first to do everything – to sit, to stand up. And the way he says, "Goo-goo-gah!" Isn't it – oh my God – *so* funny, Ross?'

I'm like, 'Er, yeah, no, definitely.'

'So what about your two?'

Lauren's like, 'Oliver's no trouble. Sleeps ten hours straight. And his brother is so good with him.'

'Awww, little Ross! How is he?'

'He's so funny. He keeps pestering us at the moment – he wants to enter one of those American beauty pageants that are suddenly all the rage!'

I tut – it's, like, an *automatic* thing?

I go, 'Tssst!' and Lauren looks at me – the first time she's properly looked at me since we all sat down – and I end up having to make the sound a few more times, pretending that I'm trying to get rid of a poppy seed from my teeth.

No one buys it, I suspect.

We study our menus, even though *I* don't need to? I always get the same thing in Shanahan's. The New York Strip. Eighteen focking ounces of it.

Lauren and Christian are suddenly in deep consultation with each other.

She's going, 'I don't know whether to have the loin of lamb with goat's cheese polenta and young summer vegetables or the whole baked turbot and creamed fennel with samphire.'

Christian's there, 'I'll tell you what – you get one and I'll get the other. That way, you can try both of them and decide which of the two you like best.'

I'll tell you something, you wouldn't catch me offering to do that. The dude is going beyond the focking call to keep his marriage together, even though I'm saying fair focks.

Sorcha is smiling at me like an idiot.

It's nice – I agree – that the two of them are making the effort with each other. It's possible that I even played a port in them sorting shit out. Maybe Lauren had a look at what else was out there – namely, people like me – and decided that she actually had it good.

The waiter takes our orders. Like I said, I order my usual steak, Lauren the turbot, Christian the lamb and Sorcha a twenty-four-ounce, bone-in rib-eye, French fries, creamed sweetcorn, crispy fried onion strings and a copper pot of bacon-enhanced, creamed spinach.

'This is going to be my last major pig-out for a while,' she goes. 'I definitely want to lose my baby weight before Amie with an ie's wedding.'

Amie with an ie is marrying some randomer from Galway, by the way, who has literally no interest in rugby.

After a bit more blah, Lauren stands up to go to the jacks and Sorcha goes, 'Oh my God, good idea!' because, as we all know, women are unable to piss in ones.

As soon as they've gone, I turn around to Christian and I go, 'It's fantastic, by the way – seeing you two getting on again. Although that thing where she gets to choose which of your two dinners she prefers – I think that's taking the piss.'

'It's just a nice thing to do,' he goes. 'We're both making an effort, Ross.'

'Don't get taken advantage of – that's the point I'm trying to make. There's making an effort and there's taking the piss. I kind of think that's taking the piss. You pick a dinner and you eat it. End of.'

'This guidance counsellor we're seeing, she just thinks we need to try to put each other first occasionally.'

'Well, I'm going to let it go, because it's nice to see the two of you not shouting at each other for once.'

'Well, we've both agreed to put the past behind us – including . . .'

'Continue.'

'I told you, the whole Tinder thing.'

'Oh, yeah, definitely. Brilliant. I think you're doing the right thing. It'd be best forgotten. It was probably a moment of madness that the girl immediately regretted. Let's all move on from it.'

Our food suddenly arrives and there's, like, still no sign of the birds. Sorcha's order – I'm not shitting you – takes up one entire half of the table.

Christian goes, 'She's never going to eat all of that.'

And I'm there, 'Don't underestimate her at the moment – Dude, give me a hand here.'

I reach across and I grab literally a handful of Sorcha's deep-fried onion strings and I shove them into my mouth. Then I grab her plate and I cut a massive chunk off the side of her steak.

'Quick,' I go, 'help me eat this.'

He's like, 'Ross, what are you doing?'

'Here, eat half. I'm trying to save Sorcha from herself. Horse into her onion strings there as well. And give me over that creamed corn.'

He does exactly as I tell him. He always did. That's why it was such a joy to have him as my inside-centre.

He goes, 'Just tell me why we're doing this.'

I'm like, 'Have you not noticed how much weight Sorcha has put on?'

'Like she said, she's still carrying a bit of baby weight.'

'Very diplomatic. She's a total focking porker, Christian. I'm calling it. Cruel to be kind. Blah, blah, bah. Get into the creamed spinach there before she comes back – quick.'

He lashes into it. I throw another two handfuls of onion strings into me, then have another crack at her steak.

Christian goes, 'Has she tried, like, appetite suppressants?'

I'm there, 'Unless they come deep-fried in batter, with a side of chips, I don't think she'd be interested. Have more onion strings – we've barely made a dent in them. What are appetite suppressants anyway?'

'They're just, like, tablets,' he goes. 'You get them in the chemist and, like, health food shops. I think most girls basically live on them for the six months before they get married.'

'And, what, you just buy them over the counter?'

'Yeah, no, I think there's caffeine in them. They're supposed to help with, like, *cravings*? Shit, they're coming back!'

I swallow what's in my mouth, then I wipe my lips with the back of my hand.

'The food's here!' Lauren goes. 'Christian, you shouldn't have waited for me. You must have been sitting here starving!'

He goes, 'I didn't want to stort until you decided whether you wanted the lamb or the turbot.'

'I think I'll have the lamb. I just remembered that I don't like turbot. I was mixing it up with trout.'

See? There's trying to make your marriage work and there's being a focking doormat.

Sorcha takes one look at her food and goes, 'Oh my God, *what* is the story with the portions?'

I'm there, 'What do you mean, Babes?'

'That doesn't look like a twenty-four-ounce steak. Look, it's actually smaller than yours!'

'Maybe the weight is in the bone.'

'In the bone?'

'Yeah, no, that might be it. Might be all in the bone.'

'Well, what about the onion strings? Usually, you get, like, *twice* that many?'

'They might be cutting back on the portions. I'm just remembering that thing you were saying the other day about how food waste is actually a bigger environmental threat than, I don't know, something else.'

'Our reliance on fossil fuels.'

'That was it – it really impressed me that you knew that statistic.'

She doesn't say anything. She picks up her knife and stares sadly at her dinner, which – I'm not shitting you – is now about a third of the size of what originally arrived.

Me and Christian exchange a look, which is all that has ever been necessary. That's the relationship between a number ten and a number twelve.

'Oh, well,' Sorcha goes, 'it looks like the diet storts tonight!'

Fair focks to the old biddy in the health food shop. She's trying to explain to me how appetite suppressants work. She's had, like, two or three cracks at it, but I'm only picking up the occasional word.

'Okay,' I go, 'explain it to me like I'm an eight-year-old boy.'

She's there, 'Well, have you ever heard of serotonin?'

'Okay, that's not going to work,' I go. 'Explain it to me like I'm a five-year-old boy.'

She laughs. I know a lot of Senior Cup players who buy their Creatine in here. She's obviously used to dealing with thick focks.

'Serotonin,' she goes, 'is the happy hormone.'

And that's when the penny suddenly drops.

'Ahhh,' I go, 'you always hear birds mentioning serotonin when they've got their . . . okay, I'm trying to think of a nice way of putting this . . . when the safety cor is out – you may or may not be an Fı fan – and they're horsing into the Galaxy.'

She goes, 'Well, chocolate *is* one of the things that increases the body's production of serotonin.'

'It's an amazing thing, science, isn't it? This conversation is actually making me want to improve my mind.'

I look at the tub in my hand. It's, like, the size of a jam jor and on the front it says, Size-Busta!

'So, serotonin,' I go. 'Continue on from there.'

She goes, 'Well, you've seen people binge-eat when they're unhappy.'

'Yes, I have. And it's not pretty to watch.'

'When our mood is low, our appetite – essentially our desire to increase our serotonin levels through food consumption – increases. So it stands to reason that if we stimulate our body's production of serotonin, our appetite diminishes.'

'Yeah, no, you're losing me again – a lot of big words in there. Just tell me what's actually in it?'

'Well, Size-Busta is one of the most popular dietary supplements on the market. It contains – have you heard of kumquats?'

'Hey, we're never out of Superquinn.'

'So you know what they are then. It contains Nagami kumquat extract and caffeine.'

'Caffeine? Caffeine as in coffee?'

'Yes, just regular caffeine. When combined with the kumquat extract, it confuses the brain into thinking that the stomach is full. It's also been found to speed up the process of fat burning.'

'Hey, these sound exactly what I'm looking for.'

'Are they *for* you – do you mind me asking?'

I actually laugh in her face.

I'm there, 'Yeah, no, you're right to ask. If someone with a body like this came in looking for diet pills, you'd have to wonder did that person have mental issues. No, they're actually for my wife. She – let's just be kind and say – *piled on the weight* while she was pregnant and then afterwards as well. We had triplets.'

'Well, like I said,' she goes, 'they're perfectly safe, one hundred percent natural and effective in the vast majority of cases.'

'And would she be able to taste them if I ground them up and put them in her tea?'

She's pretty shocked by the turn the conversation has suddenly taken.

She's like, 'What?' big focking saucer eyes on her.

I'm there, 'What I mean is, if I crushed them up into, like, powder, then I put them in, like, a hot drink, would she cop it? I'm noticing here on the packaging, it mentions that they're tasteless.'

She goes, 'I . . . I . . . I really wouldn't recommend giving them to someone without their knowledge,' and I can suddenly sense her becoming a little bit judgey, so I slap fifty snots down on the counter, put the tablets in my sky rocket and I get the fock out of there immediately.

Five minutes later, I'm walking along Stephen's Green on the way back to the cor, which I threw in, like, Fitzwilliam Square.

I'm about to ring Ronan to find out how he got on this morning. He had, like, Maths or French – one of those. And that's when I spot Fionn about fifty yords ahead of me, ducking into the old Shelbourne Hotel.

I cross Kildare Street and into the Shelly I go. I check the bor first, except he's not in there, then I find him in the Lord Mayor's Lounge, where my old dear always took afternoon tea until the management asked her to stop sitting so close to the window, because people looking in thought it was a fat farm.

Fionn is sitting with this bird in, like, an actual business suit. I think she's a ringer for Bérénice Marlohe. There's all that, like, awkwardness of a first meeting between them. *He's* talking with his hands a lot and *she's* sitting forward, pretending to find what he has to say interesting.

Again, Fionn isn't wearing his focking specs. And, again, he's dressed like the Rossmeister – from the boat shoes right up to the tip of his quiff.

I tip over to them. I'm like, 'Hey.'

She goes, 'Oh, hello – can I get an oolong tea, please? Fionn, what are you going to have?'

She thinks I'm the focking floor staff. I *am* wearing a black shirt, I suppose.

I'm there, 'Yeah, no, I'm actually a friend of this dude here. Although I barely recognize him these days without his goggles. Ross O'Carroll-Kelly is the name?'

She goes, 'Oh, hi, I'm Rowena – Rowena Stagles.'

She's English, by the way.

I'm there, 'The pleasure's mine, Rowena,' laying on the chorm and at the same time having a sly look down her shirt, admiring her grillework.

'Fionn's just been telling me about his ordeal in Uganda,' she goes. 'I'm fascinated to know how someone could survive an experience like that.'

Fionn goes, 'Rowena's over from London. Her company is interested in making a movie about the kidnapping.'

Neither of them has asked me to sit *down*, can I just mention?

I'm there, 'Cool. I wonder who'll play me. Possibly Jack Reynor, provided he buffs up.'

She goes – I swear to fock – 'Oh, were you in Uganda as well?'

I laugh. I end up *having* to? I turn around to Fionn and I go, 'Tell her.'

And that's when *he* says *the* most un-focking-believable thing.

'Yeah, he was there,' he goes, 'but it was at the very, very end, when it was as good as over. I'm not sure if he's strictly germane to the plot.'

I end up just, like, staring at the dude – whose focking life I *saved*, by the way? I should point that out, except I'm too in shock to even open my mouth.

This focking whatever-her-name-is goes, 'Do you know what I've been re-reading for the last few days, because I knew I was meeting you today – *An Evil Cradling*?'

Fionn's like, 'Oh, it's one of my favourite books of all time.'

'I actually see a lot of parallels between your story and what happened to Brian Keenan. Have you read it, Ross?'

I'm just, like, still staring at Fionn, giving him the filthy of all filthies.

'No,' I go, 'I haven't.'

She's like, 'Oh, you really should read it.'

I'm there, 'Unless he played rugby for Leinster and/or Ireland, I can tell you now that it's not going to happen.'

'I mean, the story is so awful – but at the same time it's also uplifting.'

'You're wasting your time still talking about it,' I go, talking to her, but still staring at Fionn, 'because I'm never going to focking read it. Now let's just agree to differ.'

She picks up on the vibe that there's suddenly, like, an issue here and that it's between me and Fionn, because she makes an excuse to leave.

She goes, 'I'm just going to go to the ladies' room. Ross, if you're not here when I come back, it was very nice to meet you.'

Then off she jolly well focks.

'Dude, what do you want?' he has the actual balls to go. 'I'm trying to have a meeting here.'

I'm there, 'Are you focking shitting me? *Ross was there at the very, very end, when it was as good as over. I'm not sure if he's strictly something to the plot.*'

'You *were* there at the very, very end.'

'I focking rescued you. *We* focking rescued you. We risked our lives. Me, Christian, Oisinn and JP.'

'Well, I haven't decided how you fit into the story yet.'

'Fit into the story?'

'It's the story of one man's ordeal at the hands of brutal captors, Dude. I don't want to risk crowding the narrative with too many peripheral characters.'

'You've got balls like focking church bells.'

'What do you think of her, by the way?'

'What?'

'Rowena – what do you think?'

I would let Mathieu Bastareaud punch me repeatedly in the face for an hour and a half just to drink the run-off from the washing machine that laundered her smalls.

I wouldn't tell Fionn that, though. I wouldn't give him the pleasure.

I'm there, 'She's okay? I'd say she's a seven – tops.'

He's like, 'Do you have any condoms on you?'

Again, I'm just, like, stunned into silence. It's like your granny asking you to get her donkey porn.

He goes, 'Ross, give me a condom. I'm going to suggest to her that we take the meeting upstairs to her room.'

I'm like, 'Jesus, Fionn, what the fock has happened to you?'

'Go on,' he just goes, 'get the fock out of here. She's coming back from the jacks.'

Sorcha doesn't seem to believe me and I'm struggling to explain it to her. I'm like, 'The only thing I can compare it to is when Spiderman became *Bad* Spidey?'

She just shakes her head. I think I might have watched that movie on my own.

She tries to go, 'What happened to him in Africa, Ross, it's bound to have changed him.'

I'm like, 'But not in a good way. I met him in The Queens last week and you'd want to hear the way he red-corded this bird. Then in the Shelbourne the other day – he was talking about this woman in a very disrespectful way.'

'And that upset you, did it?'

'Well, you know how much of a gentleman I can sometimes be.'

'You *can* be a gentleman,' she goes. 'Especially the past three days – oh my God, bringing me tea in bed every morning!'

I can't look at her. I've got one of those faces that tends to, I don't know, *incriminate* me?

I just go, 'Being married to someone is not a reason to stop making the effort, Sorcha.'

This is us sitting in the waiting room, by the way, waiting to see the famous Siofra focking Flynn. Sorcha is flicking through an old *Woman's Way* with, like, Bláthnaid Ní Chofaigh on the cover. Sorcha has literally no interest in Bláthnaid's skincare secrets, though. She just keep stopping on pictures of food, going, 'Look, Ross – bacon and pea cheesy risotto!' and, 'Look, Ross – creamy salmon tagliatelle!'

Three days on the tablets and her appetite is still exactly as it was – in fact, if anything, it's possibly *worse*?

I did read somewhere online that a huge port of it is actually psychological. So I then try to work that whole angle with her.

I'm like, 'Why are you constantly thinking about food, Sorcha?'

She's there, 'I don't know. I'm just, like, *storving* at the moment?'

'But *are* you, though?'

'What do you mean?'

'Think about it – are you *actually*?'

'Yes, Ross, I focking am.'

Her knee is bouncing up and down, by the way, and she's talking at twice the normal speed, which is possibly the caffeine. It says on the box that one of the possible side effects is, like, *jitters*?

I change the subject.

I'm like, 'Why the fock are we still coming here, do you mind me asking?'

She goes, 'Ross!' because the receptionist is listening. I don't *give* a fock. She knows I think her boss is a spoofer. 'Siofra told us from the beginning that we should see the programme through.'

'But I thought you'd come around to the view that Honor was, like, cured.'

Honor, I should mention, is over the other side of the waiting room, telling this totally random little girl that she has pretty hair. I think the poor kid is a little bit freaked out by the intensity of the attention Honor is giving her.

'Isn't her hair pretty, Mommy?' Honor keeps going. 'Oh my God, I'd love to have hair like that!'

Sorcha honestly can't see through it.

She goes, 'The way she mixes with other children now! It's so lovely to see.'

I'm there, 'That's why I don't see why we have to keep coming here. The first Lions Test is on this weekend. I can't give the game my proper attention during the week if I know I have to come here.'

A buzzer sounds and the receptionist goes, 'Doctor Flynn will see you now.'

Doctor Flynn! You'd have to admire the woman's balls.

In we focking go. Siofra's full of it, as usual. She's there, 'Hi, how has your week been?' and all the rest of it.

We sit down and Sorcha talks the woman through the last seven days in the life of the world's most perfect child. Honor sits through it, her two hands on her lap, grinning like a shot kangaroo.

Sorcha mentions that the two of them drove to Monart for a mother–daughter spa day and Honor – oh my God – had her first ever facial and her first ever mani-pedi. Then they had a movie night and they watched, like, *Brave* and *Madagascar 3*, snuggled up together under the duvet in Honor's room. Then Sorcha talked her through the book of recipes that her old dear gave to her and that Sorcha hopes Honor will one day pass on to her own children.

'And next week,' Sorcha goes, 'we're going into town to see

Barack Obama. He's doing, like, a whole speech thing in College Green.'

Honor goes, 'He's, like, *such* an inspiring man, isn't he, Mom?'

Sorcha's there, 'Absolutely. And I was a major, major supporter of his, even before anyone over here had heard of him, wasn't I, Ross?'

I'm like, 'Er, you were, yeah. They're saying he's from Offaly now – although I, personally, think he's full of shit.'

'And do you know what the really, really lovely thing is, Siofra? I actually feel – as mother and daughter – that Honor and I are, like, totally up to date on each other's lives.'

Seriously. Spare me.

'That's wonderful,' Siofra goes. 'Would you have imagined, even six months ago, that you would get to enjoy such a mutually reward-ing relationship – I'm actually going to use the word friendship – with each other?'

Sorcha's like, 'I'm going to be honest with you, Siofra, and say that it was my dream. But it was a dream I didn't think was ever going to be realized.'

Honor pipes up then.

She goes, 'Can I just say, Siofra – from *my* point of view? – I just feel – oh my God – *so* guilty about what I put my Mom and Dad through for all those years.'

Siofra goes, 'We talked about guilt in our one-to-one sessions, didn't we, Honor? And what did we say? It's the most useless of all emotions – because every day is a chance to start over.'

'I know. It's just, I can't believe it's taken me this long to realize how actually lucky I am to have the mom and dad that I have. They are literally the best parents in the world.'

I'm actually disappointed in Siofra, not seeing through this horse-shit act.

'Okay,' the woman goes, 'now can I talk to you, Sorcha, about something that's been, well, troubling me about your case?'

Shit. She *has* seen through it.

'Troubling you?' Sorcha goes, the full dramatic voice. 'Oh my God, Siofra, what?'

Siofra goes, 'Well, you've been coming to see me for, what, five or five and a half months now? So even though I've never paid you a home visit, I think I have a fairly good grasp on your domestic – shall we say – landscape?'

'Siofra, where's this going?'

'Your family situation is rather unconventional. I hope you'll forgive me for saying it. You, your husband and your four children living with one set of in-laws.'

'But that's what modern family *is* these days. Oh my God, Siofra, you of all people should know that.'

'Well, I'm a firm believer in the principle that children need strong adult role models who are, shall we say, in harmony with each other?'

'I believe that as well.'

'I'm rather concerned about the role of your mother and father in your home – especially your father. I know from our many conversations in this room that there is a sort of tit-for-tat battle of wills going on between him and Ross.'

Sorcha turns to me. She goes, 'You're making an effort to get along with him, aren't you, Ross?'

I'm there, 'I'm not actually – certainly not consciously.'

The next thing to come out of Siofra's mouth nearly floors me, because I genuinely thought the woman hated my guts.

'Actually,' she goes, 'I don't think the problem is that Ross doesn't get along with your father. What I'm suggesting to you is that your father's presence in the house is disrupting the happy equilibrium of your family life.'

I actually laugh out loud. That's how happy I am to hear it.

Sorcha goes, '*Excuse* me?' and she's all of a sudden the same Sorcha I remember from her days on the Model United Nations, defending the decision to send an Observer Mission to Angola.

Of course, I'm there, 'Let's hear the woman out, Sorcha. We're paying her enough. Carry on, Siofra – you were saying . . .'

But Sorcha's on her like a pigeon on vomit.

'I happen to have amazing, amazing parents,' she goes, 'and they have been – oh my God – *such* an unbelievable support to me. Who do you think is looking after the triplets today? Have you ever tried rearing triplets, Siofra?'

'I'm not saying you don't need help,' the woman – in fairness to her – goes. 'What I *am* saying is that, as it now stands, Honor has two fathers and two mothers.'

'A lot of people would consider that a good thing.'

'Well, as a child behavioural expert with seven years' experience, I *don't* consider it a good thing. Especially since your father seems to have difficulties severing the Oedipal bond between you. And that's manifesting in two ways – one is his constant hostility towards Ross and two is your constant undermining of Ross as a parental role model.'

I'm there, 'Can I just say, that this is all muesli to my ears.'

Sorcha goes, 'Shut the fock up, Ross!' and she literally uses those words.

I notice Honor straining to keep a straight face during all of this. The poor girl looks fit to burst.

Sorcha goes, 'Siofra, I think you're actually overstepping the mork there.'

Siofra goes, 'You came to me for professional help. I'm trying to give you – like I said – the benefit of my long experience. I don't think it's a good idea that your father continues to live with you. I think it's destabilizing your marriage and it's destabilizing the family unit.'

Sorcha stands up. It looks very much to me like we're done here.

I'm there, 'Sorcha, keep an open mind on this – there might be something in it.'

'My father is literally bankrupt,' she goes. 'And you are suggesting, what, that I put him out on the street? Come on, Honor, we're going.'

Honor stands up and I end up having to do the same.

Siofra goes, 'Please, sit down.'

Sorcha's like, 'No, we're finished here. Thank you, Siofra, for helping Honor become the daughter I've always wanted. But I'm not going to let you tear my family aport.'

She storms out of there, followed by Honor and then me. I'm the one apologizing – can you believe that? – to Siofra.

Sorcha says fock-all during the drive home, except three or four times when she goes, 'Oedipal? Did you hear her say that?'

I'm like, 'I did. I've no idea what it means, though.'

'It's disgusting.'

'Should we not even consider what she said, though? They could move back to Sandyford – maybe live with your sister.'

'Don't even, Ross. And I mean that – don't even.'

We finally arrive home. Sorcha storms straight up the stairs and I hear the bedroom door slam.

I follow Honor down to the kitchen. She opens the fridge and looks inside. 'Why is there never anything to eat in this house?' she goes. 'I'll answer that – because *she* focking eats it all.'

I just smile, not agreeing with her, but not disagreeing with her either.

I'm like, 'That went well, I thought.'

She goes, 'Stop trying to suck up to me.'

'I'm not trying to suck up to you. I'm just mentioning that it couldn't have gone better. Think about it. We don't have to go see that so-called Siofra anymore. And a supposedly qualified child psychiatrist has told her that it's not healthy having her old man living here.'

'If you think she's going to throw him out, you're deluded.'

'The seed has been planted, Honor – that's the point I'm making. I think we should definitely stick together, though.'

'You *are* trying to suck up to me.'

'I'm not.'

'I told you – you've made an enemy out of me and you're going to focking regret it.'

'If you've already done something, Honor, I wouldn't mind knowing what it is. Because I have to be honest with you here, *not* knowing is actually killing me?'

And it's at that exact moment that the house is suddenly shaken to its very foundations by the sound of Sorcha's blood-curdling screams.

I take the stairs like I'd take the Kardashian sisters – in threes and without actually looking at them.

By the time I reach our bedroom, Sorcha is literally trashing the place. She's, like, flinging open wardrobes and sweeping everything out of them onto the floor. She's pulling out drawers and tipping their contents onto the bed. She's turning over pieces of furniture and genuinely not giving a fock if they break.

It's, like, a full-on freak attack.

My first thought is that she's found the diet pills in my jacket pocket. I'm just about to say something along the lines of, 'You admitted yourself that you've got chunky, Babes – I was just giving you a gentle hoosh.'

But she goes, 'They're gone, Ross! They're gone!'

I'm there, 'Thank fock for that. What's gone?'

And that's when she says it.

She's like, 'My wedding and engagement rings.'

She continues turning the room over until it looks like Lindsay Lohan stayed the night.

I'm like, 'Are they not in that little drawer? I remember you not being able to get them on because your fingers were – okay, I'm going to say it – too fat.'

'No, they're not in the focking drawer,' she literally roars at me. 'That's why I'm turning the room upside-down.'

It suddenly hits me then. A feeling I can sum up in a single word. Focking Honor. This is her work. I suddenly know it like I know where the posts are on a rugby pitch.

I turn around and there she is, standing in the doorway of our bedroom, sobbing – or at least *pretending* to?

'Oh, Mommy!' she goes. 'I'm sorry! I'm so, so sorry!'

Sorcha looks up. She's like, 'Honor, what is it?'

'It's my fault! It's all my fault!'

Sorcha runs to her and she storts, I don't know, comforting her, giving it, 'What is it, Honor? What is it that has you this upset?'

It's some performance by the girl, in fairness to her.

She goes, 'It was a couple of weeks ago, Mommy – when Daddy brought those disadvantaged children to the house.'

Sorcha's there, 'Are you talking about Lamar and Tequila?'

Honor just nods.

She goes, 'We were playing Here Comes the Bride. And I remembered you saying to Daddy ages ago that you wished I used my imagination a bit more, so – oh my God, I'm so, so sorry, Mommy – I borrowed your rings from the drawer.'

Sorcha's like, 'You *borrowed* them?'

'It was just to help with the make-believe, Mommy. But I put them back. I swear to you.'

'Where did you put them back?'

'In the drawer. But now I'm thinking . . .'

'What, Honor? What are you thinking?'

'Tequila saw me put them back – and so did Lamar.'

Without even looking at me, Sorcha goes, 'Ross, get the cor keys.'

I'm there, 'Sorcha, I don't think we should go leaping to any conclusions here.'

'Ross!' she goes. 'Get! The focking! Cor keys!'

Down the stairs we chorge – me, followed by Sorcha, followed by Honor, going, 'Mommy, maybe Daddy is right. Maybe it's wrong to just assume that those *poor* children stole them.'

Sorcha's like, 'Come on, Honor – put your coat on.'

We bump into Sorcha's old pair in the driveway outside. They took the boys down to the beach in the big fock-off stroller while we were out seeing Siofra.

'We have to run,' Sorcha goes. 'It's an emergency.'

Into the Nissan Leaf we pile – me, Sorcha and Honor, like a South Dublin Frodo Baggins and his mates, setting off for a dangerous land in search of a valuable ring, except we're searching for two and we're in an electric focking cor.

The entire way there, Sorcha keeps going, 'Ross, can you *please* drive faster?'

And I'm like, 'You were the one who insisted on buying an environmentally friendly vehicle, Sorcha.'

Over the Liffey we go. The sky seems to dorken. Every time we pass a Cash for Gold shop, Sorcha turns hysterical.

'For someone who's, like, so clued-in politically,' she goes, tears streaming down her face. 'I'm also, like, *so* naive. I want the world to be this – oh my God – idealistic place.'

261

I'm there, 'We don't know that Lamar and Tequila took the rings, Sorcha.'

'Ross, did you *see* the smiles on their faces when they were leaving the house?'

Jesus, I did, now that she mentions it.

Honor's there, 'No, I'm to blame for this. It's all my fault.'

'It's not your fault,' Sorcha goes. 'And I do not want this to affect you, Honor. Because I do not want you to grow up in a world where you're frightened to trust.'

'Oh my God,' Honor goes, 'there's another Cash for Gold shop, Mom!'

The waterworks come on again.

It takes us the best port of an hour to get to Dordeen's gaff.

We pull up outside and I go, 'Look, can we *not* morch straight in there and stort throwing allegations around?'

'Ross,' Sorcha goes, 'do you have any idea what those rings are worth?'

I do. I was the one who focking paid for them.

She gets out of the cor. I turn around in my seat and I look at Honor. I'm there, 'Did you give those rings to those kids? Because now would be a good time to mention it.'

She goes, '*Excuse* me?'

I'm there, 'Is this it, Honor? Is this how you're getting back at me for taking away your credit cord privileges?'

'I'm sorry,' she goes. 'I'm too upset to talk,' and she gets out of the cor and follows her mother up to the door, where Sorcha is busy looking for a bell or a knocker or anything to rouse Dordeen from her famous afternoon television.

I just shake my head, get out of the cor and join them.

'You have to knock like this,' I go and I hammer on the door with my fist.

Thirty seconds later, Dordeen answers the door. It looks like she's been sleeping. Three o'clock in the afternoon.

Mind you, I'd normally be doing the same thing.

Sorcha goes, 'I'm sorry to disturb you, Dordeen, but can I speak to you, please?'

Dordeen goes, 'You can do whatever you waddent,' all easy-breezy.

Sorcha's like, 'Inside?'

Dordeen rolls her eyes and shakes her head and opens the door to let us in.

Into the sitting room we go. She was watching *Botched: When Plastic Surgery Goes Wrong* on TV3.

I try not to be judgemental about people, but they've got to meet me halfway.

'There's no nice way of putting this,' Sorcha goes.

I'm like, 'There might be, Babes – have a think about it before you open your mouth.'

There's a woman on the TV screen with a set of gams like bowling balls.

Sorcha goes, 'Your grandchildren stole my engagement ring and my wedding ring.'

Oh, Jesus Christ.

Dordeen thinks she's still focking dreaming.

She's like, 'Begga peerdon?'

Seriously – she thinks she's still asleep in front of the telly.

'They took them,' Sorcha goes, 'when they were at my house.'

Dordeen's there, 'How fooken deer you?'

'They were using them to play Here Comes the Bride. They saw Honor put them back in my drawer and they stole them. I'm sorry, Dordeen, I'm not one of those people who thinks poverty is an excuse for criminality.'

'Poverty?' Dordeen goes. 'You've some bleaten fooken cheek, meerchin in hee-er with yisser Southside fooken . . .'

'You can become as aggressive as you want, Dordeen. But I am not leaving this house without my rings.'

'Unless they've *fenced* them,' Honor goes – she has all the lingo, but I don't think it's going to help the situation.

Dordeen doesn't move. At the top of her voice, she just goes, 'Lamar! Tequila!' and five seconds later there's the sound of feet running down the stairs.

They burst into the living room. When they see Honor, they're all smiles. They're like, 'Ah, howiya, Hodor?'

Except Honor just turns her head. She won't look at them.

She goes, 'I can't believe you would do something like that. I thought we were friends.'

The two kids look bewildered, in fairness to them. They're either very good actors or they're, like, totally innocent.

Dordeen goes, 'They're accusing yous of robben.'

I'm there, 'Can I just say that *I'm* not? I'm very much keeping an open mind.'

'Robben what?' it's Tequila who goes.

'My wedding and engagement rings went missing from the house,' Sorcha goes. 'You were the last one wearing them – when you were playing Here Comes the Bride.'

Lamar goes, 'Hodor put them back in your droe-wer – when we were fidished eer gayum.'

'You *saw* her put them in the drawer?'

'I was looken at her, yeah.'

'Then as soon as her back was turned, you stole them, didn't you?'

'I dirn't.'

'One of you did.'

I'm like, 'Sorcha, we might dial it down a little bit – what do you think?' because I'm actually convinced now that they had fock-all to *do* with it?

Dordeen wants us out of the gaff. She's making that pretty much obvious.

She goes, 'You heerd what they're arthur saying. Thee ditn't touch your bleaten rings. And if there's one ting moy gerrant childorden ardent, it's loyers.'

But it's like Sorcha has suddenly lost all sense of reason.

'Children learn what they see at home,' she goes.

Dordeen's like, 'What's that apposed to meeyun?'

'Well, their grandfather is in prison, isn't he? For, like, *insurance* fraud? And their father – I'm presuming he's in jail as well, because he's certainly not on the scene.'

I'm like, 'Sorcha, we should go.'

'Yeah,' Dordeen goes, 'that'd be veddy woyuz.'

Sorcha's like, 'You have until the weekend. If you don't get those rings back from whatever Cash for Gold place you sold them to, I'm calling the Gords.'

Tequila and Lamar are like, 'The wha'?'

'The Gords!' Sorcha goes. 'The Gorda Síochána!' and then she turns and storms out of the gaff, followed by Honor, looking back over her shoulder at Lamar and Tequila and shaking her head in, like, a disappointed way.

'Yissuv some bleaten neerv,' Dordeen goes to me.

I'm just there, 'Hey, I can't keep everyone happy – I'm not a jor of Nutella.'

I feel bad for the two kids, because they're, like, nice kids and I know this is all port of Honor's evil plan. I reach into my pocket, whip out a roll of fifties and I peel one off.

'We don't want yisser chaddity,' Dordeen goes. 'Now get the bleaten fook out of this house.'

The reaction from Sorcha's old man is exactly what I *expected* it to be?

He's all, 'They did *what*?' at the top of his voice.

This is in the kitchen.

Sorcha goes, 'They stole my rings. And they may have . . . Ross, what was that word that Honor used?'

I'm there, 'What, fenced?'

'*Fenced* them,' she goes. 'They may have *fenced* them.'

It's hilarious listening to Sorcha try to talk street.

He's like, 'Well, what the hell are we doing about it?'

Even Sorcha's old dear gets in on the act. She's all, 'Sorcha, tell me you've gone to the authorities.'

Sorcha's there, 'I've given Lamar and Tequila until the weekend to get them back. Otherwise, I *will* involve the Gords.'

'Lamar and Tequila?' Sorcha's old man goes, like they're the craziest names he's ever heard. 'Whose children are they? Because they certainly don't sound local.'

'They're Shadden's niece and nephew,' Sorcha goes.

He turns and looks at me then, like *I'm* somehow to blame?

I'm like, 'What?'

He goes, 'Bringing bloody filth like that into our home.'

I end up totally losing it with him. I'm there, 'It's not *your* home. It's *our* home. You shouldn't even be here.'

Sorcha realizes what's coming, because she goes, 'Ross!' trying to silence me.

I'm there, 'No, I'm going to say it, Sorcha, because he needs to focking hear it. Even Siofra thinks it's a bad idea you two living here – and that's no offence to you, Mrs Lalor, because you've been great with the kids. Siofra said you're, I don't know, destabilizing our marriage and something, something, something.'

Sorcha goes, 'That was just an opinion,' because she can see her old man is rattled. 'It was the opinion of a woman who's never actually *been* in our home and has never seen how the whole thing just – oh my God – works.'

I'm like, 'Hey, a week ago, you thought the woman could do no wrong. The word genius got thrown into the mix. But it's a different story when she tells you to fock him out on his ear.'

He turns to Sorcha and he's like, 'Is that what she said? I'm destabilizing your marriage?'

'Again,' Sorcha goes, 'it's because she doesn't understand the whole concept of, like, modern family?'

'Because if you want your mother and me to move out, we can go upstairs and pack our bags right now.'

'We don't! Oh my God, we *so* don't!'

I'm there, 'I actually do. I'll drop you off wherever you want to go and there'll be no hord feelings. The focking airport preferably.'

Sorcha goes, 'Don't listen to him, Dad. This will always be your home – we're talking always, always, always.'

He stares at me, a little smile playing on his lips.

He's there, 'That's a lovely thing to hear, Sorcha. Now, what are we going to do about these items you've had stolen?'

'Like I said,' Sorcha goes, 'I've given them until the weekend.'

'These kind of people don't listen to ultimatums, Sorcha. The only thing that can reach them is the sound of a judge's gavel and a cell door slamming. I know the Sergeant in Dalkey, Sorcha. Barry Burnett. I could phone him right now.'

Sorcha's like, 'No. I've always believed that everybody deserves the chance to do the right thing.'

I walk out of the room. I've heard enough. Except Sorcha's old man follows me out into the hallway. 'Nice try,' he goes.

I'm there, 'Hey, I'm just quoting an expert in the field of whatever the fock she does. She thinks you're a bad influence on our home. She said you sound like a complete penis as well.'

I'm paraphrasing, of course. He just laughs that off – or at least *tries* to?

'You heard Sorcha,' he goes. 'I'm not going anywhere. By the way, maybe it's time we revisited the issue of your vasectomy.'

Now it's, like, *my* turn to laugh?

I'm like, 'Dude, that's dead in the water. Sorcha hasn't mentioned it since that little stunt you tried to pull in Sandycove. She obviously doesn't want me to have it anymore.'

He goes, 'Well, I'll just have to work on changing her mind, too. That September appointment she originally made – she never cancelled it, you know. And it's only, what, twelve weeks away?'

JP waits until half-time in the Lions match to drop the bombshell.

We've moved outside, just to throw a few more burgers and chicken wings on the old borbie and I'm about to give the goys my analysis, which is that we're possibly playing *too* much rugby out there and that Israel Folau is being allowed to rip the proverbial piss.

And like I said, JP drops his bombshell.

He's like, 'Chloe's pregnant.'

My mouth is full of Heineken and I end up nearly choking on it.

'What? The fock?' Oisinn goes – speaking, I think it's fair to say, for all of us.

'Yeah,' JP goes, putting a brave face on it. 'She's sixteen weeks gone.'

I'm like, 'Take my advice, Dude – deny, deny, deny! You might also consider going away for a while.'

Except JP just laughs.

'Ross,' he goes, 'we're happy about it.'

I'm, like, flipping the *meat* while this conversation is taking place? I'm going, 'Happy about it? Do you even realize what you're saying? Dude, you're focked.'

'We planned it,' he goes.

Now it's Christian and Oisinn's turn to be shocked. Oisinn's there, 'I knew you two were fock buddies. I didn't think there was anything more to it than that.'

And that's when JP tells us the entire story – although making sure to keep it short, because we've still got the second half to come.

He's like, 'Me and Chloe had this deal, going way, way back – I'm talking about when we were still in school – that if we hit thirty and we were both still single, we'd have a baby together. Thirty just seemed so old back then! Anyway, I bumped into her in Cavistons on Christmas Eve. I was walking in, she was walking out. Got talking about the old days and this pact we made when we were, like, seventeen. And I just said, "What about it?" That's how it happened.'

I'm there, 'You just decided to go halves on a baby? In the middle of Cavistons Food Emporium?'

He laughs and goes, 'Yeah, that's pretty much it. I mean, Chloe hasn't had much luck with men and time was ticking on for her. And of course you know what I went through with Shoshanna.'

She was an ex of his who told him she was pregnant with his baby, except the baby turned out to be black slash African-American.

He goes, 'So we just decided, why not? I mean, Chloe's not exactly unattractive.'

I'm there, 'Yeah, no, I've ridden her a few times myself over the years.'

I stort taking the meat off the barbecue and putting it onto the plate. I notice Oisinn watching me in a kind of, like, *disapproving* way? I wouldn't be a big believer in all those TV ads that tell you to have one plate for raw meat and one plate for cooked. We're lucky enough to live in a port of the world where diarrhoea is a laugh. It's a funny anecdote to tell people.

'Anyway,' JP goes, 'she's sixteen weeks gone and she wanted me to tell you in case, you know, you see her at Amie with an ie's wedding and you all stort speculating.'

It's Christian who raises his can to toast the news. He's there, 'Congratulations, Dude,' and we all do the exact same thing.

I hand Oisinn the plate piled high with meat and I go, 'Are we going to watch this second half or not?'

Back into the gaff we go.

Fionn hasn't shown up, by the way – he wussed out on us in a big-time way.

Sorcha calls me from the kitchen – she's in there with her old man – the dick – her old dear and the three boys. She goes, 'Ross, would you take Johnny, Leo and Brian up to the living room? We've got someone coming to see us.'

I don't even ask who's coming. I just go, 'Come on, goys – let's go and see Australia getting their orses handed to them.'

Up to the living room I bring them – two journeys – and they sit with me and the goys and they watch the second half, totally glued to it, although I end up having to cover little Johnny's eyes whenever Leigh Halfpenny takes a kick, because I don't want him picking up any bad habits that might derail my coaching later on.

God, I'm such a focking competitor.

Fionn finally shows his face twenty minutes into the second half – a big, smug head on him.

He's like, 'Sorry, I'm late, everyone,' and you can tell he's gagging for us to ask what he was doing that has him arriving with only, like, twenty minutes to go.

He even, like, *yawns*?

I actually can't take it anymore.

I'm there, 'Okay, why are you late? Are you going to give us the actual reason?'

He goes, 'Do you remember a girl called Abnoba Kennedy?'

I play dumb.

'The name doesn't ring a bell,' I try to go, 'and that's me being honest with you.'

He's there, 'She's in BNY Mellon. She's the head of something or other.'

'I'm going to say fair focks to the girl, even though I don't know her. And, what, you were with her – even though we agreed that we were all meeting up to watch the First Test?'

He's not even wearing a Lions jersey – again, something that was agreed beforehand.

He's lucky any of us are still even talking to him – trying to air-brush us out of the Um Gangum story.

'Here, look,' he goes, suddenly standing up and pulling up his shirt to show us his back. It's, like, covered in scratches – deep ones as well, the kind that would maybe leave a scor. 'She couldn't go on top for the last hour because my back was in literally flitters.'

Me and Christian exchange a look. I notice JP – who's holding Leo – and Oisinn – who's holding Brian – exchange a look, too. We're all thinking the exact same thing.

He thinks he's me.

I make the mistake of trying to smack him down. I'm there, 'Are you sure you can see the screen there, Fionn, without your glasses?'

He goes, 'It's funny you don't remember Abnoba, Ross, because she said she was with you, oh, a year or two ago.'

'Like I said, the name means literally nothing to me.'

'She said you were very quick.'

'Some girls like it quick.'

'And just before you finished – wait'll you hear this, goys – just before he finished, he started shouting, "Spoiler alert! Spoiler alert!"'

Christian, Oisinn and JP all laugh – more to humour him than anything.

I'm there, 'I just wanted to warn her that it was going to be a quickie. It's called good manners, Fionn.'

'Spoiler alert!' he goes. 'Spoiler alert!'

'Yeah, no, would you mind not talking about this shit in front of my children?'

He goes, 'Yeah, whatever. Here, can I borrow your laptop? I need to send an e-mail and I don't have my phone with me.'

I'm there, 'Yeah, whatever – it's over there.'

Then the rest of us go back to watching the match. It's close – we're talking way too close to even *enjoy* it?

It's, like, a two-point game with a minute to go and all of a sudden Australia win a penalty in a very kickable position.

We're all like, 'Fooocccckkk!!!' and even Fionn looks up from my computer.

Sorcha walks into the room at literally the moment that Kurtley Beale is spotting the ball to win it for Australia.

It's like she does it on purpose.

'Focking miss!' we're all shouting. 'Focking miss!'

Sorcha goes, 'Ross, can I see you in the kitchen for a minute?'

I'm there, 'Worst possible timing, Sorcha. Let me see this kick first.'

'It's kind of important.'

'So is this, Babes – any of these goys here will tell you that.'

Beale looks nervous. I'm the first one to say it and then everyone suddenly agrees with me. He measures six steps backwards, then storts shuffling his shoulders, trying to loosen himself up.

I'm there, 'Take it from someone who knows a thing or six about kicking. He's going to miss this.'

He takes a run at the ball. And then, just at the point of contact, he slips. The ball launches into the air like a duck hit with buckshot, wobbling low and short and wide of the posts.

We start jumping around the place, going totally apeshit. Even Johnny, Leo and Brain are laughing, loving it – they've just witnessed their first ever Lions Test win.

'Ross,' Sorcha goes, 'you need to come down to the kitchen now,' letting me know that the fun is over. 'There's someone waiting to speak to you.'

So of course I hand little Johnny to Christian and I follow Sorcha out of the room, still buzzing off the result. But the feeling only lasts the length of time it takes me to reach the kitchen.

Sorcha's old pair are in there and so is Honor – still wearing the *Is Féidir Linn* T-shirt she bought the day of the Obama visit – with a look of sadness on her face that I straight away know is put on.

And opposite them – I end up literally having to do a double-take – are two Gords.

Naturally, I'm there, 'Okay, what the fock?'

I look at Sorcha's old man, looking all pleased with himself.

Sorcha goes, 'Ross, I told Dordeen that if the rings weren't returned by the weekend, I'd ring the Gordaí.'

I'm there, 'Yeah, no, but we still don't know that Lamar and Tequila took them.'

'Honor has told these two Gords what happened, Ross, and you need to do the same.'

Boggers with Badges. They've both got, like, notebooks in front of them. I'm presuming one of them is Barry Burnett, Sorcha's old man's mate.

'You saw them playing together in Honor's room,' Sorcha goes, trying to prompt me.

I'm there, 'I didn't see them steal the rings, though. And I'm still not a hundred percent sure we need to involve the Feds, Babes.'

Sorcha goes, 'I'm really sorry, Ross, because I really like Shadden, and I've always been a huge advocate for people who come from areas of extreme disadvantage, but we're talking about a family that's steeped in criminality. That's the reality of the situation.'

I look at Honor, just sitting there, pretending to look sad for Lamar and Tequila. Kurtley Beale would kill for nerves like hers.

I'm there, 'I still think we should give those kids the benefit of the doubt. They seem genuinely cool to me – actually, that can be my statement.'

'And what about my rings?' Sorcha goes. 'Should I just forget about them?'

Her old man has to stick his hooter in then. He goes, 'They're covered under the home insurance. But we can't make a claim without reporting them stolen. So I suggest that you – as the person responsible for bringing those slum children into this house – tell these two gentlemen exactly what happened.'

One of the Gords goes, 'I should have esked – what's the velue of the two rings in quistion?'

Sorcha goes, 'My engagement ring was €80,000 – it's, like, a cluster of diamonds surrounding an amazing, amazing *centre* diamond? – and my wedding ring was, like, €20,000. Isn't that right, Ross?'

I'm there going, 'Yeah, no, that's it.'

'Thet's €100,000 in tawtal,' the cop goes, looking at me. 'Eeshy tousand for one ring and twinty tousand for thother.'

And I'm like, 'Er, yeah, exactly.'

Honor cops the slight hesitation in my voice. I just know it. Sensing weakness is something she happens to have a genuine gift for. She smiles at me across the table, like she instantly knows the truth.

See, I only *told* Sorcha that her engagement ring cost eighty Ks? It was actually more like eight. And the wedding ring that she thinks cost twenty? I'm not even sure that it's real gold.

The other Gorda dude goes, 'We have all we need for now, so we do. We'll go and talk to the two kids in quistion – see will they give them beck. If they won't, then you can come to the station in a day or two to make a formal steetmint and we priss cheerges.'

And across the kitchen, Honor gives me the most unbelievably evil smile.

8.

The Lady in Red (XXL)

Sorcha arrives home from Dalkey with cream cakes from the Country Bake and a face as miserable as a cod in mourning.

I'm up since four o'clock – as in, like, four o'clock in the morning. Leo is, like, teething at the moment and when one of the boys is awake, they're all awake. What I need more than anything right now is a nice quiet morning, but there's fock-all chance of that.

'We've been to Dalkey Gorda Station,' Sorcha goes, 'and Honor has made a formal statement, saying that Tequila and Lamar stole my rings.'

Honor steps into the kitchen behind her, a picture of happy innocence – put-on, of course.

I honestly didn't think she'd take it this far.

I'm there, 'I still say we're jumping the gun. Why don't I turn Honor's room over – see if *she* possibly took them?'

Sorcha reacts like I've just said *the* worst thing that a father could possibly say about his own daughter. She's like, 'Ross! How could you? After all the progress she's made?'

Honor gets in there, quick as a flash, and goes, 'It's okay, Mom. I understand why Daddy would think that of me, given my behaviour in the past.'

She's wearing the Dolce & Gabbana Embroidered Coronation Dress that cost me the guts of a grand – she's obviously storted moving all her clobber from the eaves into her actual wardrobe.

She goes, 'All I can do is keep trying to earn his trust and hopefully I one day will.'

Sorcha looks at me with her eyebrows raised, as if this little performance is proof of something.

While this conversation is taking place, by the way, Leo is going, 'Waaaaaahhhhhh! Waaaaaahhhhhhhhh! Waaaaaahhhhhh!'

Johnny is also going, 'Waaaaaahhhhhh! Waaaaaahhhhhhhhh! Waaaaaahhhhhh!' although not because he's teething – it's more, like, lack of sleep.

I've got one in either orm, then, with my right foot, I'm rocking Brian's little baby carrier, trying to distract him, so he doesn't kick off.

I'm there, 'Did the Feds talk to them – as in, Lamar and Tequila?'

Sorcha goes, 'Yes, they did.'

'And?'

'*And* they denied everything. Which, of course, they *would* do? Just like Kadden and Dordeen denied everything, too.'

'Maybe they denied it because they're innocent.'

'Oh, please, Ross! The Gord who took Honor's statement said Kadden is never out of those Cash for Gold places. They've nicknamed her Shirley Bassey. She's got, like, forty previous convictions, Ross. They think she probably had a buyer for the rings lined up.'

Honor goes, 'I was *so*, so lucky to be born with the parents I have. Hashtag, *blessed* much?'

She's laying it on with a focking trowel.

Leo and Johnny are still going, 'Waaaaaahhhhhh! Waaaaaahhhhhhhhh! Waaaaaahhhhhh!'

He steps into the kitchen then – as in Sorcha's old man? He drove them to the Gorda station – of course he focking did.

'The question,' he goes, 'is what those two children were doing in this house in the first place.'

Sorcha goes, 'They're Shadden's sister's children.'

'Sent here by their mother with orders to steal from us. You're too trusting, Sorcha – you always want to find the better motives in people.'

'I read Maya Angelou when I was eight.'

'I'm well aware of that. But you also have to be a realist, Sorcha. Children like that – they see people like us and they resent us for everything we've got.'

'You haven't got anything,' I go – I can't help myself. 'You gambled it away on bank shares and now you're living under your son-in-law's roof, sticking your big focking hooter in his bee's wax.'

Sorcha goes, 'Ross, the issue of Mum and Dad living here is closed as a topic of conversation – thank you.'

I shit you not. That's exactly what she says. Then she gives me a serious filthy that lasts for a good ten seconds.

Honor goes, 'Well, *I'm* going to do my best not to judge those children. I just have to be grateful that *I* wasn't born into that kind of poverty,' and Sorcha smiles at her like she's just said something deep and beautiful.

'Thank God they're covered under the home insurance,' Sorcha's old man goes. 'Although I can't imagine how much your premium is going to increase when they find out you've got the bloody dregs of – God forgive me! – North Dublin scurrying around the house, helping themselves to anything shiny that catches their eye.'

Brian storts up then. He's like, 'Waaaaaahhhhhh! Waaaaaahhhh-hhhhh! Waaaaaahhhhhh!'

Sorcha's old man picks him out of his carry cot and goes, 'Come on – let's take you for a walk around the garden!' and off he focks with him.

Honor says she needs to lie down after the emotion of the morning – then she focks off as well, presumably to go and troll Kristen Stewart or Caroline Flack.

Sorcha opens the cupboard, takes out a plate and puts it on the island in the middle of the kitchen. She opens the bag from Country Bake and storts laying the cakes out on it. We're talking chocolate éclairs. We're talking custard slices. We're talking cream doughnuts. She takes a humungous bite out of a coffee slice and she ends up with, like, cream and flaky pastry spilling down her face.

I'm staring at her and I'm thinking I can't increase her diet pill dosage any higher. She'll literally have a hort attack.

She goes, 'I'm going to make tea,' and she reaches for the kettle. 'Although I think I'm going to switch to decaf. I've got really bad jitters for some reason.'

The second her back is turned, I give the plate a shove with my hand and I knock the cakes onto the parquet floor.

I'm like, 'Oops.'

'Oh my God!' Sorcha goes, spinning around and staring at them lying face-down, cream and custard and icing sugar everywhere.

I'm there, 'Sorry, I'm obviously a little bit jittery myself. What a complete disaster, though, because they're obviously ruined. On the upside, though, I think there's rice crackers in the pantry.'

Sorcha – I shit you not – gets down on her hunkers, picks up the plate and storts putting the cakes back onto it. I'm watching her in just, like, pure shock.

I'm there, 'Sorcha, don't tell me you're going to . . .'

'Ten second rule,' she goes, putting the plate back on the island, then picking off the bits of dirt and fluff and hairs that have stuck to the cream. When she's finished doing that, she picks up a chocolate éclair and sinks her teeth into it like a lion breaking an antelope's neck.

'This is going to be my last major pig-out,' she goes, with her mouth full, 'before Amie with an ie's wedding. I definitely want to be able to fit into my red Alexander McQueen dress.'

Leo and Johnny are still going, 'Waaaaaahhhhhh! Waaaaaahhhhhhhhhh! Waaaaaahhhhhhh!'

Not for the first time recently, I feel like actually joining them.

'Are we going to hold on here?' the old man goes. 'Yes? No?'

I'm watching the second Lions Test in *his* gaff?

I'm like, 'Yeah, no, it's hord to say,' because we're leading by six points with, like, ten minutes left – except Australia look like they have more in the actual tank than we do.

That's what I tell him.

I'm there, 'Australia look like they've got more in the tank.'

He goes, 'Well, I shall have to take that on board, Ross, because no one can read a game of rugby like you can.'

'Well, it's weird you should say that, because I was only thinking last weekend what a massive, massive loss I was to the game in terms of what I could have contributed.'

'Oh, the loss is incalculable! No other word for it!'

Helen suddenly arrives home from tennis. She obviously didn't know I was going to be here because she sticks her head around the living-room door all smiles and then when she sees me, her expression suddenly changes.

She goes, 'Oh, Ross. I didn't expect . . . Hello.'

I'm there, 'Hey, Helen,' because I'm very much a social animal. 'How the hell are you?'

She's like, 'Fine, thank you,' and then off she goes.

I turn around to the old man and I'm like, 'I genuinely don't think she's ever going to forgive me for what happened in Orgentina.'

He's there, 'Give it time, Ross. I'm sure she'll come round.'

'She focking better. Because she's always been one of my biggest supporters.'

'She just can't for the life of her understand why you would have kept it to yourself about finding Erika.'

'Have you tried telling her to cop on?'

'I told her that you had your own way of operating. You were the same on the rugby field, of course. You never knew *what* the angle of attack was going to be. It's a metaphor for the way he conducts himself in life, I told her.'

'And what was her reaction to that?'

'I think she might need another week or two to, you know, really think the metaphor through.'

Australia are in our twenty-two.

'I focking hate you,' I suddenly go, 'you total and utter focktard.'

I'm not talking to the old man, I probably should mention. I'm talking to Adam Ashley-Cooper, who crashes over the line after fifteen focking phases.

'You said it!' the old man goes. 'You said Australia had more in the tank!'

I'm there, 'It gives me no pleasure whatsoever to be proven totally right yet again.'

Christian Lealiifano adds the cheese and crackers to the bill and suddenly we're a point down with four minutes to go.

The old man goes, 'Helen and I are talking about going to Seattle.'

I'm like, 'When?'

'We were thinking maybe the end of August.'

'Well, I'll obviously come.'

'Em, I'm not sure if that's, um, such a good idea, Ross.'

'Why not? I found her once, didn't I?'

'I think we may have difficulty persuading Helen that it's the wonderful idea that you and I know it to be.'

What he seems to be saying is that Helen doesn't want me there. I'm like, 'We'll talk about this again.'

'Yes!' the old man suddenly goes.

We've won a penalty on the halfway line and Leigh Halfpenny has the chance to clinch the series with, like, the final kick of the game.

'Does he have the bottle?' the old man goes.

I'm there, 'Every kicker has bottle. If we didn't, we couldn't do what we do. The real question is, does he have the distance? My suspicion is no.'

I end up being proven right yet again. The kick doesn't have the legs to go over the bor and Australia have suddenly levelled the series.

The old man goes, 'I think I'm a bit of an albatross, Ross. Every time you and I watch a match together, we seem to be on the losing side.'

I'm there, 'I certainly won't be watching the Third Test with you. You're a focking jinx.'

That's when my phone goes, 'It's Kearney time!'

It's, like, a number I don't *recognize*? I end up answering it anyway.

I'm there, 'You've got Ross!' which is a new way I've storted answering my phone.

I really like it.

A bird's voice goes, 'Oh, hi, Ross – how are you?'

The old man looks at me and mouths the word, 'Brandy?'

I nod, then I sort of, like, gesture to him to make it a lorge one. He focks off to the study to get the good XO.

I'm like, 'So who is this? I have to say, the voice has me intrigued.'

She's there, 'I don't know if you even remember me. Becky McGrew?'

I laugh.

I'm like, 'Becky McGrew? I don't believe it. I was actually talking about you very, very recently.'

I put her name on the Fock It List, if you remember – although I don't mention that fact to her.

She's there, 'Oh my God!'

There was always a serious chemistry between me and Becky back in our UCD days. I think she studied International Commerce with French but ended up working in recruitment, the big focking ride.

I'm like, 'Yeah, no, I was talking to – I don't know if you remember him – but JP Conroy and your name, let's just say, cropped up.'

This is a bird who looks like Jessica Michibata, bear in mind.

She goes, 'That is *such* a coincidence, because I actually met another friend of yours the other night – Fionn de Barra?'

I'm there, 'Fionn?' already with a feeling of dread in my stomach. 'Where did you meet *him*?'

'It's weird,' she goes, 'because he actually just rang me randomly – as in, like, totally out of the blue? He said he saw a girl who he *thought* was me on Grafton Street and he was worried that he'd snubbed me.'

'Was he now?'

'Anyway, we got talking about, you know, just the old days and we ended up going for a drink in the Merrion Inn.'

That's pretty focking slick – I have to hand it to Fionn.

'Anyhooo,' she goes, in a slightly embarrassed way, 'the thing is, we exchanged numbers and, well, the number he gave me doesn't seem to be working and I'm wondering did I possibly key it into my phone wrong?'

I laugh. I have to.

I'm there, 'Okay, what number did he give you?'

She reads it out to me. It's literally nothing like Fionn's number. It's only the 0 and the 8 at the very stort that are the same. So I give her Fionn's real number. It doesn't strike her at all odd that it's fock-all like the one he gave her.

I have to say, I find stupidity a very attractive quality in a girl.

I'm there, 'Try that number,' loving that I'm hanging the focker out to dry here. 'So, er, do you actually like him?' sort of, like, probing around the edges, trying to find out did he throw her a bone.

She's like, 'I have to say, he's nothing at all like I remembered him. He's definitely a lot more confident.'

I'm there, 'Was he wearing his glasses?'

'No, he's getting his eyes lasered!'

'Yeah, no, that's certainly the talk alright.'

'I really like him. I always kind of fancied him in college.'

That's a lie. No one fancied Fionn in college.

She goes, 'And he's come through that whole kidnapping ordeal – oh my God – so well. He's, like, so, so brave.'

I'm there, 'Did he mention me at all?'

'Er, I don't think so.'

'As being someone who was involved in actually rescuing him?'

'Recuing him? He told me he escaped.'

'He also told you his number was 08 whatever the fock he said.'

'Sorry?'

'Yeah, no, nothing – forget it. Look, can I just say, Becky, the reason your name came up with me recently was that I was telling JP that I really regretted that nothing ever happened between us. You're actually on my list of, let's just say, missed opportunities?'

'Er, okay.'

'And I was wondering did you maybe fancy going for a drink some time?'

'With you?'

'Hey, if it's Fionn's feelings you're worried about, I wouldn't bother. I hate telling tales out of school, but he's actually dicking you around royally.'

'I'm not worried about Fionn. I'm thinking about the fact that you're married.'

'Married? I don't know where you get your information from.'

'You're married to Sorcha Lalor. I used to go into her shop all the time.'

'You really should get your facts straight in future.'

'Didn't you just have triplets?'

'Look, I'm going to hang up on you now. I tried to warn you off the dude, but you don't seem ready to listen.'

So I *do* end up hanging up on the girl.

Then I'm sitting there watching Warren Gatland doing his post-match interview, thinking about Fionn – of all people – ploughing Becky McGrew and I stort to experience this unusual feeling that I slowly come around to recognizing as jealousy.

And then two things suddenly hit me in quick, I don't know, succession. The first is the memory of Fionn sitting in my gaff a week ago asking me if he could borrow my laptop. The second is a realization that sends my blood literally cold.

The old man appears with two massive brandies and I end up just blurting it out, there in the room.

'Oh my God,' I go. 'Fionn has stolen the Fock It List!'

So I'm sitting in the gorden. I've got the three boys sitting in, like, a semi-circle on the grass and I'm, like, rolling a rugby ball towards them, to try to get them used to its movement.

Sorcha suddenly appears. She's eating again – a packet of focking Tayto this time.

Appetite suppressants, my focking hole.

She sees Brian with the little rugby ball in his hands and she goes, 'Ross, they have *other* toys, you know?'

I'm there, 'I just want them to have a feel for the ball so that they're never strangers to it.'

She goes, 'I'm just saying that it would be helpful in terms of their cognitive development to let them play with other toys, like building-blocks.'

I just ignore her. She's being ridiculous.

I notice that, as well as the crisps, she has, like, an envelope in her hands. I'm like, 'What's that, Babes?'

She goes, 'I've filled in the claim form for the insurance company and the Gords have signed it. Can you dig out the receipts?'

I'm like, 'What?' at the same time thinking, 'Shit!'

She goes, 'Er, the receipts for the *rings*?'

I'm like, 'Why do you need *those*?'

'Ross, they're not going to just hand over €100,000 without me providing proof of purchase.'

'I mean, who even *keeps* receipts, Sorcha?'

'It's fine. I can go to Weir's. They'll have a record, I'm sure.'

They won't have a record of us.

I probably should tell you the full story behind Sorcha's engagement and wedding rings. I played rugby in UCD with a dude called Gus Hogarth. Handsome, was his nickname. And, like me, he never actually made it in the game.

Handsome's brother happened to be a jeweller, and when me and Sorcha got engaged, he got me a deal on an engagement ring. Eight Ks he chorged me for it, even though it was probably worth fourteen. Which, back in '03 slash '04, was actually a pretty decent amount to pay for a ring. Except then a lot of Sorcha's *friends* storted to get engaged? This was in, like, '05 slash '06 – we're talking the actual heyday of the Celtic Tiger – and suddenly everyone was talking about how much their ring was actually worth, like it was a major deal.

This question had genuinely never occurred to Sorcha before. She loved her ring and she loved the fact that I picked it out myself. Or at least she thought I did. Handsome actually picked it.

But suddenly every second conversation seemed to revolve around how much this person or that person spent on their engagement ring. And the amounts seemed to keep going up all the time. Fifty grand. Sixty grand. Seventy grand.

And then – you could say inevitably – Sorcha storted asking me how much *hers* was worth?

'I don't actually *care*?' she'd go. 'I'd just like to know.'

So I was like, 'It was very, very expensive – that's all I'm prepared to say.'

But she was there, 'Are we talking more than sixty?'

And I was like, 'Hmmm.'

'More than seventy?'

'Er, yeah.'

'Eighty? Oh my God, Ross, you didn't pay €80,000 for my engagement ring?'

She seemed quite pleased by this idea, so I went, 'Yeah, no, I did, yeah. Eighty Ks it cost me – and your wedding ring was twenty.'

Her wedding ring, by the way, is a piece of shit.

Later on, when it became the fashion at, like, dinner porties to talk about clarity and carats and all that shit, Handsome's brother got me some paperwork – faked, of course – that allowed Sorcha to talk knowledgably about the stones on her finger, never knowing that she was actually talking out of her orse.

I genuinely never expected it to come up again. But now there's all this.

'Weir's?' I go.

She's like, 'Yeah, isn't that where you said you bought them?'

'Er, yeah, no, it is. Except I've actually just remembered where the receipts are. So we don't need to go bothering them.'

'Where are they? Because I want to post this today.'

'Well, I know *roughly* where they are? I'll tell you what, I'll take that claim form and I'll go and look for the receipts now. When I find them, I'll lash them in the envelope and I'll post it this afternoon.'

She stares at me for a good five seconds. It's like she's wondering if she can trust me. She decides that she can.

Like I said, I love stupidity in a girl.

She hands me the envelope and I slip it into my pocket.

That's when Honor steps out into the gorden. She goes, 'Come on, Mommy, let's go. I'm so excited!'

Sorcha goes, 'I'm coming now, Honor!' and then she turns around to me and she's like, 'Do you mind looking after the boys for a couple of hours? They're doing organic chocolate facials in the spa in Enniskerry.'

And they said that the Celtic Tiger would never be back.

'Yeah, no,' I go, 'you two go and enjoy yourselves. I might just grab a quick word with Honor first.'

If Sorcha sees anything unusual about this, she doesn't mention it. She just walks back into the house – her orse like two basketballs.

Honor goes, 'What did you just put in your pocket?'

I'm there, 'Yeah, no, that's none of your bee's wax.'

'I actually *know* what it was? It's the claim form for the insurance company.'

'Honor, you need to tell me what happened to those rings.'

'I've already told the Gords. Those disadvantaged children took them.'

I try to frighten her, then – to scare her straight.

'Honor,' I go, 'you do realize how much trouble we could all end up in if I actually post this insurance claim. If they pay us a hundred thousand euros and it turns out that the rings were never actually stolen, well, that's technically insurance fraud.'

'You and *her* will have committed insurance fraud, not me.'

'Yeah, but if we go to jail, you'll end up being taken into care. You'll be living with disadvantaged children yourself. You'll actually *be* one?'

'Yeah,' she just goes, 'spare me,' and then she turns and storts walking back to the gaff.

I'm there, 'You won't be able to keep it up, you know?'

She looks over her shoulder at me.

She's like, 'What are you talking about?'

I'm there, 'That Goody Two Shoes act you're putting on for your old dear. You won't be able to keep it up. The true you will come out. It's bound to.'

She goes, 'It's funny, our love/hate relationship has turned into a hate/why won't you focking die? one.'

She has a lot of good one-liners in her locker, to be fair to the girl.

Off she goes.

I continue rolling the ball to the boys, while trying to figure out what to do. After, like, ten minutes of solid thinking, I decide that I have no option but to look for the rings, which means basically turning over Honor's room.

I bring the boys back into the gaff. It's, like, time for their nap anyway and they're pretty wrecked after training. It only takes me about fifteen minutes to get them down.

I tip into Honor's room. I actually *literally* tip into it, even though she's not home. It's amazing how terrified I am of the girl.

I open cupboards and I pull out drawers. I look under her bed and under every pile of clothes in her wardrobe. I look between the pages of every book. I search every little box and tin on her dressing table and I search the pockets of literally every item of clothing she owns. I spend two hours turning that room over. I even crawl into the eaves and search the boxes of shit that I bought her and which she hasn't managed to slip into her actual wardrobe yet.

There's no sign of the rings.

I eventually give up. I go into our bedroom and I lie down on the bed. A lot of my, I suppose, deepest thoughts come to me when I'm, like, lying down. Unfortunately, this ends up not being one of those occasions. I try to come up with a plan, but there is literally nothing in my head.

I turn onto my side and I stort drifting off to sleep. And that's when I spot the empty Toblerone box and the little pile of silver paper on top of Sorcha's locker. That was a *full* Toblerone at, like, ten o'clock this morning.

She's eating like an unemployed person.

I end up totally flipping. I jump up from the bed. It's like a switch has been suddenly flicked in my head.

A lot of people will tell you that the secret to a happy life is to keep shit simple. I'm, like, a firm believer in that advice, even though I've never been able to follow it. Like my old man said, I've my own way of looking at the world.

I go into Sorcha's walk-in wardrobe and I find the red Alexander McQueen dress that she's planning to wear to Amie with an ie's wedding. I fold it up and I stick it into a bag. Then I wake the boys and I tell them that we're taking a little road trip.

The dude in the alterations place looks at me like I'm as mad as a wet hen. I end up having to go, 'I don't see what the issue is here. I'm just looking to have a dress taken in. That's what you do, isn't it?'

He goes, 'It's just very unusual to be asked to alter a dress without an actual fitting.'

I hate myself for having to do this. But I have no other choice. Sorcha, like her daughter, needs to be scared straight. Not that there's any danger of her fitting into the dress anyway. But I just think the bigger the fright she gets when she puts it on her, the more serious she's going to be about losing the excess poundage.

I'm there, 'I told you, my wife is too busy to come in for a fitting. She has all sorts of shit on. That's why she told me to come in and get it done for her.'

He puts on his little half-glasses and holds the dress up. 'Well,' he goes, 'how much does she want it taken in by?'

I'm there, 'Does a foot sound mad?'

'A foot?'

'Yeah, no, is that too much?'

'A foot? As in, twelve inches?'

'I've no idea how many inches are involved. You're the supposed tailor here.'

They're like chemists, these fockers. They want you to think their job involves more than it actually *does*?

'I couldn't take twelve inches off this without cutting the fabric,' he goes.

I'm there, 'Like I said, she's lost a bit of weight.'

'Has she got the Ebola virus?'

'No, she doesn't have the Ebola virus.'

'Because twelve inches is a huge amount. Let me show you.'

He folds the dress to show me what it'd look like. He's right. It's half the focking size. Michael Fassbender in *Hunger* would be spilling out of it.

'The most I could take this in,' he goes, 'without interfering with the cut of the dress is two inches either side.'

I'm like, 'Two inches?'

'Yes.'

'Okay, go on, do it.'

Johnny storts squealing then. I've got the three boys in the big fock-off stroller. I whip out a little zip-lock bag full of sweet potato fingers and I give them each one. The woman behind me in the queue is massively impressed.

'They're beautiful,' she goes.

I'm like, 'Yeah, no, thanks.'

I don't give her any more than that. Looks-wise, she's a bit of a sheep-beast.

'Okay,' the dude goes, writing me out a ticket, 'you do understand that, by not coming in for a fitting, I'll be doing this purely at the owner's risk. There's no point in your wife coming back and complaining if she puts it on and discovers that it doesn't fit.'

'Yeah, whatever. You're actually becoming a bit boring now, so I'm going to head off. When will it be ready?'

'Wednesday of next week,' he goes, then he hands me the old Lemony.

The focking dog of a woman I mentioned earlier holds one door open for me and I hold open the second one and I manage to manoeuvre the stroller out through it and back out onto Blackrock Main Street.

That's when I hear Ryle go, 'It's Kearney time!' in my pocket.

I whip out my phone. It ends up being Fionn. He has the actual balls to try to put *me* on the defensive? He goes, 'Did you give Becky McGrew my number?'

I'm like, 'Yeah, no, she rang me up and she asked me for it.'

'There's a reason I gave her the wrong one – and that's because I didn't want to hear from her again.'

'Do you know how like *me* you've suddenly become?'

'You'd no focking right to do that.'

'Well, since you brought up the subjects of rights . . .'

'What?'

'You stole something of mine.'

'What are you talking about?'

'You know what I'm talking about. The Fock It List. You took it.'

He laughs. He *actually* laughs.

I'm there, 'Don't tell me you're actually working your way through it?'

He goes, 'Do you know who I bumped into this morning? Tlachtga Ní Dhuibhir.'

'Okay, I'm calling bullshit on that one.'

'Did you know she works in a candle shop in the Westbury Mall? Well, she actually owns the place.'

'Dude, you might get lucky with one or two. But there's no way in this world you're going to go through that entire list.'

'We're going for a drink tonight.'

'Dude, these are sympathy rides you're getting. Do you hear me? Sympathy rides!'

'And if she or anyone else rings you looking for my number, tell them you don't focking have it.'

He hangs up on me.

I'm left standing there on Blackrock Main Street, literally stunned. A few seconds later, my phone goes again. At first, roysh, I think it must be Fionn, ringing back to apologize. Except it ends up being Oisinn.

He's there, 'Where are you, Dude?'

I'm like, 'I'm in Blackrock. What's the craic?'

'Have you heard the news?'

'Is this about Fionn and Becky McGrew?'

'No.'

'Because you know he stole the Fock It List?'

'It's nothing to do with Fionn. Ross, everything you ever said about Warren Gatland was one hundred percent true.'

'He's a dickhead and he knows fock-all about rugby, despite all the things he's achieved in the game. I'm just glad I had the opportunity to say it to his face.'

'He's dropped Drico.'

'Sorry, I think I misheard you there, Dude.'

'You didn't. He's left Brian O'Driscoll out for the Third Test.'

I suddenly feel like I've been punched in the solar plexus.

'Dude,' I go, 'look at the team again. Maybe he's switched him to *inside* centre. Eddie O'Sullivan did that once or twice.'

He's like, 'Ross, you're not listening to me. It's all over the news. He's going for Jonathan Davies and Jamie Roberts in the centre. Drico's not even on the bench.'

Something smells nice. I mention it as well. I'm like, 'Something smells nice.'

It's drifting up from the kitchen to the living room.

'It's my tuna Bolognese,' Sorcha goes. 'And you really should get dressed, Ross. Our guests will be here any minute.'

I'm like, 'Guests?' because I'm at a genuine loss here.

I do *listen* to Sorcha? But it's also necessary to filter out the enormous amounts of spam that tend to be part of her general convo. Sometimes important stuff gets lost in the shuffle. Like now.

'I told you,' she goes, 'Claire and Garret are coming for dinner.'

She means Claire from Bray of all places and that ridiculous focking drip she married.

I'm there, 'I think you've lost the plot, Babes. They emigrated. To Canada. I went on a three-day bender to celebrate.'

'Well, they're back for a holiday,' she goes. 'It's Claire's grandmother's ninetieth birthday and they're going to be here for Amie with an ie's wedding as well.'

I don't focking believe it.

'But why do *we* have to see them?' I go. 'I genuinely focking hate them.'

She's there, 'Because Claire is – oh my God – one of my best friends, Ross.'

I also hate dinner porties – and that's as a *general* rule? Four or five hours of shite talk about what box sets we've seen and haven't seen and aren't Polish people mad fockers for the work, to be fair to them?

I go, 'I've already said my goodbyes and good riddances to that pair of saps. I was kind of happy with the way it ended. I actually might hit Kielys. The third Lions Test is tomorrow and there's going to be a lot of people wanting to hear my analysis of how we're going to do without Drico.'

Except it's suddenly too late. The doorbell rings, Sorcha goes out to answer it and, after sixty seconds of high decibel Oh My God-ing in the hallway, into the living room they focking troop – Sorcha, followed by Claire, followed by *him*, carrying six bottles of whatever ridiculous focking piss he happens to be drinking this week.

Garret is one of those craft beer people.

I make sure to give Claire a massive hug that goes on for about ten seconds longer than just plain friendly. It drives *him* mad that I curled her toes once or twice in a previous life and I like to constantly remind him of that fact.

'Sit down,' Sorcha goes. 'We want to know – oh my God – everything about your new life in Toronto!'

I don't. I couldn't give a toss.

Claire launches straight into it, of course. She's like, 'Oh my God, we are talking, like, *total* lifestyle change? Do you remember I famously couldn't find a Pilates instructor in Dublin who suited me? Well, I found one within, like, two days of moving to Canada! And I had my allergies finally tested and it turns out that I *am* gluten-intolerant – to the point of being almost – but not quite – *coeliac?*'

She lets that hang there for a good ten seconds. I think she's waiting for us to say fair focks – congratulations.

Sorcha lets me down in a big-time way. She goes, 'Oh my God, you always suspected you were!'

And Claire's there, 'I know! And we were only in Canada, like, two weeks before I had it confirmed. So we're both gluten-free now. And Canada is such an easy country to be gluten-free in.'

I hate listening to people who emigrated during the current economic blahdy-blah coming home and telling you how shit Ireland is compared to wherever they've chosen to live instead. I'm very patriotic about my country – well, certain bits of it.

'It's a wonder you focking came back,' I go. 'I don't think anyone here would have complained if they'd never clapped eyes on you again.'

Sorcha gives me a serious filthy.

'Ross,' she goes, 'go and put Garret's beers in the fridge. Come on, Claire, come on, Garret, I'm dying to introduce you to the boys.'

She brings the two of them upstairs to look at the babies and I head down to the kitchen.

What Garret's drinking is a beer called – I'm not shitting you here – the Hairy Bishop. It's a joke. I open all six bottles, very carefully, so as not to dent the tops. I empty them all down the sink, then I fill all six bottles with Heineken and I put the tops back on them.

I go back up to the living room just as they're coming down the stairs again. Sorcha is telling Claire that tonight is going to be – oh my God – her last major pig-out before Amie with an ie's wedding.

The big day is, like, a week and a half away and she's about to eat tuna Bolognese with about a pound and a half of cheese in each serving. Seriously, those diet pills were the biggest waste of money since Michael Cheika signed CJ van der Linde. I'd bring them back, except the woman in the shop looked like she might call the Feds if she ever set eyes on me again.

Sorcha says she's – oh my God – determined to fit into her red Alexander McQueen dress, which, by the way, is back from the alterations place and hanging up in her wardrobe.

'You don't need to lose weight!' Claire goes.

Girls can be real bitches.

She goes, 'Look at you, Sorcha – there isn't a pick on you!'

And I'm there, 'If Sorcha wants to lose a few stone to feel better about herself, then who the fock are you to try to stop her?'

Sorcha goes, 'Ross, don't be rude. Yes, I've been thinking of going on one of those, like, *juice* diets? The only thing is the cravings. I've tried, like, fruit diets before and I'm always – oh my God – storving!'

Claire's like, 'Have you heard about the tongue patch diet?'

'What's the tongue patch diet?'

'Yeah, no, it's this *thing* – it's, like, huge in the States? There's a place on, like, Baggot Street does it.'

'Yeah, no, but what is it?'

'They literally sew a piece of plastic mesh onto your tongue. It makes it, like, impossible to eat solid food – well, not impossible, but, like, really, really *painful*?'

Sorcha screws up her face. 'Plastic mesh?' she goes. 'That's, like, oh my God!'

Claire's there, 'I know. It's the same stuff they use in, like, hernia repairs? I saw a girl on TV and she lost, like, twenty pounds in ten days.'

'Oh my God, that's, like, *drastic*?'

'It only takes, like, ten minutes to fit it. And then you're allowed something like 800 calories a day – except it's obviously all juice and clear broth and protein shakes, because eating solid food would, like, seriously hurt the roof of your mouth.'

'Well,' Sorcha goes, 'I hope I'm never so overweight that I need something like that!'

No one says a word.

It doesn't take Claire long to steer the conversation back around to their wonderful new life in Canada. She goes, 'I have to show you the photographs of the shop! Garret, you brought the iPad, didn't you?'

Of course he focking did. He whips it out and storts showing Sorcha all these photographs of, like, a coffee shop. It's, like, an exact replica of Wheat Bray Love, the organic bakery they wanted to open on the Quinsboro Road until the banks laughed them out the focking door. See, that was the reason they emigrated. Having never experienced a Celtic Tiger of their own, Canada's banks are apparently quite happy to pour good money down the drain.

'We're going to be opening the first week in September,' he storts going. 'See, this is what Bray *could* have had – and now Toronto's going to have it, thanks to the fact that Canada's banks are actually genuinely interested in helping small businesses.'

It's at that exact moment that Honor steps into the room. She goes, 'Oh my God, it's Claire and Garret!' and you can see from their reaction that they're expecting her to follow up with some horrible comment about Bray or something else. But she doesn't. She shakes both of their hands and goes, 'It's lovely to see you again!'

Claire's looking at Sorcha, wondering is it even the same kid.

Honor goes, 'Can I get anyone a drink?'

Garret's like, 'Er, I'll have one of my beers. I think Ross put them in the fridge.'

He really is an orsehole of the highest order.

'And I'll have, I don't know, just a glass of wine,' Claire goes.

Honor's there, 'What colour?' because that's a whole thing, isn't it – red or white?

Claire goes, 'Oh, that depends – what are we having to eat, Sorcha?'

A wine snob from Old Court or whatever focking Council-built township she was dragged up in.

Sorcha goes, 'It's fish. It's actually my famous tuna Bolognese.'

Claire goes, 'Oh my God, there's nothing in it that I'd be allergic to, is there?'

Sorcha's there, 'I used flour to thicken the sauce but it was, like, gluten-free flour.'

'Thank God,' Claire goes, 'because my small intestine cannot handle gluten! I'll have white wine, so.'

Sorcha's like, 'There's a lovely bottle in the fridge, Honor. It's a Sauvignon Blanc.'

Off Honor goes to get the drinks.

'Oh my God,' Claire goes when she's gone, 'she's, like, a totally different child – no offence, Sorcha.'

Sorcha laughs. She's like, 'I know! It's *actually* a miracle? It's all down to this amazing, amazing counsellor slash behavioural therapist we found. Although we stopped going because she was becoming a bit, I don't know, *controlling?*'

'Oh my God.'

'She wanted me to throw my mom and dad out of the house and obviously I was like, er, my mum and dad are my best friends?'

'Totally.'

Sorcha leads the way into the dining room then. The table is set up like we're expecting royalty – we're talking candles, the good Vera Wang dinnerware and everything.

He goes, 'That's another great thing about Canada,' as he sits down at the table. 'The children there are so well behaved. They're actually brought up to be respectful of other people.'

I'm there, 'Well, personally, I'm proud to live in a country where children aren't afraid to be themselves, even if that pisses other people off.'

He ignores this – refuses to take the bait.

'Canadians are very tolerant,' he instead goes, 'but they also know how to treat each other. You know they legalized same-sex marriage while the rest of the world was still debating it. And everyone just walks around so chilled out. Do you know why? Because work–life balance is something they *actually* take seriously. I could go on and on about their low crime, unemployment and income disparity rates. And their healthcare system.'

Sorcha goes, 'Oh my God, it sounds like you two have found paradise – doesn't it, Ross?'

'When you come from Bray,' I go, 'living in a bus shelter would seem like paradise.'

Garret just smiles and shakes his head, like he pities me or some shit. 'Sorcha, I hate saying it,' he goes, 'because you have to live in this country with all of its, you know, begrudgery and its negativity. But coming back here makes me feel more and more that we did the right thing getting out.'

Then he's like, 'Ireland is focked,' totally ignoring the fact that there's actually talk of another bubble.

I'm there, 'I, em, better go and see what's keeping Honor,' and I stand up from the table and tip down to the kitchen. It's empty when I walk in there. I notice Sorcha's tuna Bolognese simmering away on the hob. I go into the pantry and I grab the flour. I bring it out to the kitchen.

'Oh my God,' a voice behind me goes, nearly causing me to drop the bag on the floor.

I'm like, 'Fock!'

Honor was on the other side of the island, bending down, obviously looking for something.

She goes, 'Were you just about to put flour in that sauce, *knowing* that Claire is allergic to gluten?'

I deny it, of course.

I'm like, 'I genuinely don't know what gave you that impression.'

She suddenly flashes one of her big crocodile smiles at me, then she goes, 'You don't need to – I've already done it.'

I laugh. I actually laugh out loud. Because this is what I meant when I told Honor that she couldn't keep the Goody Two Shoes act up for long. You can't fight your true nature. It comes out.

I'm there, 'Great minds, huh?'

She goes, 'Watch the door, will you? I'm going to fill up those beer bottles of his with Heineken.'

'You don't need to,' I go. 'I've already done it.'

We exchange a look that I like to think is mutual respect. There are times when I look at my daughter and – being honest? – I'm genuinely frightened for the world. But there are times when I look at her and I see my own reflection looking back at me. And in those moments – I don't care what shit there is between us – I love her like the day she was born.

I go, 'I'm so proud of you, Honor.'

And she's like, 'Stop being a knob.'

'This isn't the Lions against Australia,' I go, speaking, I think, for everyone in Kielys. 'This is Wales against Australia.'

Oisinn goes, 'There you go, calling it again, Ross. Without fear. Without favour.'

I'm tense. I hate watching rugby totally sober. But it's, like, the middle of the morning and all they'll give us in here is coffee. I'm on cup number five and I'm wired before the first ball has even been kicked.

I'm there, 'I'd actually be cheering for the Aussies today if it wasn't for the fact that Johnny Sexton is playing and it'd kill him if the story ever got back to him.'

'Sean O'Brien would be upset as well,' JP goes, a little grin on his face. It's hord to know sometimes whether he's ripping the piss or being genuine.

I decide to take him at face value.

'Yeah, no,' I go, 'Sean O'Brien is another one who thinks the world of me.'

The day Oisinn told me the news, I drove home from Blackrock with literally tears in my eyes. And that's all I actually remember about the journey. Which, when you think about it, means that Warren Gatland, through his actions, put the lives of my children in danger.

That's going on the list of things I'll never, ever forgive him for.

Shit. We've scored a try. Inside the first minute. Alex Corbisiero. Kielys erupts. There's, like, cappuccino foam everywhere and Gatland is suddenly the greatest coach in the world. People are very – big word alert – fickle.

Up on the screen, they suddenly switch to a shot of Drico, sitting in the stand, like an ordinary punter.

'I'd have refused to wear the suit,' I go. 'I'd have thrown on either my Leinster or Ireland jersey and told Gatland to go and fock himself. See, that's the difference between Brian and me.'

'A hundred and thirty Ireland caps,' JP goes, 'forty-seven international tries, a Grand Slam and three Heineken Cups?'

He *is* ripping the piss.

I'm there, 'I'm not going to stort comparing everything he achieved in the game to everything I very nearly achieved in the game, because I think even Brian has accepted that the morgins between making it and not actually making it are measured in millimetres. The point I'm making is that Brian always had a bit of class about him that I, thankfully, never had. If Gatland had dropped me like that, he'd be watching this match with a headache and a split lip. End of.'

Christian arrives – late. He's there, 'What score is it?'

JP and Oisinn both go, 'Ten-nil,' because Leigh Halfpenny has added the conversion and then another three from the tee.

'Ten-nil?' I hear someone go. 'Man, I am happy to say that I have literally no idea what that even means.'

I look over my shoulder and I end up getting basically the fright of my life. Christian has brought his mate, the so-called focking Doog, into Kielys to watch the rugby.

'I have no interest whatsoever in sports,' he goes.

Er, in *Kielys*?

I'm there, 'What the fock are you doing here then? Actually, you answer that one, Christian, because I clearly said that it was going to be just us – as in the *goys*? Fionn's already letting us down by not being here and then you turn up with Citation focking Needed?'

You can see the staff giving him the once-over. I don't know if I've actually described him before, but he's about six-foot-something, goatee, ponytail, leather trousers, biker boots and a long, black, leather coat.

He looks like he kills backpackers for fun.

Oisinn ends up apologizing for me. 'He's still grieving for Brian O'Driscoll,' he goes. 'And he hasn't had a drink either.'

Fionn finally shows his face just before half-time, when we're, like, 19-3 ahead. *He's* got someone with him as well, I notice.

It's focking Tlachtga Ní Dhuibhir.

They head straight for the bor, not even acknowledging us. It's actually JP who cops it. He laughs. He goes, 'He really is working his way through that list of yours, isn't he?'

I'm there, 'Don't even acknowledge it. Don't give him that satisfaction.'

'How did he get his hands on it?'

'He sent it to himself from my laptop.'

JP laughs. He goes, 'It's like something *you'd* do.'

I'm there, 'I know. Get your own act – that's how I feel about it.'

'Fionn is now, officially, the new Ross O'Carroll-Kelly.'

It actually hurts to hear that. So I go, 'Hey, there's still some life in the old one – don't you worry about that.'

Right on half-time, James O'Connor gets over for a try for Australia and suddenly the lead is cut to nine points.

I'm going, 'You see?' at the top of my voice. 'This is what I predicted would happen! They're bottling it and they're bottling it in a major way! And the best player in the world is sitting in the crowd in his focking whistle and flute! Focking spare me!'

There's general agreement in Kielys that what I'm talking is sense.

Fionn finally tips over to us then, a cup of coffee in his hand, followed by Tlachtga, who has a 7-Up. He makes the introductions.

She goes, 'Oh my God,' to me, 'I remember you.'

I'm like, 'Yeah, no, I remember you. We nearly got off with each other at Ultan Fennelly's twenty-first in Greystones Rugby Club?'

'Did we?'

'Well, I was going to get off with you that night – just to let you know. But I ended up getting off with another bird called Caer Ibormeith Daly.'

This doesn't seem to impress her. There's no reason why it should, of course.

I just decide, fock it, I'm going to tell the girl the truth – just as I have to warn all of the birds on the Fock It List.

So when Fionn is distracted, I turn around to her and I go, 'So did you two end up hooking up, if it's not too personal a question?'

If Tlachtga looks like anyone, I'd say she looks like Kara Tointon.

She goes, 'Oh, he came into the shop. He was looking for a candle for his sister's birthday.'

'His sister's birthday is in November,' I go. 'I should know – I've ridden the girl.'

I look over my shoulder. Fionn is a few feet away, chatting to Citation Needed. He looks like he doesn't know what to make of him either.

I'm there, 'It's not random that he happened to call into your shop, Tlachtga.'

She goes, 'What do you mean?'

'I drew up a thing – and this is a compliment to you – called the Fock It List. It was basically all the birds I was planning to do – and you happened to be on it.'

'Excuse me?'

'Fionn stole it from my computer. And now he's going through you all one by one. He still wears glasses, by the way, just in case he gave you the laser eye surgery story.'

I watch this look of, like, anger spread across her face. She steps past me and morches straight up to Fionn.

'Is that true?' she goes.

Fionn's like, 'What are you talking about?'

'Is it true that I'm on some list you're going through?'

He doesn't even *try* to deny it? He goes, 'Yeah, so what?'

Tlachtga doesn't say anything. She just gets her 7-Up and she throws it in his face. We all cheer. It's funny. The girl storms out and Fionn just shrugs, cracking on that it doesn't bother him.

He fixes me with a look and goes, 'Lisa Strug is next,' meaning she's next on the list. I miss the old Fionn. I never thought I'd say that, but I genuinely do.

The second half storts. Within a few minutes, Christian Lealiifano has kicked two penalties and suddenly it's a three-point game. I'm going, 'Yeah, Wales bottled it in the last World Cup and now they're bottling it here.'

Again, there's general agreement that (a) I've hit the nail on the head with my analysis and (b) Gatland doesn't know what the fock he's doing.

But then, suddenly, in the space of twelve minutes, the entire game changes. First, Sexton gets over for a try, then George North and Jamie Roberts do the same. One minute the commentator is talking about a great Australian comeback and the next everyone in Kielys is singing *Bread of Heaven* and total randomers are turning around to me and going, 'You were saying?'

The Lions end up winning by something stupid. I won't even quote the score. I wouldn't give Gatland the publicity. But he's loving it at the final whistle, parading around the field, looking all pleased with himself, like a man whose decision has been – I'm going to use the word – *vindicated*?

And there's poor focking Drico, trying to look happy because the Lions have won the series. Except he looks like a dude who won the lottery and washed his chinos with the ticket in the pocket.

I notice that Christian isn't even watching. Citation Needed is in his ear about something or other and it pisses me off. I don't *know* why? It just does.

I just happen to go, 'What the fock are you two talking about? There's a focking friend of ours up there on that screen and he's hurting right now.'

Citation Needed goes, 'I'm just telling Christian that he's too forgiving.'

I'm like, 'What the fock does that even mean?'

He goes, 'I'm talking about Lauren, Man. I'm talking about her going on a date with another dude and Christian doesn't even want to know who it was and whether anything happened between them.'

Oh, fock. This is all I need.

'He's forgiven her,' I go. 'He's decided to leave well enough alone. And I admire him for that.'

He's there, 'That's what I mean. He's a bigger man than I am, because I know I couldn't do it.'

'Like I said, what she did or didn't do with whoever she met that night is irrelevant. The only thing that's important is that they're making a go of shit.'

'If it was me, Man, I'd still want to know.'

'What's your status at the moment, The Doog – or whatever the fock you call yourself?'

'What's that got to do with anything?'

'Do you have an actual wife yourself?'

'No, I'm single, Man.'

'Yeah, no focking surprise there! Why don't you leave the subject of marriage to those of us who know a little bit about it and happen to be nailing it?'

Oisinn overhears this conversation and goes, 'Calm down, Ross – we've all had a lot of coffee.'

But Citation just goes, 'I was just telling Christian that I could actually probably trace the guy. Well, I could find out whoever it was that set up the fake Facebook account under the name Richie McCaw.'

I'm like, 'You've been told to leave it.'

'I'm just saying – computers are my thing.'

'They're happy. No one needs to go poking around for answers.'

'It would take me five minutes – that's all.'

I end up totally focking losing it.

I don't remember shoving The Doog, but I must, because he suddenly goes flying backwards into a high table, sending cups and saucers and soft drinks flying everywhere. And Christian and Oisinn are suddenly grabbing me, going, 'Whoa, Ross – there's a lot of emotion in the room.'

Citation stands up, dusts himself down and storts walking towards me with his two hands up. He's like, 'What is your problem, Man?'

I'm like, 'You're not even into rugby? Why are you even here?'

Luckily, Christian thinks that this is about what happened this morning in Sydney. He grabs me in a bear hug and sort of, like, waltzes me out of Kielys, going, 'Drico wouldn't want this, Ross. He would *not* want this.'

★

Sorcha arrives home, sweating like a focking AA meeting.

She went out with the boys two hours ago, wearing her Nikes and some very unflattering Lycra pants, saying she was about to – I shit you not – *run* to Dalkey and back. I'm trying to picture her, thundering down Sorrento Road, pushing the big wide stroller in front of her. It must have been like a scene from *Dante's Peak*.

I don't say that, though, because I'm playing the role of the supportive husband. So I say the exact same thing that I said this morning when she filled up her famous Bobble and said she was going to go back to drinking eight litres of water a day, like she did in UCD.

I go, 'Fair focks, Sorcha.'

Today is the day she's going to try on the famous red Alexander McQueen dress that she's still hoping to wear to Amie with an ie's wedding. Two bottles of water and a three-mile run and she thinks she's Calista focking Flockhort.

As she's doing her stretches – warming down, they call it – she asks me if I posted the insurance claim form. I know you could make the case that I bring a lot of this shit upon myself, but I would literally kill for just one day without hassle.

'Yeah, no, I posted it,' I go. 'Last week – the day you gave it to me.'

She's there, 'It's just that I rang the insurance company this morning and they've no record of having received a claim from us.'

'The post office must have lost it. Focking useless. It's pure piss-up in a brewery stuff, that.'

'Did you register the letter?'

'Yeah, no, unfortunately not. We probably should just forget about the whole thing. Your rings are gone. I've slowly come around to accepting that fact. Maybe you should, too.'

'Excuse me?'

'I'm saying we should probably just write them off now. You said it yourself. The insurance company are going to want the receipts and I stuck them in the envelope, which now seems to be lost. Like I said – useless. Tits on a boar hog.'

'Well, I'll just ring Weir's, like I originally suggested.'

302

'It just seems like a lot of trouble to go to for two rings.'

'Two rings worth €100,000?'

'Yeah, no, even that. And there's a probably a deadline by which you have to claim – and it's probably passed. Hey, ho. Let's all move on.'

'Ross, I'm ringing Weir's.'

She hands Leo to me – he's screaming his hort out, as usual. And that's when Honor suddenly makes her appearance in the kitchen.

'No need!' she goes.

Sorcha's like, 'What?'

'Sorry, I overheard what you were saying, Daddy, about the claim form being lost in the post.'

For fock's sake. She's got it in her hand.

She's there, 'I found it in the pocket of the trousers. I remembered the chinos you were wearing the day Mom asked you to go to the post office.'

And there I was thinking that we'd genuinely bonded when we tried to poison Claire from Bray last week. See, I'm an old softie at hort.

I go, 'Well done, Honor. Thank God for that. It's a genuine relief for everyone involved.'

Except Sorcha's suddenly looking at me crooked. 'Ross,' she goes, 'why did you tell me you posted it?'

I'm there, 'I'm, er, going to let you think about that question for a minute,' trying to buy myself some time to come up with something.

Sorcha goes, 'Are the receipts in the envelope as well, Honor?'

Of course, Honor knows damn well they're not. She'll have already checked. She goes through the motions of looking anyway.

'No,' she goes, 'they're not.'

And all I can go is, 'Yeah, no, I thought I found them. I mustn't have. I'll just have to keep looking.'

Sorcha rolls her eyes and shakes her head. 'I'm giving you until tonight,' she goes. 'Now, I'm going to take a shower and then I'm going to try on my dress for this wedding.'

Upstairs she goes.

Honor smiles at me. There's, like, pure badness in it as well.

She's like, 'What's going on?'

I'm there, 'You're talking rubbish, Honor – whatever it is you're about to say.'

'Why don't you want her to see the receipts? Oh my God, because the rings are worth less than she *thinks* they're worth!'

'Like I said – rubbish.'

'Oh! My God! How much *are* they worth?'

I refuse to admit anything.

I go, 'I still maintain you don't know what you're talking about.'

'Oh my God, you are so busted. And by the way,' she goes, 'I know you searched my room.'

I'm there, 'No, I didn't.'

'Last week, when we went for our chocolate facials?'

'Okay, Honor, let's cut a deal here.'

'What kind of deal?'

'How much? For the rings?'

'I told you, I don't have the rings. Those pov kids took them.'

'Okay, let's put it another way. If you were to – let's just say – *find* them, like the way you just *found* that insurance claim form, then I would be of the opinion that you'd definitely deserve some kind of reward. And I was just wondering, you know, what do you think that reward would ideally be?'

'A credit cord,' she goes – this is without even hesitating, 'with a twenty thousand euro limit.'

I'm there, 'Honor, you're dreaming. You're *actually* dreaming.'

She smiles at me and goes, 'Okay, no deal.'

And that's when the screaming storts. Not me – although I am tempted. It's Sorcha. She's going, 'Aaaggghhh! Aaaggghh! Aaa-ggghhh!' except possibly even more high-pitched than that.

I race up the stairs, with Honor running behind. Into the bedroom we go.

It's fair to say that I'm not quite prepared for the sight that greets me – and what I mean by that is that I'm not quite prepared for the extent to which Sorcha's Alexander McQueen dress doesn't fit her.

To say that she's spilling out of it would be the understatement of the century. In fairness to the girl, she's managed to pull the zip at the back halfway up.

Nec aspera terrent, as it says on the cover of the Mount Anville Yearbook.

But her body, between her hoohas and her hips, looks like a giant Christmas ham wrapped in twine and her blood flow is so restricted that her left orm is turning literally blue.

She's crying now and I end up feeling a little bit sorry for her.

'Don't just focking stand there,' she goes – to *me*, by the way? 'See can you get the zip up any further.'

She's not thinking straight. It could be oxygen deprivation.

I'm there, 'Sorcha, I don't think it fits you. And I genuinely don't think it's going to fit you either.'

Sorcha goes, 'Oh my God, it's *so* unfair! I went for a run, Ross.'

'I know. But you might need to go for, I don't know, a lot of runs.'

'What am I going to do? The wedding is in, like, four days.'

Honor's like, 'Mommy, I'm so, so sad for you.'

Sorcha goes, 'Thanks, Honor. Oh my God, I can't feel my right orm.'

I'm there, 'We possibly should get you out of that dress.'

She sits down on the bed, looking utterly defeated. And suddenly a ripping sound is heard. It would not be an exaggeration to say that it sounds like the house is under mortar fire.

Lisa Strug works in the massive AIB headquarters in Ballsbridge. I know this because I've bumped into her a few times over the years, usually when I'm temporarily borred from Kielys for some technical infringement of the rules and I'm doing my drinking in Madigan Square Gorden.

The best way to describe Lisa is to say that she's a ringer for Ariana Grande, except with massive yams. She was a huge fan of mine back in the day. Loreto on the Green. Never missed a match. It's

genuinely mind-boggling that I never tightened the nut, even though I was with pretty much most of her friends.

She laughs when she sees me coming. She takes her lunch every day at twelve o'clock. This, I know.

She goes, 'Oh my God, don't tell me you're borred from Kielys again!'

I'm like, 'Yeah, no, things got a little heated during the final Lions Test. Two weeks, this time. Are you on lunch?'

'Yeah, I always take it at twelve.'

'I did *not* know that. Do you fancy grabbing a soup and a sandwich in the old Horse Show House? The pulled pork is supposed to be sensational.'

There was a time when she'd have had my focking orm off. Instead, she goes, 'I, em, have a few errands to run.'

I'm there, 'Can they not wait?'

She laughs. 'No,' she goes. 'Ross, what's going on?'

I'm there, 'Okay, I'm going to be honest with you. Us running into each other like this – it wasn't just a happy co-inkydink.'

'Okay, I hate that word.'

'I wanted to talk to you about Fionn.'

'Fionn de Barra?'

'Yeah, no, the very same. Have you seen him recently?'

'Actually, yes. I bumped into him yesterday. This exact spot. We went for lunch.'

'And what happened?'

'What happened? We both had the lobster bisque. He said he was interested in coming into the Bankcentre to do a motivational talk. I heard he's very good.'

'Okay, this is going to sound possibly forward, but I'm going to have to ask the question anyway – did you ride him?'

'I beg your pardon?'

'I'm guessing from your reaction that you did.'

'How dare you ask me something like that?'

'There's a reason I'm asking, Lisa, and it'll become obvious when you hear the full story. Fionn is working his way through a list.'

'What are you talking about?'

'It's a list of women – okay, this is going to *sound* bad? – that I was hoping to nail. It's called a Fock It List and you were on it.'

I don't know why I expect her to be flattered. It turns out she's not. 'You never focking change,' she goes.

I'm like, 'Whoa, horsey – I'm the one trying to stop you making a complete fool of yourself here. Fionn's changed. He's not the dude with the glasses who everybody felt sorry for back in the day.'

'Rugby focking . . . wanker.'

'Okay, don't stort saying shit about the game I love.'

'Your kind never grow up.'

She pushes past me, properly shoulder-nudging me, then she goes off to do her chores. It's pretty obvious that Fionn's been there. She's actually in tears.

I just got there too late.

I whip out the list. I'm thinking, yeah, no, I'll pop into the pub, have a few pints of the wonder stuff and decide who I'm going to warn next. And that's when Sorcha texts me.

She's like, 'Where r u?'

I'm straight back with, 'Nowhere really,' trying to avoid going into specifics.

She goes, 'Wot kind of answer is that? Where r u?'

She's like Sarah Lund – focking relentless.

'Im just in ballbrdg,' I go. 'Up 2 my eyes, c u l8r xxx.'

She doesn't take the kiss-off, though. She goes, 'Im in d merrion hotel, c u here in 10mins.'

That's it. My plans for an afternoon on the sauce are in literally tatters. I grab a Jo and I tell him to drop me to the Merrion, there being no other choice. The driver ends up being Nigerian. I hope this doesn't come across as racist, but I actually miss taxi drivers who could tell you they knew Luke Kelly.

He drops me off, then into the hotel I go. I spot Sorcha straight away. She's sitting in the lounge with a pot of green tea in front of her. I'm like, 'What's the craic, Sorcha? Who's looking after the kids?'

She goes, 'Mom and Thad.'

I'm like, 'Did you say your mum and dad?'

'Heth.'

'Okay, what the fock is going on with your voice?'

And that's when she opens her mouth and she shows it to me – a giant square of mesh in the middle of her tongue.

I'm like, 'Oh my God, Sorcha – what the fock have you done?'

9.

STD Day

Sorcha says she can't wait to see Amie with an ie's dress. Although what actually comes out of her mouth is, 'Oh my Goth, I can'th waith thoo thee Amie with an ie'th dreth.'

After four days wearing the patch, I can definitely, like, *understand* her better? Either her mouth has gotten used to it or my focking ears have, because, to me, she now sounds exactly like Ross Junior.

Speaking of who slash whom.

'Mommy,' he suddenly goes – he's sitting directly behind us in the church, 'thoo you think Amie'th dreth ith going to be a prethy dreth?'

I just stare straight ahead – at the randomer that Amie with an ie is about to marry.

'I don't know,' I hear Lauren go, 'I'm waiting to see it – the same as you.'

Despite living on nothing but fruit juice and green tea for four days, Sorcha failed to lose the five and a half stone that would have been necessary for her to fit into the red Alexander McQueen dress, so she ended up having to just buy something else – an Yves Saint Laurent trouser suit, of all things.

I still wish she'd eat something, though. I'm a little bit worried about her drinking on an empty stomach. The combination of Champagne and no food has proven lethal in the past. I'm suddenly remembering her graduation, when, having lived on a KitKat a day for four weeks, she knocked back two glasses of Veuve Clicquot and tried to beat another girl over the head with a peep-toe court when she tried to skip the queue for the jacks.

She turns into a different person. I think that's what I'm trying to say. And Claire from Bray didn't exactly help her mood when she saw her outside the church and went, 'Trousers to a wedding – oh my God, random!'

So I go, 'Maybe it's time to take the patch off, Sorcha. It might be a good idea to get a bit of nosebag into you.'

She's like, 'Roth, you can't jutht take it off. It hath to be *thurgically* removed?'

Amie with an ie is outside. The word sweeps through the church – we're in, like, *Dalkey*?

It turns out that Garret is doing the music for the wedding. Which is hilarious. It's him and Claire's wedding gift to Amie with an ie and whoever this dude is that she's marrying. I end up having to check the front of the mass booklet. Focking Kevin. I think I might have mentioned that he never played rugby in his life.

Sailing is apparently his thing.

I'm not even going to comment on that.

This is a girl who always swore she was going to marry Geordan Murphy, bear in mind, and if not Geordan Murphy, then Shane Jennings or Denis Hickie.

On the organ, Garret storts playing the opening notes of what everyone straight away recognizes as *The Luckiest*. Amie with an ie is a massive, massive Ben Folds fan. It was a J1 thing.

Everyone in the church turns around, the girls with big dumb smiles on their faces, as the girl walks up the aisle, orm in orm with her old man, who played for Wanderers back in the day and supposedly for Ireland in a match against Uruguay in 1974, even though no actual caps were awarded.

I wonder does *he* think she's just settling here.

'Oh my God,' Lauren, behind me, goes, 'she looks stunning.'

And Sorcha turns around to her and goes, 'Thtunning ith definitely the word.'

She does look well, in fairness to the girl, and I'm saying that as someone who's rung her bell on six or seven occasions.

After she walks by, Sorcha again turns around to Lauren and goes, 'Garret hath thuch an amathing voith, doethn't he?'

Lauren's like, 'Sorry?' at the same time giving her a massive filthy.

I straight away cop it. She doesn't know about the tongue patch and she thinks Sorcha is ripping the piss out of her son.

'I jutht think he'th an amathing, amathing thinger,' Sorcha goes. 'He actually *thounth* like Ben Folth?'

It's too focking funny.

I tap JP on the shoulder and I go, 'Okay, he's doing a decent version of it, but he didn't write it. Ben Folds did. I don't know why he deserves praise for that.'

JP just nods. I think he agrees with me. I look at Chloe beside him. She's really storting to show now. She's, like, nearly into her third trimester – that's what she insisted on telling me earlier on, when I asked her how she was, just making conversation.

Amie with an ie ends up marrying this dude, Kevin, and the theme of the whole ceremony ends up being, obviously, boats. The priest bangs on about how life is an ocean and it's difficult to cross that ocean singlehandedly, which is why we all need people on board to help us navigate and blahdy, blahdy blah-blah.

Kevin is apparently a member of the National – focking spare me.

He kisses the bride and *we* all clap. As they're walking back down the aisle holding hands, Garret plays the piano, while Celine Madden, Amie with an ie's complete and utter ride of a cousin, sings *Il Mondo è Nostro*, which is Spanish for *Rule the World* – as in the *Take That* song?

'Oh my God,' I hear Lauren go, 'I didn't recognize it at first!'

Sorcha turns around to her and she's like, 'Theline speakth fluent Thpannish.'

Again, Lauren's like, 'Excuse me?'

And Sorcha goes, 'She did an Erathmuth year in Barthelona.'

I swear to fock, I think I'm about herniate myself trying *not* to laugh? I even hear Christian go, 'Not here, Lauren – don't make a scene in the church.'

We drive to the venue, which ends up being the Ritz-Corlton in, like, Powerscourt. The entire way there, Sorcha keeps going, 'Why ith Lauren giving me filthieth?'

I'm like, 'Er, I don't know, Sorcha – it's a real mystery, that one.'

'Ith, like, every thime I open my mouth, she lookth she wanth to thlap me acroth the faith.'

'Maybe she's jealous because we, you know, offloaded our kids onto your old pair for the day and she's ended up having to bring hers with her, which means she can't go on the big-time lash.'

'Oh my God, I am thtorving!' she goes, then she opens the dashboard and pulls out – I shit you not – a plastic bottle containing, apparently, kale, blueberries, strawberries, oranges and a thing called chord.

This is literally her dinner for the day. And it's from that moment that I deep down know there's going to be trouble today.

We check into the hotel. Sorcha brings our bags up to the room, because she wants to reapply her make-up and, well, I really couldn't be orsed. I need a drink.

One of these days, I'm going to change my middle name to Heineken. I'm actually going to look into it.

I go looking for the goys, except it's Lauren I end up running into. She's pushing little Oliver in his stroller across the foyer of the hotel and she looks properly menstrual mad.

'What the fock is your wife's problem?' is her opening line to me.

I'm like, 'Hey, what's all this about, Lauren?' all wounded innocence.

'She's mocking the way my son speaks.'

'Oh, that – well, I did warn you that he was going to end up being bullied. And if Sorcha's ripping the piss out of him, imagine what the kids in school are going to do to him! I'm thinking in terms of wedgies. You're going to be buying him new underpants every second day.'

She goes, 'I'm going to kill her!' and that's when I decide that I possibly should tell her the truth.

'Look,' I go, 'I'm pulling your cord. She's actually had a *tongue* patch fitted?'

'A what?'

'Yeah, no, she swore me to secrecy. She thinks no one's going to notice. But that's the reason she's talking like a dope.'

'What are you talking about? What's a tongue patch?'

'They're to try to lose weight. Every time you go to eat, it literally hurts your mouth. They're big in America apparently. Like a lot of things.'

She definitely calms down a bit then. She goes, 'And you let her do that?'

I'm like, 'Hey, I didn't think there was anything wrong with the size she was, but she got it into her head that she wanted to fit into a particular dress – and actually she *didn't* in the end?'

I look over both shoulders to make sure no one is within earshot.

'By the way,' I go, 'it's great to see you and Christian making a genuine go of things.'

She's there, 'What does that have to do with you?'

'I'm only saying it because we haven't had a chance to properly chat since, you know, our date.'

'We didn't have a date.'

'Well, whatever. He knows, by the way – I didn't have a chance to say it to you before.'

'Knows? Knows what?'

'Knows you downloaded the Tinder app and met some dude with a fantastic six.'

She suddenly turns on me. She's like, 'You listen to me – this is my marriage we're talking about here.'

I'm there, 'Hey, I'm only having the craic, Lauren.'

'You ever mention that night to me again and I will literally focking kill you.'

From the way she says it, I actually believe her. And I wouldn't say her old man is a stranger to disposing of a body.

Sorcha appears downstairs. We hear her go, 'Okay, now ith time for thome bubbleth.'

Lauren glares at her, then storms off to find Christian, who's outside showing Ross junior one of the great relics of the Celtic Tiger – the helicopter landing pad slash Johnny Ronan's porking space.

God, it really was a golden age.

'Did you thee thath?' Sorcha goes. 'Lauren thefinitely hath thome kind of problem with me, Roth.'

She throws three glasses of Champagne down her in double-quick time. She says that alcohol allows the body to forget that it's hungry. It also allows the body to forget that it's pissed. And Sorcha is very pissed by the time the bell rings for dinner.

All of the tables are named after, I don't know, points of interest on the Round Ireland Yacht Race. We're on Rockabill Lighthouse, along with JP and Chloe, Sophie and some random mate of Kevin's who she's been kind of seeing – it seems like everyone is just settling – and then – oh, for fock's sake – Garret and Claire from Bray, of all focking people.

Garret might as well *not* be at our table, though? He spends practically the entire meal turned around in his chair, chatting to Celine, the bird who sang the *Take That* song in Spanish in the church. There's definite flirting going on between them, which pisses me off in a major way – like I said, I'm a fan of hers.

I don't know if I mentioned earlier that, even though the wedding is supposedly black-tie, Garret has worn red Converse with his tux and also *no* tie, just an open-necked shirt, just so he can feel like he rebelled against the dress code.

'I focking hate dicks who don't stick to the rules,' I go at the top of my voice. 'There's nothing wrong with the classic black-tie look, but there's always some knob-end who tries to give it an, I don't know, ironic twist.'

Garret doesn't take the bait. He's clearly smitten by Celine and that hasn't gone unnoticed by Claire from Bray. She goes, 'Oh my God, no offence, everyone, but I can't wait to get back to Canada!' trying to get her husband's attention. 'The lifestyle is so, so amazing over there. People work to live, they don't live to work.'

Except there's no takers.

The waitress comes around, asking us if we want beef or salmon. Claire asks her three hundred and seventy-five questions about how the food is prepared and declares seven or eight different allergies and intolerances that she has, like the woman should somehow *give* a fock.

I look over my shoulder. I wish I was sitting at the Cobh Harbour table – it's got Oisinn and some random bird he met on Tinder last night, Christian, Lauren and the kids, not to mention Fionn.

'Why thoo you keep thalking about thocking Canatha?' someone suddenly goes.

Oh, Jesus, it's Sorcha. Three glasses of Champers and one glass of red wine and she is off her face and gagging to put Claire back in her box for the crack she made in Dalkey about her trouser suit.

'I'm not slagging off Ireland,' Claire goes, trying to back-pedal. 'I'm just saying that Canada is, like, *such* a chilled-out place. People aren't worrying about – oh my God – the recession and the property tax and the water tax. It's such an amazing place to, you know, wake up in the morning and just *be?*'

That's not going to satisfy Sorcha, though. I've only seen the girl hammered – as in, like, *seriously* hammered? – about three times in my entire life.

Do you remember the scene in *Django Unchained* where the guns come out and they make shit of the gaff?

That.

'You're thocking thull of thit,' Sorcha goes – meaning she's focking full of shit.

I possibly should step in at this point and save Claire, except I think it serves her right for telling Sorcha about the tongue patch in the first place.

'Sorcha,' Claire tries to go, 'you should possibly eat something. I don't think it's a good idea for you to drink on an empty stomach.'

Except Sorcha has the bit between her teeth now – quite literally.

'You thome back here with your thocking iPath and your thocking thotographth of your thocking . . . your thocking thoffee thop . . . and you think you're thether than uth . . . you're only a thocking . . . a thocking . . . a thocking pitch!'

I'm like, 'Whoa, Sorcha,' even though I'm secretly loving where this is going. 'Go easy on the analysis there.'

'If you love Thanada tho much, why thon't you . . . why thon't you . . . thuck off pack there.'

317

'Er, because I'm here for my friend's *wedding*?'

'Your thriend? Thon't make me lath. You were thoo thocking thcabby thoo buy her a thocking wething prethent.'

'Too focking scabby to buy her a focking wedding present,' I go, helpfully translating for Claire – and for Garret, because we suddenly have his attention as well. 'I think she's referring to you ripping off Ben Folds and Gary Barlow and then trying to pass it off as an actual gift, like the total focking freeloader that you are. *Her* words, not mine.'

Garret goes, 'Sorcha, don't embarrass yourself,' because the girl, by now, is talking at the top of her voice and people from other tables are taking a sudden interest in the conversation.

'Me, embarath mythelf?' she goes. 'Whath abouth you? Thocking throwing yourthelf at Theline Mathen there! Look ath your huthband, Claire – heeth going to thleep with the girl. You juth thon't know ith yeth . . . she's a thocking . . . a thocking . . . a thocking thlut.'

I suddenly jump up from the table. Much as I'm enjoying her calling it like this, she'll be asking me tomorrow why I didn't just grab her by the ankles and drag her out of there.

I go, 'Come on, Sorcha, you need to maybe sleep it off,' at the same time helping her to her feet. Except Claire tries to have the last word, the focking idiot.

'Since we're speaking frankly,' she goes, 'I had – oh my God – *the* worst diarrhoea ever after that tuna Bolognese you cooked for us.'

Sorcha just points at Claire, going, 'Your only a thocking . . . a thocking Pray . . .'

'Don't you dare say anything about Bray,' Claire tries to go, 'that you might want to take back tomorrow.'

'A Pray . . . pitch. A thocking pitch throm Pray . . . of all pletheth . . . a thocking thithole of a thocking . . . thithole . . . thocking Pray thluth . . .'

I throw Sorcha over my shoulder and I carry her in a fireman's lift out of the function room before she storts a riot. We're only a few miles from Bray, bear in mind. I carry her into the elevator, then up to our room.

'Claireth a thocking . . . a thocking . . . pitch,' she keeps going.

'And a thocking whore . . . why thoethn't thee thock off . . . thock off pack thoo . . . Thanada?'

While I'm listening to this, I manage to get her out of her famous trouser suit, then under the covers of the bed. Literally thirty seconds later she's snoring away like a drunken sailor.

Women. You can't live with them – if they're claiming the Lone Parent Allowance. That's just a funny thing I sometimes say.

Sorcha suddenly makes, like, a gagging sound. Ever the gentleman, I roll her onto her side, wipe the saliva from her chin, then I go back downstairs to see if my beef has arrived.

I'm not a *complete* dick? I make sure that Sorcha is okay. I check on her at least every half an hour – or at least I make sure that someone does, either Lauren or Sophie or Chloe.

She's the talk of the wedding, of course. Even Amie with an ie, when she's going around from table to table with Kevin the Sailor Man, goes, 'Is Sorcha okay, Ross?' genuinely concerned about the girl, which is nice.

And I'm like, 'Yeah, no, she's pissed. She's let me down in a big-time way here. She could have totally ruined this day for me.'

I decide not to let her, though. And for a few hours at least, it ends up being one of the *better* weddings? All the goys are in cracking form. JP and Chloe seem happy enough, even though they're clearly not in love with each other. Oisinn is delighted with his Tinder date, even though he has to keep double-checking her name on his phone every hour or so. And Christian and Lauren look the most loved-up they've been for a long time. They're, like, stealing little looks at each other and smiling – and even Ross Junior, once he's finished telling the bridesmaids how much he loves their dresses, has a go at sliding across the dance-floor on his knees, like any other normal boy.

Fionn ends up making a run at Malorie Miles, who's a ringer for Alexandra Daddario, went to St Andrew's back in the day and ended up working in the Office of the Ombudsman. Although the most important piece of information, from Fionn's point of view, is that her name is on the Fock It list.

I try to give her a friendly warning when he's up at the bor. I sidle up beside her and I go, 'He's not what he seems.'

She's like, 'Excuse me?'

'Hey, I'm doing the gentlemanly thing by warning you off him. He's probably telling you all about his so-called ordeal, is he?'

'Sorry, do I know you?'

She actually says that. I possibly hurt the girl back in the day and this is how she chooses to deal with it.

I'm there, 'Yeah, no, you know me alright. Look, I meant what I said about Fionn. He has a list of names – it's probably in his tux pocket – of birds I was going to ride but who he's now riding himself.'

'I'm just having a conversation with him.'

'Don't let him ride you. That's a word from the wise. And also, bear in mind that he wears glasses. I mean, he hasn't got them on him now, but he needs them – that's the point I'm trying to make'

'Sorry, what did you say your name was again?'

I'm like, 'Yeah, no, nice try.'

Fionn says it at the exact same time as me. He's back from the bor with a vodka, soda and lime for Malorie, going, 'Yeah, nice try, Ross.'

I'm there, 'I'm just telling her not to be taken in by your horseshit.'

And without even looking at me, *he* goes, 'Are you still here, Ross?'

I just shrug. I was just trying to be a good citizen. I can do no more than that. So off I fock.

About two hours later – it must be around ten o'clock – I'm on the way to the bor when I spot Claire, sitting alone in a quiet corner, bawling her eyes out.

I go, 'What's wrong?' even though I don't give a fock – it's just a figure of speech.

'*He's* what's wrong,' she goes. 'Him and that skinny bitch,' and I straight away know, without needing to turn around, that she's talking about Garret and Celine Madden. 'Oh my God, she's, like, *hanging* out of him?'

She's very, very pissed.

I'm there, 'Yeah, no, a lot of people are commenting on the fact that they seem to be getting on very well together,' because I love twisting the knife. 'One or two wondered were they an actual couple.'

'Then on top of that,' she goes, 'Sorcha – oh my God – attacked me out of the blue. The stuff she said about me, Ross – *and* Bray.'

'You can't keep defending the place, Claire. It's a shitbox.'

'It has amazing community spirit.'

'I've never considered that a defence.'

'Did you see how many people turned out to welcome Katie Taylor home from the Olympics?'

'Look, I'm not going to fall out with you over it. Garret's the one you should be pissed off with.'

'He's a wanker.'

'Yeah, no, you're preaching to the choir. Red Converse with a tux – could anyone *be* a bigger dick? And then showing up with no present and his orms swinging. We paid three hundred snots for bed sheets and a Nuance Wine Finer. I'm only making the point.'

Something suddenly occurs to her.

'You know,' she goes, 'I haven't actually seen him – or that Celine bitch – for, like, an hour?'

'He's probably up to his nuts in her somewhere.'

'What? Do you think?'

'Definitely. Riding her bow-legged.'

The hilarious thing is that I know he's *not*? I saw him literally sixty seconds ago involved in a really serious conversation with the DJ. In fact, I heard him go, "Yeah, no, I'd actually consider myself a bit of a muso. Toronto has a really, really good live music scene. Here, it's just dead."'

I made a point of going, 'That sounds like a fascinating conversation, Dude – real edge of your focking seat stuff,' and he just shook his head and smiled at me – like he actually felt sorry for me.

Claire looks suddenly worried.

I'm there, 'I could see in the church that something was going to happen between them. She looks like Rachel Riley and there isn't a pick on her.'

I'm suddenly aware of the fact that she's staring at me very intensely. There's a little bit of Claire that will never truly be over me.

She's human.

'Do you want to maybe dance?' I go.

I can actually *see* Garret – still over by the DJ box.

Claire just nods. I take her by the hand and I lead her out onto the dance-floor. The song is *Blurred Lines* and practically everyone is up dancing. I manoeuvre her so that we're smack bang in Garret's line of vision.

'The dude must have rocks in his head,' I go, 'cheating on some-one like you.'

She's there, 'That's a really nice thing to say,' and she's dancing with me now in a seriously flirty way.

This song is definitely the song of the summer.

'I mean, I've always found your accent a bit off-putting,' I go, 'but you're not bad looking and you've a tremendous little body on you.'

She's there, 'Sometimes I wish that me and you had, well, you know . . .'

I stort dancing closer to her. I put my hands on her hips. I look over and I notice Garret suddenly staring at us, his mouth sprung like a greyhound trap.

I'm there, 'You wish me and you had what?'

She goes, 'You know.'

'I don't – go on, say it. It's possible I might be feeling the same thing.'

'I mean, don't get me wrong. Sorcha's, like, my best friend and everything, but I always thought there was this – oh my God – connection between us.'

She stops dancing and just, like, stares into my eyes.

She smells of Bacordi and desperation. Fortunately, I like both.

I smooth down her hair and she closes her eyes and tilts her head, in anticipation of being kissed. I actually smile at Garret and give him a wink.

I have no intention of throwing the lips on the girl – not in front of this many witnesses. I just want Garret to know that I could if I wanted to – and now he's seen that.

Claire opens her eyes. She's like, 'What?'

And I'm there, 'Look, I'm very flattered, Claire, but I'm actually married.'

And speaking of which – oh, holy fock – here comes Sorcha, across the dance-floor. She's managed to put her suit back on, although she's still clearly shit-faced, moving towards us like a shopping trolley with a wonky wheel.

I put my hand on Claire's chest and I give her a shove. She staggers backwards and falls onto a chair.

Sorcha obviously hasn't seen what was going down, because she throws her two orms around my shoulders and goes, 'Are you thoming upthtairth thoo beth?'

I'm like, 'I'm not really ready for bed, Babes. I'm not even pissed yet.'

She leans over and she kisses me full on the mouth.

I'm there, 'What are you doing?'

She's like, 'I'm *kithing* you?'

'Should we? I mean, there's people watching.'

People *are* watching. She's the talk of the place again.

She goes, 'Leth go thoo beth then. Come on, ith ageth thinth we thid anything!'

'You're telling me,' I go. 'I've nuts like focking guavas here.'

She storts, like, whispering in my ear, going, 'Come on, Roth – leth go up thoo the room.'

And that's when it happens. The first thing I feel is a tug on my ear lobe, then two or three seconds later a second one.

'Thhhggghhh!!!' Sorcha goes.

I'm like, 'What the fock?'

'Thhhggghhh!!!' she again goes – and that's when I realize that my ear lobe is trapped underneath her tongue patch.

'Tell me this isn't happening,' I go. 'Seriously – tell me it's not happening. Was there, like, a gap underneath it or something?'

'Thtop pulling!' Sorcha goes. 'Ith hurth every thime you thoo that.'

I'm there, 'I have to pull, Sorcha. Otherwise, how the fock am I supposed to get free?'

She's like, 'Aaaggghhh!!!' and then she closes her mouth, biting down on my ear.

323

I'm like, 'Fffooocccckkk!!!'

And that's when people stort to cop what's actually happened.

I'm like, 'Jesus, Sorcha, could you not have been more careful?'

She goes, 'Whath?'

'Coming at me, shit-faced, with that focking thing in your mouth.'

'Blaming me ithn't going thoo thoo uth any gooth.'

People on the dance-floor are storting to gather around us, some of them offering help, some of them actually laughing. The music suddenly stops. The DJ suddenly shouts, 'Is everything okay?'

I'm going, 'Is it bleeding? Can you see if my ear is bleeding?'

And Sorcha is like, 'Thtop being a thocking baby, Roth.'

Claire from Bray is on it like a bonnet. 'Oh my God,' she goes, the delight obvious in her voice. 'I'll phone an ambulance!'

I'm like, 'No ambulances!' because this is one story I *don't* want getting around?

Of course, it's too late. She phones it anyway.

The duty manager of the hotel arrives and tells us we have to move off the dance-floor, due to – get this – health and safety considerations.

'It's a bit focking late for that,' I go, as he ushers us – Sorcha's tongue still attached to the lower half of my ear – into a quiet corner next to the bor.

Twenty minutes later, we hear the sound of a siren outside.

The ambulance dudes try to be professional, but they can't help but laugh. It's like when nurses tell you stories about patients who turn up at A&E, going, 'I was using some ketchup in the nude when I slipped . . .'

They're kind of *entitled* to rip the piss?

I'm there, 'Yeah, no, we've all had a laugh – now can you detach me from my wife, please?'

The ambulance dude looks into Sorcha's mouth and he goes, 'What is that thing?'

I'm there, 'Sorcha, let me explain it,' because every time she talks I think she's going to tear off the lower half of my ear. 'It's a piece of gauze she had fitted to her tongue to stop her eating like a focking hippo.'

He goes, 'Okay,' staring into her mouth with a little pin torch, 'there's a tear at the front of it and your ear lobe has somehow managed to work its way underneath. The air has created a suction effect, which is why you're stuck.'

I'm like, 'For fock's sake.'

'You have two choices here. I can remove the patch or I can remove your ear.'

There's, like, total silence from my wife.

I'm like, 'Sorcha, you've got to be taking the piss.'

She goes, 'Ith wath very expenthive, Roth.'

And I'm like, 'Get it off her! We're talking now!'

I'm sitting on the floor in front of the TV with the three boys beside me on their mat and we're watching Ireland's victory over England at Twickenham in 2006.

I read somewhere – well, let's be honest, I *heard* somewhere – that people learn, I don't know, some mad percentage of the shit they know in the first five years of their lives.

'It looks good,' Nigel Owen, on the touchline, goes.

I say it at the exact same time. I know the entire script between Shane Horgan grounding the ball and the TMO going, 'You may award the try.'

I even say Ryle Nugent's lines: 'How's your hort? How's your hort?'

Little Leo laughs.

Sorcha's old man is suddenly standing at the door of the living room. He wouldn't recognize this match. I wouldn't say he even watched it at the time.

'Did you find those receipts?' he tries to go.

I'm like, 'Sorry, I didn't hear you knock,' because there's no way I'm answering his questions.

'The receipts,' he goes, 'for Sorcha's engagement and wedding rings. We need them if we're to put in that claim.'

I'm like, '*We?*'

'Yes, *we.*'

'*We* is me and Sorcha. There's no you in the word.'

'You need to find those receipts.'

'I'll discuss that with my wife. It has fock-all to do with you.'

He stares at me for a few seconds, then he goes, 'Your father is here. I just let him through the gates.'

He focks off. Ten seconds later, the old man sticks his head around the living-room door, going, 'Twickenham! The year of Our Lord, two thousand and six! You may award the try!'

You see, *he* knows.

'Shut your big foghorn mouth,' I go. 'You'll scare the boys.'

He's like, 'There they are! Taking it all in!' and he picks up little Brian. 'You'd be shocked, Ross, if you knew how much they actually learned at this age.'

I'm there, 'Yeah, no, I know all about it.'

'Is Sorcha home?'

'She's in bed. We were at a wedding last night. She disgraced herself. And me.'

'Well, I was just passing, as it happens, and I thought I'd drop in and tell you the news. Keep you in the loop and so forth. Helen and I are going to Seattle – the famous Emerald City.'

'What, to try to find Erika?'

'The first week in September. Booked our tickets this morning.'

'Two tickets or three?'

'Well, two, I'm afraid.'

'So Helen still doesn't want me going with you?'

'Sadly, Ross, you are to remain on the bench for this one.'

'Let her know that I'm seriously pissed off and remind her that she used to be a huge backer of mine.'

'I'll, em, do that, of course.'

'We'll see how she gets on looking for her precious daughter with just you to help her, you big focking dope.'

He sticks around for, like, an hour. We watch Ireland beat England in 2001 – the famous Foot and Mouth match. I've never been able to watch Peter Stringer's tap tackle on Dan Luger without crying. I discover that I still can't.

The old man eventually focks off. About half an hour after that,

Sorcha finally shows her face. She says she feels – oh my God – *so* ashamed of herself.

There aren't many times in my life when I find myself on the moral high ground. The trick is to enjoy it for as long as it lasts.

'Yeah, no, you focking disgraced yourself,' I go. 'I'm not being a dick, Sorcha, but you genuinely let yourself, and especially me, down.'

She's like, 'Did I ruin the day for you?'

'What, you mean when it took three ambulance men the guts of an hour to cut my ear loose from your tongue? No, not at all. I'd actually forgotten it even happened.'

'I shouldn't have drunk on an empty stomach.'

'Well, unfortunately, you did. And you were a mess.'

'Oh my God, I have this vague memory of being horrible to Claire.'

'I don't think anyone gave a shit about that. It was actually funny.'

'What did I say to her?'

'You called her a bitch and told her to fock off back to Canada if she liked it so much. You also accused Garret of throwing himself at Celine Madden and you called *her* a slut.'

'Oh my God, I'll have to ring them all to apologize.'

'Like I said, I actually thought that bit was funny.'

'Oh, by the way . . .'

'What?'

'The receipts for my rings.'

Shit. Her old man has obviously been in her ear this morning. I decide that attack is the best form of defence.

I go, 'You've some focking cheek bringing that up. You're lucky I'm still talking to you after your performance yesterday.'

She's there, 'Stop hiding behind that, Ross. I need to send this claim form. I going to ring the jewellers today.'

'Yeah, no,' I go, 'fair enough – just give me another twenty-four hours,' thinking I have to turn over Honor's room one more time. 'There's a few places I haven't looked.'

'One day,' she goes. 'That's all you're getting – then I'm definitely ringing Weir's. By the way, Honor wants to talk to you.'

I'm like, 'Talk to me?'

'She's upstairs in her room.'

'Can she not come down here to me – that's if she wants to talk to me?'

'Why don't you go upstairs to her, Ross? It's lovely that she suddenly wants us as her friends.'

Which is horseshit, of course. But up the stairs I go.

She's lying on her bed with her phone in her hand and a really big smile on her face that should tell me instantly that the girl has something on me.

I'm there, 'Were you looking for me?' leaning against the frame of the door.

She goes, 'Yes, I was. See, I knew how desperate Mom was to find the receipts for those rings. So I had a look myself.'

'And did you find them?'

Of course she didn't. They don't focking exist.

'No,' she goes, 'but I did find *this* in your sock drawer.'

She suddenly produces it from under her pillow and my hort is suddenly beating in double time. It's the bottle of diet pills that I was feeding her mother.

I try to spoof my way out of it, of course. I'm there, 'Yeah, no, I've been trying to, em, lose a few pounds. It's in case I go back playing rugby. Seapoint have been sniffing around me. One or two other clubs as well.'

She goes, 'That's why you were making her tea every morning. You were crushing them down and feeding them to her.'

'Again, I'm sticking to my original story. It's actually quite flattering that a club like Seapoint would think I'm capable of coming back and straight away playing at AIL level.'

'Okay, I'm going to call Mum up and see what she thinks.'

At the top of her voice, she goes, 'Mooommmyyy!!!'

I'm there, 'Okay, okay – what do you want? How much for your silence?'

She goes, 'You know what I want.'

'Honor, I can't give you your own credit cord. Not until you're at least sixteen.'

'Then I'm going to tell her that you were spiking her tea. Oh, I've got something else on you as well.'

'What else?'

'Okay, a couple of weeks ago, I was going through *her* wardrobe. I was looking for the red Alexander McQueen dress that she was going to wear to Amie with an ie's wedding, because I was going to put, like, *moth* larvae on it?'

'Keep going. I'm listening.'

'The dress was gone.'

'You've got one hell of an imagination, do you know that?'

'Then a few days later, I heard you tip-toeing up the stairs. I knew you were up to something, so I looked through a crack in that door and I saw you walking along the landing, carrying a dress bag.'

'You and your conspiracy theories.'

'So then, when I was poking around your room, I also found this.'

She holds it up, between her thumb and finger.

Oh, fock.

It's the receipt from the dress alterations place.

I play dumb. I'm like, 'What the fock is that supposed to be?'

She goes, 'You had her dress taken in to make her think she was fatter than she actually was.'

'Seriously – you should be writing episodes of *Gossip Girl* or one of those!''

'Mooommmmmmyyy!!!'

'Okay, okay, I did. You're right. She said herself that she wanted to lose a few pounds and I was trying to come up with ways to sort of like, egg her on. Motivation. Blah, blah, blah.'

'I want my own credit cord.'

'Look, I'll tell you what, Honor, I'll make you an offer.'

'You're not in any position to bargain with me.'

'If you give me back your old dear's rings . . .'

'I told you I don't have her rings.'

' . . . if you give them back to me, then also forget what you know about me spiking her tea and – yeah, no – getting her dress taken in to try to frighten her off the Toblerone, then I'll give you a credit cord with, say, two grand a month on it.'

'Five grand.'

'Honor, I'm not giving an eight-year-old girl five grand a month. Three and a half grand.'

'I'm going to tell Mom, then.'

'Okay, five grand a month.'

I know when I'm beaten. I can always get the money from my old man, I suppose.

She goes, 'Go and get me your shoes.'

I'm there, 'My shoes? Do you mean my Dubes? I'm wearing them.'

'I'm talking about your *actual* shoes. The ones you wore to the wedding yesterday.'

I just shrug. I have no idea where this is going. I go into our bed-room and I grab the old brogans. I bring them back into Honor and I throw them on the bed.

She picks up the right one, twists the heel, then turns it over. And from a secret compartment that I never even knew was there, they drop onto Honor's duvet.

Sorcha's engagement and wedding rings.

It would be an understatement to say that Sorcha is surprised when I produce them the following day.

'Oh my God!' she goes. She says it more than once, in fact.

I'm like, 'Yeah, no, I found them down the back of the bed, if you can believe that. So let's have no more talk about receipts and ring-ing Weir's.'

She goes, 'The back of the bed?'

'Well, I told you I was going to turn the place over one last time. I pulled out the bed and there they were. So it's a definite case of relief all round.'

'Oh my God. You said it wasn't Lamar and Tequila – and you were right!'

'I honestly don't know why I don't get listened to more. I've got all this knowledge.'

Sorcha's old pair are clearly dubious, though. Her old man is looking at me like I'm the woman who dropped the cat in the wheelie bin.

'I pulled out the bed,' he tries to go. 'And so did your mother. And there was no sign of any rings. I searched that floor – we both did – on our hands and knees.'

Sorcha's old dear nods, backing him up.

I'm there, 'I just think we should be grateful that they've been found and let's not worry about the whos and the hows and the whys of it.'

'Something's going on,' he goes. 'And I'm going to find out what it is.'

'Another option would be to keep your focking hooter out of my family's bee's wax. I'm just throwing that out there.'

'Sorcha, are you going to let him speak to me like that?'

Except Sorcha doesn't say anything. Instead, she slides the rings onto her finger and that's when she gets the second surprise of the afternoon. They actually fit her.

She stretches her left hand out in front of her, admiring them along the length of her orm. She goes, 'I'm just so, so happy to have them back,' and then she's like, 'We need to apologize. To Lamar and Tequila. For accusing them in the wrong.'

I'm like, 'We? I was the one who said they were actually good kids.'

'Well, then *I* need to apologize.'

Sorcha's old man doesn't think it's such a great idea. 'I'm really not sure it's necessary,' he goes. 'Or advisable.'

I'm there, 'Exactly. When I said they were good kids, what I meant was, okay, they didn't do this, but they'll have done something else. Or they will in the future. I wouldn't let it bother you, Sorcha.'

'One of my all-time heroes has always been the Dalai Lama,' she goes. 'Dad, you know that, don't you?'

He just nods.

She's there, 'The Dalai Lama once said, "If you are honest, truthful and transparent, people trust you. If people trust you, you have no grounds for fear, suspicion or jealousy." That's an actual quote, Ross.'

I'm there, 'I take on board what the dude is saying, but have you ever thought that the exact opposite might *equally* be true?'

'Ross, come on, let's go.'

'Go? We're actually *going* to Finglas?'

'Yes, we're going to Finglas.'

'Could you not, like, text them that you're sorry?'

'No, I want to do it in person. Call Honor.'

'Honor's coming?'

'She was there when her mother levelled a false accusation against two innocent children, Ross. It's only fair that's she's there to hear me say that I was wrong and I'm sorry. I want to be a role model to my daughter, remember?'

Sorcha's old man goes, 'I think this is a very, very bad idea.'

But there's no talking to the girl. We're going to Finglas and that's all there is to it.

Fifty minutes later, we're actually there.

We pull up outside the gaff. There's a fridge on its side in the front gorden that wasn't there the last time we were here. Whenever a household appliance stops working, the Tuites just open the front door and fock it out. They're too lazy to dump it on the green in the middle of the estate like everyone else.

'When you accuse someone in the wrong,' Sorcha goes, 'you apologize, Honor. That's what I'm here to do.'

Honor goes, 'You really are the best mom in the world!'

I genuinely don't know how she keeps a straight face.

I hammer on the door with my open palm. Two minutes later, after repeated banging, Dordeen finally opens it. I presume she was waiting for an ad break in *Judge Judy*.

She looks at us like we're here to check her TV licence.

'Hi, Dordeen,' Sorcha goes, in her poshest voice. 'Is this a convenient time for you to talk?'

Dordeen's like, 'Begga peerden?'

'I was wondering were Tequila and Lamar here? There's something I wanted to say to them.'

Dordeen calls them without taking her eyes off Sorcha.

Ten seconds later, the two kids come running down the stairs. They stop dead when they see us. We did put the law on them, I suppose. That's a capital offence in this port of the world.

Sorcha goes, 'Hi, kids. Okay, the last time I was here, I made certain allegations that have since proved to be unfounded . . .'

I'm there, 'Sorcha, maybe let me do the talking here. We're not saying these kids are angels or anything like it. But in this case, it looks like Sorcha might have been wrong.'

'She *was* wrong,' Dordeen goes. 'She has her rings on her fingor, lookit.'

I'm there, 'Exactly. They were found. So we're just saying, you know, no hord feelings, bygones be bygones.'

Sorcha goes, 'I'm saying more than that, Ross. I'm saying sorry. I'm saying sorry, Lamar. I'm saying sorry, Tequila. I accused you both in the wrong.'

Something totally unexpected happens then. The living-room door suddenly opens and out of it steps K . . . K . . . K . . . Kennet, Dordeen's husband who's supposed to be doing a stretch for insurance fraud.

Dordeen goes, 'You heert that, did you, Kennet?'

He's there, 'I c . . . c . . . c . . . certainly d . . . d . . . d . . . did. They're arthur admittin slandorden the nayums of ear gerrand childorden unj . . . j . . . j . . . justly.'

I'm like, 'Okay, what the fock are you even doing out?'

He goes, 'Ine on temper doddy release. And I gorrout of the Joy to foyunt Kadden's kids – two noicer k . . . k . . . k . . . kids you c . . . c . . . c . . . c . . . cootunt ebber meet – being interviewed by the Geerds. Accused of all s . . . s . . . s . . . sorts.'

'We'll obviously talk to the Gords,' Sorcha goes, 'and we'll withdraw our complaint.'

Kennet suddenly whips out his mobile phone and takes a photograph of Sorcha's hand, the two rings sporkling on her finger.

'That's alls I n . . . n . . . n . . . need,' he goes. 'P . . . p . . . proof that the rings you accused my famidy of sthroking have turdened up s . . . s . . . s . . . safe and well. Which means that statement you

333

made to the Geerds was defamation. You're gonna be hearton from
ear s . . . s . . . s . . . solicitodder.'

Under her breath, I hear Honor go, 'Oh my God, hillair!'

She doesn't seem at all worried. I'm there, 'Sorcha, we could end up
losing the house.'

She actually laughs. This is, like, three days later.

'It's not going to come to that,' she tries to go. 'Dad was a barrister, remember? He says he'll wipe the floor with them if it ever
comes to court.'

'He says he wants a million yoyos.'

'Well, if that's the price we have to pay for doing the right thing,
then so be it. Do you know how many years Aung San Suu Kyi
spent in captivity?'

There's no real answer to that.

I'm there, 'I still say we should have kept our mouths shut. Hong
Kong-whatever-she's-called never had to deal with human filth like
the Tuites.'

We're in Arnotts, by the way, to get Honor's uniform and various
other bits for going back to school. Sorcha has been looking forward to this day all summer and when Honor steps out from behind
the changing-room curtain in the famous green skirt and jumper,
not to mention the turquoise shirt, her eyes fill up with tears.

'Oh my God,' she goes, her hand slapped over her mouth, 'I honestly never thought I'd see the day when you were accepted back
into Mount Anville. Honor, I'm so proud of you. I'm so proud of
the daughter you've become.'

She bends down and kisses Honor on the top of the head. The
kid wants to offload. I can see it. But she swallows down what
she actually *wants* to say and goes, 'I just can't wait to get back
there, Mom. The Overseas Awareness Initiative. The St Vincent
de Paul Dress-Up Day. The Philippines Disaster Raffle. It's all ahead
of me.'

It's killing her. I can see it.

Sorcha goes, 'You're going to have the most – oh my God –
amazing experiences, Honor,' and then she looks down at the list

again. 'What else do we need to get? Coat, shoes, gum shield, sheet music stand, Chinese–English dictionary . . .'

Honor goes back into the changing room. She looks at me over her shoulder. Sooner or later, she's going to crack.

Sorcha links my orm.

She's there, 'I just can't believe she's going to get to enjoy all of the same things I enjoyed during my school career. Lunch-time musical recitals. The Transition Year 1930s Fashion Show. Sister Gregory's drama module. Do you know who I'd – oh my God – *love* to witness this?'

I'm like, 'Who?'

'Siofra.'

'Okay, I don't like where this conversation seems to be going, Babes.'

'Ross, we owe it all to her. She's the reason we've ended up with this perfect, perfect daughter.'

'Do you not remember the way things ended between us? You told her to horse off.'

'I didn't tell her to horse off, Ross. We had a disagreement because she felt my dad was undermining our marriage. And that's because she's never been in our home and she's never seen how it all just *works*?'

'So what are you actually saying?'

'I think we might invite her for dinner.'

'Again, Sorcha, I'd be in favour of leaving well enough alone.'

'We'll invite her and her husband – his name is Linus, according to the acknowledgements at the back of her book – and obviously little Jack, who looks like such a gorgeous, gorgeous little boy.'

'I don't suppose there's any point in me trying to talk you out of this?'

'There isn't. I want Siofra to see the amazing little girl that Honor has become. Oh my God, I'm going to do my famous pork fillet with sage and apricots.'

'Iseult,' he goes.

This is Fionn ringing me at, like, three o'clock in the morning.

335

I'm like, 'What are you focking talking about?'

'On the Fock It List,' he goes, 'it just says *Something Garrigan with the massive chebs*. Her name is Iseult.'

I'm there, 'You woke me up in the middle of the night to tell me that? Wait a minute, are you about to ride her?'

'No,' he goes, 'I've just ridden her.'

'You're full of shit.'

'That's twelve off the list. Sixteen down – thirty-four to go.'

'You're focking full of shit.'

Sorcha suddenly wakes up, going, 'Is that your dad?'

Do I really talk to my old man like that?

I'm like, 'No. It's Bad Fionn – he's just ridden a bird I know.'

Fionn goes, 'A bird you were mad about!'

'I wasn't mad about her. In fact, I don't know why I even put her on the list. A cracking set of hufties – I'll give you that – but she's got a focking face on her like a monkey's ormpit.'

Sorcha goes, 'Can you please go into another room to conduct that conversation?'

Fionn must hear her because he goes, 'Tell Sorcha I'm sorry for waking her. Iseult's gone to the jacks and I'm looking for a way out of this apartment.'

'We're vegetarians,' Siofra goes.

Jesus. This is *as* Sorcha's putting the dish down in the middle of the table.

She's there, 'Linus and I haven't eaten meat for – what? – ten years?'

And Linus – who seems like a bit of a drip to me – goes, 'It's more like fourteen. Jack has never so much as tasted it.'

Little Jack, by the way, looks exactly the same as he does on the cover of *So Your Kid is a Prick* – blond, pudding-bowl haircut and black polo-neck jumper. He hasn't opened his mouth once in the hour since they arrived. He just has his head down, looking – I don't know – *sullen*?

'Oh my God,' Sorcha goes, 'I should have asked you was there anything you didn't eat. Oh my God, I'm so embarrassed!'

Siofra's like, 'Don't be silly. There's more than enough here for us to eat. Look at these salads, Linus,' and she helps herself to the puy lentils with parsnips and walnuts.

Sorcha's old dear goes, 'Those are Edmund's parsnips – he grows them here, in the garden.'

'How wonderful,' Siofra goes, just making conversation, 'you've got green fingers, have you?'

And he goes, 'Growing vegetables isn't difficult. There *are* people, of course, who want to turn it into some kind of pseudo-science. Rather like the job of raising children.'

That's a dig. That's a definite dig. He's letting her know that he hasn't forgiven her for telling Sorcha to fock him out on his ear.

Sorcha tries to change the subject. 'So, Siofra,' she goes, 'Honor is storting back in Mount Anville next week and it's all thanks to you.'

Siofra's there, 'I didn't do anything. I just wrote a letter saying I was very satisfied with the progress I'd seen. Did you have a nice summer, Honor?'

Honor's like, 'Yes, thank you. But I have to say, Siofra, I'm really looking forward to going back to school.'

She's some actress. She's wearing her *Is Féidir Linn* T-shirt again and her butter-wouldn't-melt smile.

Sorcha goes, 'We bought her a brand-new piccolo yesterday. And don't worry, Siofra, we're not spoiling her. She saved up enough points on the Honour Board. Do you play a musical instrument yourself, Jack?'

And Jack goes, 'I play the viola.'

'Oh my God, the viola was *my* instrument, too!'

'I also play the piano and the glockenspiel and I'm learning the saxophone.'

Sorcha looks at Siofra and she goes, 'Oh my God, he's *so* gorgeous, Siofra!'

Still, there's, like, a weird atmos around the table. There's definite tension between Sorcha's old man and Siofra.

Sorcha tries to keep the conversation jollying along.

'So,' she goes, 'has everyone thought about how you're going to vote in the referendum to abolish the Senate?' and we end up

337

talking about that for a good, I don't know, twenty minutes. Linus says he agrees with the idea of having a single legislative house in principle, but he doesn't agree with the way the issue has been handled – like any of us should give a fock.

It's as we're finishing the main course that Sorcha's old man finally turns around and goes, 'I'm sorry, while this is all very interesting discussing Constitutional amendments, I think we all need to acknowledge the rather sizeable pachyderm in the room.'

Sorcha goes, 'Dad, please!'

He's like, 'I'm sorry, Sorcha, I have to say it. A few months ago, Siofra, you ventured an opinion to my daughter, to the effect that it would be better for Honor's emotional well-being if Sorcha's mother and I moved out of this house.'

Siofra looks at Sorcha and goes, 'I didn't come here so that we could continue that conversation. My work with Honor is finished. You decided to end our sessions.'

'No, no, no,' *he* then goes, 'you don't get off with it that easily. You told Sorcha that this would be a happier home if she put her parents out on the street. Now, I'm asking you, as a professional working in the area of mental health, how you arrived at such a determination?'

Sorcha goes, 'Oh my God, Dad, you're not in court!' trying to suddenly lighten the atmos.

Siofra's there, 'I didn't say that just Honor would be happier. I said *everyone* would be happier.'

I'm like, 'Continue, Siofra – I like where this is going.'

She goes, 'Based on what I heard from both Ross and Sorcha in our group sessions, and from Honor in our one-to-ones, you are an undermining influence in both their marriage and their efforts to parent their children.'

He's there, 'Oedipus was mentioned, I believe.'

'Yes, I do think – again, from the stories I heard over the course of the months I saw Honor, Sorcha and Ross – that you have difficulties severing the father–daughter bond. I don't think it's healthy for in-laws to play such a hands-on role in parenting their grandchildren – that's in my book.'

338

He laughs – a big, arrogant barrister laugh.

'Oh,' he goes, 'if it's in your book, then it must be true. Let me say something to you – look at Honor.'

Siofra does. She's eating salad and smiling sweetly. It's focking killing her – I can see it.

He's there, 'Does she look like a girl living in an unstable family environment?'

Siofra doesn't answer, except to go, 'Sorcha, I really wouldn't have come here tonight if I'd thought . . .'

Sorcha's like, 'Siofra, I just wanted you to see how what we have here just, like, *works*?'

He, again, goes, 'Does Honor look like a girl living in an unstable family environment?' a bit louder this time.

When Siofra doesn't answer, he goes, 'I rest my case!' like the complete and utter focking knob-end that he is.

Sorcha brings in the cheese course and Sorcha's old dear says that, no matter how bad the economy sank in the last few years, you still had to queue up to get into Sheridan's on South Anne Street and there's general agreement that that's a very good thing. But the conversation around the table never really recovers and I can see that Siofra and Linus are keen to be off.

She has a nibble at the Comté, then she mentions that they have to be up early tomorrow – Jack, apparently, has piano practice – and she goes to stand up.

Sorcha is watching the perfect evening she had planned go up in smoke. She's like, 'Please don't leave yet. I was going to ask Honor to play something for you on her piccolo.'

Linus is there, 'No, it's already late.'

'Please,' Sorcha goes. 'I was thinking, Jack could accompany her on the piano.'

To cut a long story short, that's what ends up happening. Honor is sent upstairs to get her new piccolo, then little Jack sits down in front of the piano and he asks her what tunes she knows.

Honor goes, *'Gabriel's Oboe,'* and little Jack – I swear to fock – rolls his eyes and shakes his head and goes, 'Okay, music for beginners.'

I watch Honor's little jaw tighten. She clearly wants to say something to him, but she decides not to and, instead, she storts playing the opening notes and *he* storts tinkling with the piano keys.

After, like, thirty seconds, he stops playing and goes, 'Wait!'

And Honor takes the piccolo away from her lips, looking suddenly confused.

He goes, 'Sorry, *what* is that tune you're playing?'

She's like, 'Er, *Gabriel's Oboe?*'

'Yeah,' he goes, 'as it's never been heard before! Why are you playing it so fast?'

'I wasn't playing it fast.'

'Yes, you were. Please listen to my playing and keep in time.'

I don't even need to tell you what Honor's face looks like when she hears this. She looks fit to put her hands around little Jack's throat and choke the focking life out of him.

Siofra turns around to Sorcha and goes, 'I'm sorry – he's a bit of a perfectionist!'

Sorcha's like, 'It's only by receiving constructive criticism that any of us improves.'

They stort again. Sixty seconds in this time, Jack again stops.

'Okay,' he goes, 'now you're playing it too slow.'

Honor's there, 'No, I wasn't,' in fairness, fighting her corner.

'You're playing it like it's a funeral march. Did I not tell you to watch my playing and keep in time?'

'Yeah.'

'Then why are you ignoring my instructions?'

Honor looks suddenly flustered. Her face is red. She goes, 'I need a drink of water.'

She walks over the table and she grabs her glass and she knocks back two or three mouthfuls.

Jack looks at his old dear and just, like, shakes his head. 'I mean, it's *Gabriel's Oboe*,' he goes, 'not Rachmaninoff.'

I look at Sorcha. She's still has a smile on her face, but suddenly it looks painted on. Because, for all of Siofra's supposed expertise in the area of child rearing, one thing is suddenly obvious.

Little Jack is a focking dickhead.

'Okay,' he goes, as Honor returns from the table, 'let's see can you get this right before one of us dies of old age.'

It's at that exact moment that I decide to have a nibble of the old Comté myself. But when I reach for the cheese knife, I notice that it isn't *there* anymore?

I look down at my feet, wondering did I possibly drop it, but then a sudden feeling of dread hits me – and it hits me like a sixteen-wheeler truck, because I suddenly realize that Honor didn't come over to the table for water.

She was tooling up to stab Jack.

I look up just in time to catch the little flash of silver hidden in her hand. I'm up off the chair like *it's* on fire and my orse is catching.

Jack is sitting at the piano and, suddenly, Honor is holding the cheese knife like a dagger.

Sorcha goes, 'Oh my God!'

Honor pulls back her orm, getting ready to plunge the knife into Jack's shoulder. Everyone is frozen to the spot, totally powerless, except for the Rossmeister.

I literally throw myself at her, grabbing her by the wrist and I take her down like *I'm* Sébastien Chabal and *she's* Chris Masoe.

We're suddenly rolling around on the floor. She's kicking and screaming and biting and scratching, basically like a feral animal, going, 'I'm going to kill him! I'm going to focking kill the little prick!'

Honor has some serious strength in her. But I manage to get the knife out of her hand and I throw it onto the table, even as she's going, 'Baaassstttaaarrrddd!'

I sit on top of her to pin her down, as Siofra stands up, fixes Sorcha's old man with a look and goes, 'You asked me does Honor look like a girl living in an unstable family environment? Do you still want me to answer that question?'

And then she goes, 'Jack, Linus – come on, we're leaving.'

Sorcha can't even look her old man in the eye. 'Ross and I have been talking,' she goes.

341

I'm there, 'And wait till you hear what it means for you!'

He looks at me, then he looks at Sorcha, except she can't find the words to say what she has to say, so *I'm* the one who ends up saying it?

I'm there, 'We've discussed it – my wife and me – and we've come to a decision. You're out – the two of you. Sling your focking hook.'

Her old man totally blanks me and just addresses Sorcha.

He's like, 'Is that what *you* want?'

She doesn't say yes *or* no. Instead, she just goes, 'Honor isn't better at all. In fact, she's right back to square one again. Unfortunately, we have to consider the possibility that Siofra was right all along.'

He laughs – he genuinely can't believe this. He goes, 'So this is all down to me – is that what you're saying? Honor trying to stab that little boy is down to me, is it?'

I'm there, 'Yeah, that's exactly what we're saying. Now pack your bags and focking hop it.'

I've always been a bad loser, but I'm an even worse winner.

He still refuses point-blank to look at me.

Sorcha's old dear goes, 'What about the boys? How will you cope with them?'

'We'll manage,' I go. I take Brian out of *her* orms and I take Johnny out of *his* – Sorcha's already holding Leo. 'Although we'll probably end up getting a nanny or two. Preferably from Eastern Europe.'

Her old man goes, 'It gives me no pleasure whatsoever, Sorcha, to see you making the same mistakes over and over again.'

He tries to emotionally blackmail her then. He's like, 'Where are we supposed to go?'

I'm there, 'Doesn't your other daughter have that aportment in the Beacon South Quarter? It's got two bedrooms. I presume she'll let you have the other one for the time being.'

He goes, 'Sorcha, don't do this,' because the place was still a focking building site when they lived there.

I'm like, 'I saw those gaffs described as "well-apportioned" and "excellently serviced through a range of public transport links" recently. You'd have to think that the economy is picking up with that kind of talk, wouldn't you?'

'This is – oh my God – *so* hord for me,' Sorcha goes. 'And, Dad, I hope you'll forgive me in time. I just want what's best for my daughter.'

Her old man just nods. He's beaten and he knows it.

'Can you give us a few days,' he goes, 'until we sort something out?'

Sorcha's like, 'Oh my God, take as much time as you need.'

I'm there, 'We'll give you a week – then you better be gone,' and I walk out of the room, grinning like a focking hero.

I take Brian and Johnny upstairs and I put them down for their afternoon nap. Brian is out like a light. Johnny only takes, like, five minutes before he's finally asleep.

I tip down the passageway to Honor's room. She's staring at her phone – either texting or tweeting. I stand in the doorway and she eventually notices me. She goes, 'What the fock do you want?'

I'm there, 'I'm proud of you, Honor.'

It's definitely not what she expected to hear.

She's there, 'Proud of me?'

I'm like, 'Yeah, no, I'm not proud of you for trying to stick a knife in that kid – even though was being a complete dick and a lot of people would have said he deserved it. I'm proud of you because Sorcha's old pair are moving out.'

That instantly cheers her up.

She's like, 'I'm so focking happy.'

I'm there, 'I thought you'd be pleased. You probably remember that I predicted all of this last Christmas. I was the one who backed you up. I said you were a bitch because that's what you wanted to be. If they'd all just accepted that, then we wouldn't have had to go through all the shit that we did.'

'I was good for a little while.'

'Exactly. I mean, I could see you struggling with it. It looked exhausting at times, but you proved that you *could* actually do it? I'm going to say something else to you, Honor. I know you might have very nearly killed that kid, severed a major ortery, blah, blah, blah, but I still love you. And I don't want you to change at all. I think you're perfect just the way you are.'

345

See, the Siofra Flynns of this world would probably tell you that what I'm doing here is bad parenting. They can think what they want. I know how to bring up my daughter. If you buy her whatever she asks for, blank out the really hurtful shit that she says to you and keep her away from anything that could be used as a weapon, there's really very little to worry about.

I can see only positives, in fact.

'What's *she* saying?' she goes. 'She said she needs time to think of an appropriate punishment for me.'

See, this is, like, the following *day*?

I just smile at her. I'm there, 'I, personally, don't think she'll do shit. That's my genuine belief. And don't forget, I'm going to be behind the scenes, constantly defending you and putting your case.'

On the bright side, she storts back at Mount Anville next Wednesday – at least then she'll be someone else's problem during the daytime.

As I turn to leave, she ends up saying one of the most incredible things I've ever heard.

She goes, 'You're the only real friend I have.'

It's a lovely thing to hear.

I'm there, 'I'm sure that's not true, Honor,' even though I know it is.

She's like, 'No one likes me except you.'

'And that's never going to change,' I go. 'I'll take your side, Honor, no matter what you do.'

I tip downstairs feeling like the best father in the world. And that's when my phone storts going, 'It's Kearney time!'

I look at the screen and it ends up being Fionn.

I answer it by going, 'Okay, I don't want to know who on the Fock It List you've ridden now. I'm having one of my best days in a long time and I'm in cracking, cracking form.'

He goes, 'Hey, Ross,' and I can straight away tell from his tone that something is wrong.

I'm like, 'Dude, what is it?'

We've obviously had our differences, but I'd still walk through a plate-glass door for the goy. That's rugby. Live with it.

He goes, 'Ross, can I talk to you?'

I'm there, 'Of course.'

'I'm at the front gate.'

'*My* front gate?'

'Yeah, I'm outside.'

'Hang on a second – I'll buzz you in.'

'No,' he goes, sounding suddenly sheepish, 'can you maybe come down to me?'

I'm there, 'Come down to you?'

He's like, 'Please, Ross.'

So that's what I end up having to do. I walk down to the front gate. He's sitting in his old dear's Honda Civic, having never actually owned a cor of his own.

He leans across and opens the front passenger door. I hop in.

I'm like, 'You're still driving this heap of shit, I see.'

He takes, like, a deep breath. He has something to say, although he ends up taking his focking time about it.

He goes, 'Can I show you something?'

I'm like, 'Yeah, no, what is it?'

And suddenly, without any pre-warning, he unzips his fly and storts rummaging through the fruit bowl.

I'm like, 'Whoa, whoa, whoa – what the fock are you doing?'

And he goes, 'I think I've got something.'

'What do you mean?'

'I think I've got, you know, a sexually transmitted disease.'

I actually laugh.

I'm there, 'Delighted! I am focking delighted! Oh my God, this is turning into *the* most perfect weekend.'

He goes, 'Can I show it to you?'

I'm like, 'Fock off – go and see a doctor.'

'I just thought, you might be able to, you know, confirm it for me.'

'What, just because I've ridden probably two or three thousand women in my time, I'm bound to have had every disease going? You've some focking cheek, Fionn.'

'Please, Ross.'

I sigh and I shake my head.

'Go on then,' I go, being basically too nice for my own good. It's nothing I haven't seen before. Like I said – we played rugby together. 'Whip it out there.'

And that's what he ends up doing. He pulls it out through his fly and I look at it, lying limp in his hand, all dork and shrivelled and miserable, like something you'd see in Columbo's ashtray.

I stare at it, spotting one or two giveaway lesions on, like, his foreskin.

'Does it hurt to piss?' I go.

He's like, 'Yeah – it's agony.'

Again, I laugh. I'm there, 'You've got Chris Rea's brother – Gonner.'

He's like, 'Shit.'

'Yeah, no, it's the clap. Here, put your mickey away – this is a respectable street.'

'I don't believe it.'

'It serves you focking right.'

'What am I going to do?'

'Like I said, go and see a doctor. Here, I'm having a great weekend – and this is the cherry on top.'

'I can't go to the doctor. I'm embarrassed.'

'What's there to be embarrassed about? Go in, whip it out and treat it like it's a big joke. Come on, it's a few tablets. You'll probably have to go off the drink for a couple of weeks as well. Trust me – you and the doctor will end up having a laugh about the whole thing.'

'My doctor's a woman, Ross. She's one of my mother's best friends.'

'Oh, this just gets better and better.'

'I've had discharge as well.'

'Okay, too much information, Dude. There's other doctors, you know? Why don't you go to the Wellman Clinic?'

'Will you come with me?'

I'm there, 'You're kidding me, aren't you? I wouldn't miss it for the focking world.'

IO.

The Curse of Tinderella

Honor's first day back at school ends up being the usual emotional rollercoaster. We're talking tears. We're talking tantrums. We're talking anxiety. And that's only Sorcha trying to decide on an outfit for the school run.

Honor ends up sleeping through the worst of it, while I'm prodded awake in the early hours of the morning to advise my wife on such vital matters as whether it's too early in A/W13 for cashmere and whether a Cartier scorf is a bit 'fock you' – especially given that they didn't *have* to take our daughter back?

School-run fashion, it turns out, is a serious, serious business and the first day of the new school year is *the* most important day of all for fashion-savvy moms. You don't get a second chance to make a first impression. At the gates of Mount Anville, you barely get a first.

'What you wear on the day that school storts will define you for the rest of the year,' Sorcha goes. She's lost, like, two stone over the course of the summer, which has given her even more options. 'If you get it wrong on Day One, you can spend the next few weeks overcompensating, and before you know it, it's Christmastime and the other mothers are talking about you behind their hands.'

'About that,' I go. 'Do you not think we should possibly, I don't know, declare what happened at the weekend?'

She goes, 'What are you talking about?'

I'm like, 'Er, our daughter went for another kid with a cheese knife?'

'We don't know for sure that she was definitely going to stab him,' Sorcha goes. This is what we've decided to tell ourselves. 'You heard her, Ross. She said she only picked up the knife for her own

349

protection, because she felt threatened by Jack constantly hectoring her over her playing.'

What she means is that if we told the school about the incident, they wouldn't let her through the gates of the place.

'Besides,' Sorcha goes, 'we're dealing with the matter ourselves.'

Her old pair are moving back to the Beacon South Quarter next week – to an aportment next door to Sorcha's sister. It was described online as bijou, which in French means focking tiny.

Sorcha says she thinks it might be easier to choose an outfit if she listed what she calls *paradigms*?

'I'm thinking of three,' she goes. 'Über Rugby Mom, Career Mom in Slim Tailoring and Gym Mom with Full Make-Up.'

This is at, like, five o'clock in the morning, bear in mind.

I actually nod off. It's a case of the spirit being unwilling and flesh not really giving a fock. But Sorcha shakes me awake again and, when I open my eyes, it seems we've moved on to a fourth paradigm.

'But if I decide to go with the Keeping Down with the Joneses look,' she goes, 'would High Street come across as, like, sarcastic?'

After several hours of this, I'm like one of those Guantánamo detainees that you see in, like, movies. I'd say yes to any question I'm asked in exchange for even five minutes of sleep.

Just before eight o'clock, Sorcha finally settles on an outfit for the morning: we're talking a delaine twill blazer in antique rose by Theory, dork blue skinny jeans by Current/Elliott – she cries actual tears when she realizes they actually fit her – and nude Chloé ballet pumps.

And then it's suddenly time for me to get up.

I swing my feet out of the bed. The bedroom floor looks like a mad bull has run loose in BTs.

I grab a Munster farmer's breakfast – a long, open-mouthed stare at myself in the bathroom mirror and a drink of water straight from the tap – then I throw on the first clothes that I can find and I go to wake Honor.

I'm surprised to find her already wearing her uniform and sitting on the end of her bed. I'm there, 'Are you okay?'

She gives me a tight little nod.

I'm like, 'You're not nervous, are you?'

She goes, 'No,' but I know she is.'

I'm there, 'Do you want some breakfast? Or even just a coffee?'

She shakes her head. 'No,' she goes, 'I just want to get the first day over with.'

I totally understand that.

Fifteen minutes later, the three of us are in the cor. Deciding on a look for the morning doesn't seem to bring Sorcha any happiness. Every minute of the drive to the school, we have to listen to her outpourings of outfit remorse.

'Maybe I should have worn a statement colour,' she goes. 'You know my Michael Kors wool-crêpe blazer in cobalt blue? It's just I'm wondering now is antique rose possibly a bit, you know, *meh*?'

This is at the traffic lights outside the old Spirit of Negative Equity.

Honor goes, 'Yeah, it's not all about *you*, you know?'

Sorcha's there, 'I know it's not all about me, Honor. I'm actually doing it for you. I don't want to let you down on your first day back.'

The lights have turned green, but, having had pretty much no sleep, I don't notice until the dude behind me in a white Mitsubishi Colt gives me an angry blast of his horn. I give him the finger out the window, then I carry on.

And so does Sorcha.

She goes, 'Now, I haven't completely settled on a bag yet.'

I'm there, 'What the fock are you talking about? We've already left the house.'

'I put three or four in the boot. To choose from. The bag is the most difficult thing to get right. A clutch makes it look like this is the only thing I have to do today. I don't want people to think that. Even though it *is* the only thing I have to do today. And then, by the same token, something over-the-shoulder can totally misshape a blazer. Oh my God, it might even end up actually being no bag at all.'

Of course, nothing settles a woman's doubts about her own outfit quite like seeing another woman who's made a total pig's ear of hers. We're pulling into the school, making our triumphant return, when the critiquing of the other mothers storts.

'Oh my God,' Sorcha goes, 'both of you, look at Granuaile Sweeney's mum! What I'm saying is, look, but don't make it *obvious* that you're looking?'

I'm like, 'What's wrong with what she's wearing?'

'Er, a black maxi dress and Converse? She's trying way too hord to look like she doesn't give a shit.'

'Maybe she *genuinely* doesn't?'

'Oh, please! Look at her hair. She's had that done somewhere this morning. Oh my God, is that Penny Osborne? It *is* Penny Osborne. Just smile and wave, Ross. Oh my God, *how* many seasons ago were ponchos in?'

I'm there, 'I don't know, Babes,' as I pork the cor. 'I've lost track.'

'Unless they're, like, *back* in,' Sorcha goes, 'and I somehow missed it. Honor, have you heard anything about ponchos being back in?'

Honor doesn't answer her. She just opens the back door and she gets out and me and Sorcha end up getting out as well.

Sorcha goes, 'Oh my God, good luck, Honor,' except Honor just totally blanks her. She throws her schoolbag over her shoulder, picks up her piccolo case and walks off in the direction of the school building.

I can see a lot of mothers and their children checking her out. Our daughter being back here is obviously massive, massive news, especially given her history.

But then something suddenly occurs to me. Something isn't right. There isn't any of the, I don't know, fear that I expected to see in the eyes of the other children and parents. As a matter of fact, they're all grinning from ear to ear as Honor walks past them and into the actual school.

Sorcha cops it as well. She's like, 'Ross, are they – oh my God – *laughing* at her?'

They're brave focking kids if they are.

I look around at the various mothers standing around. Most of them are looking in our general postcode and *they* seem to be finding something funny as well.

'Hi, Sorcha,' Keelin Massey's old dear goes, struggling to keep a straight face as she walks past us.

Then Blaise Banagher – whose daughter, Eva, used to be in Honor's class – also goes, 'It's lovely to see you both,' at the same time laughing – as in, like, really struggling to hold it together.

Sorcha thinks it's her outfit.

'Oh my God,' she goes, 'maybe I should have just made it a plaid shirt with jeans and knee-high boots.'

That's when I look up and I notice Honor coming back out of the school and walking towards us. She's got, like, her iPhone in her hand and a face like thunder. Not that there's anything unusual in that.

'If you're wondering what everyone's laughing at,' she goes, 'it's this!' and she hands her mother her iPhone.

I look over Sorcha's shoulder and I'm in literally shock.

It's a video of us on the dance-floor at Amie with an ie's wedding, with Sorcha's tongue surgically attached to my focking ear.

'Garret,' I go, because I'm pretty sure I saw him filming it at the time. And he obviously waited until now to post it to cause us maximum focking shame. 'This is going to literally break the Internet.'

Sorcha's like, 'Oh my God. I mean, literally, Ross, oh my God!'

Honor goes, 'You don't want to let me down on my first day back at school?' and she shakes her head. 'You two are a focking embarrassment.'

'Yes, it's just as I thought,' the doctor goes. 'It's gonorrhoea.'

I laugh. I can't help it. Me and Sorcha go viral in the same week that Fionn goes bacterial. The goys have been ripping the serious piss out of me over becoming a YouTube sensation. I'm glad the focus is off me all of a sudden.

The doctor's there, 'Do you find this funny?'

And I'm there, 'I do. I genuinely do.'

He doesn't even crack a smile. Of course he sees this kind of shit all day, every day – there must come a point where it stops being genuinely hilarious.

Fionn puts his thing away and he zips up his fly. The doctor suddenly seems a bit interested in *me*, for some reason? 'Okay, pull down your trousers,' he goes, 'and I'll take a look at you now.'

I'm there, 'Me? Why do you want to look at me?'

'Well, I would have thought that if this chap here has gonorrhoea, then you, as his partner, would be concerned that you had it as well.'

'Portner?'

'Pull your trousers down and sit up on the table there.'

It's Fionn who ends up having to put him wise. 'He's not my partner,' he goes.

I'm there, 'I'm very much a ladies' man.'

The doctor looks confused by that. He's like, 'Well, if you're not his partner, then why are you here?'

I'm there, 'Why do you think? For a focking laugh!'

The dude just shakes his head – he obviously thinks I'm immature – then he turns back to Fionn. 'Can I ask you about your, em, lifestyle?' he goes.

I'm there, 'He's asking you what you've been up to, Fionn. He's asking about your carbon cockprint.'

Fionn's there, 'Yes, thank you, Ross.'

The doctor goes, 'How many partners have you had in the last, say, twelve months?'

I sit forward. I'm interested in hearing this myself.

Fionn goes, 'Somewhere between sixteen and twenty.'

I'm like, 'Jesus Christ! Just to put that into prospective for you, Doctor, until about a year ago he couldn't get a ride if his life depended on it. Birds found him boring and a geek.'

The doctor goes, 'Did you have unprotected sex with all of these women?'

Fionn's like, 'No. Yes. Some of them. I mean, in a lot of cases – shit – I can't remember.'

'Well, you know what the responsible thing to do is, don't you?'

I laugh again. I'm there, 'Are you telling him he needs to tell all these birds he nailed there's a chance they may have caught something off him?'

He addresses his answer to Fionn rather than me – I suppose he would, though, wouldn't he?

'In most cases,' he goes, 'they'll know if they have something. But gonorrhoea doesn't always present symptoms in women. It still needs to be treated, though. If it isn't, it can cause all sorts of serious health problems later on.'

'This just gets better and better,' I go.

The doctor goes, 'You might, em, take the morning to draw up a list of all the . . .'

'No need,' I go. 'He's already got one.'

I stand up. Fionn's jacket is hanging on the back of the door. I reach into his inside pocket and I whip out his copy of the Fock It List. It's, like, folded in four. I open it out. A lot of the names are highlighted using a yellow morker pen. I'm guessing they're the ones he's, like, *been* with?

'What's that?' the doctor goes.

I'm there, 'It's called a Fock It List. And I wouldn't mind but it's not even *his* Fock It List. It was originally mine. Jesus, look how many he's worked his way through.'

I show it to him.

I'm there, 'Come on then, Fionn – as Father Fehily used to say, a good stort is half the work.'

'Ross,' Fionn tries to go, 'this is something that needs to be handled, you know, sensitively. I think I'd rather do it on my own.'

I'm like, 'Dude, you've got two choices here. Either we tell them together or I tell them myself.'

The doctor writes Fionn out a prescription. Five minutes later, we're sitting in his old dear's Honda Civic. I'm staring at the list, trying to work out what order to do it in – there could be, like, seven or eight hours in this job. Fionn, meanwhile, is just staring into space, feeling sorry for himself.

He's going, 'I am so ashamed. I am so ashamed of myself.'

I'm there, 'Dude, I wouldn't beat yourself up over it. Like I said, you were someone who couldn't get kicked in a focking stampede. Then suddenly women were interested in you, mostly out of sympathy.'

'It was like I became someone else.'

'It went to your head. The thing I'll possibly never forgive you for was trying to, I don't know, airbrush me and the rest of the goys out of the story. We put our focking necks on the line for you.'

'I know. Look, it was all the attention. It was the audiences and the applause. It was the talk of books and movie deals. I just became a different person.'

'Okay, can I suggest something here?'

'What?'

I open the glove box and straight away I spot the little black case. I take it out and I open it up. Inside are Fionn's glasses.

'Put these on,' I go.

He's there, 'I was going to get my eyes lasered.'

'Dude, forget getting your focking eyes lasered. This is you, Fionn. You're glasses. You're literally just glasses and books and shit like that. If you want to go back to being the man you used to be – the one we all respected, the one that birds had literally no interest in – you have to put them back on.'

He considers this for a good, like, ten seconds. Deep down, he knows I'm talking sense. He takes them from me, stares at them for a moment, takes a deep breath, then he hangs them back on his ears.

He looks like a complete focking dork again.

'It's like the old you is suddenly back,' I go. 'Now, who's first on the list? I was thinking maybe Tlachtga Ní Dhuibhir?'

She's the one who threw a 7-Up in his face in Kielys. She'll have a shit fit.

He takes a second or two to compose himself, then he storts the cor and points it in the direction of town. We pork in the Brown Thomas cor pork, then we walk up Clarendon Street and into the Westbury Mall we go. We stop outside the candle shop where she works – although I think he mentioned that she might actually *own* it?

We look in. The shop is actually rammers. There's hope for the country if people are spending thirty snots on smelly candles again. Tlachtga is behind the counter.

Fionn goes, 'Ross, will you let me handle this?'

I'm like, 'Of course. I'll wait out here.'

Into the shop he goes. I can see Tlachtga – she really is a little honey – looking at him oddly when she sees him coming. You can tell she's totally thrown by the glasses.

You can tell she's thinking, 'Oh my God, he didn't look like that the night I rode him – luckily for him.'

I can see that Fionn is, like, trying to find the words to tell her what he has to tell her. Except he's making a total meal of it. He can't even make eye contact with the girl. He keeps pushing his glasses up on his nose and his face is all red with embarrassment.

That's when I stick my head around the door of the shop. 'Tlachtga,' I shout – this is in front of, like, ten or fifteen *customers*, bear in mind? 'He's got Knob Rot. There's a very good chance that he's given it to you. Get yourself checked out.'

Everyone in the shop's jaw just drops.

I'm like, 'Now hurry the fock up, Fionn – this is a long list we've got to get through!'

'I acted in a way that was less than chivalrous,' Fionn is telling Ealga Gary an hour later.

Less than chivalrous? Oh, he's definitely back to his old self.

He goes, 'I treated you very cruelly and very dismissively and for that I am truly sorry.'

We're in, like, Ealga Gary's gaff. She lives in one of those aport-ments on the Stillorgan dualler, next to the Applegreen.

Ealga just shrugs. She goes, 'Yes, I was annoyed that you never returned my calls. But don't flatter yourself – I didn't exactly fall in love with you, Fionn. I mean, you weren't the greatest lover in the world.'

I laugh. Have to.

I'm like, 'Did you hear that, Dude? You weren't the greatest lover in the world!'

I know I'm in no position to talk, but it's still funny. Ealga turns on *me*, then?

She's like, 'Sorry, why are *you* here?'

357

I'm there, 'I'm trying to be a friend to the goy and to offer him a bit of moral support. You haven't even heard the best bit yet.'

'What are you talking about?'

'Ross,' Fionn goes, 'can you please stay out of this?'

I'm like, 'He has the clap, Ealga. That's what he's here to tell you. The dude you chose over me – can I just remind you? – even after I opened my hort to you and told you that you were someone I always regretted never making an actual move on. You chose him and your reward is possibly the clap.'

She just, like, stares full-on at Fionn. She's there, 'Is this true?'

'Look,' he goes, 'I'm ninety-nine percent certain I didn't have it when we . . . you know . . .'

I'm there, 'What he's trying to say is that you were the first bird he rode off the Fock It List.'

She's like, 'The what?'

'It was, like, a fantasy list – of all the women I wanted to ride and that's a compliment to you, Ealga, because there were some real crackers on it. I don't know if you remember a bird called Becky McGrew? That's the calibre we're talking about. We're going to see her later this afternoon.'

Fionn tries to go, 'Ealga, you and I used protection when we did it – well, certainly at first.'

The girl just shakes her head.

She goes, 'I don't believe this. I don't actually believe it.'

He goes, 'You probably still should see your doctor, though – as a precaution.'

Ealga suddenly slaps him across the face. The hilarious thing is that Fionn actually sees her hand coming – he always had good reactions on the rugby field, in fairness to him. But he obviously thinks it's something he deserves, roysh, because he makes no attempt to duck it, block it or even just ride it. He closes his eyes and he takes it.

She catches him beautifully. There's, like, an almighty crack and his glasses go flying across Ealga's kitchen floor.

I end up having to chase after them. I pick them up, look them over and go, 'Careful, Ealga – these are a vital piece of his personality.'

'You're an asshole,' she goes.

He's there, 'I didn't conduct myself at all well,' as I hang the glasses back on his head. 'For that, I am very, very sorry.'

I'm like, 'The other thing is, Ealga, that he's not a hero. I was the one who rescued him from Africa. He blubbed like a focking baby. Anyway, your time is up. Like I said, we've got a lot of names to get through.'

So this is how we spend the entire day – driving around South Dublin, breaking the news to sixteen girls that they may or may not have the drip. Fionn tries to give me the slip once or twice, but I stick to him like the stink on vomit.

The last name on the list ends up being Iseult Garrigan. She works in the Deportment of Communications, Energy and Natural Resources on Adelaide Road. We ask for her at the front desk, the receptionist makes a call upstairs and five minutes later she comes clip-clopping across the lobby – I think I mentioned she has tremendous tartugas, even though the face isn't great – squinting her eyes, wondering does she know us.

She's another one who's confused by the glasses.

'Fionn?' she goes, once she's standing practically in front of him.

I'm there, 'He has a bit of news for you.'

She goes, 'News?'

And I'm like, 'Yeah, he's pregnant.'

I'm just trying to lighten the atmos.

'Ross,' Fionn goes, 'just once, would you let me do the talking?'

I'm like, 'Hey, you fire ahead, Dude.'

'Okay,' he goes, turning to Iseult, 'you remember the night we were together?'

She's there, 'Do you mean the night I went to the bathroom and when I came back you'd opened a window and climbed out?'

Another one of my moves. I wish people would just get their own acts.

She goes, 'Yeah, I vaguely remember that night alright.'

'Well,' he goes, 'there's a possibility that I may have, well, given you something. For what it's worth, I'm very ashamed of myself.'

She's like, 'When you say something . . .'

'When I say something,' he goes, lowering his voice to a whisper, 'I mean, you know, a sexually transmitted infection.'

'Gonorrhoea,' I go. 'He's focking riddled with it. And I'm only saying that, Fionn, because the girl deserves the full facts.'

Iseult takes this news surprisingly in her stride. In other words, she doesn't *react*? She doesn't scream at him or slap him across the face or say that being with him was the biggest mistake of her life, like all the other girls.

She actually just looks away and goes, 'I have it, too. I got the results from the clinic yesterday.'

'All I can do,' Fionn goes, 'is to tell you again that I'm truly, truly sorry.'

And that's when Iseult drops her bombshell.

'You didn't give it to me,' she goes. 'I gave it to you.'

He's like, 'You?'

I laugh. He got it from the last bird he rode. Which means none of the others has anything to worry about. Which means the last six hours we spent driving around town telling birds to get themselves checked out was all for nothing. I end up having to leave the building because I'm laughing so much.

Fionn joins me outside a minute or two later. I'm leaning against a wall, literally weak from laughter.

He goes, 'Apparently, she got it from her ex-boyfriend. He was on a stag in . . .'

He doesn't even bother finishing his sentence. It doesn't really matter where the stag was. He was probably going to say Newcastle.

We stort walking down Adelaide Road, back towards the cor.

I go, 'I suppose, looking back, the sensible thing would have been to stort with the most recent case and work your way backwards.'

He just nods.

'No,' he goes, pushing his glasses up on his nose, 'I think I needed to do it. It was my punishment.'

I'm like, 'The big lesson for you, Fionn, once again is to stick with birds who are *in* your actual league. I've always seen you ending up with a really, really plain girl with a good coat.'

He's like, 'Thanks.'

He looks so sad. I decide to take him out of his misery.

I'm like, 'Dude, seriously, I wouldn't sweat it. Another day or two and this will just be a funny anecdote. Trust me. I'm already thinking about all the people I'm going to tell.'

We're suddenly back at the cor.

I'm like, 'Pint?'

'No,' he goes, opening the cor door, 'I'm going to go home to start working on my book. The *true* account of what happened in Uganda.'

I'm there, 'I better focking be in it.'

And he smiles sadly at me and he goes, 'Don't worry, Ross – you will be.'

The old man and Helen have their bags packed and waiting in the hallway. 'Dublin to John Fitzgerald Kennedy International,' *he* goes at the top of his voice, a giant turd of a cigor smouldering between his fingers, 'then from John Fitzgerald Kennedy to Seattle-Tacoma International!'

I'm there, 'Fair focks. I'd obviously drop you to the airport, except, well, you know . . .'

I let my voice trail off. I couldn't be focking orsed is the actual reason. If Helen doesn't want me on this trip, then they can make their own way to the airport.

'Don't you worry about a thing,' the old man goes. 'We have transportation arranged. I shall keep you in the – inverted commas – loop, *vis-à-vis* developments and so forth.'

'*Vis-à-vis*. You're such a focking tool. Do, though. Definitely tell me what's happening. And if you need me to go over there – again, bear in mind that I already found her once.'

'Well – and this is strictly *entre nous*, Ross – Helen and I already know where Erika is. We've known where she is all summer.'

'*Entre* focking *nous*. I'm actually stunned that I'm even related to you. Continue.'

'Well, do you remember a chap she was in college with – name of Colm?'

'Colm Lernihan? Yeah, no, I played rugby with Colm Lernihan. She had a major thing for him. Except he was gay.'

'Well, they stayed in touch, you see. He moved to Seattle. Ten years ago – or something of that order.'

'You wouldn't even know about Seattle if it wasn't for me.'

'Quite right, Ross. Well, when you mentioned Seattle, that got Helen thinking about why Erika would go there, and then she managed to track this chap down. This was just after we got back from Buenos Aires. It seems he has his own restaurant over there. Done very well for himself.'

'And she's with him?'

'She's working for him as a *maître d'*.'

'Jesus, I could weep for the girl. Is Amelie still with her?'

'Yes. And she's being very well cared for. Colm's been wonderful. Helen explained the situation to him – what she's been going through. What we've all been going through. And he's been talking to Erika, preparing the ground, if you will, for her eventual return. Well, it seems the poor girl's head is all over the place and she just needed her – what's this you young people call it – *space*?'

'Does she know that you've been talking to him?'

'No, no, it's all been very much on the down-low, to coin a phrase. Well, we're just terrified that if she finds out we're onto her, she'll flee again. Like I said, this Colm chap has been trying to persuade her that she needs to see her family and he thinks he's managed to win her trust. He says now would be a good time for us to come.'

'Like I said, you wouldn't even know about Seattle if it wasn't for me. So I deserve a lot of the credit – that's what I'm saying.'

'Yes, of course you do. Any word from young Ronan?'

I check my phone.

I'm there, 'Yeah, no, still nothing.'

The Junior Cert results are out today and the old man was obviously keen to find out how he got on before he left the country.

He goes, 'Why don't you try his number again?'

I'm there, 'I did. It keeps going straight to voicemail.'

'You don't think . . .'

He means, do I think he failed?

I'm like, 'Of course he didn't. This is Ronan we're talking about. Yeah, no, he's probably just having a few pints to celebrate.'

'Pints? He's sixteen, Ross.'

'Well, cans, then. I'm sure we'll hear from him soon.'

That's when the doorbell all of a sudden rings. We look at each other, then we both go racing out to answer it. I get there first.

My turn of pace over the first ten yords is something that has never left me, even in Dubes on a maplewood floor.

I reef open the door and he's standing there with an expression that I can't actually read.

I'm like, 'Ro, what's the deal? I've been ringing your phone all morning.'

He goes, 'Me batter doddy ren out.'

'Well, what's the focking Jack? Did you pass or not?'

I suddenly notice that he's not smiling. In fact, he's just staring down at the doorstep. He has a piece of paper in his hand. He obviously doesn't want to show it to us.

Oh, fock. It was all those weeks he put into trying to track down that ancestor of ours who blew the focking shit out of the supposed heroes of Nineteen Whenever. He spent so much time on it, when the exams came around he had fock-all energy left.

I'm like, 'Ro, exams aren't the be-all and end-all. Look at me, just as an example. Most of my exams, I wrote down my exam number and left after half an hour. Look at the gaff I'm living in today.'

He looks up at me and he holds my stare for a good, like, twenty seconds, then he smiles, hands me the piece of paper and goes, 'Ine arthur getting all A's, Rosser.'

This, like, wave of relief suddenly sweeps over me. I punch the air. My old man throws his orms around Ro and I stort literally dancing around the front gorden, going, 'My son is a genius! My son is a basic genius!' not giving a fock what anyone on Ailesbury Road thinks.

Ronan goes, 'Here, Rosser, I loved your little speech theer, "Exams aren't the be-all and end-all – look at me."'

'I know,' I go. 'You'd want to be really hord up to take any consolation from that,' and then I stort shouting at the sky again. 'My son is a focking genius!'

Helen steps outside then. She goes, 'What's all the shouting about?'

Ro goes, 'I got all A's in me June Yidder Ceert, Mrs Joseph.'

She smiles.

She's like, 'Congratulations, Ronan,' and then – this is a nice touch – she goes, 'Congratulations, Ross.'

It's the first nice thing she's said to me since Orgentina.

I'm there, 'Yeah, no, I'll take that, Helen – thanks.'

She turns to the old man and she's like, 'You checked in, did you?'

'Did it online,' he goes. 'The wonders of the modern world and so forth! The car should be here any minute.'

Helen goes back inside to grab their bags.

I turn to Ro. I'm like, 'So you'll probably want to get shit-faced on the strength of this,' and then I turn to my old man and go, 'Give him some money to get shit-faced, will you?'

The old man reaches for his pocket.

'No, no,' Ronan goes, because he's a great kid. 'Ine throying to mebbe lay off the geergle for a bit. I've been thrinking a bit too much lately.'

I'm there, 'Who's to say what's too much, Ro? There's an awful lot of shite being talked about drink at the moment. They're trying to say that three pints is a binge now. That used to be a storter. I mean, if these health freaks had their way, I'd be having my last pint on an international match day before *Ireland's Call*, my hangover during the second half and my morning-after fry-up at six o'clock in the evening. They're being ridiculous and they know it.'

'We're habben a birrof a peerty in the gaff – you know yisser self. Shadden's trowen it for me.'

'And obviously I'm not invited because Shadden's old pair are suing us for slander.'

Ronan just shrugs. He's like, 'It's a teddibly awkward situation, Rosser. Ine caught in the middle of it.'

That's when the old man says a suddenly surprising thing. 'No one is suing anyone,' he goes. 'It's all been sorted out amicably.'

I'm there, 'What?'

'Well, I knew that you'd had this misunderstanding with the Tuites over Sorcha's rings. I took it upon myself – I hope you don't mind, Ross – to go and see the famous Kennet in person. Well, we go back, of course.'

They shared a cell in Mountjoy back in the day – either a cell or a landing.

He goes, 'I mean, I thought the chap was still – italics – *inside*!'

Ronan's like, 'He was lerrout on temper doddy release.'

'Well, I had a word with the chap and I asked him if there was anything I could do to help make this *temper doddy* release of his a bit more permanent. He said he needed to find a job. I said, "I think I can help you with that – provided you drop all this slander nonsense, of course."'

The next thing any of us hears is a voice behind us going, 'Th . . . Th . . . Th . . . Theer yar, Cheerlie, me oawult boy!'

I turn around, roysh, and there, standing outside on the road, next to the old man's Jag, in a black jacket, trousers and a hat, everything about six sizes too big for him, is the famous K . . . K . . . K . . . K . . . K . . . Kennet!

I laugh. I'm there, 'You've hired him as your driver?'

'That's right!' the old man goes. 'Well, Helen and I are getting to that age in life, Ross, where it's rather nice to be chauffeured about the place. Plus, I'm on ten penalty points and I'm bound to lose my licence any day soon.'

Kennet goes, 'Ine g . . . g . . . g . . . going sthraight this toyum, Rosser. An hodest's day's woork for an hodest day's pay is alls I ebber wanthed ourra . . . l . . . l . . . life. Me auld mate Cheerlie hee-er is arthur gibbon me back me self-respect. So you can tell Surrogate we'll forget about eer little b . . . b . . . b . . . birra b . . . b . . . b . . . bodder.'

'Hurrah for that!' the old man goes.

Ronan's like, 'Yeah, feer fooks, Kennet.'

'Monta fook, Cheerlie,' Kennet goes. 'We'd want to getting on the roawut if you're gonna make yisser faloyt.'

★

I've got Brian, Johnny and Leo sitting on their play mats on the floor of the kitchen and I'm rolling the ball to them again. I can see them watching the way it wobbles, really taking in the fact that a rugby ball is not like any other ball.

'Like the good Lord Himself,' Father Fehily used to say, 'it moves in mysterious ways.'

I can hear Sorcha's old pair moving around upstairs, packing all their shit into boxes. They're moving out tonight and we're going to stort interviewing for a new nanny next week.

Sorcha asks Honor to put her breakfast dishes into the dishwasher and Honor goes, 'You focking do it if it means that much to you.'

It's nice that things are getting back to normal around here.

'Will I go and ask your old pair if they need help packing?' I go. 'Be definitely quicker with an extra pair of hands.'

Sorcha goes, 'You've already offered twice, Ross. My Dad told you they didn't need your help.'

'He's too proud – that's his problem. One of his problems. One of his many problems.'

'He thinks you're just rubbing their noses in it.'

'Anyone who knows me would tell you that's not how I roll.'

Honor gets up from the table.

'Where are you going?' Sorcha goes.

Honor's like, 'Er, *school*?'

'I told you to put your bowl and your glass into the dishwasher?'

'Yeah, I think I've already made myself clear on that point. If it bothers you that they're on the table, then do something about it.'

'Just to let you know, we're going back to using the Honour Board.'

'Yeah, focking spare me.'

She doesn't care. She knows she's got the five Ks I've promised her every month.

Sorcha goes, 'Ross, please speak to your daughter.'

I'm there, 'I'll put them in the dishwasher, Honor. You go up and put your uniform on.'

Like I said, things are returning to the way they were. It's nice.

366

'So that's the answer now?' Sorcha goes, as soon as Honor is out of the room. 'We're going to go back to letting her do whatever she wants.'

I'm there, 'I just think it's easier all round. We just need to buy her the things she asks us for and then ignore her when she's being horrible to us. Just as an example, she called me a sad sap and a total focking loser last night when she saw me scribbling down some thoughts I had about rugby in my famous tactics book. I just went, "Yeah, no, you're right, Honor – I'm probably both of those things," and she literally didn't know what to say. I just think her problems are manageable. We possibly should put a lock on the knife drawer, though.'

'Can you actually hear yourself? A lock on the knife drawer?'

'Look, I've said it all along, Babes – there's no perfect way to parent a child. I think that's one thing we definitely learned from Siofra Flynn. I mean, the famous Jack turned out to be a little bollocks, didn't he?'

I put Honor's dishes into the dishwasher. It only takes a few seconds. In future, me and Sorcha can take turns doing it.

'I'm finding it – oh my God – so difficult to be here,' Sorcha goes, 'while Mum and Dad are packing. I know *he's* still furious with me.'

I'm like, 'Fock him.'

I tip upstairs to get dressed myself. I stick my head around the door of what used to be Sorcha's old pair's room. They're both in there, like I said, packing.

I can't resist the urge to showboat, of course.

'If I was to have one criticism of the way you're packing,' I go, 'it's that you're being a bit too, I don't know, careful with your shit. Why don't you just fock everything into the boxes. You're only moving to Sandyford Industrial Estate.'

He ends up totally flipping. 'Can you please leave us in peace?' he practically shouts at me.

I walk off, actually laughing, which might sound horsh, but then he was the one who tried to have me neutered, as he put it.

I go into my room and while I'm throwing on my clothes I stort thinking about my old man and Helen. I'm wondering how they're getting on in Seattle and I'm still feeling a bit, I don't know, pissed off that they decided to go without me.

Like I said, they wouldn't have even known about Seattle if it wasn't for me.

On a whim, I decide to try Erika's number again. It's something I've done maybe four or five times since we got back from Buenos Aires, though more in hope that she'd answer it than expectation. It rings, like, six or seven times, except this time, instead of going to, like, voicemail as usual, it ends up being answered.

I'm like, 'Hello? Erika, is that you?'

She goes, 'Will you just leave me the fock alone?'

I've no idea what time it is in Seattle. It's possibly the middle of the night.

In the background, I can hear a baby crying.

I'm like, 'Is that Amelie?'

'You ruined everything,' she goes.

I'm there, 'Erika, I wasn't going to let my niece be raised in a strange country by a couple who don't even speak English.'

She actually shouts it this time. She goes, 'You focking ruined everything!'

There's, like, silence then. After twenty seconds of neither of us saying anything, I find myself suddenly going, 'They're in Seattle, Erika – as in, like, Helen and the old man? They've gone there to find you and hopefully bring you and Amelie home.'

She's like, 'I'm not in Seattle. I only told you that to throw you off the scent. And like an idiot, you believed me.'

I suddenly hear myself go, 'You're in Seattle and you're working as a *maître d'* in Colm Lernihan's restaurant.'

I instantly regret saying it. There's, like, silence on the other end of the phone. I've landed poor Colm in it. He was one of the best second rows I've ever played with, by the way – not that it's relevant to the story.

Erika goes, 'Have you been talking to him? He promised me. He focking promised . . .'

I remember what the old man said about her possibly pegging it again, so I end up going into verbal overdrive.

I'm like, 'Look, Helen and the old man are over because they're worried about you and because they love you and because that's what you do when you have a kid and you think they're possibly in trouble. The ends of the Earth – blah, blah, blah. They've been going out of their minds, Erika. Especially your old dear. She's half the woman she was a year ago and it gives me no pleasure to say that.'

I'm there, 'If you could only just for once swallow your pride. Look, no one cares that it didn't work out between you and Fabrizio Focking Fock Features. You were always out of his league. Someone like you deserves to be with a rugby player – and I'm talking one with an IRFU contract. What I'm also saying is that, you know, you have nothing to be embarrassed about. There are a lot of people here who think the focking world of you, Erika – me and Sorcha being chief among them. We all just want you home. You *and* Amelie. And I'm sorry if you think I focked things up for you.'

And that's when the line goes suddenly dead.

It's the middle of the afternoon when I suddenly realize that today is a special day. And I don't just mean it's the day that Sorcha's old pair are moving out. It's also the day that my latest ban from Kielys of Donnybrook is lifted.

It's actually three o'clock when I get the text from the staff to say that the sin-binning is over and wondering where the hell I am. I laugh. It's the greatest focking pub in the world.

Then I decide to Hailo a taxi.

John storts pulling a Heineken for me the second he sees my big, ugly mug.

'Welcome back,' he goes.

I'm there, 'How did you know I was going to ask for Heineken? Maybe I wanted something else – a pint of Carlsberg or possibly Guinness.'

'Don't be ridiculous,' he goes and I laugh as I put my credit cord down on the bor. They know me too well.

The place is empty. But then it's, like, four o'clock on a weekday afternoon. You have to keep reminding yourself that it's not 2005 anymore.

'We don't want any trouble in here today,' John goes and I end up having to laugh again. I could literally find trouble in an empty bor.

I grab my pint and I disappear into the corner. I make pretty short work of it as well. I end up knocking back, like, two-thirds of it in just two mouthfuls and I suddenly realize that I'm in cracking, cracking form.

I'm sitting there thinking how well everything is all of a sudden going. Honor is back in Mount Anville and we don't have to go to see Siofra focking Flynn anymore. The triplets are literally obsessed with rugby and my son got all A's in his Junior Cert. Sorcha has lost a couple of stone, even though I think she could still do with shedding a bit more, and the Tuites are no longer suing us. The original date for my vasectomy operation is tomorrow and it's been totally forgotten about. And right now, my interfering in-laws are packing their shit and moving out of my gaff.

If my life got any better, I'd have to take on staff to help me enjoy it.

I even have a little chuckle thinking about the YouTube video of Sorcha's tongue attached to my ear and the one point three million hits it's managed to rack up on YouTube. I'll get Garret back in time.

I knock back the rest of my pint and I get another one in, then another one after that.

At some point, I whip out my phone and I think about texting Fionn to see if I can change his mind about having a few scoops. That's when I notice the Tinder app on my screen and I think, fock it, one more time – go on, just for the craic.

I mean, just because you look at the menu, it doesn't mean you have to eat.

So I call up the famous app and twenty seconds later I'm checking out today's specials.

It's the usual craic, of course. The first five or six pictures look like Store Street focking mug shots. Then they stort to get less horrendous. Suddenly one jumps out at me. A bird called Sunniva. She's an absolute cracker as well.

I'd very nearly describe her as a flat-chested Diora Baird and that's possibly not even doing her justice.

My thumb hovers over the button for a good, like, twenty seconds, then I think, fock it, what's the worst that can happen? I'm just finishing my third pint when I'm told that I have officially clicked. In other words, I like the look of Sunniva and Sunniva likes the look of me.

She messages me and asks me if I fancy meeting up. I tell her where I am and she says – oh my God – she loves Kielys! I message her back and tell her to get down here then. She says she'll be about half an hour.

I order a fourth pint. This is officially a 'binge' in new money and I'm still sober, which just goes to prove how wrong all these anti-drinking freaks are.

I'm thinking, okay, whatever happens with Sunniva, it's going to have to happen quickly, because I want to be there when Sorcha's old pair are leaving the house, even just to say goodbye and good riddance.

The time passes quickly and I'm just finishing my fourth pint when the door suddenly opens. But it ends up not being Sunniva at all. It ends up being – of all people – Christian.

I laugh.

I'm like, 'Hey, Dude – great timing. I'm about to meet this total cracker I met on Tinder. I think she looks like Diora Baird except with, sadly, smaller roundies.'

Of course, I still haven't copped it. I'm so slow, you could roast your Christmas focking turkey by me.

'I knew it,' he goes, staring at me from the doorway.

I'm there, 'What are you talking about? Are you getting the pints in or what?'

'It was you,' he goes. 'It was you that Lauren met on that date.'

Oh, shit. The penny finally drops. My orse is straight away up off the stool. I'm suddenly backing away from him as he comes stalking across the floor of the pub towards me, his fist cocked, like he's actually getting ready to hit me.

I'm there, 'Dude, I don't know where you got your information. I'm meeting up with a bird called Sunniva.'

He's like, 'There *is* no Sunniva. Sunniva is The Doog's sister. We used her Facebook account to set up a fake Tinder profile to flush you out.'

Shit.

'That was a bit sneaky of Citation focking Needed, wasn't it? He never liked me – can I just remind you? – even before I nearly decked him in this place. He's obviously managed to poison your mind against me. That just makes me feel incredibly sad.'

I'm standing behind a high table. Christian is on the other side of it. He throws a punch across the table at me. I manage to duck away from it. Then he literally pushes the high table out of the way and it hits the floor with a thud.

Poor John behind the bor must be wondering will I ever repay his faith in me.

I run to the next high table. Again, I get on one side of it. Christian is on the other.

'Dude,' I go, 'nothing happened between us. Lauren was as morto as I was. I think, if anything, seeing the kind of shit that was out there scared her into trying to fix her marriage. In a weird way, you should be thanking me.'

He's, like, seething. I haven't seen him this angry since, well, since I rode his mother.

He throws a stool out of the way, then he grabs the sides of the table and I take off on my toes again. He goes to follow me, except he ends up slipping in his Dubes on the hordwood floor and he hits the deck with a loud crash.

I run for the main door, as John shouts, 'Three months this time!' after me. Just as I'm reaching out for the door, it suddenly opens and there, standing in front of me, looking very focking pleased with himself, is Citation Needed.

He's obviously here to lend a bit of muscle.

I don't even have time to plan my next move. I tackle him waist-high – hooomph! – and we crash through the doors out onto

Donnybrook Road, landing in a pile of flailing limbs on the actual footpath.

I'm the first to my feet. No surprises there. I'm the athlete, bear in mind.

I put my orm in the air and I manage to hail a passing Jo. I jump into the back, tell the dude to bring me to Killiney and then I breathe a sigh of relief.

Twenty minutes later, I'm home. We pull up outside the gaff. I hand the driver a fifty and I don't even wait for change. It's just like the old days. I key the code into the pad, the gates open and up to the house I go.

The front door is actually open.

Sorcha's old pair are coming down the stairs, carrying their suitcases. There's also a pile of boxes in the hallway.

I'm there, 'Are you two not gone yet?'

Upstairs, Honor is playing Paul Brady's *The Long Goodbye* at full volume and on permanent repeat. In that moment, I love her like I love myself.

Oh, shit.

Someone is suddenly kicking the front gate repeatedly and screaming abuse at the top of their voice.

'Oh my God,' Sorcha goes, 'who's that? It sounds like Christian. Ross, is that Christian?'

Fock it. I didn't think he'd actually come to the gaff.

I'm there, 'Don't ask me. I'm as much in the dork here as everyone else.'

She goes outside and walks down the driveway towards the gate. I follow. We all follow – we're talking me, her old pair and even Honor, who's going, 'Oh my God – *what* have you done now?'

I'm there, 'Don't listen to him, Sorcha, whatever it is he's about to tell you. He looks hammered to me.'

Sorcha reaches the gate. Christian is still kicking it. Three inches of solid oak, though – even Mike Ross wouldn't get through it.

'Christian,' Sorcha goes, putting her ear close to it, 'it's Sorcha. What's wrong?'

He's like, 'I want to kill your husband. I literally want to kill your husband.'

'Kill him? Christian, what did he do?'

I'm there, 'I swear to God, Sorcha, I have literally no idea what he's about to say. Could be anything with the state he's in. The pisshead.'

He goes, 'He went on a focking date. With my wife.'

It's, like, shocked expressions all round. Except from Honor. She laughs in a really, I don't know, wicked way.

'Nothing happened,' I go, through the gate, 'just to put your mind at rest – as in, I didn't ride her. I was in the pub one night and I was fluting around – yes – with that dating app that Oisinn told me about. If it's anyone's fault it's his. I arranged to meet some randomer – again, it was for a laugh more than anything – and the randomer ended up being your wife.'

'Open the gate,' Sorcha's old man goes.

I'm like, 'Sorcha, please don't open the gate.'

'I'm going to kill you with my bare focking hands,' Christian goes.

I'm there, 'I don't think you will, Dude. I think you'll eventually forgive me and that's because of a thing called rugby.'

He goes, 'I'm going to rip your focking testicles off!'

And that's when I notice Sorcha's old man staring at me with a little smile playing on his lips.

'Isn't it tomorrow?' he suddenly goes. 'That appointment you originally made, Sorcha – for his vasectomy?'

I'm there, 'Okay, I don't see how me having a vasectomy is the solution to any of this. Like I said, I think Oisinn has one or two questions to answer.'

'No,' Sorcha suddenly goes, her face full of resolve, 'you're having it.'

I'm like, 'Sorcha, this is crazy talk,' as her old man breaks his hole laughing.

Except she goes, 'You're having a vasectomy, Ross. Or *you* can go and pack your bags as well.'

374

Christian keeps hammering on the gate, going, 'Ross, come out here now!'

As Sorcha stomps off in the direction of the house, her old man turns to me and goes, 'You took away the most precious thing in the world to me. And tomorrow, you're going to find out how that feels.'

The old man won't answer his phone. I've left him, like, five or six voice messages, last night and again this morning, going, 'Dude, it's actually happening. They're taking my balls – what am I going to do?'

Sorcha's old man thinks it's hilarious, of course. He steps into the day ward with a big smile on his face.

'Look at you,' he goes. 'Even at this late hour, you think this is something you can worm your way out of.'

I'm like, 'Have you not got better things to do – like unpacking your stuff in your new gaff?'

No, he's here to make sure I end up definitely going through with this thing.

Sorcha steps into the day ward then, pushing the boys in their stroller, followed by Honor. Johnny and Leo both laugh when they see me sitting on the end of the bed in my hospital gown – they obviously don't know what's about to go down here.

Honor laughs as well – she *does* know what's about to go down here.

Sorcha goes, 'Ross, get into the bed. You heard the nurse – the anaesthetist is on his way.'

I'm there, 'Yeah, no, I might just sit here for a second,' and my eyes automatically stray towards my Dubes in the corner.

Honor goes, 'He's thinking about making a run for it,' and she picks up my shoes.

'Don't even think about it,' Sorcha goes.

And I'm like, 'Yeah, no, I *wasn't*?'

I look down at my phone. Still nothing from the old man. I'm like one of those dudes you hear about on death row, waiting for a phone call from, I don't know, the Governor's office to say there's been, like, a last-minute reprieve – fair focks.

'Is everyone getting their messages?' I go. 'I might just go down to the end of the corridor to see if the signal is any better down there.'

'Ross,' Sorcha goes, 'you are not leaving this ward.'

And then it's too late anyway, because the anaesthetist suddenly arrives.

'Into the bed,' he goes.

He's Indian. I hope that doesn't come across as racist.

I look at Sorcha and I go, 'Please don't make me do this. If this is your revenge for me going on a date with one of your friends, I already told you I'm sorry.'

I can nearly hear the anaesthetist thinking, 'Did I really just hear him say that?'

Sorcha turns down the sheets. 'Into the bed,' she goes.

And I end up having to do as I'm told. There are times when even a born winner like me has to accept that he's beaten.

'Can I film the operation?' I hear Honor go.

Sorcha's like, 'No, you can't film the operation, Honor.'

The anaesthetist swabs the inside of my orm with an alcohol wipe, then he produces a syringe. I end up nearly passing out at the sight of it. I look away. I feel a bit of a prick. But then that's only natural with my wife, kids and father-in-law staring at me.

The anaesthetist pushes the needle into my orm. 'Count back-wards from ten,' he tells me.

I'm like, 'Ten, nine, eight . . .'

And at the same time I hear Sorcha's old man go, 'It has to be done, Sorcha. It's the most humane thing, in the circumstances.'

And that's the last thing I remember. After that, I'm out of the game.

I'm woken by the sound of Ryle Nugent going, 'It's Kearney time!'

At first I'm wondering has the focker come to visit me, but then I realize that I'm in the recovery room and it's actually my phone.

I try to, like, summon up the strength to reach across and grab the thing off my locker. Except I just feel flattened. It's obviously the drugs. The thing rings out.

I'm suddenly aware of this, like, dull pain south of the border. I lift the sheets and I look down. I can see the bandaging. The job has been done.

'It's Kearney time!'

It storts up again. This time, I manage to get to the thing before it stops. It ends up being *him*. Too focking late now, of course.

I answer by going, 'What do you want?'

He goes, 'Some regrettable news to impart, Kicker!'

I'm there, 'Is it about Erika?'

I feel instantly shit.

'Yes,' he goes. 'I'm afraid she's gone again.'

'Gone?'

'Had it away on her toes in the middle of the night. Colm thinks she somehow got wind of the fact that we were in town and she didn't show up at the restaurant two nights ago. He went to her apartment and it's been cleaned out.'

'That's, er, shit.'

'No sign of her *or* little Amelie. And the great shame is that, well, he thought he'd gotten her trust. Helen and I were going to go to the restaurant to see her that very night.'

'Like I said, that's annoying. Is Helen pissed off?'

'Well, she certainly was. We had the most terrible row yesterday.'

'Well, I hope she dumped you – finally got sense – you big focking let-down merchant.'

'Like I said, the most awful row. About something and nothing. And I said, "We have to consider the fact that Erika doesn't want us to find her! And we're putting our own happiness on hold. Let's just get married, Helen! Let's just damn it all and bloody well do it! Here! As soon as it can be arranged!" Because Helen is still a US citizen, don't you know.'

'I seriously hope the punchline to this story is that she kicked you to focking touch.'

'The punchline to this story is that she said yes, Kicker! Which is what I'm ringing to tell you! Helen and I are to be wed this Saturday in the beautiful city of Seattle.'

'Are you focking serious?'

'Well, of course, I'm disappointed that it's not happening in Sandy Lane, Barbados, but Dermot Desmond and the other chaps will just have to understand that sometimes in life a man has to seize the moment. The announcement will be in tomorrow's *Irish Times*, Ross. Ms Helen Joseph and Mr Charles O'Carroll-Kelly will be tying the proverbial knot at the Woodmark Hotel on Lake Washington!'

'Sorry – and all of this affects me *how* exactly?'

'Because I want you, Ross, to be my best man!'

I'm left literally speechless by that. It's an incredible honour.

'You can shove it up your focking hole,' I go. 'I've just had major surgery – while you were ignoring my phone calls, by the way.'

'Oh, come on, Ross,' he has the actual balls to go, 'you've only had a vasectomy! You'll be back on your feet in twenty-four hours!'

'Yeah, no, well, I'm not going to Seattle. You can ask some randomer to be your best man. I'm focking finished with you.'

'Excellent! I want you all here, Ross. You, Sorcha and all of my beautiful grandchildren. I'll have Hennessy call you. He's making all the arrangements.'

It's a beautiful day. The temperature is up in the seventies. And the view is something I can't even begin to describe. The still lake. The deep, blue sky. The snow-capped mountains in the background. This place is, like, screensaver beautiful.

The pain from the operation has mostly disappeared. All I can feel now is the pain of, I don't know, *longing*? The sense that I'm missing something, if you know what I mean – the ability to create, I suppose you'd have to say, life.

It's definitely affecting me. I don't feel like the same Ross O'Carroll-Kelly anymore. Still, I have to keep reminding myself that this day isn't about me.

There's, like, forty or fifty white chairs set out on the lawn where my old man and Helen are going to be married, although we only need, I don't know, a fraction of them. *I'm* here obviously, then Sorcha and the boys, Honor, Ronan, Shadden, little Rihanna-Brogan,

Hennessy and then a surprise guest who my old man tells me about as I'm straightening his cravat.

'She should be here any minute,' he goes.

And, automatically, I'm like, 'Are you serious?' thinking it's going to be Erika.

I left her a voice message last night when we landed, telling her that we were all in Seattle and that her old pair were getting married at eleven o'clock this morning at the Woodmork Hotel – if she wanted to be there.

'That's down to me,' I go. 'The hero of the hour, I'm tempted to say, yet again.'

'Ah,' the old man says, looking over my shoulder, 'here she comes now!' except when I turn around, it ends up not being Erika at all. It ends up being my old dear.

'Fionnuala!' the old man goes, sort of, like, holding her at orm's length to get a proper look at her. 'You look absolutely wonderful! Doesn't she, Kicker?'

I don't commit myself either way, other than to say, 'She looks like she always looks – bet-down.'

They sort of, like, embrace each other. She's going, 'I'm so happy for you, Charles! I couldn't *be* any happier!'

'Careful,' I go, trying to prise the two of them aport, 'you're going to end up with half her focking face on the front of your jacket.'

She turns her attention to *me* then? She's all, 'Hello, Ross.'

And I'm there, 'Yeah, no, I'm supposedly doing best man here, so I'm probably going to be limited in the amount of time I can spend talking to you today.'

She smiles. It's a horrible sight. She has a face like a roadkill rabbit. 'You have time to say hello,' she tries to go.

So I'm there, 'Hello,' and then, a few seconds later, I go, 'Are you clean?'

She's like, 'Yes, I'm clean, Ross, and thank you for asking. If you must know, my life is very, very wonderful at the moment. In fact, I've met a darling new man named Ari . . .'

'He must be desperate for company.'

'He's a financier, a widower and he's worth billions. I've been spending a lot of time at his house in Malibu writing my memoir. He knows someone who knows Oprah and she said she might read it. Anyway, I'll not go on – this is your day, Charles. I'm so pleased for you and Helen.'

And she lets out a squeal and goes, 'Oh, look at all these beautiful babies!' meaning her grandchildren and also her great-granddaughter, although it'd kill her to call them that, of course, because that would mean acknowledging that she's focking ancient. Which is why she's never bothered to learn their names.

'Oh,' she goes, looking at Johnny in Sorcha's orms, 'look at this . . . little one.'

I hear Sorcha tell her that she looks – oh my God – *so* amazing.

'I've met a darling, darling man named Ari,' the old dear tells her. 'He's a financier.'

I turn to the old man. I go, 'When you said you had a surprise guest coming, I genuinely thought it was going to be Erika, not Angelina focking Stoli.'

The celebrant arrives. His name is Dave and he has a beard. He seems cool enough.

Suddenly, the string section storts playing *There's No Other Like My Baby*, which was my old man and Helen's song back in the sixties.

It makes me automatically smile.

The old man turns around. We all turn around. Helen is standing, like, thirty or forty feet away, in a white dress, looking seriously, seriously well for a woman of her age.

She smiles, then storts walking towards us, holding a bouquet of flowers and linking orms with Hennessy, who's going to give her away.

'Oh! My! God!' Sorcha goes. 'She! Looks! Stunning!'

Even Honor looks up from her iPhone for about five seconds.

Tears stort rolling from my old man's eyes. I tell him to get his shit together – because that's one of my duties on the day – just as Helen arrives beside us.

'Well, you took your time,' the old man goes, because she's nearly an hour late.

And *she* goes, 'I had to wait fifty years for this day. I thought the least I owed you was to make you wait fifty minutes.'

Everyone laughs. It's a definite moment. There's no doubt about that. But then it's nothing compared to the moment that's about to come, just as the ceremony is about to begin.

The first thing that alerts me to it is the sound of Sorcha, at the top of her voice, going, 'Oh! My God!'

That's so often the case.

I look over my left hammer. And there, standing in the exact spot where Helen stood just a minute ago, is Erika.

She looks incredible – and I'm saying that as her half-brother – in a little red dress that really showcases her legs and her tremendous double whammies. And she's holding Amelie.

For a few seconds, everyone is just, like, frozen to the spot, not knowing what to do or say.

All hell suddenly breaks loose. Helen and the old man go running towards her and the four of them – Amelie included – disappear into a scrum and all you can hear out of it is, 'I love you!' and 'I missed you!' over and over and over again.

I'm turning around to people – Sorcha, Hennessy, the old dear and this Dave dude – going, 'Yeah, no, I was the one who texted her to say this was happening here today,' just making sure I get the recognition I deserve.

Twenty minutes later, we all take up our positions again, as Dave goes, 'Ladies and gentlemen – and children, because I notice that, as grown-ups, we *are* rather outnumbered here – we are gathered today to celebrate the marriage of Helen Angela Joseph and Charles Bertram Algernon O'Carroll-Kelly . . .'

Erika is sitting beside me in the front row. She's holding Amelie in one orm. Her free hand reaches down and grabs mine and that's how we end up watching most of the ceremony. And every so often, she squeezes my hand really tightly, which I know is her way of saying thank you.

In terms of emotion, I'd put it up there with the birth of my children and obviously winning the Leinster Schools Senior Cup in 1999. There isn't a dry eye in the house, except obviously in the case of my old dear, who hasn't had tear ducts since a botched crow's-feet operation performed in international waters back in 2005.

She *tries* to cry, in fairness to her, even though it just makes her look constipated.

When it's all over, we tip down to the lake for photos. The old man and Helen. The old man, Helen, me and Erika. The old man, me and Hennessy. The old man, Helen and all their grandchildren and great-grandchildren, with Honor giving the cameraman the old one-finger salute. Then everyone together.

We're some focking family. That's what I'm thinking as we all make our way towards the morquee, where the actual *reception* is going to happen? The old man and Helen are just, like, strolling along, orm in orm, the happiest I've ever seen them. Sorcha and Erika are exchanging baby stories – Erika is admiring the boys and Sorcha is admiring Amelie – the two of them looking just as close as they ever were. The old dear is telling Hennessy that she's met a darling, darling man named Ari, who lives in Malibu and who's a financier. Ronan and Shadden are telling Honor that they'll take her up in the Space Needle tomorrow and Honor is telling them that it sounds really boring and she'd much prefer if they took her to the mall.

I'm pushing Brian, Johnny and Leo in the stroller and do you know what I'm thinking? I'm thinking, maybe the vasectomy was a good idea after all. Maybe this is all the family I'm ever going to need.

'Did you see how thin Erika is?' Sorcha goes – this is while we're putting the boys into their high-chairs before the meal is served. Sorcha looks pretty alright herself, considering that three months ago she had a focking trunk on her like a Nissan Xterra.

She smiles at me. It's one of those days. She'll probably even forgive me for the whole Tinder thing before it's over.

'Are you still sore?' she goes.

She's talking about my nuts.

I'm there, 'Yeah, no, not really. The painkillers are pretty good. It's more, I don't know, *psychological*? It's an adjustment, isn't it? Knowing that, you know, I'm suddenly shooting blanks. I had one of my famous deep thoughts in the shower this morning. I was thinking that having sex after the snip is like playing rugby in Division 2B of the AIL. You're having fun and everything, but there's also a nagging voice in the back of your mind, going, "Why the fock are you even bothering here?" '

Sorcha kisses me on the lips. It's, like, a big lingering one as well.

'Well,' she goes, 'maybe playing in Division 2B of the AIL will be more fun than you think.'

I smile – although that's just to humour her. The girl wouldn't know a rugby ball if it hit her on the focking head.

I tip up to the bor and I order a beer, deciding I'm definitely going to get shit-faced here. Suddenly, Hennessy is at my elbow.

He goes, 'How's the speech coming along?'

I'm like, 'I didn't write one. I just thought, you know, I'd talk from the hort. They've always been my best speeches. People still talk about the one I gave in the dressing room before we beat New-bridge College. I didn't have a note in front of me and I'm talking literally.'

He goes, 'That's good.'

'I'm just going to tell it like it is. Yes, he can be a dickhead. Yes, he can be a knob. Yes, he can be a complete tosspot. But he's also – weirdly? – the best friend I've ever had.'

'Yes, he is.'

'I mean, the whole parenting thing. You get all these experts – the Siofra focking Flynns of this world – and they tell you that you need to do more of this and less of that, but at the end of the day, a lot of it is just guesswork. Bringing up kids is as big a mystery now as it's ever been. Take me and Sorcha. We've given Honor everything she's ever wanted. A few weeks ago, she tried to stab another kid with a cheese knife. Explain that to me. A lot of it is just random.'

'Yeah, that's, er, very deep.'

'Yeah, no, I'm in that kind of form today. I never know when it's going to strike. At the end of the day, I think the most important thing is to be a best friend to your kids and vice versa. That's what the old man has always been to me. He's the one person in the world who always believed in me despite all the evidence that there was probably no actual point. And I can put my hand on my hort and say that very rarely in my life did he ever let me down.'

Hennessy asks the borman for brandy. 'None of this measures shit,' he goes, 'just fill the fucking glass.'

Then he turns to me and goes, 'I would say he *never* let you down.'

And I'm like, 'Hmmm,' remembering all those frantic calls I made from the hospital, looking for him to bail me out, like he used to in the old days.

Hennessy goes, 'I've been saying to Charlie for a year now, what can I get you as a wedding present? You see, I've always loved your father like a brother and I wanted to get him something to reflect that.'

'He loves a nice decanter,' I go. 'That's what I was thinking of getting for him. Eventually.'

'So he rings me the other day and he says, "Hennessy, old scout, I've thought of something. Kicker is in trouble. He's being forced to have a vasectomy – against his will, I might add – by that father-in-law of his. And for once in my bloody well life, I can't be there to bail him out. If you were to help him, old friend, well, I could think of no better wedding gift from you to me."'

I'm like, 'Okay, what are you even talking about?'

'I rang the clinic,' he goes. 'Turns out the surgeon doing your operation was Eddie Chassay. Played hooker for Terenure when I played loosehead. Fucking asshole. But, well, I hid a lot of money for him back in the eighties.'

'Rugby,' I automatically go. 'It's the greatest sport in the world.'

'So I rang him up and I said, "Hey, asshole," because that's how we talk to each other. "My best friend's idiot son is having his tubes cut today. I would consider it a final repayment for debts owed – both on and off the rugby field – if the operation, for whatever reason, was not a success."'

I'm like, 'What are you shitting about? I *had* the snip – I've got the scors.'

'You got scars,' he goes, 'because he made a few cuts. Said he had to make it *look* real, then he could always claim later that the operation just didn't take.'

I'm there, 'Are you saying what I think you're saying?'

He's like, 'Your equipment still works. And, hey, I know there's no real point in giving you this warning – but be careful what you do with that thing.'

Acknowledgements

My thanks to Rachel Pierce – it has been my great fortune to have her as my editor; to Faith O'Grady, the best agent in the business and a rock of good sense; to Alan Clarke – I can't tell you how excited I am when the finished artwork drops into my e-mail inbox; to Michael McLoughlin, Patricia Deevy, Cliona Lewis, Patricia McVeigh, Brian Walker and everyone at Penguin Ireland – you are a great team to play for, a Castlerock College among publishers; to editors past and present, especially Ger Siggins, Matt Cooper, Paddy Murray, Orna Mulcahy and Kevin O'Sullivan; to my father, David, and my brothers, Mark, Vincent and Richard, for the happy times; and to Mary, my wife, with all my love.